Praise for *Luck and Last Resorts*

"Expertly crafted and brimming w_____ *Re-sorts* is a beautiful romance that is _____ ___le. I adored Nina and Ollie, and all _____ ____de their second-chance love story so _____ _____g I could experience it again for the first time."

—Libby Hubscher, author of *If You Ask Me*

"*Luck and Last Resorts* hits every beat of a second-chance romance to per-fection. Its hero and heroine are complicated and emotionally messy and so carefully drawn that you finish the book feeling as though you've just spent several hours in the company of real people whose lives and personal histories are as complex as your own. Both funny and deeply emotional, this is a lovely, utterly memorable romance."

—Martha Waters, author of *To Marry and to Meddle*

"Luck and Last Resorts has every ingredient for the perfect contempo-rary romance—engaging writing, delicious heat, charming and compli-cated characters who face deeply felt questions of how much love to gamble on life's risks."

—Emily Wibberley & Austin Siegemund-Broka,
authors of *The Roughest Draft*

"With a perfectly saucy heroine and a delightfully grumpy Irish hero, it's easy to fall head over heels for Sarah Grunder Ruiz's lovable leads. *Luck and Last Resorts* is full of yearning, hope, and hard-earned romance. This book will have your heart doing cartwheels."

—Bridget Morrissey, author of *Love Scenes*

"*Luck and Last Resorts* is my favorite sort of love story—one where the feelings are as strong and complicated and euphoric and messy as they can be in real life, and one where the characters, in all their flawed and frustrating humanity, are given the space to experience them all. Sarah Grunder Ruiz's writing is absorbing and affecting, perfectly tuned to the voices that populate this story."

—Kate Clayborn, author of *Love at First*

"*Luck and Last Resorts* is hands-down one of my favorite books I've read all year. I wish I could zap it from my memory just so that I can read it all over again for the very first time, savoring every page of Nina and Ollie's laugh-out-loud banter, sizzling steam, and Sarah Grunder Ruiz's God-tier unfolding of events in the characters' past as they come together again in the present, hitting every emotional note just right. It's the perfect second chance romance AND it's the perfect enemies to lovers romance. I don't think I'll ever get over the charming and hilarious Nina and Ollie; they have my whole heart."

—Sarah Hogle, author of *You Deserve Each Other* and *Just Like Magic*

"I devoured *Luck and Last Resorts* in two sittings, and was instantly transported from a cold, grey London to the tropical warmth and blue skies of Florida aboard the Serendipity super yacht. This book has the perfect ingredients of flawed but lovable characters, warm-hearted humor and gorgeous, swoony romance, with a generous side helping of witty banter. I defy anyone not to fall in love with Nina and Ollie; this is the vacation read you NEED to pack."

—Freya Sampson, author of *The Last Chance Library*

"You need to pay careful attention when you read *Luck and Last Resorts*. On the surface it's a tangle of second-chance and friends-to-lovers between two beautiful people set on a yacht. Beneath this, however, lies an aching and poignant examination of the choices we make—or refuse to make—as we enter our thirties and decide what parts of ourselves we will carry on into the next stage in life. Grunder Ruiz has honed her writing and it is so smart you almost miss the skill. This is a deeply satisfying romance at the same time it's a compelling novel about the reality of "starting over" and the tenacity of love in the face of a person's obvious flaws. People may not be perfect, but this is a perfect romance."

—Elizabeth Everett, author of *The Perfect Equation*

Praise for Love, Lists, and Fancy Ships

"*Love, Lists, and Fancy Ships* is a delightful love story about setting and settling goals, about the journeys of the heart, and about how you have to let go of the past in order to move forward. You'll be rooting for Jo from the first page."

—Jodi Picoult, #1 *New York Times* bestselling author of *The Book of Two Ways*

"This book is a love letter to letting yourself feel your feelings instead of pushing them away, or pushing away those who want to love you through it. Sweet, beachy, and emotional, you will want to read this one with a box of tissues."
—Sarah Hogle, author of *Twice Shy*

"*Love, Lists, and Fancy Ships* is funny, touching, swoony, and brimming with heart. Sarah Grunder Ruiz writes characters you'll cheer for and fall in love with, and leaves you wanting more."
—Trish Doller, author of *Float Plan*

"An incredibly moving and beautifully told story about the importance of being open even after encountering loss. Sarah Grunder Ruiz masterfully weaves together heartbreaking moments with lighthearted fun as Jo attempts to move forward and complete her bucket list. I laughed, I cried, and I became super invested in Jo's delightfully slow-burn romance with the single dad known as Hot Yacht Chef. This is the perfect beach read, as long as your beach bag contains a box of tissues."
—Kerry Winfrey, author of *Very Sincerely Yours*

"Charming and hopeful, with a tenderness that underscores every scene. I adored headstrong, secretly vulnerable Jo, her chaotic teenage nieces, and Hot Yacht Chef, all of them beautifully written, fully realized characters trying to make sense of their own heartbreak. This debut is utterly irresistible—the kind of book that's impossible not to hug to your chest after finishing."
—Rachel Lynn Solomon, national bestselling author of *The Ex Talk*

"Sarah Grunder Ruiz's *Love, Lists, and Fancy Ships* is a book with enormous heart, and one that balances family grief with truly delightful witty banter. It made me laugh, it made me cry, and it made me swoon from all the delicious pining between Jo and Alex. It's a wonderful debut, and I can't wait to read more from her."
—Olivia Dade, author of *Spoiler Alert*

"Sometimes hilarious, sometimes devastating, and always heartwarming, *Love, Lists, and Fancy Ships* is an amazing debut about picking up the pieces after loss. With a complicated (but ultimately loving) family, fully realized friends, and a very handsome chef, this beautiful book shows how being generous with your heart can help mend it. I loved it!"
—Farah Heron, author of *Accidentally Engaged*

Also by Sarah Grunder Ruiz

LOVE, LISTS, AND FANCY SHIPS

Luck and Last Resorts

SARAH GRUNDER RUIZ

JOVE

New York

A JOVE BOOK
Published by Berkley
An imprint of Penguin Random House LLC
penguinrandomhouse.com

Library of Congress Cataloging-in-Publication Data

Names: Ruiz, Sarah Grunder, author.
Title: Luck and last resorts / Sarah Grunder Ruiz.
Description: First Edition. | New York: Jove, 2022. | "A Jove Book".
Identifiers: LCCN 2021057426 (print) | LCCN 2021057427 (ebook) |
ISBN 9780593335444 (trade paperback) | ISBN 9780593335451 (ebook)
Classification: LCC PS3618.U55 L83 2022 (print) |
LCC PS3618.U55 (ebook) | DDC 813/.6—dc23
LC record available at https://lccn.loc.gov/2021057426
LC ebook record available at https://lccn.loc.gov/2021057427

First Edition: August 2022

Printed in the United States of America
1st Printing

Marco, this one is for you.

1

~~~~~~

June

Returning home from months at sea is like waking up from one dream right into another. Charter season is four months of sunshine, the bluest water that has ever existed, and lots and lots of money. But it's also sixteen-hour shifts, sleep deprivation, and late nights scrubbing the vomit of hungover billionaires from white carpet. At the end of the season, we always come to Mitch's, an Irish pub that puts the *dive* in dive bar. Mitch's is dirtier than someone who cleans a twenty-million-dollar yacht for a living would like, and the dust on the bookcase beside our table is likely a health violation, but seeing as it's the first mess in months that isn't my responsibility to clean, I couldn't care less.

Some people never experience déjà vu, but I feel it all the time. More and more as the years pass. Every time I slip into this booth at Mitch's, for instance. Jo, the *Serendipity*'s second stew and my soon-to-be *former* best friend, says I'm just bored. But I disagree. How can I be bored when I work on a giant boat and run away to the Caribbean four months a year? How can I be bored when I get paid to see the places most people only dream of? As Jo's nieces would say, I am *living the dream*. Usually, I don't disagree.

Usually.

But as I stare across the table at Jo, *nightmare* is the word that comes to mind. I can see her mouth moving, but I don't hear a word. I'm distracted by the ache in my bad knee, which, after the last four months working barefoot, is aggravated by even the lowest of low-heeled wedges. In a few days, my knee will adjust to life on land along with the rest of me. All I have to do is ignore the pain until it fades. But what Jo's just told me? I won't adjust to it. I refuse.

"Nina?" Jo's voice comes back into focus, and the feeling of déjà vu slips away. Her gaze darts from me to her fiancé, Alex, beside her.

"It's an awful idea." It's all I can manage, because this is the most ridiculous thing I've ever heard. Jo quitting the yacht? To help Alex run a restaurant?

Jo frowns into her drink. "That's all you have to say?"

"You can't even cook, Josephine. They don't pass out Michelin stars for knowing how to operate a microwave. How are you going to help this man run a restaurant? Sure, he makes a good cheese Danish, but the sex can't be that good."

"I'll try to focus on the part where you compliment my cooking," Alex says.

I shoot him a glare. "Don't."

Jo twirls the straw in her glass. "I won't be cooking. I'll help manage the place," she says.

Alex puts an arm around Jo's shoulders, and though I love him for loving Jo, I also want to punch him in the ribs. Not hard enough to break one, but enough for him to understand how all this is making me feel.

A better friend would smile, buy a round of shots, celebrate this new phase of her friend's life. But I am not Jo's better friend. I'm her *best* friend. And as such, I can't help but think of all the things I'm losing. *You're upset because she's choosing him over you*, the voice in my head says. The voice isn't wrong. Of course Jo is choosing Alex over me. He's the fiancé. I'm the best friend. That's what happens when people get engaged, or land their dream job, or find something else they can't resist.

"This is worse than a secret fetus," I whisper into my drink.

Alex tenses. "A what?"

I wave a hand at Jo. "I thought you may have impregnated her. She's been acting weird all week."

Beer dribbles down Alex's chin when he turns to look at her.

"I'm not pregnant," she says. "You've seen me drinking all season, Nina. We shared a fishbowl at that weird pirate bar—"

"Davy Jones's Locker is *festive*, not weird." I fiddle with one of the dangling unicorn earrings I take off only to shower and sleep. "You could've been pregnant. I don't know your life. How am I supposed to know if you adhere to CDC guidelines?"

"You *do* know my life," Jo says. "Which means you also know I never planned to work in yachting forever. I never planned to work in yachting at all."

The three of us fall silent. Mitch's walls are littered with photographs, and ticket stubs, and dollar bills, making me feel as if I've stepped into a stripper's scrapbook. I glance at the wall beside us, my heart cartwheeling in my chest when I spot the Polaroid of me, Jo, and Ollie, the *Serendipity*'s chef before Alex. I decide that our current chef, Amir, is my new favorite. His food isn't as good as Ollie's or Alex's, but at least Amir has never broken my heart.

Ollie and I started on the *Serendipity* the same year, when both of us were new to yachting. We worked together for eight charter seasons, and it was in this very bar, almost a year ago to the day, that I'd found out he was leaving to become sous chef at Miami's illustrious Il Gabbiano.

Don't think about him, the voice in my head chides. But how can I avoid it when he's staring right at me from that damn Polaroid? I lean over and grab the photo, yanking it free from the wall with one sure pull.

"Nina," Jo says. "What are you doing?"

I shove the photo into my bra. "Souvenir," I say. I'm not sure what I'll do with it: burn it, tuck it into a book, sneak back here in a week and staple it to the wall again.

"Shots!" Britt, the *Serendipity*'s third stew, appears beside the table with four shot glasses crowded in her hands. She grins at us, completely oblivious to the tension she's walked into.

I take two of the shot glasses and glare at Jo. "I need this more than you." I tip Jo's shot down my throat before chasing it with mine.

Britt scoots into the booth energetically, nudging me against the wall and blocking me into this hellscape.

"Leave some room for the Holy Spirit, won't you?" I shove Britt over until half her ass hangs out of the booth. "Lord help me sitting next to you all night. Where's RJ? He'd let a girl have some peace and quiet."

Britt snorts. "I doubt it."

I've never heard RJ, the *Serendipity*'s bosun, string more than one sentence together at a time, and I've known him for as long as I've been in yachting. Jo and I exchange a look that says, *What's that supposed to mean?* But I look away when I remember she is now my *former* best friend.

"Shouldn't you be somewhere mooning over Amir anyway?" I ask Britt. Their love affair had done nothing positive for the efficiency of the interior crew this season.

"I'm letting him miss me," Britt says. Her gaze is unfocused, and I wonder how many shots she's had already. "What is it with stews and chefs?" she muses. "Is it the knives? I mean, it's got to be more than a coincidence. Me and Amir, Jo and Alex, you and—" I raise an eyebrow. She mimics my expression and realizes her mistake. "Uh, Chrissy Teigen."

I twirl the two empty shot glasses before me on the table. "Is Chrissy technically a chef? There was a robust debate about it on Twitter a few weeks ago, and I don't remember what the consensus was." Alex opens his mouth to answer, but I cut him off. "Rhetorical question, Alex. I don't want to hear anything from you. It's bad enough you've stolen away my former best friend."

Jo looks stricken. "Former?"

Britt sighs unsteadily against the table and nearly topples out of the booth. "They told you, huh?"

"You knew about this?" I say.

"Britt!" Jo hisses.

Britt flashes drunken jazz hands at me and shouts, "Surprise!"

"She's taking over for me," Jo explains.

Which means Xav, our captain, already knows too. "Next you'll tell me RJ found out before me."

"That may be my fault," Britt slurs. She grabs Jo's unfinished margarita, but I pry it from her hands and pass her my water instead.

"She wasn't supposed to tell anyone," Jo says.

"RJ made me tell him." Britt leans forward to catch the water's straw in her mouth and misses.

I ignore the revelation that RJ actually converses with someone and turn to Jo. "When?"

"Why would I know when she told him?"

"When are you *leaving me*?" I say.

Jo bites her lip but doesn't answer.

"Two weeks," Alex says, putting Jo out of her misery.

Two weeks? No, no. Clearly, she hasn't thought this through. "Britt can't take over for you," I say. "She always does Med season." Almost every photo Britt posts is of her on either the *Serendipity* or the *Talisman*, the superyacht she works on in the Mediterranean Sea after we finish charter season in the Caribbean. The woman is only on land four months a year. I nudge her with my elbow. "Tell them," I say.

Britt rests her head on the table and mumbles, "Screw Med season."

As I look from Britt to Jo, the cartwheels in my chest become back handsprings. "You're drunk," I tell her. "You're all drunk!" I look at Britt and sigh. "But she's the drunkest. Seriously, she needs to hydrate." I make her sit up so I can shove the straw in her mouth.

Jo worries her bottom lip, and I realize my reaction is hurting her. I take a slow breath and tell myself I can walk this back. I can still save the post-charter-season celebration and Jo and Alex's big announcement. I can be Jo's better friend *and* her best friend.

"I'm just teasing," I say. I force a smile on my face I'm not sure Jo buys. "You're my past, present, and future best friend. I'm happy for you, Jo. Really."

It's true. I'm happy for Jo, even if I'm not *happy*.

Jo grabs my hand from across the table. "You don't have to worry about you and me, you know. Just because I won't be around at work doesn't mean—"

"I'm not worried!" I squeeze her hand before letting it go to fidget with my empty shot glass. "I never worry. I don't know how. We're on land, and on land, I only know how to have fun."

"And are you happy for me?" Alex says. "Getting my own place. Lifelong dream coming true and all."

I squint at him. "Depends on how many cheese Danish I get out of it."

Alex tilts his head as if lost in thought. "How about two dozen?"

"Make it three and you've got yourself a deal," I say.

"Done."

Jo rolls her eyes. "Three dozen cheese Danish? That's all I'm worth to you?"

I shrug. "They're really good cheese Danish."

Jo drops her gaze to her drink. "And you're fine with this. Really?"

I don't know if I'm *fine* with it, exactly. It's not like I have any other choice. I don't love the idea of not having Jo at work anymore, but I don't actually expect her to plan her life around me. "I'm not fine *now*, but I will be."

I hope I seem calm on the outside, because inside, I'm freaking out. I have always known my emotions are bigger than most people's. Years of gymnastics training helped me to develop the discipline necessary to keep them in check, a useful skill when your job requires catering to the whims of the wealthy. Normally I do better than this. But Jo and I have been through everything together over the last six years. Now she has Alex and his fourteen-year-old daughter, Greyson—a real family to go through everything with. I know Jo and I will still be best friends, but things are changing, although I was perfectly fine with how they've been. I thought I'd at least have her at work, even if her life outside of it became a bit more complicated. It never crossed my mind that she'd quit, that one change would ripple outward, washing over everything.

Too much, I think. I need to step away for a minute. I force Britt to sit up and move out of my way so I can escape the booth.

"Where are you going?" Jo says.

"I'm getting champagne, of course," I say. "This is a celebration, is it not?"

Jo looks at me for a moment, but she must believe me, because the hesitation on her face eases. "Thanks, Nina."

"Don't thank me," I say. "I have plenty to celebrate myself. Like the three dozen cheese Danish in my future."

When I leave the table, I don't go to the bar right away. Instead, I prowl the perimeter of Mitch's, running a hand over the dozens of dollar bills that jump out at me from the mess of photographs on the walls. What a shame to leave all this money here, stuck but still valuable. I look around the pub and wonder how much money has been left here. I certainly hope Mitch doesn't plan to use it as his retirement fund. It seems a rather risky investment strategy.

A corner of the Polaroid of me, Ollie, and Jo jabs into my skin. I face the wall and discreetly adjust the photo inside my bra. As I do, I spot a dollar bill that's been defaced to make George Washington look like a zombie. When I reach out to touch it, the dollar is so worn, it feels like fabric beneath my fingertips. I think of how good it felt to rip that photo from the wall, and without checking to see if anyone is watching, I tug at the thumbtack pinning Zombie George in place, then fold the dollar in half and stuff it into my bra beside the photograph.

Maybe I should feel bad, but I don't. It feels good to take something for myself, something that would be useless otherwise. It's what I love about thrifting. One woman's trash is another woman's treasure. I put the thumbtack back in its place and scan the wall again. Perhaps I'll grab a few more. Instead of returning to the table, I'll have the champagne sent over and I'll disappear. I'll go down the street to the gas station and buy a pack of cigarettes even though I haven't smoked in years.

"One charter season without me, and you turn to a life of crime?" a familiar voice says from behind me.

Ollie. I didn't know he'd be here, but part of me had hoped. I won't give him the satisfaction of turning to face him, though. I don't want to seem too eager. "What are you doing here? You aren't part of the crew," I say.

"Alex invited me. He's not crew anymore either. Mitch's is open to the public, yeah?"

I should've known this was Alex's doing. He and Ollie have become *buds* over the last year. They even have matching T-shirts with Gordon Ramsay's face on them that say *Where's the lamb sauce?* I don't get the joke, and I don't want to. All I know is Ollie talks to Alex about me, and I don't like it.

"How's the form, Neen?" Ollie says.

His breath is warm against my skin, and he smells like the mint tea he drinks obsessively. My instinct is to lean into him, but I'm not sure if being around him will make tonight better or worse, so I try not to move.

"I used to be a professional gymnast, Oliver," I say. "My form is excellent." I know that's not what he means. I've picked up more Irish slang over the years than I let on. This is just part of the game we play.

"You know I don't like being called Oliver," he says, like he often does when I use his full name.

"And you know I don't care," I reply, like I have hundreds of times. Thousands, maybe. Same old barbs. Same old reactions. I like to think of them as the grooves of our relationship. We settle into them when we're around each other just to remind ourselves they exist. If we stick to the lines, we can play this game for as long as we like. If we follow the rules, no one gets hurt.

Ollie wraps his arms around me and rests his chin on my shoulder. I hate how I don't mind it. How I can't help but rest my weight against his chest. Before Jo, it was just me and Ollie. A whole lifetime ago, it seems. He and I have more history than I care to admit. And though Jo is my best friend, my relationship with Ollie means just as much, albeit in a vastly different and infinitely more complicated way.

Ollie's barely-there stubble scratches my cheek when he speaks. "You good, Neen?"

I keep my eyes on the wall ahead of me. "Why wouldn't I be?" I say. *Better*, I think. *Being around him will make tonight better.*

"Heard you might've got some bad news," he says.

So even Ollie found out about Jo and Alex's plans before me? *Worse,* I decide. "I'm marvelous," I say.

Ollie's nose nudges my neck. I ignore the way it makes me weak in the knees, and not just the bad one. "I've missed you," he says, not at all the way you tell your ex-coworker you miss them.

I want to put some space between us, but Ollie is too comfortable, and I can't drag myself away. "Where's your girlfriend?" I ask. Sondra? Samantha? Tall. Redhead. I like her.

"Don't have one anymore."

No surprise there. The man goes through girlfriends faster than I can snap up a pair of vintage Levi's off the rack. "What was wrong with this one?"

"She wasn't you," he says. His breath raises goose bumps on my neck. So, he wants to play *that* version of our game.

I pull his arms off me with a sigh. "Not tonight," I say.

"It's true."

I turn, getting the first good look at him I've had since I left for charter season. He's unchanged, everything about him as in-between as ever. His hair, between blond and brown, between straight and curly, short on the sides and longer on top. He isn't tall, but he isn't short either. Even his outfit, a navy button-down, jeans, and white sneakers, falls somewhere between formal and informal. That's not to say Ollie is plain, because he isn't. There's something striking about the balance of him. Beautiful, really.

The only out-of-balance feature on Oliver Dunne is his eyes. Blue, but not like the sky or the ocean. They're an intense, impossible blue that reminds me of the blue-raspberry Slurpees I shared with my father after gymnastics practice when I was a kid. We'd stop at the 7-Eleven, and I'd stay in the truck while my father disappeared inside. He kept a lucky quarter in the cupholder between our seats, and I'd warm it between my palms while I waited for him. When he returned, I'd pass him the quarter for his scratch-off ticket in exchange for the Slurpee. Every now and then, the smell of quarters and scratch-off dust washes over me, making me sick. I thought my father and I were playing a game. I suppose we were. But that didn't mean there weren't consequences.

All this is to say, I've encountered many attractive people in my life, ones who wanted exactly what I did—no feelings, no strings attached—but none of them drove me wild like Ollie does. At first I thought it was the accent. But even with his mouth shut I want to kiss him. I tell Jo I don't love him. I tell *him* I don't love him. But of course I do. If soul mates exist, Oliver Dunne is the closest thing I have to one. But that doesn't mean we're good for each other. It doesn't make either of us immune to the damage we can inflict on one another. It doesn't change the rules.

Ollie looks me up and down. "Nice dress," he says. It is nice. A knee-length color-block dress with matching buttons down the front. Vintage Liz Claiborne. One hundred percent silk. He catches the hem between his fingers, and his knuckles brush against my thigh. "Where'd you get it?"

"Do you really care?" I should step back, but my muscles are frozen. I blame the bad knee.

"Maybe I do," Ollie says, his eyes on the fabric between his fingers.

"Butch, of course." Butch, the owner of my favorite thrift store, knows exactly what I like.

"The one and only Butch. You make me jealous when you talk about him."

When he lifts his gaze to mine, I force myself not to look away. I hate when he looks at me that way. It makes me feel stark naked when I'm obviously overdressed.

"You *should* be jealous. Butch is the man of my heart."

"And Jo is the woman, I know."

"Not anymore." I look beyond Ollie. Amir, RJ, and some of the other deckhands have joined Jo, Alex, and Britt at the table. Amir says something that makes everyone but RJ laugh. The look RJ gives him could fillet him alive. At least I'm not the only one who's miserable tonight.

Ollie doesn't say anything else. When I look up at him again, I catch the soft smile he saves only for me. Being near him is like sighing into my couch when I first get home from charter season. We haven't spent much time together since he moved from Palm Beach to Miami. He's only an hour and a half away, but the restaurant keeps him busy, and I've avoided driving down to see him ever since the last time I ended up in his bed.

For the last year, my friendship with Ollie has consisted of phone calls on his drive home from work. Most nights, unless I'm working late on the boat, he calls just as I've gotten into bed. I always put the phone on speaker and close my eyes as we talk, mostly about nothing. The restaurant, the yacht, weird Craigslist listings. By the time I hear Ollie unlock his apartment door, I'm half-asleep, lulled there by the sound of his voice.

It sounds like a capital-*R* Relationship, but it's not. I don't know what to call it. The phone calls and occasional hook-ups are all I can give. They're enough for me. But this phase, the one in which we can be friends, lasts only so long before Ollie is itching for more, something with a label. And when I refuse, he'll pull away from me again. We won't talk for months, maybe a year. He always says he's done, and sometimes he finds someone else, someone he really likes. But it's no use. We always find ourselves back here, walking this in-between place like a balance beam.

"Did you miss me?" he asks.

"We spoke yesterday. Though you failed to mention you'd be here."

"Wasn't sure I'd come. But I like to see the faces you make when you tease me."

"Teasing? Me? Never." I rest my hands on his shoulders. "You're built like a hunky fridge," I say. My hands slide down his arms to give his biceps a squeeze. He laughs, and I shoot him a glare. "What? You're frigid, and bulky, and occasionally provide food." I'm making quite the spectacle of myself tonight. Maybe it's time to give up the tequila.

"That face. Right there," Ollie says. He presses his thumb to my mouth. "And you say you don't tease me."

My heart is doing moves now that would be physically impossible for anyone but Simone Biles. I take Ollie's hand in mine and squint at his palm like a fortune-teller. I know the callus at the base of his forefinger. I can map out the small scars and discolored burns that run up his hands and arms. Even when I don't want to, I think of them whenever someone else touches me. It's a real mood killer.

"No new injuries, I see."

"Not on this hand."

"And the other?"

He puts his other hand in mine, and I spot a new burn right away, just behind the knuckle of his pinky finger. "New line cook doesn't look where he's fecking going," he says.

"I wish you'd be more careful," I say, but I regret it as soon as Ollie's smile becomes a smirk.

"So, you did miss me."

"I didn't say that." And really, what does he care if I missed him or not? What would it change about anything?

"I'm seventy percent sure you did," Ollie says.

Ollie's hands feel so good in mine after months apart that I don't care that what I'm about to suggest will only make the situation between us murkier. "Do you want to play a game?" I ask.

"What game?"

"Truth or dare."

He raises his eyebrows. "Oh. Sure." He squints at me. "Truth or dare, Nina Lejeune?"

"No," I say. "I go first."

Ollie rolls his eyes. "Why do you always get to make the rules?"

"Because I suggested the game."

"All right, all right. You go."

"Truth or dare?" I ask.

Ollie's eyes are bright with mischief. "Dare," he says.

"I dare you to come outside with me," I say.

"Done."

"Marvelous." I drop one of his hands, keeping a tight grip on the other as I pull him through Mitch's and toward the door that leads to the back parking lot. I'm only distracting myself from one problem by blowing up another. I know that. But I'm not very good at listening to reason, especially my own.

As soon as we step outside, I press my hands to Ollie's chest and push him against the brick exterior of Mitch's.

"You smell like a tin of Altoids," I say.

"Probably taste like them too."

"This means nothing."

"Sure thing, kitten."

When I lift myself onto my toes and kiss him, Jo's news and the ache in my bad knee are all but forgotten. Kissing Ollie is like working a charter—familiar, but never boring. At first the kiss is soft, almost sweet. He tastes exactly as I remember. I'd bet all my tips from the season he has a still-warm tumbler of mint tea in his car. When Ollie slides his fingers into my hair and pulls me closer, my hands find his shoulders again. Really, does the man do anything besides swear, and cook, and work out?

When we pull apart, Ollie grins. "Now I'm ninety-nine percent sure you missed me."

I roll my eyes and lean in to kiss him again, but Ollie catches my shoulders and holds me back. "Uh-uh," he says. "It's my turn."

I sigh. "Fine. Go."

"Truth or dare?" he says.

"Truth," I say.

Ollie's expression turns serious. He caresses my cheek with the back of his hand. "What's this really about?"

I glare up at him. *This* is not part of the game. We don't talk about *why* we do things. We just do them. "I've been at sea for four months; what else could it be about?"

"Come on, kitten. You're obviously upset. Talk to me." His voice is so gentle it makes my chest ache.

When I don't say anything, Ollie pushes my hair, down from its usual high ponytail for once, over one shoulder. He tugs gently at one of my unicorn earrings. "These give a man false hope, you know."

My eyes leave Ollie's to run over his gently sloping nose, his mouth, the wrinkle between his eyebrows. "Please don't," I say, surprised to find myself blinking back tears.

How do I always end up kissing Oliver Dunne in secret? Despite what he says about missing me and breaking up with his girlfriend, this thing between us is not serious. It shouldn't be, anyway. And I should be inside celebrating the next chapter of my best friend's life. But instead, I'm in a bar parking lot making out with Ollie so I can forget about it.

Ollie's hand drops from my ear. He pulls me to him, and I think he's going to kiss me, but instead he tucks my head beneath his chin and holds me against his chest. "It's all right," he whispers. "Nothing has to change. You and Jo will be the same as ever."

I want to believe him, but Ollie is wrong. I can feel it. My entire universe is being reordered, just like when he quit the boat last year. The distance between us grew, and these days we hardly see each other. My bad knee is throbbing now. It's the same feeling I get when I'm on the *Serendipity* and know a storm is coming. The sky may be cloudless and calm, and RJ and Xav can tell me there's nothing on the radar until they're blue in the face, but I'm never wrong about storms. It's like they're part of me.

Ollie can pretend he doesn't feel it too, but I know he does.

Everything is about to change.

2

~~~~~~~

**Eight months later, February,
first day of charter season**

"Well, aren't you a ray of sunshine?" Jo says when I fling myself into the passenger seat of Alex's van.

It's a bright February morning. The perfect day to set sail and escape South Florida for a few months. I shoot Jo a glare before dropping my sunglasses over my eyes. "Why must you drive the man van, Josephine? Just because we're in our thirties doesn't mean we have to act like it. Please tell me you've discovered you despise the restaurant business and have changed your mind about charter season."

I know she hasn't. The restaurant, Serendipitous (a little on the nose, if you ask me), had its grand opening the other night. The food was brilliant, and Jo looked happy, completely in her element. I'd nearly gnawed off my arm to punish myself for being such an asshole about it when she'd told me she was quitting the boat. Of course Jo would make a great manager. Why wouldn't she? The woman is marvelous at everything but cooking. She was made to please difficult people. Like the guests on the yacht. Like picky eaters at a restaurant. Like me.

Jo ignores my plea. "The van is all part of the soccer mom vibe. You can't be mad at me in this. Look, I'm even wearing the shirt."

She stretches out the shirt she's wearing so I can read it, though I already know it says *I only raise BALLERS #soccermom*, seeing as I'm the one who bought it for her. Man, she's really laying it on thick. Jo knows my three favorite things are her, Craigslist, and soccer moms (in that order). Target clothing and minivans aren't my personal aesthetic, but I can't deny that caffeine-fueled rage and aggressively blunt bobs have a certain allure.

"That shirt is a lie," I say. "You're ten months from becoming a track-and-field mom, thanks to your future stepdaughter. One day you're bringing snacks in a cooler, and the next you're buying matching USA Olympic Team tracksuits for the whole family."

Jo laughs. "As if Alex would let me do snacks. Besides, I don't know a thing about running."

"You don't know a thing about running *yet*. All I'm saying is there's a seedy underbelly to the sports-parenting world. It changes a person. I'm doing you a favor by warning you." I'm reminded of a photo of myself at twelve years old, wedged between my parents in our—you guessed it—matching Olympic tracksuits. It was taken not long after I'd started competing in gymnastics at the elite level. That sweat-wicking fabric haunts my dreams.

"Sports-parenting world? Seedy underbelly?"

"Just get on the boat, Josephine."

Jo sighs in her seat, eyes on the road as we drive toward the marina. "Are you going to be mad at me forever?"

"Possibly. But don't worry, it won't detract from my love for you. I'll deduct the love points from Alex."

"You're ridiculous," Jo says. She navigates through a roundabout and eyes me when we come out on the other side. A flash of nervous energy passes over her face. "Will you promise me something?"

I hold up three fingers. "On my honor, I will try: to serve captain and crew, to help my primary at all times, and to not replace Jo Walker as my best friend."

"Not that."

My hand drops into my lap. The road runs alongside the ocean, but I look at Jo instead. I'll have plenty of time for ocean gazing over the next few months. "What, then?"

Jo bites her lip. "Promise you'll be open to any new opportunities that arise. Or, you know, old ones."

What the hell is she talking about? She's wearing the same twitchy look she had at Mitch's right before telling me she was quitting. "What sort of opportunities are you referring to?"

"Adventure? Friendship? Love?" Her eyes dart in my direction.

"Friendship? Do you *want* me to replace you as my best friend?"

"Of course not."

"And love? Are you trying to set me up with RJ? Because it's never going to happen."

Jo laughs, but there's something off about it. Before I can say anything, she turns up the volume on the radio as the theme song to the *Whacked Out News!* segment of our favorite morning talk show begins. I watch her, not singing along like I usually do.

"So many people on meth!" Jo sings, tapping out the end of the jingle on the steering wheel.

I'm suspicious. Not about the meth song. Typical Florida. What's stranger than today's *Whacked Out News!* is Jo's behavior. She isn't the sort to toss platitudes around all willy-nilly. *Live, laugh, love! Carpe diem! Dare to dream!* But she sounds like a goddamn *Happy Planner* sticker today. Has she truly taken to a soccer mom identity? Is this how far she'd go to prove she loves me?

"What are you hiding?"

"I'm not hiding anything." Jo stares straight ahead as she pulls into the marina. She's lying to me. I know it. But we've parked before I can grill her properly, and I'm running late, so I let it go.

"This is it, Jo." I clap her on the shoulder once we've stepped out of the van and she's helped me lug my suitcase from the back. "If I die at sea, know I was very angry with you when it happened. My ghost will haunt you for all eternity."

"I look forward to it. The haunting part. Not the *you dying* part."

I roll my eyes, and Jo squeezes the breath out of me with a tight hug. "I'm going to miss you, Nina."

I try to lift her off the ground when I hug her back, but I'm too short and don't quite manage it.

"Don't be mad if Britt and I emerge from charter season as best friends," I say.

"It's more likely you'll toss her overboard. Take it easy on her. She's a baby."

"Not as much of a baby as one of my new junior stews. She's so green Xav hired an extra stew to make up for it. I don't care how experienced she is, it sounds like just one more person's drama to manage, if you ask me. Britt and I will get along just fine so long as she keeps her mess contained to her bunk. I pride myself on running a tight ship, you know."

"I know," Jo says.

A voice calls my name from the dock, and we turn to face the water. Sunshine bounces off the *Serendipity*'s blindingly white exterior. I worked a day charter for a retirement party a few days ago, but it's different knowing I won't be back home for four months. I'm sailing away from so many things I love, like Jo, and a predictable schedule of nightly phone calls with Ollie, and World Thrift, all so I can fold myself into a tiny shared bunk and serve wealthy strangers. But I also love charter season, and it's a perfect sailing day. For the first time since Jo quit the yacht, the old excitement washes over me. Maybe it won't be so bad.

The voice calls my name again, and I spot the *Serendipity*'s captain, Xav, staring us down with his arms crossed over his chest.

"You better get going," Jo says.

I sigh and take one last look at her. "I'll be refreshing your blog every ten minutes. Alex was totally right about how entertaining it would be reading about your doomed attempts at cooking." Jo sticks out her tongue, and I pinch her cheek before turning away to wheel my suitcase through the parking lot and toward the dock.

"Be good!" Jo calls after me. "Play nice and make new friends! And remember what I said about opportunities!"

When I step onto the dock, my thoughts turn to Ollie. Last night he called me on his way home from work and asked if I remembered the day we met. *I'll never forget the look on your face when you knew I'd caught you doing handstands out in the marina parking lot,* he said. I asked him how I'd looked. *Fecking scary, but beautiful,* he said. Half-asleep, I asked him what had been so scary about me. *I knew right then if I spent too much time around you, I'd fall in love,* he said. I tried to laugh it off, but Ollie said only, *You still scare me, Neen. I'm terrified all the time.* I didn't know what to say to that, though I was suddenly wide awake. I hardly slept at all.

My phone weighs heavily in the back pocket of my shorts as I make my way down the dock. Service can be spotty on board, and my hours will be unpredictable. I'll hardly have a moment to breathe, let alone manage nightly phone calls with Ollie. I stop in the middle of the dock and pull out my phone, thumb hovering over the call button beside his name on my favorites list. *What would I even say?* Nothing has happened since last night, and even if something had, he and I have nothing new to say to each other. We are old news, a tabloid cycling through the same stories about Bat Boy each year.

Instead of hearing his voice and risking whatever feelings it might set off, I hit the message icon and tap out a text.

Getting underway. Don't miss me too much. xx.

I stare at the screen, delete the double *x*, and press send before shoving my phone back into my pocket.

"Nice of you to finally join us," Xav says once I haul my suitcase on board.

"Leave me alone, old man," I say. "Where's a deckhand when you need one?" I don't like the way Xav's looking at me, like I'm a child. That's the problem with working for someone for so long, they get to know you too well.

"You're late."

"I'm always late."

"And I ought to fire you for it."

I shrug. He wouldn't dare.

Xav braces the rail and sighs. "Get your ass in the crew mess and greet your team."

"Do I have to?"

"I think you ought to see what you'll be dealing with this season."

"I don't understand why you continually hire greenies."

"It got you a job," he says. "Not all my new hires are green this season."

"Yeah, yeah. Like I said, just one more person's drama to manage."

"I suggest you toss that attitude overboard before you get down there."

"I can't lose something that is my very essence, Xav." He raises his eyebrows in warning. "Fine, fine, I'm going."

Laundry and to-do lists crowd my mind as I make my way through the main salon. My phone buzzes in my pocket when I reach the staircase that leads belowdeck. *Ollie*, I think. He doesn't always reply so soon. Late nights at the restaurant mean he usually sleeps during the day. I push my sunglasses on top of my head and fish my phone from my pocket.

Sure enough, the text is from Ollie. But it's not what I expect.

I won't.

My excitement at the sight of his name on my phone flickers out like the candles I light whenever we have a proposal on board. I always end up running around in circles, one candle blinking out just as I've lit another. It's exhausting. What do I care if Ollie misses me or not? I've been begging him to move on for years. Maybe he's decided to listen to me for once.

It shouldn't bother me. It *doesn't* bother me.

Except it definitely does.

I shove my phone away without replying and continue belowdeck. Every year I strive to be the last crew member to board the yacht on the day we set sail. It's atypical for a chief stew and drives Xav crazy, but I have my reasons. I like to give the crew time to get to know one another before I arrive and ruin all the fun. Once I get down these steps, I will no longer be fun Off-the-Boat Nina. I'll be Boss Nina, No-Nonsense Nina. The Nina you love to bitch about on your break.

The crew mess is bustling with activity as everyone waits for Xav to start the all-crew meeting that will kick off the season. RJ sits at the table beside Simon, a South African man who's worked as a deckhand the last few seasons. Watching them from the other side of the table is a woman I don't recognize, but who must be Eglé, our new deckhand from Lithuania, if her toned biceps are any indication.

Britt stands beside the counter, talking animatedly with a young Black woman with a shaved head and a white woman with carrot-colored hair wrapped around her head in intricate milkmaid braids. My new stewardesses. I scan the crew mess and tally everyone up.

Someone's missing, but I'm too tired to figure out who. Coffee. I'm going to need a lot more of it to get through sailing, and introductions, and showing my new stews around.

I try sneaking behind Britt to the coffee maker without being noticed. But I've never had great luck when it comes to avoiding conversations I'd rather not have, so of course Britt spots me right away.

"Nina! You're here!" she squeals. She acts as if she hasn't seen me in ages, though we worked together only a few days ago.

I toss Britt her famously overused jazz hands. "Surprise," I say.

Britt turns to the two women standing beside her. "This is Nina, our chief stew. She looks mean, but it's just resting bitch face. She's actually really nice."

"I don't have resting bitch face. I really am a bitch," I say. "Especially when I don't get my coffee."

It's not a joke, but everyone laughs anyway.

"Alyssa," says the woman with carrot-colored hair.

"You worked on an eighty-footer before, right?" I say.

"Correct," Alyssa says. "I've been chief stew on the *Why Knot* for the last six years."

She's adorable.

And definitely high maintenance. I can tell.

"Looking for a change of scenery?"

"Figured I'd see if bigger actually is better."

"Oh, well I can tell you the answer to that right now," I say.

"And?"

"It depends."

"On what?"

"On how much you can handle." I give her a polite smile and turn to the other woman. "And you must be Nekesa."

"Coming to you from a four-hundred-footer," she says.

I give her a blank stare.

"A four-hundred-square-foot Starbucks in a mall," she explains, lip twitching at the joke.

Britt cackles. Alyssa gives her a hesitant side-eye.

"I know who I'll be putting on breakfast service, then," I say. "Rich people like *wet* cappuccinos, FYI."

"So they like lattes but insist on calling them cappuccinos. Noted," Nekesa replies.

Funny. "Speaking of coffee," I say. "If you'll excuse me, I'd like to have some."

A loud whistle cuts through the crew mess.

"Asses in chairs, people. Let's get this shit shoveled."

Xav, of course. I glance at the time on the microwave and fight back a yawn. Eight a.m. on the dot. Right on schedule.

The conversation lowers to a simmer as the rest of the crew, eager to please, finds their seats. But me? I won't be in the mood to please anyone until I get some caffeine.

I've just reached the coffee maker when Britt lets out a high-pitched squeal that makes me wish I'd unpacked my earplugs already. If another goddamned seagull has somehow found its way belowdeck, RJ can deal with it. I still have nightmares from the last time.

But I forget all about seagulls and coffee when I turn to see what's causing the hysterics. At the edge of the crew mess, having just emerged from the hallway leading from the sleeping quarters, are broad shoulders and bronze hair I could pick out in the middle of a cruise ship safety drill—not that I'd ever set foot on a cruise ship.

Ollie.

"Hello, darlings," he says.

Britt lunges forward to wrap him in a hug. "What are you doing here?" she says. "Have you been here this whole time?"

I have the same questions. Because by my calculations, the only crew member missing is . . .

"I'm back as the chef this season, of course," Ollie says.

He rests his chin on Britt's shoulder, but he's looking at *me*. The corner of his mouth tips up into a half smile, setting off the cartwheels in my chest like it always does.

I expected a lot of things this morning. Chaos, laundry, more laundry. But Oliver Dunne smiling at me belowdeck was not one of them.

3

~~~

I was twenty-three years old when I stepped on board the *Serendipity* for the first time. After pulling into the marina parking lot, I sat in my father's pickup truck and kneaded my knee through the thick wool fabric of my forest-green dress pants. The pants were a bit warm for winter in South Florida, but paired with a white silk pussy-bow blouse and nude heels, I hoped I'd come across as both memorable and professional. And besides, these pants were lucky. I'd found them drowning in a sea of black and navy Ann Taylors at a Goodwill a couple of years ago and realized they were designer quality as soon as I touched them. Brunello Cucinellis, and in my exact size too. That day I'd felt as if wonderful things could be anywhere—maybe everywhere—if I only looked hard enough.

I caught sight of my résumé on the passenger seat, and the magic of my thrifted designer pants faded. This was an awful idea. I wasn't qualified to work on a yacht. I couldn't just pack up my life—what was left of it anyway—and ship out with a bunch of strangers for four months, could I?

My fingers fluttered beside the keys in the ignition. I could drive away right now. I could forget this whole yachting thing and go to Walmart. I'd buy a beanie and a pair of scissors, come back here, and rob the boat instead.

But I'd already spent money I didn't have on ink to print copies of my résumé. Jobbery instead of robbery would have to do.

I let my hand drop back to my knee and gazed out at the boats on the water, spotting the *Serendipity* right away. One hundred and fifty feet hadn't sounded like much last night, but the yacht towered over every other boat in the marina. I'd spent a long time scrolling through photos of the yacht before deciding to apply for the junior steward-ess position. Though *apply* might not be the most accurate choice of words. Technically, I hadn't applied. Plenty of other people had. Over a hundred. Which was why I'd printed my résumé and driven down here as soon as I'd woken up this morning, hopeful I could march right in (or was it on?) the boat and demand a job I was clearly un-qualified for.

Worst-case scenario? Captain Rodriguez would laugh me off the boat. Nothing I couldn't handle. I snatched my résumé from the pas-senger seat and pulled my keys from the ignition.

But as soon as my heels hit the asphalt, anxiety set in. I wasn't sure why. I'd done back handsprings in front of a panel of Olympic judges. I'd busted my ass in front of them, in front of everyone, on live TV. This was nothing. If this didn't work, I'd find something else.

Except there was nothing else, nothing that could solve all my problems, most pressing of which was finding a place to live that wasn't my parents' house. Unfortunately, I hadn't found any apartments in my price range, none that would take me after a credit check, anyway.

I took a deep breath and pulled my ponytail tighter. Last June, when I'd botched my standing Arabian salto on beam during Olympic trials and shattered my knee, I'd lost my confidence along with my career. My entire life until then had been gymnastics. It was a family affair. My father was my coach. My mother was a former Olympic gymnast herself. I'd already failed to make the team four years before. Everyone knew this was my best shot. I was at the top of my game, dominating competition after competition. Making the team was inevitable. And then . . . in a moment, everything I'd worked so hard for amounted to nothing.

It had happened in an instant. I couldn't have told you what went wrong. I hadn't watched the video to find out, though millions of strangers had. I pretended I was fine. Months of physical therapy had gotten me mostly back in shape, and I probably could have recovered enough physically to compete again, but it was the mental game I couldn't overcome. Whenever I stepped on beam, anxiety, something I had never truly encountered in my life until then, sparked within me like a hungry flame, making it impossible to shut out everything that could go wrong. And so I retired from gymnastics. *My career would have ended soon enough anyway*, I told myself. But in truth, I was shaken. Not only because I'd been at the top of my game and had it all pulled out from under me, but also because during my recovery, I'd discovered my credit was abysmal. It hadn't made sense. I didn't have student loans. I'd hardly ever used my emergency credit card. Eventually, I'd learned the truth, that my father had a gambling addiction my parents had been keeping from me for years. In addition to tanking his own credit, he'd maxed out credit cards in my name. Defaulted on loans using *my* information. He'd ruined my life in what felt like a moment, though it had been years in the making. I'd never forget the look on my father's face when he told me we needed to talk. Ever since, a loop of

Now what? Now what? Now what? had invaded my brain, never quiet long enough for me to think clearly.

And there it was, running through my mind again. I couldn't walk onto the boat like this. I needed to calm down. I sighed and threw open the truck door, then slipped off my heels, setting them on the seat along with my résumé. Whenever my mind went racing ahead of me, skipping like a scratched CD over the same thought, there was only one solution: to quiet it with my body and take as much control as I could.

I swung out my limbs, getting my body warm and loose. After scanning the parking lot to make sure no one was watching, I flipped into a handstand right there beside the truck. The bow of my blouse flopped onto my face, but I concentrated on feeling balanced, on the strength in my arms and shoulders. I held the handstand until the noise in my head subsided. *Better*, I thought. Once I righted myself again, I wiped my hands on my pants and slipped on my heels, then grabbed my résumé and made my way down the dock before I could change my mind.

"You better get them fecking shoes off," a voice said when I took my first step on board.

I turned to find a bronze-haired man staring at me from where he leaned against the railing. I'd been so busy hyping myself up that I hadn't noticed him. Had he been there the whole time? And why was he so . . . pretty? He watched me with the bluest eyes I'd ever seen. Something about them drew me toward him, but everything else—his body language, the tone of his voice—radiated an intensity that seemed to say, *Stay away.*

"Excuse me?" I said.

The man nodded to my feet. "You'll feck up the teak with them stabby shoes," he said, and I registered the Irish accent. "Haven't you ever been on a yacht before?"

"No, actually," I said. I slipped the heels from my feet. Suddenly, I was three inches shorter, forced to stare up at this rude stranger. I felt like a ridiculous party girl with my heels dangling from my fingers. "This is my first time on a yacht."

"Yeah, I sort of guessed that," he said.

I scowled. "Can't say I'm loving the experience so far."

The man continued to stare at me, his entire body still except for the fingers of his left hand, which rolled an unlit cigarette back and forth. The craving for a cigarette ghosted across my tongue, one of the many bad habits I'd picked up since smashing my knee, and I wanted to snatch it from him.

The man squinted at me. "You're a wee little thing, aren't you? You look familiar. Have we met?"

"No."

"You sure?"

"Positive."

"Nice little show you put on there, by the way." He nodded to the parking lot.

I followed his gaze to my father's truck, dusty and pitiful-looking beside all these fancy ships. When I turned back to him, the corner of his mouth was tipped up in a half smile, but only for a moment. He shoved the unlit cigarette between his lips and tamped the smile down. He was *laughing* at me and trying to hide it. I was sure of it.

It shouldn't have bothered me. What did I care what this guy I didn't even know thought? But it was that little smirk and the way he'd stamped it out when he realized I'd seen it that pissed me off. It would've been better if he had just laughed in my face. Concealment. I was tired of it.

I nodded to the unlit cigarette in his mouth. "You'll kill yourself," I said. "Haven't you been scared straight by the Tobacco Free Florida commercials?"

The man drew his brows together. "The what now?"

"The anti-smoking ads. You know the ones. Wheezing voice-overs, lungs covered in tar. I bet yours are all shriveled up by now."

"Can't say I know what you're talking about, but I bet you're real fun at parties."

"I am, actually. I'm delightful."

"I can see that."

"More delightful than you, anyway."

He turned so that his entire body faced mine, one arm resting against the railing to support his weight. "I don't need to be delight-ful," he said.

"And why's that?"

"I'm a chef," he said, as if that explained anything. When I didn't respond, he added, "Don't need to be delightful when you've got food."

I wanted to argue with him, but he had a point.

He sighed. "Listen, love—"

"Don't call me love."

He took the cigarette from his mouth and waved a hand. "Don't know your name."

"Nina Lejeune," I said. I waited for him to tell me his, but he didn't.

He bit his lip as he looked me over. "Nina Lejeune," he repeated. "You sure we don't know each other?"

"I'm pretty sure I'd remember meeting my least favorite person in the world."

His eyes widened. "In the whole *world*? Already? Hell, that's gotta be a record." His gaze dropped to the cigarette between his fingers, then bounced up to meet mine again. "Well, Nina Lejeune, as lovely as it is having a stranger berate my life choices at nine in the morning, it'd be great if you could just . . . piss off. What are you doing here anyway?"

Right. *Right!* I was here to get a job. I didn't need any distractions. Especially not of the infuriatingly attractive asshole variety.

"I'm here to see Captain Rodriguez about the junior stewardess position," I said. I stood as straight as I could in an attempt to project the confidence I'd faked my way into feeling. The heels would've helped.

"Grand," he said, but he looked as if he didn't think it was grand at all. He unclipped a walkie-talkie from his pants and held it up to his mouth, his eyes on my face as he held down the talk button. "Cap. Cap. This is Ollie."

Ollie, I thought, storing the name away just in case I happened to land this gig.

"Go ahead," a voice replied.

"There's a Nina Lejeune here to see you. Says she's got an interview for the junior stew position."

No, no, no. Could he have said anything worse? The captain wouldn't know my name, seeing as I hadn't *actually* been called in for an interview.

Ollie must have noticed the panic on my face. "What? I say something else wrong?"

"It's just that . . . well, I don't actually have an interview."

"What do you mean?"

I held up my résumé. "I just thought I'd print out my résumé and head down here. Apply in person." Which had definitely been a mistake. What did I think I was doing just showing up and demanding a job?

"Ah, dock walking, are you?" Ollie said. "Or dock handstanding, in your case, I suppose."

"I'm sorry, dock . . . what?"

"Dock walking. You know, walking up and down the dock looking for work."

I narrowed my eyes, unsure if he was making fun of me or not. "That's a thing?"

"It sure is, darling," he said. "You don't know a thing about yachting, do you?"

"I know enough."

"Yeah, sure." He watched me with a look I couldn't place. Annoyance? Incredulity? A mocking disregard? I held his stare, not wanting to let this infuriating man with his bad attitude, and windswept golden hair, and broad shoulders, and blue eyes dressed in impossibly thick lashes think he'd gotten one over on me. The pause was only seconds but felt much longer, and I'd begun to seriously consider stabbing him with one of my heels and jumping overboard when the captain's voice came over the radio again.

"Bring her to the wheelhouse."

Ollie sighed and clipped the walkie-talkie back to his pants. "There goes my fecking smoke break," he said as he tucked the unlit cigarette into his shirt pocket.

"Sorry for giving you back eleven minutes of your life," I said. "Truly, I am."

He raised an eyebrow.

"Every cigarette you smoke takes eleven minutes off your life," I explained.

"Are you on about that Free Florida Tobacco shite again?"

"Tobacco Free Florida," I corrected.

"Well, I wouldn't worry too much about extending my life, seeing as you'll clearly be the death of me if you get this job." He turned away from me then and set off down the main deck.

For a moment, I couldn't move. I watched him walk away, indecision freezing me in place. He was right, I knew nothing about yachting. I didn't even know to take off my shoes or that dock walking was an actual thing.

Ollie paused a few feet away and glanced at me from over his shoulder. "You coming or not, Nina Lejeune?"

It was the amusement on his face that made the decision for me. I couldn't run away when he clearly didn't think I should be here at all. I couldn't fail when that was exactly what he expected me to do. My false confidence became real determination, and I raised my eyebrows in challenge as I took my first step after him.

That hesitant smile flickered at the corner of Ollie's mouth again before he continued down the main deck. I followed after him, neither of us speaking. There was too much to see. He turned a corner and led me through what looked like a large luxurious living room to a spiral staircase. I ran my hand along the intricate wooden railing as I climbed after him. The staircase was beautiful. Everything on the *Serendipity* was clean and tasteful and expensive-looking.

When we reached the next landing, Ollie set off down a short hallway and stopped before a closed door.

"Here you are," he said. He rested a hand on the door handle and swung it open. "Good luck, Nina Lejeune. You'll need it." He winked and turned away. I watched him go, not sure what to think. The man was confusing as hell. And annoying. And damn, he had a nice ass.

Ollie looked back over his shoulder and caught me staring. I looked away quickly but heard him laugh as he disappeared down the staircase.

A throat cleared behind me. I turned back to the wheelhouse. Inside, two leather-padded swivel chairs stood before an array of screens and panels. Large windows looked out over the bow of the ship and the marina parking lot. At a small table to the side of the room sat the source of the throat clearing.

Captain Rodriguez was a Hispanic man who looked to be in his late fifties. He wore a blue polo with the word *Serendipity* embroidered on it in gold letters, white slacks with sharp creases, and boat shoes that didn't have a single scuff mark. The man was the very definition of put together. There wasn't a wrinkle in sight other than on his sun-weathered face, though most of it was covered by a neat white beard.

"Captain Rodriguez," I said, reminded of my purpose. A few sure steps found me beside the table, and I stuck out my hand. "Nina Lejeune. I'm here to discuss the junior stewardess position."

He shook my hand and gestured for me to take the seat across from him. "Good morning, Nina. Please, call me Captain Xav."

I set my shoes on the floor and took my seat, feeling childish with my toes hanging in the air. I needed to pretend being a yacht stewardess was my heart's desire if I wanted to beat out the other applicants. But even after hours of web searches, I wasn't sure what all the job entailed. The duties of a yacht stewardess seemed to vary depending on the boat. All I was certain of was it would get me what I needed: money, a place to live, food, an escape.

Pretend you're trying to break the beam. The thought, a mantra from my gymnastics days, was a well-worn track in my brain. Even before I'd shattered my knee, beam had been my hardest event. The only way to succeed on beam was to let go of fear and go hard. It required intensity, total focus. Captain Xav didn't speak when I slid my résumé across the table, and I could tell that navigating this conversation would be a lot like that. I had to release any doubts I had about myself and this job and go hard.

"So," I began. "Like I said, I'd love to be considered for the junior stewardess position."

He glanced at my résumé. "You don't have any relevant experience," he said. "Your only work experience is as a children's gymnastics coach."

"Yes, but the skills I gained as a coach would be an asset to—"

"Let's just get to the point," Captain Xav said. He leaned toward me over the table. "What are you really doing here?"

I blinked at him. "Pardon?"

He tapped a finger against my résumé, which sat on the table between us. "No offense, kiddo, but you don't look like someone who knows a lot about yachts."

Break the beam, I reminded myself. I lifted my chin. "I was under the impression that yachting guests weren't all that different from young children."

Captain Xav's eyes narrowed as he looked me over. "They have their similarities." He glanced at my résumé again. "You've got quite an interesting history, despite the lack of relevant experience. Second in the US Gymnastics National Championships. First at the American Cup. You're young. Why not continue competing?"

The man clearly knew nothing about gymnastics. If he did, he would've recognized my name and known why I was no longer competing. "I injured my knee," I said. "All good now. Not gold-medal good, but good enough to work as a stewardess."

Captain Xav scratched his beard, his expression unreadable beneath it. I bet that was why he'd grown it in the first place. "What makes yachting the alternative? Why do you really want this job?"

"I already told you," I said, then paused when Captain Xav raised his eyebrows. "But you want the truth."

"That's what I asked for."

I stretched my toes until they brushed the floor, grounding me somewhat. I could tell the truth. Part of it, at least. "There's been an . . . unfortunate . . . turn of events in my life. I need to get away. I need to make money. And I need a place to live. This is the only job I've found that can give me all three."

"And what would this turn of events be? We don't hire felons,"

Captain Xav said. He held up his hands. "Owners' rule, not mine. I'm sure you understand. This is a twenty-million-dollar yacht, after all."

Twenty million. I lifted the tips of my toes from the floor. "Do I look like a felon to you?"

Captain Xav shrugged. "Why not? Criminals can look like anyone."

I bit back a laugh. If I'd learned anything in the last month, it was that. Criminals could look like people you loved. They could look like the last person in the world you'd think would hurt you.

"I'm not a criminal," I said.

"Then?"

I dropped my gaze to the table. Other than to my parents, which was unavoidable, I hadn't spoken about what had happened to anyone. Not even my friends. They were off doing marvelous things—competing, moving to new cities, getting married, landing dream jobs, traveling. I had always been the fun friend. The one who was always up for a late-night drive to the beach when you were bored or couldn't sleep, or who'd take you thrifting and give you a makeover after a bad breakup. I didn't want to bring anyone down with my problems. If I spent too much time around my friends, they'd know something was off, and I didn't know how to explain what had happened. I didn't want to be a burden. All I wanted was a solution. One that wouldn't tear my family apart.

Captain Xav, however, seemed prepared to sit there staring at me for the rest of the day.

I lifted my head. "If I tell you, can I have the job?"

Captain Xav laughed, and for a moment, he seemed like a different person entirely. Someone who'd grab a beer with you and shoot the shit after a long day. "Depends on what you have to say. I can't make any promises, but I do value honesty on this boat."

"I'm honest," I said. Besides, what did I care what this salty old man thought? "I accumulated a . . . substantial amount of debt after my knee injury," I said. It was *mostly* true. The injury wasn't the main reason I was in debt, most of it had come before, but my knee was why I'd found out about it in the first place. "I couldn't keep up with it, and now I can't get approved for an apartment, or a car, or anything. I have nowhere to go. I need to get away from here for a while, and I need a job that will give me a place to stay while I start piecing my life back together as cheaply as possible."

I couldn't read Captain Xav's expression as he looked me over. Perhaps he was one of those people adept at reading body language, someone who could sniff out a lie from a mile away. If so, I had nothing to worry about. Everything I'd said was true, even if I'd left out a few details.

Even so, I half expected him to ball up my résumé and toss it at my head, to say he didn't give a shit about what *I* needed. Wasn't the point of a job interview to sell yourself, not to convey your personal desperation? But then he nodded slowly, seeming to have come to a decision. "There are two courses you'll need to take in order to be certified," he said. "The Greens, the boat's owners, will pay for them. I'll have our bosun, RJ, email you the information. We set sail February first. Does that work for you?"

What's a bosun? I thought. I opened my mouth to ask, but paused, realizing what he'd said. "You're giving me the job?"

"Do you want to argue about it?"

"Not really. Just . . . why?"

Captain Xav took my résumé from where it sat on the table between us. He folded it into a square and stuffed it into the pocket of his polo. "You don't get to that level of athletics without hard work. And even though I shouldn't, I like your attitude. I don't recommend bringing it on the boat with you, though. You seem like a kid who needs a lucky break. Everything else you can learn."

The leather of my seat squeaked unattractively as I jumped to my feet. "Thank you! Thank you so much!" I stepped around the table and jolted toward him with my arms outstretched, then froze. "That was inappropriate," I said, letting my arms drop back to my sides. "I'm a professional. Really." I gave him a salute, then grabbed my shoes and turned to leave before he could change his mind.

"You didn't answer my question," he called.

"Oh, right." I spun to face him. "What was the question again?"

"We'll be at sea from February first to June first. That works for you, right?"

"My availability is wide open. As it turns out, drowning in debt makes filling one's social calendar quite the challenge."

He looked as if he were trying to hold back a smile beneath his beard of secrets. "Be on the lookout for that email from RJ," he said.

"I will," I said, and reached for the door.

"And, Nina?"

I paused. "Yes?"

"It was nice to meet you."

I turned to face him. "Thank you," I said. "It was nice to meet you too."

Captain Xav waved me away, and I raced down the spiral staircase, nearly dizzy with relief by the time I reached the bottom step.

"What do you look so pleased about?" Ollie said, startling me when I stepped from the staircase into the main salon.

At the sight of him leaning against a doorway a few feet away, my happiness faded. I'd forgotten getting this gig meant being stuck at sea with this asshole for four months. I peered beyond him and caught sight of the galley's clean surfaces and stainless steel, as cold and intense-looking as the chef who worked in it.

My eyes flicked to his. "You might want to get started on that funeral planning," I said.

"He gave you the job?"

"Yep."

"Knowing you don't know a fecking thing about yachting?"

Jesus, this guy was a real pain in the ass. I squinted at him. "I recommend going closed-casket, just to be safe."

Ollie rubbed his chin. "Well, fuck me," he muttered.

"No chance of that happening."

"Are you sure you're more delightful than me?"

I gave him a hard stare. "Look, I'm not thrilled at the idea of spending four months on a boat with you either, but—"

"I never said—"

"Let's think of this as an opportunity."

Ollie paused. "An opportunity for what?"

I pressed my palms together in front of me and said, "To grow in patience."

"More like impatience," Ollie muttered.

"You think you're funny."

He shrugged a shoulder. "I'm delightful."

"I thought you didn't need to be delightful."

"Don't. Never said I wasn't."

I sighed. "Well, now that we're telling blatant lies, I think it's time for me to go."

"Great idea. Oh, before you go, what flowers should I get?"

"Flowers?"

He tapped his fingers against the doorframe. "For the funeral," he said.

"Poison ivy."

Ollie snorted, and I walked away before he could say anything else that annoyed the crap out of me.

When I stepped off the yacht and onto the dock, I slipped my heels on, feeling more hopeful than I had in months. I could fix my problems. I could fix everything. I'd get my life back on track, maybe even sooner than I'd planned. And no one, especially not a smug Irish chef with a nice ass, would get me off course.

4

~~~~~

"All right, all right," Xav says. "Asses in chairs *now*. That includes you, Nina."

I give the coffee maker one last longing look before abandoning it to pull up a stool behind RJ and the deckhands. I try not to stare at Ollie as he makes his way to the opposite side of the crew mess table, introducing himself in a *mostly* polite way to the crew he doesn't know and cursing at the ones he does.

Ollie settles into a seat beside Xav and catches my eye, a ridiculous little smirk on his lips. I think back to the text he sent only minutes ago about not missing me. Is this what he meant? He can't be here for charter season, but he said it himself, he's the chef. Why else would he be here?

"There are a lot of little rules and two big ones," Xav says.

All the veterans, including myself and Ollie, chorus his next line: "Don't embarrass yourself and don't embarrass the boat."

Xav laughs. "Well, at least you know them. I don't want to hear otherwise when one of you dipshits inevitably does both."

I have to keep myself together, and that means trying to pay attention to Xav's kick-off speech, though I've got it memorized by now. *Follow the chain of command, no drinking when guests are on board, fuck up and you'll earn yourself a one-way ticket home.* I lean between RJ and Simon to grab a yellow legal pad and pen from the crew mess table. I doubt I'll need to take notes, but I can at least pretend that's what I'm doing so I don't end up spending the entire meeting staring at Ollie like some sort of mouth-breathing middle schooler.

True to form, by the end of the meeting I have a page of nonsensical notes before me. Some gems from the margins include: *WTF?* and a poorly drawn caricature of Ollie.

"Nice note-taking skills, chief," Britt says.

I clutch the notepad to my chest and turn to find Britt, Alyssa, and Nekesa standing behind me.

Perfect. Ollie has been here for all of five seconds, and I'm already off my game. I try not to notice him as he moves around the crew mess and chats with the others as if his surprise arrival is no big deal.

And maybe it isn't. We've worked eight seasons together. Sure, we fight the whole time and occasionally hook up in the laundry room, but I fight with every chef, and the hookups are a great stress reliever. Ollie being here is *more* normal than his not being here. It's not like anything has changed.

"Nina?" Britt says, snapping me back to attention.

"Right," I say. "Still haven't had that coffee." I reach into my pocket and pass Britt the to-do list I wrote the night before. "Once you three get unpacked we can get started. Alyssa, Britt will show you around since you already know what the job entails. Nekesa, come find me once you're settled in your bunk and I'll show you around the laundry room. Keep your radios on you at all times," I add, swiping mine from the table.

The way Britt wads up the to-do list like a used tissue and shoves it into her pocket makes me cringe. "Now get out of here," I say, waving them away. "I don't want to see anyone until I've had so much caffeine I'm literally vibrating."

"She means it," Britt says. She sticks one arm through Nekesa's and the other through Alyssa's and drags them to the far wall, where the rest of the crew is ogling the bunk assignments.

I make my way back to the coffee maker and stretch up onto my toes to reach for the highest shelf in the cabinet, where I stow my favorite mug so no one else will use it. But before I can blindly hook my fingers into the handle, Ollie is beside me placing it into my hands. It's a seemingly boring white one that says *Aruba* in gold letters, but when you pour coffee into it, hot-pink flamingos appear.

He grabs a mug from the cabinet, humming to himself as he makes his tea. Once he's finished, he leans a hip against the counter and turns to me. "Haven't seen you in ages, Neen."

"It's been a month." I grab the coffeepot, watching him from the corner of my eye as I pour.

The last time I saw Ollie was New Year's Eve. I was about to leave for a party when he showed up at my door without warning, pale and disheveled. *Are you going out?* he said. His eyes were red-rimmed, making them seem even bluer than they normally were. *No*, I lied. I knew *he* knew I was lying, but for once he didn't argue with me about it.

I let him inside and changed into my pajamas. I found him stretched out on my couch, his eyes glued to the TV. When I asked what was wrong, he said everything was fine, but that was a lie too. I didn't push him about it. I spent the evening watching TV with his head in my lap, running my fingers through his hair the way I know he likes and wondering what was wrong. Had something happened at the restaurant? He was inventive. A perfectionist. I couldn't imagine him doing anything but thriving at Il Gabbiano. Or—my stomach dropped at the thought—what if he *had* found some other woman he really cared about, and she'd broken his heart? I tried not to think about that possibility. One, it was too painful. And two, I'd kept him at arm's length for so long that I had no right to be hurt if he had found someone else.

I never found out what was bothering him. Other than mumbling *fuck* every now and then, he hardly said a word the whole night.

We didn't mark the passing of one year into another. No jokes about balls dropping, not a single ill-advised midnight kiss. That night, he dozed in my lap, seeming almost childlike. I spent more time watching him than the TV. When his eyes fluttered open, it was after two in the morning. "Sorry," he said, his voice hoarse. *For what?* I wanted to ask, but I only smiled and ran a hand through his hair again. When he left, he paused to kiss me on the forehead on his way out the door. I didn't hear from him for days after that, not even when I called to wish him a happy birthday. When he finally called me on his way home from work a week later, neither of us brought up that night. The whole thing was like a fever dream.

Ollie lowers his voice. "Surprised to see me?"

I shrug and take a sip of my coffee. "That was a mean text," I say, tapping a fingernail against the side of my mug. "Don't you have a restaurant to run off to?"

He laughs and runs a hand through his bronze hair. His eyes meet mine with a softness that makes me restless, and I look down into my mug. Ollie has always dealt with anxiety, but you wouldn't know it from looking at him. In public he is loud and brash and confrontational. When we first met, I was sure he wanted nothing to do with me, but I soon realized he liked to keep people from getting too close. But today, despite the teasing tone, I see the vulnerability that was in his voice last night when he told me he was terrified.

He drops his gaze to his mug, fingers fidgeting with the string of the tea bag. "I quit the restaurant," he says.

I still with the transformed flamingo mug halfway to my lips. "What do you mean you *quit*? That place can make you. I thought you were going to be head chef once what's-his-face left."

He sets the mug on the counter and lifts his eyes to mine. "Maybe I don't want to be the person it would make me. Maybe I want to be someone else."

"What happened to being done with yachting? *I'm a restaurant man now, Neen,*" I say, giving him my best Irish accent.

He shoves his hands into the pockets of his jeans. If I turned them out, I know what I'd find. In the back right pocket: his wallet, flattened and worn. Front left: two saint medals threaded onto a chain. Saint Dymphna and Saint Valentine. He's had the Saint Dymphna one for as long as I've known him, but once upon a time, the Saint Valentine medal belonged to me.

Ollie drops his voice to a whisper and leans closer. "I'm not here because I care about yachting, Nina. I'm here for you."

Here for me. My heart vaults into my throat as I watch him pick up his mug again and blow across it, wafting steam in my direction.

"I'll be home in June," I say. "We go months without seeing each other all the time."

Ollie takes a sip of his tea. He winces at the heat and sets the mug back down. His skin is still warm from the mug when he reaches for one of my unicorn earrings and his fingers graze my neck. "I'm here for you," he says again.

The warmth of his touch jolts right through me. Doesn't he realize we're in a room full of our coworkers? "Well, you found me. Surprise! I'm right where I always am."

I can't deal with this right now. Certainly not in front of the rest of
the crew. I abandon my coffee on the counter, grab my suitcase, and
start toward the sleeping quarters. There's too much to do. I suppose
we've moved on to the part of our game in which Ollie insists he wants
more, and I tell him I can't give it to him. It's too bad. We were having
so much fun.

"I'm serious," Ollie says, following me down the hall. "You might
not be going anywhere, but I am. If we aren't together by the end of
charter season, I'm going home."

Home? I whirl around to face him. Muffled laughter sounds from the
crew mess, but it's quiet here in the hallway. Ollie looks . . . wild. Desperate. He's always intense, but this is different. I've seen this look on
him before. He looks like a man out of options. "What do you mean
home?"

"I'll move back to Ireland," he says.

Ireland! He wouldn't. He's only been to Ireland once since he left
nearly fifteen years ago. "That's ridiculous."

Ollie steps closer. "Maybe it is, but I don't care. I'm done with all
the games. I'm done pretending you aren't the only reason I'm still
here."

"I'm not the reason you're here, Oliver." We've toed the line between friends with benefits and something more ever since our first
charter season, but we were clear about our intentions from the outset:
It was casual. A mutually beneficial arrangement. We were too young
for something serious. I was too in debt and too hurt by my parents'
betrayal to trust anyone with my heart, no matter how much I liked
them. Ollie, for his part, had something to prove. He'd left his family,
his country, his whole life to start over here. Neither of us was interested in commitment. Or so we said.

We're not as young as we were then, and our circumstances have
changed. I'm no longer in debt. Ollie has his career. Or *had* it until

today anyway. Even so, loving someone and being with them, to do the whole for-better-or-worse thing, are not the same. I don't do commitment. Ollie knows that. It's been almost ten years, but people don't really change. And by people, I mean me. *I* don't change. Not for anyone. Not even Oliver Dunne.

"What do you mean by *together*?" I say. "We get *together* all the time. What more do you want from me?"

"I want something real."

I laugh. "Feels pretty real to me."

"You know what I mean."

"We spoke on the phone last night," I say. "You didn't think to say any of this then?"

Ollie sighs and looks up at the ceiling. "I thought about it, yeah, but I wanted to talk in person." He settles his gaze on me. "I thought maybe we could . . . go out."

"Go out," I repeat.

"Like on a date."

I snort out a laugh. "A date?"

"What's so funny about that? I've never taken you on a real date before."

"Just . . . no."

"Why not?"

"Because I'm *fine* with the way things are."

"And what if *I'm* not fine with it?"

"Oh, I don't know, Ollie. Find a way to be fine with it. Look. Seeing as we are currently at *work* and will be stuck on this ship together for the next four months, let's put a pin in this, shall we? A very sturdy one that's impossible to remove. Take a little breather. Avoid each other for a few days. And then you'll see how utterly ridiculous this scheme of yours is." I turn away before he can respond and drag my suitcase to my bunk.

"Just let me take you to dinner," Ollie says, following after me.

"No!" I call over my shoulder.

"But we need to talk. Off the boat."

I stop before the closed door to my room, ignoring the panic that phrase, *we need to talk*, sets off. Nothing good ever happens in a conversation preceded by it. As soon as I swing open the door to my bunk and spot the shamrock-green suitcase inside, I rest my forehead against the doorframe with a groan. I feel Ollie behind me but don't turn to see the shit-eating grin I'm sure he has on his face.

"What's wrong, Neen?" he says.

"Nothing," I mumble.

"You sure? Because it looks to me like you've just realized who you assigned as your roommate. Wasn't even part of my plan. Don't know how I lucked out."

So much for avoiding each other for a few days. I ought to march up to the wheelhouse and give Xav a piece of my mind. Last week, when Xav and I sat down to make the bunk assignments, he told me he still hadn't hired a replacement for Amir. Instead of a name, I'd written *Chef* right beside *Nina*. I mentally curse Amir for quitting to become a traveling food vlogger. Next I curse myself for assuming the devil I didn't know would be better than the devils I *did*. I should've guessed I'd know all the devils.

After another deep breath, I lift my head. "This can easily be rectified. I am chief stewardess, after all." I turn around and wheel my suitcase past Ollie and back toward the crew mess.

"Where you going, love?" he calls out after me.

"Away!"

I hear Ollie sigh and the sound of the bunk door opening and closing. Once he's out of view, I dip into the laundry room, reveling in its quiet. Soon the machines will be in constant motion. There's so much laundry. It never ends when we're at sea. Sheets. Tablecloths. Uniforms. Guest clothing. My mind is whirling with thoughts of Ollie, and Ireland, and how ridiculous this is. I'll be thirty-three in two months, but suddenly I feel as young and adrift as the day I started this job. I never could have guessed back then that I'd still be here. I couldn't have guessed Ollie and I would even be *friends*, let alone whatever we are now.

My phone slips from my pocket when I sink onto my suitcase. It clatters to the floor, and the lock screen lights up, displaying a photo of me and Jo from the night she and Alex got engaged. I swipe my phone from the floor. *Damn it, Josephine*, I think, and find her contact info in my favorites.

"Did you know about this?" I hiss when she answers.

"Know about what?" Jo says, but I hear the smile in her voice. *So much for being my best friend.*

"Josephine," I say, giving the dryer a good kick.

"Maybe I knew."

"Oh my *God*, Jo. I can't believe you would let this happen and not warn me! If I didn't love myself so much, I'd drown myself in the marina so I can start haunting you earlier than anticipated."

"Just give him a shot."

"I'll give him a shot, all right. Bang! Bang!"

Jo's laugh is both beautiful and infuriating. "You two have been obsessed with each other for as long as I've known you. Probably longer," she says. "Ollie loves you. I'm not sure if you love him in that way or not, but think of this as an opportunity to decide."

"I don't *need* an opportunity to decide. I love him! I hate him! I think he's a foul-mouthed butthead with an excellent head of hair and lovely blue eyes! It doesn't mean I want to be in a relationship with him. And besides, you know the rules."

Jo sighs. "Your rules are . . . questionable, Nina."

"How? In what way?"

"They're impossible!" Jo says.

I disagree. For the last ten years I've lived by two rules: One, always have fun. Two, don't rely on anyone but yourself. Impossible? No. Challenging? Sometimes. Not the first rule. How hard is it to have fun? I've broken the second rule only once and don't plan on making the same mistake twice.

"Don't encourage him," I say. "He's threatened to leave for Ireland if we're not together by the end of the season. I don't believe it for a second, but do you really want to be responsible for sending him away? Do you have any idea what he went through to be here in the first place?"

"For someone who doesn't care about Ollie, you sure don't want him to go anywhere," Jo says.

"I'm going to punch you in the boob the next time I see you."

"It won't hurt if you're a ghost," Jo says. "Your arm will just . . . go right through me."

"Oh, what do you know about ghosts anyway?"

The radio at my hip crackles to life when Xav calls for me, RJ, and Ollie to come up to the wheelhouse in fifteen minutes for a preference sheet meeting. I squeeze my eyes shut. "I've got to go. Preference sheet meeting, and I haven't even started unpacking," I tell Jo. "I can't believe you aren't here. You're the worst. I love you," I say, hanging up before she can respond.

Re: the bunk situation. My choices are limited, even as chief stew. I could try to get someone to swap with me, but my options aren't great. Britt is a complete slob, and I would most definitely murder her if we roomed together. I don't know Nekesa or Alyssa very well, but I can't imagine either wanting to room with me, their boss, or with Ollie, a man they don't know. That leaves RJ and the deckhands, and it's best I don't get involved in RJ's domain when I can help it. Rooming with Ollie isn't ideal, but it will only be for a few months. We'll be so busy we'll hardly have any time to spend together anyway. It's the best of all possible options.

"Welcome home, darling," Ollie says when I return to our room.

"Absolutely not," I say when I spot his suitcase beside him on the bottom bunk.

Ollie follows my gaze to the suitcase and gives it a pat. "Oh no you don't, kitten. Bottom bunk's mine. First come, first served. That's your rule, I believe."

He's right, but still. "Don't be ridiculous. Look at me."

He smiles so wide his dimples appear. "Don't mind if I do," he says. I hate those dimples. They make me feel things in places where I am busy trying not to feel anything.

Ollie settles the suitcase at the head of the bed before stretching out and using it like a pillow.

"*Excuse* you, that is *my* bunk." I take hold of one of his ankles and try to pull him off the bed but can't drag him an inch. He sits up on his elbows and takes off his shirt before stretching out again with a sigh. I try to resist running my eyes over his lean stomach and muscled chest, but it's no use. Even though it's been almost ten years since we met, he looks as good—no, better—than he did then.

"What are you doing?"

Ollie puts his hands behind his head. "Distracting you with temptation."

"What makes you think anything about you is tempting to me?"

Ollie's eyes shine in amusement. "You're breathing awful fast. Some might say you've got a heaving bosom."

I lean over and jab his bare chest with a finger. "You are a barnacle, Oliver Dunne." I jab him again for emphasis. "A barnacle on my life."

"But I'm a sexy barnacle, yeah?" He pulls my finger from his chest and kisses it. A little thrill zips through me. I'm disgusted with myself. Fingertip kissing is not sensual.

"That's unsanitary." I wrench my hand from his grasp and take a step back. Five seconds in this ridiculously small cabin, and we've already got our hands on each other. "And no, you are not a sexy barnacle. You're the ordinary kind. The kind that gets stuck to the bottom of a cruise ship. A *cruise ship*, Oliver!"

Ollie laughs and sits up.

"Give me the bottom bunk," I say. "I'm barely five-two. You're five-eight."

He shoots me a glare. "Nine," he corrects.

I know exactly how tall he is, but I also know he hates it when I pretend I don't. "The point is, it'll be much easier for you to get on and off the top bunk."

He picks up a fitted sheet from the foot of the bed. "You can do one of those pole-vaulting thingies and get up there."

"Pole-vaulting is track and field, not gymnastics."

"Same thing," he says, though I know he knows the difference. He turns the fitted sheet over in his hands, trying to work out which way is which.

Ollie knows I like the bottom bunk, and not only because I'm short. I like having access to the porthole so I'm in charge of the amount of light that comes through. We've never bunked together during charter season, but I've heard enough from his former bunkmates to know Ollie likes to keep the cabin as dark as his soul, even during the day. No way I'm willing to give him that much control over my environment for the next four months. I'm like a plant. I need sunshine or I'll wilt away. When I tell Ollie this, he rolls his eyes and says he believes I'm half plant because I'm as stubborn as a tree.

"Come on, Ollie. I'm desperate." I drift closer to him again. Not hard to do, given it's only a few feet from the door to the beds. A single step, and I'm right in front of him. The door is open, which makes it feel a little less claustrophobic in here, though I don't love that the rest of the crew is probably getting an earful right now. I can hear laughter and conversation floating in from the other bunks. That could've been me if I hadn't been so bent on not rooming with any of the other crew.

"Nah," he says. When he looks up at me, heat in his eyes, I am desperate in so many ways. He drops his gaze back to the sheet and stares at it like it's a Rubik's Cube.

"Are you serious?"

Ollie shrugs. "I want the bottom bunk. You want the bottom bunk. Why don't we share it?"

"Funny," I say.

"Suit yourself." He gets to his feet, forcing me to take a step back.

"I'm a higher rank than you," I say. I try to yank the sheet from him but end up playing a pathetic game of tug-of-war. I'm doing the tugging. Ollie is doing the standing and laughing.

"You're not, darling. We're the same rank."

"But I've been here longer."

"I started five months before you did."

"And then you *quit*," I say, giving the sheet another yank and gaining no purchase. "You haven't worked here for over a year. I officially have more experience than you do."

"Don't think that's how the chain of command works on yachts, kitten."

"Why won't you do this for me? Wouldn't this all fit into your master plan of winning me over?"

Ollie looks at me with an expression I can't place and yanks the sheet to him. It pulls me along with it, and I careen right into his bare chest. He tips his face down and his nose almost brushes against mine. His breath smells like that fucking mint tea, and I nearly push myself onto my toes to kiss him. His eyes drop to my mouth, and I marvel at how long his eyelashes are. I almost let go of the sheet and reach out to touch them.

"Okay," he breathes.

"Okay what?"

"You can have the bottom bunk."

"Really?" I sigh in relief. "Thank you. You have no idea—"

"On one condition."

Of fucking course. Suddenly I don't give a shit about his eyelashes, as unfairly gorgeous as they are. I look away, and my vision snags on his shoes in a heap beside the door to the world's tiniest bathroom. I used to complain about that when we had an apartment together, how he'd just kick off his shoes anywhere. What did he think the point of the shoe rack was? But after he moved out, I remember thinking my shoes looked so lonely without his on the floor nearby.

"What's the condition?" I say.

"You go on that date with me tomorrow night." He tucks a loose strand of hair behind my ear.

"No."

He pries the sheet from my hands and takes a step back. "You enjoy the top bunk, then. I'm thinking we'll need a schedule for the porthole. How about we keep it closed from sunrise to dusk, and you can have it open from sunset to dawn?"

"How about I shove that sheet into your mouth hole and keep the porthole open twenty-four seven?"

"Easy now, killer," he says.

"I thought you wanted to win me over. How's this helping?"

"I'll never get a second alone with you on this boat. You'll run away to the laundry room, or call Britt, or jump into the ocean, or pretend to be asleep whenever I'm in here."

I would. It's true. In the past, I've done all these things to avoid him.

Ollie settles the sheet around his neck and turns away from me to begin unpacking his things into our shared closet, if one can even call it a closet. It's more like a kitchen cupboard with drawers.

"Oh, stop." I nudge him away from the suitcase. He's just tossing things onto shelves. "I won't have enough room for my things if you do it like that."

"Nina, don't."

I ignore him and take one of his T-shirts from the suitcase. Dolce & Gabbana. I run my fingers over the pilled fabric. I gave it to him five Christmases ago. One of the few items of clothing I've ever bought new. I spent far too much money on it, but Ollie wears it all the time, so I suppose the investment was worth it, though he never washes it the right way. I set it on one of the shelves before grabbing another.

Ollie takes hold of the shirt in my hands. "Nina, stop."

"It's easier if I do it," I say. It's childish, but I need something to do.

"I'll do it right this time. Just. Let. Me. Do. It," he says, tugging on the shirt with each word.

"Fine." I let go of the shirt at the same time Ollie pulls. It surprises him, and he stumbles back, banging his head against the top bunk. His suitcase tips over, and everything inside spills onto the floor.

"Oh shit." I drop to my knees so I can scoop his things back into the suitcase. "Sorry, Ollie. I didn't—"

"I've got it, Nina." He sinks to his knees across from me and massages the back of his head with his hand.

"Don't be ridiculous," I say. "You've hurt yourself. I'll clean this up, and then you can knock yourself out unpacking." I glance over at him. "Sorry, that was a bad joke. Don't actually knock yourself out."

"Nina, I can—"

"Hush up and let me do it." When I look down at the mess on the floor, my eye is drawn to a folder that's fallen open. A stack of papers spills out on top of a pile of Ollie's underwear. My name jumps out at me from the top sheet.

"What's this?" I say.

"Don't—"

We reach for it at the same time, but I'm quicker. I glance down at the paper in my hands and immediately wish I hadn't.

"Ollie, what is this?" I feel as if I've sailed through the Bermuda Triangle and into another reality.

"This is why I wanted to talk off the boat," he says.

I open my mouth but don't have a single quip ready to fire. All I can do is stare at our names written in Ollie's neat block letters, so different from my slapdash cursive.

In re: The Marriage of

OLIVER DUNNE
                    Petitioner

And

NINA LEJEUNE
                    Respondent

I tear my eyes away and look up at him. There's a resolve in his expression that freezes me straight through. This isn't a joke or a game. This is real.

"You want a . . . divorce?"

5

~~~~~~~~~

Ollie winces at the word *divorce*. He gets to his feet and steps around me to pull the door to our cabin shut before sitting on the bottom bunk. I stand up and pace the room, staring at him as he rubs his hands over his face. How long has he been planning this ambush? Showing up for charter season unannounced, giving me this ridiculous ultimatum, and now *this*, bringing up the secret we've kept for nearly a decade.

He drops his hands into his lap. "I don't *want* a divorce," he says. "But I'm done pretending. We make this real now or never."

"We don't talk about this," I say, though apparently that's no longer true. The word *divorce* falling from his lips shouldn't sting, but it does. I shouldn't care if we're legally married or not. We've pretended this doesn't exist for years. I've told him to move on more times than I can count. I should nod, congratulate him on finally coming to his senses. And yet . . . staring at the paper in my hands is somehow worse than all our pseudo breakups, and seeing him with other women, and the months we dropped out of each other's lives combined, because I always knew, deep down, that we had this. We'd never really be done with each other as long as we were still legally married. We couldn't *be* together, not really. Not in the way Ollie wanted. But I was under the impression we'd made a silent agreement *not* to get divorced. Wasn't that why neither of us ever mentioned it?

For months, before I found out my father stole my identity, I'd been inundated with calls from debt collectors. I brushed it off because it was obviously a mistake, and I was too busy competing and training. At first I assumed it was a stranger who'd ruined me. I never once considered it was someone I knew. My father and I were so close. Ever since I was a little girl, he'd told me no man would ever love me more than he did. But if ruining my life was how he, the man who loved me most in the world, treated me, then what did that say about everyone else?

And not only was I worried about my life slipping out of my control again, but I also didn't want to risk losing what Ollie and I had. What if actually being together ruined the good thing we had going? The phone calls and unspoken understanding. Before he moved to Miami, I used to swing by his place unannounced, and he'd get in the car without asking where we were going. Sometimes I had a plan, a random event or item I'd found on Craigslist that I just had to see, but other times I didn't. When we drove around Palm Beach in my convertible, it was as if no one else existed. What if we lived by the vows we hadn't meant to keep and it took away the magic? What if it took all the fun and spontaneity out of things?

But that didn't mean I *wanted* a divorce. Because as long as we were still legally married, I knew we'd be in each other's lives and do our little on-and-off dance. Round and round and round. But if he's willing to get a divorce petition and fill it out, then maybe he's willing to file it and move home to Ireland.

Maybe he really is ready to cut me out of his life forever.

"I can't keep doing this, Neen," Ollie says. "I love you. I have for years. You know that. You love me too."

"Not like that," I lie.

"If you don't love me, why didn't you ask for a divorce after I moved out?"

"Divorces are complicated," I say. It's the excuse I always give myself when the existence of our marriage forces its way to my attention, which is about once a year, when Ollie sends me his information so I can do our taxes.

"Ours would be simple enough."

It probably would be. It had to be less complicated than this shit we put ourselves through, anyway. And still . . . actually going through with it is unthinkable. I don't want Ollie to leave, but I can't give him what he wants. I just want everything to stay the same.

"You never asked for one either," I say.

"I didn't want one."

He takes the divorce petition from my hands and slips it back into the folder before setting it inside his suitcase. I take in the groove of a wrinkle between his eyebrows. The fine lines at the corners of his eyes from squinting in the sun or, hell, all the glaring at me he's done over the years. We're no longer the kids we used to be. And yet we're still here, bickering on this godforsaken yacht.

"You won't move back to Ireland," I say. My eyes focus on that odious suitcase. I ought to fill it with rocks and dump it in the ocean. "You hate Ireland. You haven't been there in years."

Ollie shakes his head. "Never said I hate Ireland. But it'll be better than staying here if you won't have me."

"I don't believe you."

He lifts his eyes to mine. "If you really don't want me, I'll file the papers as soon as charter season ends and take the next flight to Ireland. I already broke the lease on my apartment."

"I don't believe you." My voice sounds false, even to me. I don't know what I think. If he hadn't handed me that divorce petition, I'd never believe he'd go back to Ireland. Ollie has said a lot of ridiculous things over the years, but this is the most ridiculous of them all.

Ollie pulls out his phone and starts scrolling. "Here," he says, pressing it into my hands.

On the screen is a text exchange between Ollie and his landlord about moving dates and the safety deposit.

I pass back the phone. "This proves nothing. How do I know that's actually your landlord and not some rando you've roped into this scheme? How do I know you don't already have another apartment waiting for you?"

Ollie shrugs. "You want to call him? Check my bank accounts? Or, I don't know, take me at my fecking word?"

"Ireland!" I say. "You'd really just pick up and leave your entire life behind because I won't be your . . ." I can't even say the word.

"Wife," Ollie says. "If you won't be my wife—and you *are* my wife, Nina—then we'll get divorced, and I'll get out of your hair for good. If we're nothing, I don't see what the big deal is."

"I never said we were *nothing*. We're friends."

He shakes his head. "We're not friends, Nina. I don't know what you think we are, but we aren't that."

"You don't have to *leave* for *Ireland*."

"But I will," Ollie says. He fidgets with the zipper on his suitcase. "If you won't have me, I've got nothing here. I'm done waiting."

"I never asked you to wait." My hands are trembling now. I set them on my hips to try to still them. "I *told* you to move on. I've told you a dozen times! I'm perfectly fine doing . . . this."

His eyes flash to mine. "And what is *this*, Nina?"

"I don't know! Just . . . Nina and Ollie." I turn away and start hurling his clothes into the drawer closest to me. Right now, I don't care if they're neat or not. I just need something to keep my hands occupied. "We do that arguing thing, get in an actual fight, make up, make *out* sometimes too. And, you know." I hold up one of his shoes and whirl it around in a circle. "Lather, rinse, repeat."

"You're freaking out," he says.

"You think *this* is me freaking out?" I say, chucking the shoe into the drawer. "If you think this is me freaking out, you clearly don't know me well enough to marry me."

"We're *already* married," he says.

I shush him. "Everyone will hear you. Can we please not talk about this right now? Or, I don't know, ever?"

"This is why I wanted to talk about it off the boat," he says.

When I turn to him, I have his other shoe aloft in my hand. "Why? So you could corner me?"

Ollie groans. "Oh, I don't know, Neen, I thought springing it on you while we're stuck on the boat might've felt like cornering you, which was why I wanted to have this conversation on land, at dinner, off the clock."

I hurl his other shoe into the drawer. "Gee, how thoughtful of you! You just showing up for charter season with an ultimatum doesn't feel at all like being cornered! Well, there's no need to go to dinner now because there's nothing to talk about."

"Then why the hell do you keep me around?"

"Don't be ridiculous. I don't *keep* you around. You live almost two hours away. You even date other women! You have great taste, by the way."

"But you know I'm still yours."

"You're not *mine*—"

"You know I'll come running as soon as you call. You know I'd leave anything, anyone, if you asked."

"I've never asked—"

"I wish you would."

I still at his words, a pair of his boxer briefs in my hands. He says it so seriously, I can't even laugh it off. "You *wish* I'd ask you to leave something you want? You want me to rein you in? To take something from you?"

Ollie nearly bangs his head against the top bunk when he gets to his feet. "Yes! For fuck's sake, yes!"

I hurl his underwear into the drawer. "How hard did you hit your head?" I say. "Do you have a concussion? Do I need to call RJ down here? Because you're making absolutely no sense."

Ollie continues as if he hasn't heard me. "At least then I'd know I matter enough for you to ask. I feel like I live in a fecking funhouse. I *asked* you if I should apply for the Il Gabbiano job. You told me to do what I wanted, then freaked out when I actually took it. You act like you don't care, but you're miserable when I leave. We talk every night, we fuck—"

"It's just sex."

He laughs. "That's why you keep me around? For sex every now and then? C'mon, kitten, you can do better than that."

"I don't *keep* you around," I say.

"Do you want the divorce or not?"

This is a trick question. I should want a divorce, but I don't. At the same time, I don't want to be his wife or girlfriend. I just want to be . . . Nina. I want us to stay the way we are now. If I could explain it to Ollie, maybe I would. But I hardly understand it myself.

"It's unnecessary," I say. I turn away from him to face the drawer I've filled with his things. God, I've made a mess. I sigh and toss the shoes by the door where they belong and start refolding his clothes.

"This is exactly what I don't get, Neen," Ollie says. "How many times have you said you can't be with me? How many times have you told me to move on? Here I am, offering you exactly what you want, and you're *pissed off* about it."

"That's not why I'm pissed off."

"Then tell me why."

"Because you're being ridiculous! What's wrong with what we've been doing this whole time? What's wrong with just having fun together?"

"Look at me," Ollie says. When I turn to face him, his eyes dart to my mouth. For a moment, I think he's about to kiss me. If he did, I'd kiss him back, even though I shouldn't. I've got a Pavlovian response to that fucking tea.

Ollie leans toward me, pausing when his mouth is a mere breath away from mine. "I don't want to *only* have fun with you, Nina. I'm not *capable* of only having fun with you."

"Then what do you want?"

He pulls away with a sigh. "Everything. Jesus, girl. Why is that so hard to understand?"

There is a beat of silence as we stare at each other, and Ollie's anger flattens into an unnerving calm.

"I have a theory," he says. "Do you want to hear it?"

I don't say anything, because I do want to hear it. I want someone to explain to me why I'm incapable of either taking him or letting him go.

"You're scared."

"I'm not scared."

Ollie continues as if he hasn't heard me. "You can't admit you love me because it feels like giving up control. So you just keep doing the same thing over and over again, bringing me as close as you can stand and then shoving me away. You're stuck, Nina, and I can't do it anymore. I love you, but once charter season is over, I'm done."

The word *stuck* smacks me over the top of the head like one of his precious cast-iron frying pans. "Stuck?"

"Think, Nina. What about your life has changed over the last ten years?"

"My life is perfect."

"Oh, it's perfect, all right. Perfectly in control. You pretend you're all fun and games, but you're not, Nina. You're calculating. You and your fecking rules. Are you even having fun? Because I don't think you are. Not really. I get why you feel like you can't risk the chance of something going wrong. I do, but—"

"But what? I'll say, *Yes, Ollie, let's be together!* and suddenly I'll have a whole new life? Be a whole new person? Is that what you want? I've worked incredibly hard to get to where I am, and my life might not *look* different to you, but I can assure you that not drowning in debt, not having anyone else's mistakes tying me down, *feels* different."

Ollie's expression softens. "I know—"

"I know you do. You know exactly what it's like to be hurt again and again by the people you trusted."

"I won't hurt you."

"You don't *want* to hurt me. Intentions are wonderful, Ollie, but they aren't real."

He throws up his hands. "Fine! I can't promise I'll never hurt you. But you can't live like this, Nina."

"I can live however I want. That's the point." I finish organizing Ollie's drawer, then grab his sheet and nudge him aside so I can fit it around the mattress on the bottom bunk.

"Nina, stop."

"Why?" I tuck the first corner of the sheet swiftly into place. "Go ahead. Have the bottom bunk. Plunge us into darkness for the next four months. What do I care?"

"C'mon, Neen, don't be like that."

I yank the second corner so hard it makes the first come undone. Ollie falls quiet. When all four corners are in place, I smooth the sheet and turn to face him. His eyes are as humorless as they were on New Year's Eve, and I want to run my fingers through his hair and soothe the hurt I see in them. But I can't. Not now. Not when I'm the cause of it.

Xav's voice breaks the silence when it comes on over the radio. "Nina, Ollie, this is Xav."

"The preference sheet meeting," I say. I unclip my radio from my shorts. "Nina and Ollie here, over."

"Quit dicking around and get up to the wheelhouse. *Now*."

I shoot Ollie a glare. "Already on our way."

Ollie yanks on a shirt and storms from the room. I watch him go, then take a deep breath before I step out into the hallway and face the confused expressions of my crewmates.

This is exactly why Ollie and I can't be together. We can't only have fun. I'd have to take on the inevitable disappointment and hurt. There would be expectations. I'd have them for him, and he'd certainly have them for me.

I have to ignore this. It's the only shot I have at making it go away. By the time charter season is over, he'll realize I'm not worth all the trouble. He'll stay, and eventually things will go back to normal. He's clearly having an early midlife crisis. Someone needs to buy that man a sports car.

Britt bounds over like a gossip-sniffing golden retriever. "What was that about? I didn't hear the details, but it sounded intense. Do you need some girl talk?"

Nekesa and Alyssa give each other bewildered looks from where they stand behind Britt.

"Don't you worry about Mom and Dad," I say, and pat Britt on the top of her head. "Can you train Nekesa on laundry for me? I've got a preference sheet meeting. Think you can handle making up guest rooms, Alyssa?"

Alyssa nods, and I shoot the three of them a smile, grateful to step away until I arrive in the wheelhouse to find Xav, RJ, and Ollie waiting for me at the table. Suddenly girl talk sounds like the better option.

I glare at Xav. "You think you're funny, don't you?"

Xav shrugs. "Sure. Don't know what this has to do with the preference sheet meeting, though."

"You're full of it," I say. There's no doubt in my mind that Xav helped orchestrate this. I turn to RJ. "I never thought I'd say this, but you're my favorite."

RJ wrinkles his brow. Ollie stares down at his hands. Xav rolls his eyes before telling me to sit my ass down. I take a seat near RJ, something I have never purposefully done twice in one day.

It's going to be a long charter season.

6

Nine years earlier

The day before my first-ever charter guests arrived, I skipped up to the main deck and spotted Ollie as soon as I pushed through the galley doors. He was bent over the island counter, scribbling furiously with a pencil as he glanced from a notebook to three preference sheets, the contents of which included a photograph of each guest along with their likes, dislikes, and special requests.

He didn't look up from the preference sheets when I stepped inside. He hadn't paid me any attention when everyone had assembled for the all-crew meeting the other day either. All I'd gotten was *You again, huh?* I'd replied with *Well, hello to you too, Mr. Delightful.* Ollie had only shaken his head before taking the seat across from me at the crew mess table.

Awkward greeting aside, I was hopeful Ollie and I could get off to a better start now that we were docked at Simpson Bay and charter season had officially begun. Seeing as we'd be stuck on this boat together for the next four months, what other choice was there?

I crossed the galley and stood on the opposite side of the island from him. "Lovely seeing you again, Oliver."

He flicked his gaze over me before returning his attention to the preference sheets with a sigh. "It's Ollie. Not Oliver."

He straightened before I could say anything else and bounded to the pantry. He stuck his head inside, muttering under his breath when he returned to the counter and wrote something in his notebook. Back and forth he went, acting as if I weren't there. Counter, pantry, counter, pantry. Peek inside, scribble, scan the preference sheets.

After a few rounds of this dance, Ollie stuck the pencil between his teeth and stared at me. "Can I help you?" he said, the words warped because of the pencil in his mouth.

"Quinn sent me to help you go shopping for the items that were missing from the provision delivery yesterday," I explained.

Ollie let the pencil drop to the counter and started writing again. "And I already told Quinn I don't need any fecking help."

I held back a sigh. I didn't give a flying fuck whether *Oliver* needed my help or not. My only concern was keeping my job, and seeing as *Quinn* was chief stewardess, and Ollie wasn't, he could deal with my company for a little while. Unlike me, he didn't have a superior to answer to other than Captain Xav.

I plucked the pencil from his hands, wishing I could shove it up his nose. "That's too bad, Gordon Ramsay, because I'm going anyway."

Ollie stared at the pencil in my hands before dragging his eyes up to meet mine. *What pretty eyes! What a pretty mouth!* I thought, and imagined him replying, *The better to eat you with, my dear.*

"Can't tell if that's a compliment or not," he said. He pried the pencil from my fingers to flourish one last line on the page before tearing it from the notebook. When he shoved the page into the pocket of his T-shirt, he gave me a weary look. "Nice chat. See you later, love."

"Don't call me love," I said.

"Don't get flattered. I call everyone love." I watched him kick off his boat shoes and grab a pair of beat-up sneakers from the pantry.

"Hey!" I called, following him as he strutted from the galley. "Where are you going?"

Ollie didn't reply, but the answer was obvious. I looked down at my bare feet. Did he seriously think I'd let something as simple as a pair of shoes keep me from missing out on my first chance to explore Saint Martin?

"Oh hell no." I didn't know why Ollie didn't want me tagging along. I should've given up and turned around. I could've explained the situation to Quinn. But Ollie winning meant *me* losing, and after the last few months, I really needed a win.

I swiped Ollie's boat shoes from the floor and followed him, infuriated by how he looked up at me coolly when he stopped beside the gangway to tug on his sneakers. "No shoes? Sorry, *love*. My taxi should be here any minute, and I'm in a hurry. Maybe you can come next time."

"Oh, I've got a pair of shoes," I said, grinning as I shoved my feet into his boat shoes.

"What the fuck do you think you're doing?"

"Helping you go provision shopping."

I stepped around him, racing down the gangway and onto the dock. Ollie swore and shot to his feet. "Don't you dare," he said, and followed me down the dock. When I reached the end of it, I stepped into the parking lot without hesitation.

Ollie swore. "I can't believe you just did that!" he said when he caught up to me. "I won't be able to wear those on the boat now with you tromping around God knows where, picking up God knows what!"

I gave him a look of feigned innocence. "Oops! Silly me. I had no idea!" I continued through the parking lot. "Gosh, I just know absolutely nothing about yachting! However did I get this job?"

Ollie fumed at my side. "Jesus, you can't still be mad at me for saying that, can you? You *didn't* know anything about yachting. It was a statement of fact."

We exited the marina and halted beside the main road to wait for the taxi. A car whizzed past, kicking up a stray grocery bag that wound itself around Ollie's ankle. I tried not to laugh as he attempted to shake it loose. Eventually he gave up and bent over to pull it off. He balled up the grocery bag and shoved it into one of his pants pockets, muttering about litter under his breath.

"Forget delightful, you're about as charming as that grocery bag," I said.

Ollie glared at me. "I happen to like grocery bags. Means I can carry more groceries. You don't like grocery bags or something?"

"They're . . . fine, I guess."

Ollie snorted. "Fine? You ever shopped at an Aldi before?"

"Who hasn't?" I said, uncertain where this conversation was going.

"Always forget to bring my bags," Ollie said. "End up looking like a feckin' Muppet carrying everything up to my apartment." He turned to me with narrowed eyes. "I bet you're the sort to load all the bags on your arms so you can bring everything inside in one go."

"Am not," I lied. I kicked at a rock with one of his oversized boat shoes. "And even if I were, who cares?"

"Smashes the bread," Ollie said. "You like smashed bread?"

I ignored the question, because *no*, I did not like smashed bread. I gave him a long hard look. "Why are the pretty ones always annoying?"

The corner of Ollie's mouth twitched, and a dimple appeared. "You think I'm pretty, do you?"

I rolled my eyes. "Don't act like you don't know it. And don't get any ideas. I'm not impressed by pretty."

"Go on, then," he said. "What're you impressed by, if not my gorgeous face?"

I rolled my eyes and said the first thing that came to mind. "Snacks."

"Snacks?"

"*Yes*, snacks," I said, suddenly committed to the theory I'd only just made up. "You can tell the quality of a person's character by what their favorite snacks are. I'd explain further, but that would be doing you a favor." I turned away from him to look at the hills that rose in the distance. I'd been so distracted by Ollie that I'd forgotten where I was. A new country! An island! A world removed from my normal life!

"What are your favorite snacks, then?" Ollie asked.

"How about this: I'll tell you *one* of my favorite snacks if you tell me why you don't want me here."

Ollie looked me up and down. "Have you ever been provision shopping before?" he said.

"No."

"Have you ever been to Saint Martin before?"

"No."

He shrugged. "Then you'll only slow me down."

I glared at him, and a thought struck me. "Have *you* ever been to Saint Martin before?" I'd learned at the all-crew meeting this was his first charter season. He'd been employed on the yacht for five months, having started during the low season since graduating from culinary school in September.

His smug expression faltered. "I haven't been to Saint Martin before, no."

"Isn't that interesting?"

"Look, I can't afford any distractions."

"Oh!" I said with a laugh. "So now I'm incompetent *and* distracting?"

"I didn't . . ." The tips of his ears turned pink, and he dragged a hand through his hair. "You're ridiculous, and, yeah, it's distracting. I need this job. I take it seriously. That's all."

"You're rude," I said, and turned away to face the road.

"So? What is it?"

"What is *what*?"

Ollie groaned. "Jesus, girl. We made a deal, or did you forget already? C'mon, pony up. What's your favorite snack?"

"You don't deserve to know."

"You promised. Don't you remember what Cap said at the meeting? The three values of the boat, honesty, loyalty, and all that?"

"I'm not loyal to *you*."

Ollie leaned toward me and held my gaze for a long moment before rocking back onto his heels. "You're weird."

"So I've heard," I said, kicking at another rock. "You're kind of a dick, you know."

"I do, yeah," he said. "Just know I'm going to bother you until you tell me what your favorite snack is." He smiled then, not the smirk I'd seen before, but something genuine. The way it warmed his face startled me. I would've guessed getting a genuine smile out of Oliver Dunne was about as likely as a flock of seagulls helping me fold laundry on the yacht.

"Ridiculous eye candy," I muttered.

"What's that?"

I glared at him, feeling the heat rush to my cheeks. "I said you're . . . a ridiculous chimpanzee."

He flexed an arm. "It's the muscles, isn't it?"

I snorted. "No, it's the way I don't trust you not to rip my face off."

"Well, you're like a . . . unicorn," he said.

I narrowed my eyes. "What's that supposed to mean?"

Ollie toed the loose gravel beneath his feet and cursed at the sight of me wearing his boat shoes.

"Hope you're real proud of yourself," he said. "Now you'll be stuck shopping with me even longer so I can find some new boat shoes."

"If you'd have waited for me, I would've grabbed my own shoes," I said. "What do you mean I'm like a unicorn?"

He lifted a shoulder. "You're scary."

"I fail to see how unicorns are scary."

"An animal the size of a horse with a giant horn sticking out its head? That's scary."

"Did you just call me a giant animal?"

"Obviously you're not the size of a horse. More like a wee little pony. And I think you've got two horns instead of one. Point is you're fecking scary."

I stared at him, momentarily distracted by the reappearance of that smile. Really, his face was quite different when he smiled like that. I wasn't sure what to make of it.

Finally, our taxi arrived. When it stopped beside us, he opened the back door and gestured for me to climb in. He was a jerk, that much was clear, but at least he was a jerk with an ounce of etiquette. I couldn't say the same for most of the jerks I'd encountered.

When Ollie scooted into the back seat after me, he leaned forward to speak to the driver, and his knee knocked against mine. I pulled away, sliding as far from him as I could. I felt his eyes on me but kept my gaze out the window. I didn't want to give him the satisfaction of noticing.

But my resolve lasted for all of ten seconds. "Will you quit staring at me?" I said when I turned to him and he didn't look away.

"Not until you tell me what your favorite snack is," he said.

Insufferable. He didn't even have the courtesy to *pretend* he hadn't been staring.

The cab lurched forward to weave into traffic. At my yelp of surprise, Ollie laughed. The sound, warm and full, seemed to leap out of him. I was tempted to poke him in the ribs just so I could hear it again.

"It's pizza rolls," I said. "And in case you were wondering, I don't like you." When he laughed again, I turned to face the window, not wanting him to see the smile I was fighting to bite back at the sound of it.

"Still not sure about you," he replied. "Could go either way."

7

~~~~~~~

As it turns out, trying to ignore Ollie while sharing a tiny cabin on a superyacht has its complications. For one, my willpower is constantly under siege. At every turn Ollie is there. Rolling from the bottom bunk in the morning and blinking the sleep from his eyes, hair stuck up charmingly on one side. Right out of the shower, a towel wrapped loosely around his waist, chest dripping wet, water gleaming on those broad shoulders. Some mornings it takes everything I have not to tell him to shut up and yank him into bed with me.

And then there's the fact that as the *Serendipity*'s chef, he's just as insufferable and arrogant as I remember. I last only two charters managing polite work-related conversation with him before he annoys the ever-loving shit out of me, and I lose it in the galley.

"I'm not going to the fecking beach picnic," Ollie says. A steady thud punctuates his words as he hammers away at bloody beef cheeks on the counter. "I'll cook whatever they want, but I'm not getting in the tender and spending all day in the sun like some beachfront hibachi chef."

I know I've got an attitude, but Ollie's takes the cake. I glare at him from the opposite side of the counter, perching my feet on the bottom rung of a stool I've pulled up to it. In front of me is the trusty yellow legal pad that keeps the interior of this ship running efficiently.

I put pen to paper and mutter loud enough for Ollie to hear as I write, "Tell guests Chef doesn't know how to grill and is an inflexible asshole."

"Piss off, Nina. You know the food'll be better if you let me cook it in the galley."

"Then just *pretend* to grill it. Cook it here, for all I care. As long as they *think* you grilled it on that beach, that's all that matters."

"How am I supposed to *pretend* to grill it, Nina? It'll be a little obvious when the grill doesn't have flames and isn't smoking."

Why does he have to be so impossible? Inflexible? "I don't care *how* you do it. Grill them. Pretend to grill them. Grill some and put on a big show of it, and we'll switch them out for the ones you cooked on board. But you *will* go to that beach, stand in front of that fucking grill, and put on whatever Irish charm you have left."

"Tell them I can't do it, Neen. Who the hell wants grilled beef cheeks at a fecking beach picnic? I'm not a circus monkey."

"Correct. You're a yacht monkey. The pay is much better. It's what they want, so it's what you'll do. Go cry it out like a big man-baby, then get your ass on that beach. Either you get on the tender yourself or I'll have RJ fireman-carry you onto it."

"This is fecking ridiculous," Ollie huffs, and I know I've won this fight. He stomps across the galley to the sink with the meat tenderizer in hand, looking like he'd really like to use it on the next person who gets in his way.

"Damn, that was intense," Nekesa says from behind me.

I'd forgotten we had an audience. I turn to find Nekesa and Alyssa staring at me as they polish silverware.

"There had better not be a single water spot on those forks," I say before turning back to the legal pad to finish writing out the list of all the things we need for the beach picnic. I'll ignore Nekesa, and Alyssa, *and* Ollie, if that's what it'll take to get through this charter.

Ollie's cursing fades to a light muttering by the time Britt skips into the galley. She hops onto the counter and winds one of her curls around a finger. "I'm sensing . . . drama."

"Hey, Britt," Nekesa calls. "If Nina kills you, does that mean I get bottom bunk?"

Britt tips her head to the side. "I did say you could have bottom bunk over my dead body, so sure. But Nina won't kill me. She loves me like a sister. Don't you, Nina?"

"I'm an only child, but rumor has it I ate my twin in utero," I say, then add *Murder Britt* to the to-do list, making sure the words are big enough for her to see.

Britt snatches the pen from my hand and adds *with love*.

"Get off the fecking counter, Britt," Ollie says. He glances at Britt's addition to the list and snorts. "Good luck with that," he says, then sets the beef cheeks aside to marinate and leaves the galley.

"So . . ." Britt says, hopping back onto the counter as soon as Ollie disappears. "Are we ever going to talk about this?"

RJ and Eglé drift into the galley, dragging a large cooler behind them.

"Talk about what?" Eglé asks.

Jo was absolutely right about the possibility of my throwing Britt overboard. "Yes, Britt. Talk about what?" I touch a fingertip to the end of my pen and point it at her threateningly.

"We're talking about the elephant in the room, of course," Britt says, because, unfortunately, she has no fear of me. I ought to fire her for it.

"Elephant is right," I say. "He stomps around this boat like an elephant having a tantrum."

I've done a pretty good job pretending Ollie bringing up our legal status never happened. If I act like nothing is going on, maybe he'll give up on his ridiculous ultimatum and see it's no use. So far, it seems to be working. He hasn't brought it up since then. If I wanted to be more self-aware, I might spend some time working through the mess of my feelings for Ollie. But I refuse to shell out hundreds of dollars for therapy, much to Jo's annoyance. She's become a real therapy evangelist ever since starting family therapy with Alex and Greyson. She even goes on her own now and threatened to gift me a few sessions after the last time I stonewalled her about Ollie. I told her she wouldn't be able to afford the amount of therapy I need, and she dropped the subject.

"You're talking about Ollie, right?" Eglé asks.

"Who else?" Alyssa says.

I turn to glare over my shoulder at her and Nekesa. "Does anyone on this boat work but me?" RJ laughs from across the galley. "What are *you* looking at?" I say to him. "Don't you have a poop deck to swab?"

"Who cares what he's looking at?" Britt says. "Shoo, RJ."

"You heard her," I say, and wave him away. "Scram."

RJ rolls his eyes. "Have fun hauling the coolers on the tender yourself." He gets to his feet and leaves the galley.

"Thanks, Nina and Britt. Now he's going to be in a bad mood,"

Eglé says. "I better get back to work before he turns that angst on us lowly deckhands."

"Can we get back to the topic of Nina and Ollie?" Nekesa says.

"No," I say.

"Yes," Britt says.

Alyssa looks at the rest of us with a bored expression. "What's there to say about it? They hate each other."

"Nina and Ollie are totally in love," Britt says.

"Could've fooled me," Nekesa says.

"I don't pay you to gossip about me when I'm sitting right here," I say, and add *curse stewardesses and their future descendants* to my to-do list.

"You don't pay us. The Greens do," Britt says.

I sigh. "Either way, if you're going to continue fabricating conspiracies about myself and Ollie, I'd prefer you to do it off the clock. Let Mom and Dad work it out."

"So I'm a grown-up and not a big man-baby like you were saying, oh, I don't know, five minutes ago?"

I nearly leap out of my skin at the sound of Ollie's voice behind me. I hadn't heard him come back into the galley.

Britt, Nekesa, and Alyssa look at each other, biting back giggles.

I turn to rest my back against the counter. "Shouldn't you be somewhere crying over beef cheeks or something?"

Ollie moves between me and the girls. He faces me, the corner of his mouth twitching. It's the only hint of the truth—he loves our bickering. "Piss off, Neen."

"Grow up, Ollie."

He leans forward and braces the counter on either side of me with his hands. My breath hitches in my chest. I wait for him to say something, but the way he's staring right into my eyes makes it hard to look away. *Kiss him*, the voice in my head says. But we're working. We have an audience. And I'm still pissed at him, though now I can't remember *why*.

"I am trying to grow up, Neen," Ollie says. "You should give it a go. We can do grown-up things together."

"What are you suggesting?" I say, suddenly breathless. "This is a place of work, and you are being highly inappropriate."

He pulls back, pinning me in place with a roguish grin. "I don't see what's inappropriate about doing our taxes. Get your mind out of the gutter, girl." He reaches out and tugs gently on a piece of hair that's escaped my high ponytail in the hustle and bustle of the workday. My cheek burns where his fingertips brush against it. "I ought to make you wear a hairnet," he says.

And then he turns away and crosses the galley, humming under his breath as he pokes his head into the refrigerator. The little shit.

"That was some *sexual* tension," Britt says.

"It was nothing of the sort," I say, careening right into denial. "Which of you is keeping an eye on the guests? Wasn't it supposed to be *you*, Britt? I swear, you drive me to distraction."

"Not as much as *he* does," Britt says with a gleeful grin.

"You know what?" I toss my legal pad onto the counter. "I'd rather babysit obnoxious guests than sit here with the three of you. Alyssa, you're on beach picnic prep. Nekesa, do a load of laundry and take your break. Britt, clean the toilets."

Britt's mouth falls open. "Toilets? But—"

"*Butt* is right," I say. "If I have to put my bare ass on anything other than a perfectly clean toilet seat, you're fired."

"I have some ideas about where you can put your bare ass," Britt mumbles, making Alyssa gasp.

I close my eyes and take a deep breath. Better not to engage at this point. I turn to Ollie. "I will see *you* and your beef cheeks on that beach in an hour."

"Always knew you loved my cheeks, Neen," Ollie says.

"I will not dignify that comment with a response."

"She didn't deny it," Britt says.

"God only knows why I get on this boat year after year," I say, shooting each person in the galley a glare before I leave.

8

~~~~~~

The night Ollie and I became friends began when he knocked on the door to my bunk a month into our first charter season.

"Good, you're here," he said when I opened the door to find him standing on the other side, a mug of tea in one hand.

"You're back," I said. I was surprised to see him, and not only because we weren't exactly friends. Two days earlier, I'd woken up to find a different chef in the galley. Ollie hadn't mentioned leaving, but, then again, we hadn't interacted much. As junior stewardess, I spent most of my time on laundry duty and cleaning. Outside the galley, Ollie mostly kept to himself. If he wasn't holed up in his bunk, he was smoking on the highest part of the boat, a small cushioned area we called the bunny pad. I always knew when he was up there, because I'd start craving a cigarette before I even smelled smoke. The few times I'd been on service were enough for me to conclude that Ollie was a border collie in a human body. Loud mouth.

Intelligent eyes. A frenetic aura about him even when he was standing still.

"Did you miss me?" Ollie asked. He took a sip of his tea, then leaned against my doorframe, acting as if knocking on my door and striking up a conversation was something he did all the time.

"Not at all," I said.

The chef who'd filled in for Ollie was a quiet woman who'd personified professionalism. At first, I'd thought Ollie had quit in the middle of the charter. But my chief stew said his absence was temporary, though even she didn't know where he'd gone or why. Those two days were the calmest the galley had been all season. Even so, I'd felt a strange sense of relief knowing Ollie would be back.

Ollie ran his eyes over me. "You're a bad liar."

"I ought to shut this door in your face," I said.

The rest of the crew had gone barhopping in Saint Martin. I'd declined to join them. It was awkward, not eating or drinking when everyone else was. I only ever ordered water, and it was hard enough to part with the few dollars I left as a tip. I didn't want to explain why I was such a tightwad.

Ollie, like me, didn't go out much. I had no idea why. He was a bit of a loner. I assumed it was because he preferred his own company to that of other people.

So seeing him there at the door to my bunk was unexpected. He rocked back and forth on his heels in the hallway. "Meet me on the bunny pad in ten," he said. "I've got a plan. And bring your cigs. I'm out."

I raised my eyebrows in surprise.

He swore. "That's right, Ms. Florida Free Tobacco. I know your little secret. Your hair smells like it."

I touched a hand to my hair.

"You think you're sneaky hiding down on the sun deck when I'm smoking, but I know you're there." He shook his head. "Rushing a man on his smoke break, now that's rude." He smacked the doorframe with a hand. "Right. Bunny pad, ten minutes."

"No," I said.

He cocked his head to the side. "No?"

"I don't like being told what to do."

He rested his head against the doorframe, eyes narrowed as he looked me over. "I'd never have guessed that about you."

I gripped the edge of the door. "I really will shut this in your face."

"Wait, wait. Let me try again." He closed his eyes, looking like an actor preparing for a scene. When he opened them again, he said in a saccharine voice, "Nina Lejeune, junior stewardess of the *Serendipity*, would you do me the honor of meeting me up on the bunny pad in ten minutes and bringing your cigs?"

I glanced at the mug in his hands, then eyed him suspiciously. "Did you put drugs in your tea or something?"

"I did not," he said. He leaned closer. "So? Will you come? I have a plan, like I said. It involves snacks."

It was the promise of snacks that lowered my defenses. That, and I was bored of being alone in my room and, despite my better judgment, curious about this plan of his.

"What's the plan?" I said.

Ollie grinned. "Tell you when you get there."

"No. You'll tell me—"

"When you get there!"

I sighed in defeat. "Fine. Ten minutes."

"And the cigs?" he said.

"You have a problem."

"I've got more than one, love," he said, and turned away.

"Don't call me love!" I called after him. Ollie disappeared into his room with a laugh, and I stood in the hallway for a moment and stared at his door, utterly bewildered by the unexpected turn my evening had taken.

Fifteen minutes later—I didn't want to seem *too* interested—I found Ollie up on the bunny pad. He looked at me eagerly, his hair boyishly windswept. He seemed so young, sitting there with his arms wrapped around his knees, a whiskey bottle resting between them. At twenty-three, he *was* young. We both were.

"Did you bring—"

"I said I would." I hurled my cigarettes at him, and the carton hit him square on the nose.

Ollie rubbed his face and swore. "Are you gonna keep throwing shapes if I ask for a lighter?"

"Here's a quadrilateral." I pretended to toss one his way and sank beside him on the cushion, then passed him my lighter with a sigh. "I know you're speaking English, but I don't have a clue what you're saying."

Ollie put a cigarette between his lips. "Quadrilateral, huh? Nice one. Would've gone with trapezoid myself. Throwing shapes is like . . . acting all tough." He puffed out his chest and arched a brow. His expression was so ridiculous it made me laugh.

"So *that's* what you're always doing."

"Ha." He held up my lighter. "Thanks, Neen."

"Why can't you just call people by their actual names, *Oliver?*"

He shrugged as he tried and failed to light his cigarette. "Nina. Neen. It is your name. You don't like it?"

Neen was better than *love* at any rate. "It's not the worst name someone's called me," I said, which made him laugh. "So why the sketchy meeting? I was promised snacks."

Ollie furrowed his brow. "Hush, now. The snacks are for later. Let a man smoke in peace before getting down to business." He continued flicking at the lighter, but the wind was too strong up there. He finally gave up and held the lighter out to me with a sigh. "Do me a favor, will you?"

"You're impossible," I said, but took the lighter from him anyway. Ollie shielded the cigarette from the wind with cupped hands. I flicked the lighter beneath the cigarette, and the flame caught it on the first try.

"Thanks, *Neen*," Ollie said after taking a drag.

"Should've burned your eyelashes off."

"But then I wouldn't be so pretty," he said, and fluttered them at me.

Ollie helped me light a cigarette for myself. I watched the wind spiral the smoke away from us and into the sky, thinking about how different it felt to be sitting here with someone else rather than on my own like I usually did. The night was peaceful. The yacht was quiet, devoid of guests and crew, except for Captain Xav, who stuck to the captain's quarters on our nights off. Up here, it was easy to forget how I'd ended up on a superyacht in a Saint Martin marina, smoking beside a hotheaded Irish chef who, up until a few minutes ago, I was sure hated me. The glow of other boats gliding along the horizon blinked at me like stars. *I could be happy*, I thought, *if every moment was like this*. Back then, I'd thought it was the hum of the yacht, the gentle sound of the ocean, the murmur of voices in the marina that made me feel that way. I didn't even consider that it had more to do with the man smoking quietly beside me.

"I don't get it," I said once I'd burned through my cigarette.

"Don't get what?"

"Why I'm here. I thought you hated me."

Ollie turned to look at me. "You did? Why?"

"Oh, come on. You snapped at me on our first charter."

"I didn't *snap* at you."

"*I don't need any fecking help,*" I said. A dimple jumped out on Ollie's cheek at my impression of him. "Just last week you threatened to chop my hand off with a butcher knife when I borrowed one of your mint tea bags."

He shook his head. "I didn't need help, and I don't share my tea. You can't *borrow* a tea bag. That had nothing to do with *you*. Don't take things so personally."

"You don't like me," I insisted.

He leaned in closer, and his shoulder brushed against mine. "Listen, I like you, Nina. You're . . . amusing. You seem like a"—he tipped his head to the sky—"nice girl. No, sorry. Let me try again. Like a good person. Cool, I mean. I've never seen a yacht stewardess do a full gymnastics routine on the floating trampoline before," he said. "That's cool."

Nice girl? Good person? Cool? I took another cigarette from the carton and rolled it between my fingers to slow my heart rate.

"What I'm saying is you seem like someone I'd be friends with."

I glanced at him, skeptical, but he seemed sincere . . . embarrassed, even. "I guess you seem . . . okay."

"*Okay?* Geez." He helped me light my next cigarette, then drummed his hands against the whiskey bottle. "Are you ready for the plan?"

I narrowed my eyes, suddenly wondering what sort of plan this was. "As long as it's not a plan to get in my pants."

Ollie snorted. "No, Neen, that's not the plan. Haven't you ever heard the saying *Don't screw the crew*?" He patted the whiskey bottle between his knees. "The plan is, we drink this—"

I flicked the bottle with a finger. "I wouldn't call drinking whiskey up on the bunny pad a *plan*. It's an awful one anyway. Do you want to fall to your death?"

"I wasn't *finished* with the plan, Neen."

"Go on."

"We drink *this*." He gave the bottle another slap. "Down on the sun deck, if you like, and then you teach me to do a cartwheel."

I gave him a blank stare. "You want me to drunkenly teach you to do a drunken cartwheel?"

"I never learned."

"To do a drunken cartwheel?"

"To do any sort of cart anything. Why are you always pestering me?"

"I don't see why we have to be drunk."

"We don't, but it'll make things more interesting, don't you think? All I know is I really need a drink after the last few days, and I want to learn to do a cartwheel."

I looked him over, trying to reconcile this man with the one who'd tried to ditch me on the boat a few weeks ago. He was dressed in gray sweatpants and one of the ridiculous graphic T-shirts he always wore when he was off the clock. From what I could tell, he owned a seemingly endless supply of them. The goofy sayings didn't seem to match the grumpy, hotheaded chef in the galley. Today's shirt had an image of a cereal bowl beside a carton of milk. *Cereal Killer*, it read. I nodded to his shirt. "You can't tell me you really think these jokes are funny."

He looked down at the shirt, then back up at me, his expression serious. "It's not a joke," he said. "It's a warning. I can kill a box of Froot Loops easy. Don't even need a bowl. I just pour the milk right into the box."

I laughed, which made Ollie grin. "Froot Loops?" I said. "Everyone knows Cap'n Crunch is the superior cereal." At his offended expression, I sighed. "You're not at all what you seem, Oliver Dunne," I said.

"What do I seem, then?"

"Like a younger Irish version of Gordon Ramsay on a boat. Like a big serious grump."

"And I'm not a big serious grump?"

I paused for a moment. Ollie was . . . confusing. I'd thought he was aloof, but tonight he'd shown up at my door and invited me up here. I'd thought he was serious, but here he was in his goofy T-shirt cracking jokes. I'd thought he was angry, but here he was smiling at me with those dimples. "You are, but you're also . . ." *Interesting*, I thought. "Odd," I said.

Ollie unscrewed the top of the whiskey bottle and took a swig before holding it out to me. "So the plan, it's good, yeah?

"I wouldn't say it's *good*."

"But you'll do it."

I stared at the whiskey bottle. There was something about Ollie that seemed almost pleading. He'd said he needed a drink, and I believed he meant it. I didn't know where he'd gone or why, but the Ollie who sat beside me now seemed decidedly different from the one who'd left the *Serendipity* two days ago. He seemed . . . desperate for something. I wasn't sure what.

"Fine." I grabbed the whiskey bottle from him and took a swig. "I'll do it, but only because watching you drunkenly cartwheeling all over the sun deck sounds highly entertaining."

Ollie and I left the bunny pad and pushed all the lounge chairs to the edge of the sun deck.

"I have to show you how it's done before I get too drunk," I said. I took another swig from the whiskey bottle and passed it back to Ollie, then directed him to go sit by the hot tub. I pulled out my phone and put on some music, turning up the volume as loud as I could and setting it on one of the lounge chairs before doing a few cartwheels.

"All right," I said once I righted myself again. It felt good to have my body moving, even though I wasn't as in shape as I used to be. I smoothed my hair back into place, then walked over to Ollie and nudged him with my toe. "Your turn."

He stood with a groan and trudged over to the center of the deck, then did the most pathetic attempt at a cartwheel I'd ever seen.

He shot me a false glare. "No laughing!" he said. I laughed even harder as he massaged his groin muscles. "Jesus, that's harder than it looks. I better not get a dick hernia."

I choked on the whiskey in my mouth, coughing so hard tears streamed down my face. "A . . . what?" I wheezed. "Is that a thing?"

"What am I supposed to do with it?" he said. He shot me another glare when I dissolved into a fit of giggles. "I'm serious! Is it supposed to just be swinging around down there? That can't be right."

"I have no idea," I said. "I've never thought about it."

"Should I be wearing underwear for this? Is that what the pros do?"

"You're not wearing . . . Oh, never mind. I think the competition shirt—"

"The what, now?"

I waved a hand. "The leotard," I said. "I think it kind of . . . holds it all in place. Some of them wear tight briefs or compression shorts. I'm not . . . Oh, forget it, you're fine. You're not going to get a dick hernia," I added, trying very hard not to look at his crotch.

"You're an awful coach," Ollie said. He tried a few more cartwheels, but his shirt kept falling onto his face. Eventually he whipped it over his head and tossed it onto a nearby lounge chair. I tried not to stare at him, but the man looked . . . great. I knew he worked out. RJ, Ollie's bunkmate, was constantly muttering under his breath about tripping over Ollie's free weights and knocking his head against the pull-up bar whenever Ollie left it up in the doorway. But beneath that ridiculous graphic tee, he was much more in shape than I expected.

I tried talking Ollie through the steps of doing a cartwheel, but the lesson ended up being more physical than I'd planned. My hands were all over him—his shoulders, back, waist. I was too drunk and enjoying myself too much to feel self-conscious about it, though. At one point, when I had his ankles in my hands, he had me laughing so hard, I nearly dropped him on his face.

When Ollie finally achieved a half-decent cartwheel, he turned to me with a grin. "That was it, right? That one was good?"

"I mean . . . relatively speaking, yes."

He rolled his eyes, and I noticed a small oval-shaped medal that had fallen on deck.

I stooped to pick it up and squinted at the image of a woman with a sword in one hand and a book in the other. "Is this yours?" I asked.

"Hmm?" He looked at the medal in my hands. "Oh. Yeah."

"Who is she?"

"Saint Dymphna," he said. "Says so right there."

"Well, yeah. But what's her thing?"

"What do you mean, *What's her thing?*" he said, putting on an impressive American accent.

"Don't they all have specialties or something? What's hers?"

"Anxiety," Ollie said, sounding annoyed. He plucked the medal from my hands and shoved it back in his pocket. "Jesus, I'm langers. Better stop now before I cartwheel overboard, yeah?"

He crossed the sun deck and sat with his back against the outside of the hot tub. With the medal tucked out of sight, the amusement returned to his face, and he seemed like a totally different person from the moment before.

After I sat beside him, I nodded to his lap. "How's your . . ."

Ollie laughed. "It's wonderful," he said. "Rave reviews."

"Well, it can't be worse than your cartwheels at any rate. You're awful."

"That's not a fair assessment. You come from Olympian stock. I'm amazing for a beginner."

"I come from Olympian stock, huh?" Everyone on board knew I used to be a kids' gymnastics coach, but I hadn't said anything about my professional athletic career. If anyone knew, they hadn't breathed a word of it around me.

Ollie rubbed the back of his neck. "I, uh, looked you up after we met. Just couldn't shake the feeling I knew you from somewhere."

"Let me guess, you knew me as *that girl* from Olympic trials."

"I watched your other stuff too. I think I've seen it all now. Not on purpose . . . I don't want you to think . . ." His ears grew pink as he fumbled for words. "YouTube has that autoplay thing. You watch one video and, next thing you know, it's two hours later and you're . . ." He let the words trail off. "What I mean is, you're really good. Incredible."

I sighed. "Not anymore. As you can see, I am now retired."

"You didn't want to go back to it?"

I flexed the leg that rested against his. "Not really," I said.

His fingers grazed my knee. "Does it still hurt?"

"Sometimes." I tried to ignore how nice it felt to have his hand there. *God, I'm drunk.*

Ollie, seeming to realize what he'd done, pulled away and shoved both his hands between his thighs. "What do your parents think about your retirement?"

I shrugged. "They probably think the same thing everyone else does."

"Which is?"

I let out a bitter laugh. "My mother is an Olympic silver medalist.

My father, a highly respected coach. And then there's me: the one who took *break a leg* seriously."

Ollie looked at me but didn't say anything.

"Bad joke." I sighed. "The point is, I'm a disappointment."

"And *everyone* thinks that?"

"I obviously can't read *everyone's* mind, but I imagine that's what most people think. It's what *I* think."

"Well, Neen," Ollie said, "I can tell you with one hundred percent certainty not everyone thinks that."

"How would you know?"

"Not that it matters what I think, but as someone who really is a family disappointment, you don't seem like one to me. It sounds like you've had a lot more success than failure, and you've sure as hell had more success than most people. I don't know your parents, but I can't imagine they're disappointed in you."

"Maybe," I said. "What makes you the family disappointment?"

"Oh Jesus, a lot of things."

I waited for him to explain, but he didn't, so I figured it was better not to ask.

"To tell you the truth," I said, "I was sort of relieved when I decided to retire. I love gymnastics. You don't go through that sort of training if you don't. But the longer I'm away, the more I wonder if *competing* was what I really wanted. Did I really want gymnastics to be my entire life? Was I doing it for me or for my parents? Not that they forced me into it or anything. I used to feel so . . . grateful to them."

"And now you don't?"

I traced circles on the teak with my finger. "I don't know." Other than sending an occasional text to tell my parents I was alive, I hadn't spoken to them since leaving Palm Beach. Part of me had hoped leaving home would give me clarity about what to do or how to feel. But the time and distance had only confused me more.

Suddenly I found myself on the verge of tears. "Oh hell," I said. I dabbed at my eyes with my shirt. "This is why I don't drink whiskey, you know. I'm more of a tequila girl."

"You all right?"

"I'm fine. It's just . . . Well, to tell you the truth, I've had a falling-out with my parents. It's not even about the gymnastics stuff." I didn't know if it was the exhaustion, or the alcohol, or if it was something about Ollie I hadn't yet identified, but I couldn't shut my mouth and breeze past the subject like I usually did. "My father stole my identity." At Ollie's widened eyes, I continued. "He has a gambling addiction, and I . . . well, I had no idea. For years he'd been taking out loans in my name. He defaulted on them, of course, and it's totally fucked up my life. I'm in so much debt I'm not sure I'll ever be able to pay it back. I can't get an apartment. Or a car. I've got nothing. Except bills," I said. "I have plenty of those."

"That's . . . fuck, that's brutal," he said.

"Yeah," I said, rubbing at my bad knee again. "When I retired from gymnastics, I started looking for my own place, but no one would approve me because my credit was abysmal. It didn't make any sense. I didn't have any student debt. I never carried a balance on my credit card. So I did some digging and found out someone had been taking out payday loans and credit cards in my name, but I never thought . . ." I let out a slow breath to keep the tears at bay. "I used to be close with my parents, especially my dad. As you can imagine, that is no longer true."

"I'm sorry."

"It is what it is," I said. I tapped my fingers along the whiskey bottle. "But that's not even the worst part."

"What's the worst part?"

"The worst part is I can't bring myself to do anything about it. I'm pissed. I feel like they've sabotaged my life. I know what you're thinking. Why don't I turn him in and try to clear my name? I should never speak to them again. But at the same time, I really believe they love me. He's my dad. He's a good person, even though it doesn't sound like it. He's . . . sick. He's in rehab trying to get better. My parents, they help with the bills as much as they can, but it isn't enough. I'm not sure I can throw them out of my life forever. And I can't bring myself to turn him in and risk ruining their lives."

"Even when they've ruined yours?" Ollie said.

"I know it doesn't make sense."

"It makes perfect sense."

I looked over at him. "It does?"

He freed his hands from between his thighs and scrubbed them down his face before turning to me, his expression more serious than I'd ever seen it, without amusement or annoyance. "Nothing wrong with taking your time to be sure. Family is . . . complicated."

I nodded, then laughed when I found myself blinking back tears again. For months I'd wrestled over what I should do. From the outside, I'm sure the right choice seemed obvious. But *complicated* was exactly the right word. "I don't normally cry this much," I said, and pushed the whiskey bottle over to him. "Think I can at least win gold for the most fucked-up family event?"

"You mean between the two of us?" Ollie said.

I shrugged, too drunk and emotional to know what I'd meant. It was just a joke. But Ollie was quiet for a moment.

"Nah," he said. "I've got you beat."

Again, I waited for him to explain, but he didn't.

"Did you see the floor routine I did to that instrumental version of 'Low' by Flo Rida?" I said to break the silence.

Ollie smiled. "Yeah, I did."

"Dad about killed me for that. I told him I wouldn't compete at all if he didn't let me. That was my defiant phase."

"Which you never grew out of, obviously," he teased. "You were, what, thirteen?"

"Fourteen. Floor was my favorite event. It was the only one where I could really interact with the crowd, you know? Everything else you had to have tunnel vision for, but floor"—I sighed, smiling at the memory of how it felt to be out there—"it was just . . . pure fun. The music, the dance elements, song choice. There's nothing like getting out there and performing, knowing the crowd is feeding off your energy and you're feeding off theirs."

"Which of your floor routines was your favorite?"

"'Feel Good Inc.,'" I said. "I wanted to put this blue streak in my hair, but I would've gotten docked for it."

He laughed. "So you were a weirdo back then too, huh?"

I leaned my head against the side of the hot tub and closed my eyes. "Yup."

"Good."

I turned my face toward him. "What about you? Were you a weird kid?" I couldn't imagine Ollie as anything other than the man sitting beside me now. It was easy to pretend the day I met him was the first day of his life, that he didn't have a past at all.

"Dunno," Ollie said. "Probably."

Once again, I waited for an explanation that didn't come. The silence between us stretched on, this time broken by my stomach growling.

"Ugh," I groaned. "Where are those snacks you promised? I'd cut off my right pinky toe for some pizza rolls."

Ollie rubbed his hands together. "You're in luck. That's what I was planning to make. Only took me a fecking month to perfect the recipe."

If I hadn't been drunk, maybe I would've wondered what was happening between us. Being around Ollie was comfortable and thrilling at the same time. It was as if I'd known him my entire life. Out on the boat during those first few months of our friendship, it felt like anything was possible, like our lives outside it weren't real at all.

But of course they were. Life on deck was the dream, and we were sailing steadily toward the end of it, where everything we'd been running from was still waiting for us.

9

～～～

When I wake up an hour before my shift on earlies is supposed to begin, I peer over the side of my bunk and find Ollie's bed empty. I can guess where he's gone. Ollie has always been a light sleeper, but some nights, he hardly sleeps at all. The first time I found him up on the bunny pad at sunrise was years ago, but I'll never forget how he told me watching the sun come up was as restful as an hour of sleep. Right now, sleep sounds like the better option to me, but when Ollie can't sleep, it's usually for a reason. Maybe he had a nightmare. He could be up there having an anxiety attack. I won't get any rest worrying about it, so I slip from bed and change quickly into my uniform, tossing on a cardigan before I leave our bunk. When I pass through the crew mess, the light on the electric kettle is on. Ollie and his tea, of course. He's probably already gone through a mug of it but is too tired or upset to come back down for another. I stifle a yawn and start a pot of coffee for myself and the rest of the crew. While I wait, I make a mint tea for Ollie.

Sure enough, I find Ollie staring out at the ocean when I reach the bunny pad. The wind is gentle today, ruffling his hair in the early-morning light. It's a thrill to see him up here, looking so pretty, especially when I thought I wouldn't see him for months. We've had our ups and downs since charter season started, but in this moment, he's my golden boy, literally and figuratively.

"I thought I might find you here," I say.

Ollie turns to me, bleary-eyed. "Hi."

"Hi."

I take a sip from my coffee, and Ollie nods to the mug in my other hand. "Is that . . ."

"Yup," I say, and hold it out to him.

"You're an angel." Ollie sighs as he takes the tea from my hands and moves the empty mug to make room for me beside him.

"I'm most certainly not," I say, and sit down. "I'll never understand your need for that stuff. It doesn't even have caffeine."

"I love a lot of things that don't make any sense."

"Aren't you cold?" I pull my cardigan tighter around me. The coffee in my hands warms me as we gaze out at the ocean. We're anchored at sea halfway through our fifth charter. There's nothing but water all around us. How can five weeks have passed so quickly? The way time stretches and collapses in on itself during charter season is something I am never prepared for, no matter how many times I've experienced it. How is it that every day can feel eternal, and yet the weeks ripple by in moments? Three months until Ollie either changes course or . . . leaves.

I'd rather not think about that possibility. There's enough to worry about. Crew drama, demanding guests. But up here watching the sunrise with Ollie feels like a moment outside of time. With all the guests and the rest of the crew asleep, it's as if Ollie and I are the only two people in existence. The sun has only just made its appearance over the horizon, bringing with it all my favorite colors—oranges and reds and pinks—to chase the night blues away.

"It's gorgeous out here," I say.

"Sure is," Ollie says, and I can feel him watching me. "Are *you* cold?"

"A little."

Ollie puts his arm around my shoulders, and I let myself relax into his side. This moment doesn't count. It doesn't mean I've changed my mind. Ollie knows that. At least I hope he does.

"Couldn't sleep?" I ask.

"Not really."

"Do you want to talk about it?" Most people don't get to see this side of Ollie. He'd rather show them the perfectionistic asshole in the kitchen. But I know that is only one piece of him. It bobs on the surface, distracting everyone from what's underneath.

"I was thinking about my da," he says. His voice is so quiet that at first, it takes me a moment to understand what he's said.

Ollie doesn't talk much about Ireland, especially his family, even to me. I know the basics. He grew up in Cobh, a pretty little harbor town in County Cork. His family owns a pub called the Local. He hasn't talked to his parents or his brother, Jack, who is ten years his junior, since he left for culinary school. His father was . . . cruel. I look at Ollie and spot the small, almost invisible scar just below his chin. All he told me about how he got it was that his father had smashed a glass against the kitchen counter in a fit of anger. *I think it was an accident*, Ollie had said as he'd rubbed his thumb along the scar. That *I think* broke my heart. Whenever I notice the scar, I'm tempted to try to kiss it until it disappears. For all the stories Ollie has told me, I'm sure there are a dozen he hasn't.

Ollie catches me staring at him, and I drop my eyes to the mug in my hands. "What were you thinking about your dad?"

He takes a long drink of his tea. My mind is whirring with questions, but I keep silent and lean against him with a bit more pressure. Sometimes he needs a few moments before he can say something hard. The silence gives him space to think, but a little contact—my hand on his arm, my weight against his side—can help him work up the courage to say whatever he needs to get off his chest.

Ollie sets down his tea and rubs the scar beneath his chin. "I was thinking about how I only applied for that job at Il Gabbiano because of him."

"What do you mean?" Last I knew, Ollie wanted that job because it was a good career move.

"I got an email from my da a few months before I quit the *Serendipity*. I don't know how he tracked me down. It was . . . odd. It started with him saying how much he and Mum and Jack missed me. And then . . . well, he said he hoped cooking for rich bastards on fancy boats was worth abandoning my family."

"He can't say that. He doesn't get to say that." A life goal of mine is to one day sucker punch that guy as hard as I can.

Ollie shrugs. "Well, he did."

"As if he doesn't know why you left."

He fidgets with the string of his tea bag. "If he was trying to make me feel guilty about leaving, he needn't have bothered. I've felt guilty for the last fifteen years."

"You shouldn't feel—"

Ollie shakes his head, and I fall silent midsentence. I don't need to tell him not to feel guilty. He knows he shouldn't. Doesn't keep him from feeling guilty anyway.

"It was just another way for him to try to control my life," Ollie says after a stretch of silence. "I can't believe I fell for it, but I thought . . . It sounds stupid now, but I thought if I had some impressive job, then I could show him I'd made myself into somebody without him. I'd been offered the gig at Il Gabbiano a few months before that and turned it down."

He . . . what? This was news to me. "You were offered the job before?"

Ollie nods. "But I turned it down, like I said."

I shake my head. "Why the hell would you do that?"

He gives me a pointed look.

Oh. I search for something to say but come up empty.

"I didn't regret turning that job down once until that email. It made me feel like a fecking kid again. Da would get all pissed off at me, and I just had to show him he was wrong, even though I *knew* nothing I did would ever be enough for him. Didn't keep me from trying."

"But Il Gabbiano . . . I thought you loved it there. I'm still shocked you quit."

Ollie laughs bitterly. "Hated every second. Thought it would get better once I got used to it, but it never did. When I took the job, I finally emailed my da back and told him I didn't work on yachts anymore. Told him I worked at one of the best restaurants in the Southeast. I shouldn't have sent it, but I thought he'd see I'd made myself somebody."

"You already were somebody," I say.

"Thanks, kitten," he says, and presses a quick kiss to my hair. "Anyway, he emailed me back the day I started the job. You want to know what he said?"

"I'm guessing I won't like it."

"All it said was 'Good luck.' Didn't hear from him after that. Any time there was an article about the restaurant in the paper, I'd save it in this folder on my computer. It was like collecting evidence to prove I'd done the right thing leaving Ireland, and then leaving the boat, leaving *you*, to work this job I hated. Whenever I wanted to quit, I'd imagine sending it to him."

"Did you ever do it?"

He nods.

"And?"

"Never heard back."

I rest my head against his shoulder. "You should've told me."

Ollie sighs. "Wouldn't have changed a thing, kitten."

"It might've made you feel better."

"I don't think so." He squeezes me tight against him before dropping his arm from around my shoulders. "You remember when I asked you if I should take the job?"

"I told you to do whatever you wanted." I didn't *want* him to go, of course, but who was I to tell him what to do? The next I'd heard about it was at the post–charter season celebration when Ollie told me he'd taken the job and was quitting the yacht. "If you didn't want the job, you should've said. I don't know why you asked *me*. It's *your* life."

Ollie shakes his head. "Because I *wanted* to know what *you* wanted. I was hoping you'd say no. I was hoping you'd tell me to stay. But you didn't, so I figured you didn't care either way."

"You can't be serious."

"What do you mean?"

"I'm not a fucking mind reader, Oliver."

"Don't like it when you call me—"

"Telling you to do whatever you want doesn't mean I don't *care*. I didn't want to sway you from the job if you wanted it. I didn't *want* you to leave, but I couldn't take an opportunity like that away from you. How could I tell you to stay, when I can't . . ."

"When you can't what?"

I wish he would drop it. I wish he would simply let things be. "When I can't give you what you want."

"Can't or won't?"

I wave the question away. "The point is that our current . . . arrangement . . . gives you total control over your life."

Ollie laughs. "Darling, if you think you have no sway over my life just because you won't admit to being in love with me, you aren't paying attention."

I don't spend a moment considering whether or not he's right. I'd rather not know. "Well, let the record show I never told you what to do. If we don't have any expectations, we won't have any disappointments. With the way things are, we have nothing to lose."

Ollie doesn't say anything. The sun climbs the sky quickly now, bathing everything in golden light. Moments like this are usually my favorite. They fill me up with enough peace to get through even the worst charter.

But today, with the words *we have nothing to lose* hanging between us, I don't feel at peace. I feel . . . unsettled.

Because when I look at Ollie beside me, when I think of waking up to find his bunk empty, I know I'm lying not only to him, but to myself too.

10

~~~~~~~

Nine years earlier

It was strange and terrifying how quickly Ollie and I became friends. Four months in close quarters had a way of intensifying everything. The smoke breaks, late nights talking in each other's rooms, the bickering in the galley. I'd meant to keep our friendship casual, but somehow, whenever the line between late and early blurred, I'd end up telling him things I'd never told anyone else. I told myself it was because being on charter felt like being in a separate universe, one completely removed from reality. But I couldn't deny it also had something to do with Ollie himself. He was a good listener. He knew when to laugh and when to keep his mouth shut. When to call someone a motherfucking shitehawk and when to call me on my BS.

Two weeks before the end of our first charter season together, I slipped down into the bilge to find decorations for a casino party we were throwing in the Sky Lounge but discovered Ollie sitting on one of the costume bins with his face buried in his hands.

He didn't see me at first, and I hesitated, unsure whether I should make myself known or leave before he found out I'd seen him. I thought back to the night we'd become friends and how he'd seen me cry and said exactly what I needed to hear. It was only fair I return the favor if that was what he wanted.

"Ollie?" I said. I pulled the door shut behind me. Whatever was happening here, I didn't want anyone else walking in on it.

When Ollie dropped his hands and stood, he turned his face from me. "Don't you have work to do?" he said. He cleared his throat and glanced over at me as if trying to assess how much I'd seen.

"Are you . . . all right?" I said.

Ollie folded his arms over his chest and paced the bilge but didn't answer.

"Ollie—"

He halted suddenly and sank back onto the costume bin. "I'm fucked, Neen."

"What do you mean?" I crossed the bilge and nudged his shoulder until there was enough space for me to sit beside him.

"It's my visa," he said.

"What about it?"

"I'm here on my student visa for culinary school," he said.

"But you graduated from culinary school last year."

"They authorized twelve months of post-completion practical training. That's this gig."

"Okay . . ."

"And my twelve months are up at the end of July."

"Oh," I said. "Well, that should be easy enough, right? Don't most international crew get a B-1/B-2 visa?"

He picked at a loose thread at the hem of his shirt. "Yeah, well, not me."

"Why not? I know you think you're special, Oliver Dunne, but you're not."

He side-eyed me. "You know how I left for a few days in March?"

"Of course I do. They were the best part of the whole season."

"Smartass," Ollie said. "I was in Ireland for a few days for my visa interview, but it got denied. I've been trying to sort things out since, but . . ." He shook his head.

"But you've got a job already. Why would they deny you?" Despite being the most commonly used visa for yachting, the B-1/B-2 wasn't designed for it. I'd heard getting one could be tricky. It all came down to the specific person you interviewed with, but Ollie already had a job. He'd studied in the US for years. I'd have thought his getting one would be no problem.

"They don't think I have enough ties to Ireland," he said. "If they so much as suspect you're trying to get around the legal immigration process, you're fucked."

"Oh," I said.

Ollie sighed. "They're not wrong. I don't have any ties back home. Hadn't been there in four years. Don't have any property, a car, not even an apartment. Don't have a single piece of mail from there. I don't talk to anyone back home either . . ." He buried his face in his hands and groaned. "I'm so fecking stupid."

It frightened me to see him so distressed. "I'm sure things will work themselves out," I said. "You've got time. Maybe Captain Xav can ask the owners to sponsor you."

Ollie shook his head. "Cap asked, but he told me this morning that the Greens said no."

Earlier Captain Xav had found me and Ollie sitting together at the bow of the boat, our legs swinging off the side as we rested our arms on the railing and looked out at the sea. He asked how I felt about becoming chief stewardess of the *Serendipity*, seeing as neither of the other stewardesses could stay on for the low season. Thrilled at the opportunity, I'd accepted right away. I'd been so excited that I hadn't thought anything of it when Captain Xav asked to speak with Ollie privately.

"Shit," I said. "But I'm sure you'll find someone who will. You're certainly not the worst chef in the world."

Ollie rolled his eyes. "I've applied to . . . geez, everything," he said. "But no one will even look at me because of the sponsorship thing."

"And you don't want to go back to Ireland."

"I can't," he said. He chewed on his lip, silent for a moment as he stared across the bilge. I had no idea what to do, but I needed to do something. So I took his hand in mine and squeezed.

Ollie seemed to snap out of whatever thought he'd gotten lost in. He glanced at me, and then dropped his gaze to our laced fingers and squeezed my hand back. "You know how you told me you weren't sure you could cut off your parents, even with all they'd done?"

"Yeah," I said, unsure what my family drama had to do with this.

"Well, I really did cut my family off." He paused, but I could tell he had more to say. I rested my chin on his shoulder, and finally he sighed and continued. "My da's not a great guy. He'd . . . well, he'd knock me around and stuff. Ma. Jack too."

"Jack . . ." Ollie had mentioned his parents now and then, vague offhand comments, but I'd never heard the name Jack before.

"My brother," Ollie said. "He's ten years younger than me. I haven't spoken to him since I left for culinary school, but I . . . When I went to Ireland, I saw him. Couldn't resist driving down to Cobh from Dublin. I didn't know what I'd do if I did see them, but Jack was the only one I saw, anyway. He was riding his bike down our street and . . . Jesus, he's tall now. He looked happy too. At least right then. People hide all sorts of stuff, you know. It felt like watching someone else's life or some TV show I'd seen before but didn't remember the details of. Anyway, he seemed okay, and I didn't want to ruin it, so I just . . . got in the car and drove right back to Dublin. Drove six hours round-trip just to spend thirty minutes in Cobh, because I'm a fecking coward."

"You're not, Ollie."

He shook his head. "I am. When I got into culinary school, I thought, *This is it. Ma and Jack can come with me and we can get the fuck out of here.* I didn't know how I'd manage them staying. I even got them their visitors' visas. Fecking expensive, they were, saved every penny I made working at the pub. I told myself it'd be easier to figure out a long-term solution once we were gone. I was tired of us all walking on eggshells all the time, you know. Ma even agreed to come with me. We told Da that she and Jack were just coming to help me settle in. But when I woke up the morning we were supposed to leave, Ma and Jack weren't home. She'd left a note saying she'd meet me at the airport, something about an errand, but"—he shook his head—"I knew something wasn't right."

I squeezed his hand tighter. "And then what happened?"

"She never showed. When I finally got ahold of her, she told me she was sorry. Just said she loved me and to be good. All those years I'd thought she never left because she didn't have the opportunity. It never crossed my mind that she didn't leave because she didn't want to. I know it's more complicated than that, of course, but I was angry ... I'm still angry. Anyway, I got on the plane, left, and never looked back. You're a better person than me, Nina. I cut them all off. Even Jack. Once I was gone, I just ... didn't know what to say. I didn't want to leave them, especially not Jack, but I didn't know what else to do. I couldn't take him with me. Maybe I should've stayed, been nearby, kept watch over them, but ..."

"You did what you had to do."

"Wish I could believe that. Da and me always butted heads the most. Could never keep my mouth shut, you know. He always acted like I was the problem, like it was my fault he would get so angry. As fecked-up as it sounds, I hope he's right. I wouldn't feel so guilty if I knew my leaving had fixed everything. Who knows? Maybe it did. Maybe Jack really is happy. Maybe they're all happy now."

I didn't believe that, but I didn't know what to say. Both options seemed miserable: to believe you were the cause of your family's misery and had solved their problems by leaving or to carry the guilt of leaving them, knowing it had fixed nothing.

"I'm so sorry," I said. I kept my hand in his and my chin on his shoulder. I couldn't move away. I didn't want to.

Ollie rested his head against mine. "Don't be sorry for me."

The situation was awful, but I couldn't help but admire Ollie for being able to leave and start a new life. "You're not going back," I said. "We'll figure it out. I promise."

He lifted his head with a sigh. "You can't promise that."

"You forget who you're talking to."

"Trust me, when I'm talking to you, I never forget."

My hand ached from how tightly I was holding on to him. I flexed my fingers, loosening our grip on each other. Ollie seemed to notice it too and gently pulled his hand from mine to muss up his hair.

"Well," I said, smoothing my polo when I got to my feet. "Just in case you *do* forget, I'm Nina Lejeune, failed professional gymnast and future chief stew of the *Serendipity*. Nothing is impossible for me, so I hereby declare, you are not allowed to return to Ireland."

Ollie laughed. "All right, Nina Lejeune, you tell that to Immigration. See what they have to say about it."

"Maybe I will. We've still got time to figure this out, so stop worrying," I said, as much to myself as to him.

All week, after finding Ollie in the bilge, I turned his dilemma over and over, racking my mind for a solution. I couldn't shake the look he'd had on his face when I walked in on him. *Trapped*, I'd thought. I knew the feeling. It was how I felt whenever I thought about the end of charter season, whenever a voice mail from a debt collector or one of my parents popped up on my phone.

Maybe I should have asked myself why I cared so much. But the truth was, I liked Ollie. We'd grown extremely close over the last few months. As much as I tried to deny it, the thought of his leaving and my not knowing when I'd see him again, the thought of not seeing him every day, made my chest ache as bad as my knee often did.

We were friends. I cared about what happened to him. And, yes, I'd had friends before, but none like him. None who got me without my having to explain. None who always knew when I was joking and when I was serious. None who listened to the ridiculous things I said without batting an eye. Now that I'd had a taste of something like that, it seemed impossible to live without it.

"Fecking proposals," Ollie said when he stormed into the galley after a preference sheet meeting a few days later. "Hate when they do it the first night. The rest of the charter will be awkward if she says no."

Later, I watched as he painted dozens of roses on a cake, his hand steady and deliberate as he dipped a paintbrush into food coloring and hunched over it. "You're an artist!" I squealed, startling him and nearly ruining the whole thing. He threw me out of the galley on a wave of curses, but I didn't care. It was worth it to see the way his eyes lit up when I said it again. "You're a marvelous artist, Ollie, even if you're rather moody."

That night I watched from nearby as Ollie set the cake on the table in front of the primary's girlfriend. When he leaned away from the table, I caught his eye and mouthed *artist* at him. Ollie shook his head, tamping down a smile that fought to make an appearance at the corner of his mouth.

I turned my attention to the primary. He wiped a cloth napkin over his brow and opened his mouth to begin his big proposal speech, and it was at that exact moment when the solution to Ollie's problem came to me with dizzying clarity.

"Bunny pad. Ten minutes," I said to Ollie once we'd finished breakfast service the following day. I'd hardly slept the night before, unable to shake the plan from my mind. It was ridiculous. *Illegal.* I'd spent hours researching, trying to weigh all the risks involved.

Admittedly, there were many.

Not that they made a difference. As soon as I'd thought it up, I knew nothing could deter me.

I just had to convince Ollie.

When I reached the bunny pad, Ollie was already waiting.

He pointed his cigarette at me. "You're late."

"Marry me," I said, too excited to keep it in any longer.

The cigarette slipped from between Ollie's fingers, making a black mark where it dropped onto the cushions. "Fuck," he said, and scrubbed at it with a finger. "RJ's gonna kill me. Do you think he's killed someone before? He has that look."

My pulse thudded in my ears. "Did you hear what I said?"

Ollie continued rubbing at the singed cushion without looking up at me. "Nina, I think you're great, but—"

I covered my face in my hands. Maybe I should've led with an explanation instead of diving right in. "You're not understanding me. Marry me so you can get your green card. Then you'll never have to worry about this visa stuff again. You can even get your citizenship. Stay as long as you like." I sat beside him. "I'm offended by your reaction to my proposal, by the way."

Ollie searched my face as if trying to decide if I was joking or not. "Are you proposing we commit immigration fraud and risk the two of us going to jail?"

"Oh please," I said. "It won't happen. It's not like we met online or anything. People know us. Half the crew thinks we're sleeping together, anyway. I'm telling you, it will work."

"I don't think so, Neen."

"People get married after just meeting all the time."

Ollie finished his cigarette and immediately lit up another. "Not only is what you're suggesting a felony, but it's absolutely bonkers. What do you get out of it?"

"You need a green card, and I need a roommate."

He looked at me as if I'd sprouted a second head. "I don't get it."

"Without someone, I'm stuck. I'll marry you so you can stay, and, in exchange, you make me an authorized user on your accounts. I don't even need the passwords, just the credit boost. Be my roommate. Co-sign for me on a car loan."

"I'd help you without doing this absolutely horrible idea."

I grabbed the cigarette from his mouth and stuck it in my own. "You can't help me if you aren't here. And before you ask—no, I don't have anyone else. As ridiculous as it sounds, you're the best friend I have. Maybe the only one I have left. It isn't like I can get help from my parents."

Ollie looked away from me to rub at the burn mark on the cushion. "What if you meet someone?"

"I'm never getting married," I said. "For love, anyway. Believe me, I've seen what a marriage built on love can do to you. I'm not interested."

"Yeah," Ollie said. "Yeah, I guess you're right."

"So?"

"You really want to go around acting like we're . . . married?"

"That's the best part. We won't tell anyone. I've looked it up. You don't need a witness to get legally married in Florida. No one has to know. We can fake it all. We'll take the happy couple pictures. We'll elope. No one but the immigration officer has to see them. There's an interview we'll have to get through, but we'll have plenty of time to get our story straight, and since we'll be roommates, I don't see why we can't practice for it. You can get your green card in a year, but it'll be with conditions. Two years after that, you can apply for citizenship or just stick with permanent residency. Whatever you want. We'll get divorced as soon as you're in the clear."

Ollie paused. "You'd really do this?" he said, the first sign he was actually considering it.

"Yes." It was ridiculous. Dangerous. Wildly fucked-up and ethically wrong on so many levels. But I pushed all that aside.

"I always expected I'd end up in a loveless marriage," he said.

"Does that mean you're in?"

He sighed, a spark of hope in his eyes when they met mine. "I'm in. Let's do it, Nina Lejeune. Let's get married."

11

~~~~~~

In what comes as a surprise to absolutely no one, the charter season from hell does not improve. Almost halfway through the season, we get a primary who runs a music-streaming start-up and has brought his girlfriend, cousin, and two of his coworkers along for the fun. All the men seem to think they are God's gift to women. The dinner conversation is appalling. I'm not sure I've ever had my ass so openly ogled at a dinner table before, and I have plenty of experience.

By the third night of their six-day charter, I've had enough of the primary's creepy comments to the girls—asking Britt if she can do breakfast service in a bikini, pretending to micromanage Alyssa as she wipes down tables so he can stare at her ass. The final straw was when he grabbed Nekesa by the arm as she was clearing dessert plates and said he bet they'd make beautiful babies.

"I've already got two kids, and they're hideous," Nekesa deadpanned back.

The primary, too drunk to figure out if she was serious or not, let go of her arm and took a long sip of his mojito, unaware of his girlfriend's glare from across the table.

I hoped that if the girlfriend married the guy for money, she'd at least take out a good life insurance policy before suffocating him in his sleep.

Sexual harassment is an unfortunately common aspect of the job. Most of our guests are respectful, especially the ones used to chartering yachts. But inevitably we have a few charters that are complete duds. The guests think the money they've paid to be here means they can do whatever they like, and nothing gets them off quite like having a bunch of young women catering to their every whim for a few days.

Simply put, these situations are dangerous and complicated. The only times I've ever felt truly trapped on this boat were when I was out fending off lewd comments from a drunken asshole in international waters. No cell signal, no escape. How can you tell the difference between an inappropriate joke and an actual threat? When should you risk a thirty-thousand-dollar tip, disappointing the rest of the crew, and the possibility of everyone thinking you're overreacting to tell the primary he's a skeevy perv?

It can feel impossible to speak up.

But it's my responsibility to protect the girls. Nekesa is supposed to work lates, but the guests are still up, still drinking, and the primary is becoming more predatory by the minute. There's no way in hell I'm leaving any of them to babysit the guests tonight.

Once we've given the guests fresh drinks and they've wandered up to the hot tub, I pull Britt, Alyssa, and Nekesa into the galley for an emergency meeting and instruct them to avoid the primary as much as possible for the remainder of the charter. I swap shifts with Nekesa and send her to bed, telling Alyssa and Britt to do the same once they've pulled everything we'll need for breakfast tomorrow.

Nekesa slumps onto the counter in relief. "Thank *God*. I was really worried I was going to have to pretend I had two ugly kids for the rest of the night. I even found a few pictures on Google just in case. It took me *three years* to get a job in yachting. I'm not letting some creep ruin it for me."

All her humor aside, I know it can't be easy for Nekesa to be here. When she says it took her three years to get a job, I believe it. The industry is painfully white. "Don't worry. I've handled more creeps than I can count over the last nine years."

Once the girls leave the galley, I disappear down into the crew mess and nab one of the deckhands' Red Bulls from the fridge.

"I thought my coming back meant you'd renounce your life of crime," Ollie says.

I chug the rest of the can, which has Simon's name written in large letters on it, and turn to find Ollie watching me from where he leans against the doorframe that leads to the crew quarters.

I set the can on the counter and pad over to him. I've been up since six thirty, and from the looks of the guests, the party isn't stopping anytime soon. God, I'm tired. So tired that Ollie looks like the perfect comfort right now, damn the consequences. I touch him low on his stomach, walking my fingers slowly up to the center of his chest as I speak. "I think if I were to analyze the history of my criminal tendencies . . . the fault would land squarely on you," I say, and tap his heart.

He squints down at me, looking as if he's unsure what to say. "You're that tired, huh?"

"I'm that tired." I wrap my arms around his neck and sway into him, resting my cheek on his chest.

Ollie hesitates before circling my waist with an arm and pulling me closer. "So why aren't you in bed?" he murmurs into my ear.

I sigh and let my eyes drift shut for a moment. "I took Nekesa's shift so she wouldn't have to be around that pervert all night."

"You did what now?"

"Can't leave any of them alone with him. He's awful."

"So *you're* planning to be alone with him?" Ollie says.

"Mm-hmm."

"If he's that bad, you need to tell Xav."

"It's not that easy."

"Like hell it isn't."

"Shhhhhh."

Ollie groans and pries my arms from around his neck. He pulls me back so that I'll look at him. "Nina, you need to talk to Xav."

Well, there goes my five minutes of rest before the Red Bull kicks in and I have to throw myself into the fray again. I pinch my cheeks to try to wake myself up. "All he's done so far is make a bunch of creepy comments. He hasn't *done* anything—"

"*Yet*," Ollie says.

"Relax, Ollie. This isn't my first rodeo."

"Didn't like any of the others either."

"I'm aware." I take a step back, regretting how easily I'd fallen into his arms. How do I always forget how quickly Ollie can go from being a comfort to a nuisance? It isn't like his worrying can change the situation. "Lovely chatting with you, Oliver. But I really better head back up there."

But when I take the steps up to the sun deck, Ollie follows after me. "Really, Ollie, go to bed. I can handle it. You've got breakfast in the morning."

"Won't sleep a wink knowing you're with that gobshite."

I turn away without another word and keep climbing the steps. It's no use arguing with Ollie. As stubborn as he says I am, he's just as bad. Maybe worse.

The primary's eyes slide over me when I step onto the sun deck and find the guests in the hot tub. "Nina, Nina, Nina," he says. I hate the way he says my name, like it's an item on one of Ollie's tasting menus.

"Hello," I say. "Everyone doing all right?"

"I'd be a lot better if you joined us," he says.

"She's not allowed," Ollie says from behind me.

The primary's eyes leave me and focus on him. "Whoa, Chef. You can't tell the lady what to do. She's an adult."

"She's. Not. Allowed," Ollie says again. "Boat policy."

"Boat policy," the primary mimics, butchering Ollie's accent and making everyone but his girlfriend laugh.

She lifts herself from the hot tub. "I'm off to bed."

"Can I get anyone a drink?" I say, trying to ignore the tension that practically radiates from Ollie. After taking orders for another round of mojitos, I step into the Sky Lounge to make the most watered-down version I can get away with.

Ollie enters the Sky Lounge a few minutes later and stretches out onto the couch.

"You need to cool it," I say.

"No need to finish those drinks, love," Ollie says. He settles one couch pillow beneath his head and clutches the other to his chest before closing his eyes. "They've gone to bed."

I pause in my pouring and set the bottle too hard on the bar. "What do you mean?"

"They decided they were tired."

"Really? They decided they were tired right after ordering mojitos?"

"Guess so."

"And did you by any chance *help* them make this decision?"

"I wouldn't say I *helped* them. I simply suggested it might be time to call it quits for the night, and they agreed, so I assisted them in making their way down to their rooms, that's all."

I stare at him. "What the fuck, Oliver?"

Ollie cracks an eyelid to look at me. "Keep it down, kitten. I'm trying to sleep."

I glance out the sliding glass door to the now-empty hot tub. "I don't know what you said, but if you cost us our tip—"

"I don't give a flying fuck about the tip," he says. He closes both eyes again and settles deeper into the couch.

I leave the bar, abandoning the half-made mojitos to glare down at him. "I didn't need your help," I say. My voice is raw and frayed. Damn those energy drinks. They never make me any less exhausted, only more fragile.

Ollie opens his eyes and sits up. "Neen, c'mon. I was only—"

I hold up my hands. "Just stop," I say. "Stop talking. Stop with the jokes and the tough-guy attitude. This is *exactly* why we can't be together. I *asked* you to let it be, but you seem to think you know what I need better than I do. You think you can just swoop in here and solve all my problems. But you *can't*, Ollie, because all you ever do is make more problems. *You* are the problem."

Ollie is so still that I wonder if I've actually said what I think I have. But then he blinks, and the hurt in his eyes is clear. I wish I could rewind the moment and reel the words in. I knew what I was doing. Ollie's greatest fear has always been that he is a burden to the people he loves, that he can't help them because there's something fundamentally wrong with him that makes him incapable of it. It's why he left Ireland in the first place. It's why he hasn't been home in almost ten years. It's not true. Why didn't I keep my mouth shut for once and walk away?

I cover my face in my hands. "I didn't mean that," I say. I know I should say more, but I'm too tired to know how to fix this right now.

"Go ahead and take the bottom bunk tonight," he says. "I'll sleep here."

I peek at him through my fingers. "Don't be ridiculous." But Ollie is no longer listening. He stretches out on the couch again and turns his back to me. "Fine," I say, trying to keep my voice even as I focus on gathering up dirty glasses from around the Sky Lounge. "If you wake up with your back thrown out, you'll only have yourself to blame."

I pause and wait for a response, but Ollie is silent.

I leave for the galley and wash the glasses. True to his word, Ollie's bed is empty when I slip inside our room. I can't take the bottom bunk. It smells like him. *This was what you wanted*, the bitchy voice in my head says as I settle beneath my comforter. But this isn't what I wanted at all. I didn't want to hurt him.

Though lately it's all I seem to do.

I soon discover that Ollie isn't the only one I've pissed off on this charter. The next morning, I find myself in the Sky Lounge with Alyssa, the vacuum quiet at her side as she glares at me.

"It looks better with horizontal lines," she says. "That's how I did it on the *Why Knot*." She's got her arms crossed over her chest, attitude rolling off her in waves. The vacuum, which I unplugged as soon as I stepped into the room and saw her with it, rests quietly against her leg. Tiny wisps of hair float around Alyssa's face, having escaped her always-neat milkmaid braids. Seems the junior stew life does not suit dear Alyssa. Surprise, surprise.

"And all I'm saying is that this isn't the *Why Knot*." I tap the name embroidered across my polo. "This is the *Serendipity*. I don't want to come up here and find you wasting time vacuuming the already-clean Sky Lounge because you don't like the direction of the lines. You don't need to like them. *I* need to like them. There are a million things to do, like the things I *asked* you to do. Have you made up the guest beds?"

Alyssa begrudgingly nods.

"And are there other tasks on the list I gave you?"

She nods again.

"And is re-vacuuming the Sky Lounge on that list?"

Alyssa doesn't respond.

"Then I don't see what the issue is. Seems I've made it very clear what you ought to be doing."

"Someone's got to pick up the slack around here," Alyssa mutters when she bends over to wind up the vacuum cord.

I suck in a breath through my nose, because if I open my mouth too soon, this will end badly. "Remind me, who is the chief stewardess on this yacht?" Alyssa keeps her attention on the vacuum cord and doesn't answer. "Oh right. *I'm* chief stew," I continue. "And whether you like it or not, you answer to me. If you want to do things the way they're done on your old boat, then *Why Knot* go back?"

Alyssa is spared having to respond when Xav's voice comes on over the radio. "RJ, Nina, this is Xav. I need you in the wheelhouse ASAP."

I sigh and bring the radio to my lips. "Nina here. I'm on my way." I clip the radio back to my skirt and turn to Alyssa. "Since you love vacuuming so much, why don't you do the main salon next. Go wild. Do a chevron pattern on the carpet if you want."

I can feel Alyssa glaring at my back as I leave the Sky Lounge, but I don't waste a second more of my time dwelling on her power dynamic issues. Instead, I'm rehearsing what I'll say when I get to the wheelhouse. This has Ollie written all over it. I know, because only ten minutes ago I heard him radio Xav to ask if they could have a chat, and after last night, what else could it be about?

The regret over what I said to him last night fades a little as I near the door to the wheelhouse. Why Ollie feels the need to get involved in the running of my department is beyond me. I ought to break out the masking tape and mark off his area of the boat to remind him of his place. Galley: Ollie. Everywhere else in the interior: Nina. It's simple, really. You'd think he'd get that after working with me this long.

I've got peak bitch face in place when I step into the wheelhouse. Xav and Ollie are already seated, but I've arrived before RJ. Neither Xav nor Ollie looks happy, which works for me. At least there's something we can all agree on.

"Take a seat, kiddo," Xav says.

I don't look at Ollie when I sit, leaving an empty chair for RJ between us. Normally I'd walk in here and demand to know what the surprise department-head meeting is all about, but I already know and wish I didn't. No one speaks until Xav sighs a minute later and mutters, "Where the hell is RJ?"

Xav leaves the table to look out the wheelhouse windows. When he pulls out his radio to call for RJ again, I lean toward Ollie. "You had *no* right to interfere."

"Come off it, Neen. That's not even—"

"I had everything under control. There are only two days left of this charter and—"

I'm interrupted by RJ's arrival to the wheelhouse. "Sorry, Cap," he says. "Guests wanted the slide."

Xav's beard twitches in annoyance. "I don't care if they want you to set up a dick-measuring contest; when I say to get your ass to the wheelhouse ASAP, you stop whatever it is you're doing and drag yourself up here. Got it?"

RJ nods. Xav gestures to the table and returns to his seat. RJ settles in between me and Ollie. Perfect. Never in a million years did I think I'd rather look at RJ's face than Ollie's. But I suppose some things do change after all.

"This is going to be uncomfortable," Xav says. He settles his gaze on each of us in turn.

I peek around RJ to glare at Ollie, who seems to be very purposefully *not* looking at me.

"I hate to do this," Xav continues. "Especially when everyone's worked so hard, and we've almost made it through, but I've got no choice. We're ending the charter early. As soon as we're done here, we're setting sail back to Simpson Bay."

Fucking Ollie and his meddling. "I don't know what Ollie said, but it's really not that bad."

"Neen—" Ollie starts.

"We've got less than forty-eight hours," I say. "I've dealt with worse, honestly."

"Not that bad?" Xav says. "Do you know what'll happen if we get caught with drugs on board? It doesn't matter *who* they belong to. Forget this charter, the whole goddamn season will be over."

"Drugs?" I look from Xav to Ollie to RJ. RJ is the only one who looks as surprised as I am.

Xav fishes something from his pocket and smacks a small plastic baggie containing white powder onto the table. "This was found in the primary's bathroom this morning," Xav says. "Beats me why Chef is bringing it to my attention instead of you, Nina. Whatever is going on with interior needs to work itself out, because if I have to get involved, no one will be happy."

"Oh," I say. I can't unglue my eyes from the baggie on the table. Why had Ollie been the one to bring this to Cap? What was he doing in the guest rooms?

"Chef," Xav says, "we won't get back to the dock until after lunch, so you'll still have to cook for the little asshats, but don't put too much effort into it. Nina, RJ, I don't want the guests finding out what's going on until we have to tell them. Clue in your departments but instruct them to keep it quiet."

"Copy," RJ says.

Xav looks at me. "Copy," I say weakly.

"Right," Xav says. "Now get your asses back to work so we can get underway. At least you'll have two extra nights off before the next charter."

Ollie is up and across the room before I can stop him, not that I'm sure *what* I'd say, because *sorry* doesn't feel like enough. I've really fucked up this time. I think of what I said to him last night and want to lock myself in the bilge for the rest of the season.

"Nina," Xav says.

I blink, finding myself alone in the wheelhouse with Xav. He stands at the helm, watching me. "Yes, Cap?"

"You okay, kiddo?"

I stand and smooth my skirt. "I'm fine," I say. "Just tired."

Xav looks like he doesn't quite believe me. "We've worked together a long time, haven't we?"

"You can say that again. Have you added me to your will yet? That's the only reason I'm still around."

Xav laughs and runs a hand over his beard. "I know I'm hard on you, but I think of you as a daughter. You know that, right?"

He's said it before, but right now, when I feel like my life has become nothing but balancing plates that are destined to break anyway, it hits me harder than it usually does. "I know."

"All I want is for you to be happy," he says. "And if that means this gig is no longer for you, I'll understand."

Now I know he's going senile. I shake my head. "Nina Lejeune without yachting? I don't think so."

Xav shrugs. "Just something to think about."

I have no idea where this is coming from. Yachting isn't the problem. This *season* is the problem. My crew is the problem. These guests are the problem. Everyone acting like I've got a problem is the problem.

I join Xav by the helm and rest my head on his shoulder, the two of us looking out at the empty sun deck below. There's nothing before us but sea and sky. A perfect day. "I'm good, really. And besides, who'll cover for you when you start losing it and they try to take this thing from you?" I say, giving the helm a pat.

"You won't need to cover for me. I'll happily retire."

I snort. "Yeah, and I'll happily hand my job over to Britt and let her run interior."

Xav laughs and gives my shoulder a squeeze. "All right, kiddo. Moment over. Get your ass downstairs before I fire you."

"You'd never," I say, taking in the view for one last second before I turn to go.

12

~~~~~~

A week after the end of my first charter season, I sat beside Ollie in the wheelhouse, sure we were both about to get fired when Captain Xav slid the marriage license application we'd filled out the day before across the table.

"Care to tell me what this is about?" Captain Xav said.

Shit. I took the paper in my hands and tried to keep my cool. "Where did you get that?"

"I found it where one of you dipshits left it in the crew mess."

I glanced at Ollie, but he only raised his eyebrows. We'd been living on the yacht temporarily until we could move into our new apartment at the end of the month. One of us must have left the application out, and it sure as hell wasn't me. No one was supposed to know about our plan, which included a simple courthouse wedding. But, as I'd quickly learned that season, secrets didn't stay secrets for long on board a superyacht.

Everything had gone according to plan so far, and now this. Desperate to think my way out of it, I grabbed Ollie's hand in mine and tried to give Captain Xav my most earnest expression. "We're in love," I said. "Isn't that right, Oliver?"

"I . . ." I squeezed Ollie's hand hard, and he cleared his throat. "That's right, Cap. We're in love. We want to get married."

Captain Xav looked between the two of us before leaning back in his seat with his hands behind his head. "And this doesn't have anything to do with Ollie's visa trouble?"

"No!" I said, gripping Ollie's hand tighter. I hoped I didn't look like I was panicking because I definitely was. I thought about Ollie leaving, of packing my bags and having to move back in with my parents . . . I hadn't even spoken to them since returning home.

Captain Xav held my gaze. "Do you remember the values of this boat?"

"Of course, but we're not—"

"I *really* value honesty, you know," Captain Xav said.

There was a beat of silence in which the three of us just looked at each other.

And then Ollie swore and pried his hand from mine. "You're right, Cap."

"Ollie!" I glared at him. How could he go and ruin things before doing so was absolutely necessary? Clearly, I could never ask him to help me bury a body.

"It's not Neen's fault," Ollie said, resting his elbows on the table. "I . . . talked her into it. It was my idea. I didn't think. I was just—"

"It was my idea!" I said, and smacked him on the shoulder.

Captain Xav held up a hand, and the both of us shut our mouths. "You act like I ought to be surprised by this, but you two are as transparent as a glass-bottom boat. I didn't need to find this," he said, nodding to the marriage license application, "to know what was going on. One minute Ollie tells me he's out of options and going back to Ireland, and a few days later he tells me he's got it all worked out? You two are inseparable. It wasn't hard to figure out."

"Why didn't you say anything?" I said.

Captain Xav shrugged. "Didn't want to lose the best stewardess and chef I've ever had."

"So why all the drama now?"

Captain Xav leaned toward us over the table. "Because you two are clearly incompetent." He shook his head. "Leaving it in the goddamn crew mess. Where are you getting married?"

I stared at Captain Xav. This conversation was . . . not going the way I expected. "The . . . courthouse . . ."

Captain Xav sighed and looked up at the ceiling before settling his gaze on us again. "The courthouse."

"What's wrong with that?" I said.

"I think you two need a little help," he said. "Fortunately, you have me."

Which was how I'd ended up wearing a thrifted wedding dress on board the *Serendipity* a week later as Captain Xav took photos of me and Ollie after performing the shortest wedding ceremony of all time. The dress was a gorgeous little thing. Off-white and with a soft neckline and pencil skirt, it was somehow elegant and casual at the same time. If it weren't for Captain Xav's running commentary, it would've been easy to pretend it wasn't a wedding dress at all.

"You've got to kiss," Captain Xav said. I shot him a glare. "What's that look for?" he added, lowering Ollie's phone. "Not very bride-like."

"You're having fun with this, aren't you?" I said.

"What's the immigration officer going to think when you show them your wedding photos and you look like you've been sucking on lemons? A kiss will sell it, but if you want to take that risk, so be it."

I glanced up at Ollie and shrugged. He shrugged back.

"Great," Captain Xav said. He held up Ollie's phone and motioned for us to scoot closer together. "And maybe I am having fun with this. Why shouldn't I?"

Ollie and I faced each other. "I think I hate him," I said under my breath.

"For making you kiss me? Gee, thanks," Ollie said.

"Don't act like you want to do this any more than I do," I said.

Captain Xav cleared his throat.

"Will you cool it?" I said to Captain Xav, though I didn't take my eyes off Ollie. "We're doing it, okay?"

Ollie took a step closer and rested his hands on my waist. It was a typical South Florida summer, hot as could be, and the way he held me only made me feel warmer all over.

"Nina, you look like you're being kidnapped," Captain Xav said.

I ignored him and wrapped my arms around Ollie's neck.

"Hey," Ollie said, his voice a whisper.

I stared up into his eyes, hoping he couldn't feel how fast my heart was beating. "What?"

"Did you ever find out the underwear thing?"

"What underwear thing?"

"You know, how male gymnasts keep their junk from swinging around."

"You're thinking about . . ." I shook my head and laughed, pressing my face into Ollie's shoulder. I could feel his breath against my cheek as he laughed along with me. It loosened me up a bit, making me feel as if I'd just finished warming up before a competition, though the stakes were just as high, if not higher, that day than they'd been when I competed.

As soon as I caught my breath and lifted my face to Ollie's, he took my face in his hands and kissed me. It took me by surprise. I suppose that had been his plan all along, to make me stop thinking about it.

And boy, did it work. Maybe a little too well. Ollie's mouth was soft on mine, softer than I'd ever imagined, not that I'd imagined it all that much. Only sometimes. It was the least chaste closed-mouth kiss I'd ever experienced. For a moment, I forgot about Captain Xav, and the fact that none of this was real, and was actually illegal, and could very well ruin both our lives more than they were already ruined.

Instead, all that ran through my mind was a steady rhythm of *Ollie, Ollie, Ollie*, as if his name kept my heart beating. I thought he felt it too, because we both pulled away at the same time, blinking at each other as if we were complete strangers.

Ollie looked away first. His hands dropped from my face, and the tops of his ears turned a furious shade of pink. I touched a hand to my cheek as I stared at him, certain my skin was warmer than it ought to be.

"That was . . ." Ollie said.

"Fine," I said, sure my voice sounded higher than it normally did. It was this weather. It would make us both sick if we had to stand out here any longer. I turned to Captain Xav, hoping to dispel the awkwardness that had fallen between myself and Ollie. God, I hoped that stupid kiss wouldn't ruin our perfectly platonic marriage the second it began. "It's fine, right?"

"How the hell would I know?" Captain Xav said. "I've done plenty of kissing in my day, but—"

"Not the *kiss*, you fool. The *photo*."

"Ah, yes, the photo." He shielded his eyes and looked down at the phone. "Photo's perfect," he said. "That'll really sell it. Hell, *I* almost believe it. You don't get shots like this at the courthouse."

Ollie raised his eyebrows at me, and I raised mine back. My heart was knocking around in my chest like it had been thrown into rough seas, but there was no turning back now. The ceremony had taken a mere moment, Captain Xav had signed the marriage license, and now we had the photos to prove it. All we had to do was drop off the marriage license and we could start working toward the whole reason we'd done this in the first place: getting Ollie his residency.

"Thanks, Cap," I said when he handed Ollie his phone.

"I think you can just call me Xav now, Nina," he said. He clapped both me and Ollie on the shoulder. "Enjoy the honeymoon."

"Take a hike, *Xav*," I said.

"So," Ollie said as we watched Xav make his way down the dock to the parking lot. To think I'd ever been afraid of that silly old man. "We should . . ."

"Get off this boat for a while," I said. I stepped away from him when I realized our arms were touching. "We can drop off the marriage license and have the least romantic dinner of all time. What's the least romantic place you can think of?"

"Gas station," he said.

"Disgusting. Get changed and we'll go. Oh, wait a sec." I turned my back to Ollie and pushed my hair over my shoulder to expose the zipper of my dress. "Unzip me before you go, or I'll never get out of this thing."

Ollie grumbled but stepped closer. I was miserably hot but didn't mind the warmth of his fingers at the nape of my neck or how it skimmed along my back as he tugged the zipper down.

I'd only meant for him to unzip it a little, just enough for my fingers to catch hold of the zipper so I could do the rest myself, but I didn't say anything when he kept on going. He stopped once the dress was fully unzipped, and neither of us moved or said anything for a moment. But then Ollie cleared his throat. "That should do it," he said. I turned to thank him, but he'd already turned away, heading belowdeck as if he couldn't get away from me fast enough.

Half an hour later, we sat side by side on the hood of his car, trying to distract ourselves from what we'd just done by listening to music we hated and eating 7-Eleven chili dogs.

"Do we really have to listen to this again?" Ollie said.

I held up a finger, chewing a too-big bite as quickly as I could. I'd been playing the same Nickelback song on loop from my phone. Ollie reached over me to try to grab it, but I swatted him away.

"*Yes*, we have to listen to it again."

"Why?"

"Because."

"Because why?"

"Because I want to."

"Why do you want to listen to this?"

"Fuck off, Ollie. Stop repeating me. What are you, five?"

Ollie rolled his eyes and took a slurp of the large blue-raspberry Slurpee we shared. His hair, having grown blonder after months on the yacht, fell into his eyes, and I pushed it from his face without thinking.

"You need a haircut," I said when he raised an eyebrow at me. I looked away from him and shoved another bite of chili dog in my mouth, needing to make myself feel as disgusting as possible.

Ollie laughed. "So much for wedded bliss—"

"Shh," I said. "Don't even talk about it."

Ollie rolled his eyes. "You look absolutely miserable. We can always get an annulment before—"

"Shh!" I said, and clapped a hand over his mouth. "I'm fine. Or I will be if you'll just shut up about *you know what*."

Ollie pulled my hand from his mouth and set it in my lap. "It's the kiss, isn't it? That's why you're freaking out?"

"I'm freaking out because we just dropped off the license for our . . ." I paused to make sure no one was in earshot and dropped my voice to a whisper. "*Fraudulent* marriage!"

"The kiss didn't mean anything," he said. "We had to do it."

"Oh my God, Ollie. Please stop talking about the kiss. It was no big deal." *Then why does it feel like a big deal?* the voice in my head said.

"Fine. No more talk about the kiss," he said. "I . . . uh, got you something." Before I could respond he leapt from the hood of the car and grabbed something from the center console, then returned moments later with a small black box in his hands.

"A little late for a proposal, don't you think?" I said.

"It's a thank-you gift."

I laughed when he passed the little box into my hands.

"What?" he said, his ears turning pink again. "What's so funny?"

"It's just . . . well, we must be spending too much time together, because I got *you* something too. It's in the trunk. Here." I pushed the box back into his hands and leapt from the hood of the car like he had a minute earlier.

When I handed the gift to Ollie, he tugged at the curled ribbon on top. "Yours looks nicer than mine," he said.

"I'm a yacht stewardess," I said. "It's my job to make things look pretty. It's nothing big. Open it."

"Fine," he mumbled, slipping off the ribbon and undoing the paper as if preparing molecular gastronomy for a picky guest on the yacht.

"Oh, you can go ahead and rip it open."

He glared at me. "I don't want to ruin your hard work!"

"It wasn't that hard!" I reached over and tore part of the gift wrap so he would just *open it* already.

When he finally got all the wrapping paper off, he lifted his eyes to mine. "Is this a shoe box?"

"Just open it, Oliver."

He returned his attention to the shoe box. As soon as he lifted the lid and saw the boat shoes inside, he shook his head and laughed. "You're something else, Nina Lejeune."

"I feel bad, okay? I can't live with this guilt. I had to replace the ones I ruined." I reached into the box and grabbed one of the shoes.

"These are top-notch. You wouldn't believe how much research I did to find these."

"Thank you," Ollie said. He put the shoe away, then pushed the little box into my hands again. "Your turn. I just . . . saw them and thought of you."

"Well, if it was something that reminded you of me, I'm a little frightened to find out what's in here." I grinned at him and flipped the box open. "Oh!" I said at the sight of pink earrings resting on the velvet inside. Each was shaped like a unicorn reared on its hind legs. They were the most ridiculous things I'd ever seen. They were utter perfection.

"You hate it," Ollie said. "It's . . . weird. I can take them back. It's only . . . you're always wearing those long tangly earrings, and these ones reminded me of—"

"The day you called me a big scary animal," I said.

A look of alarm passed over his face. "That's not what I—"

"Relax, Oliver. I took it as a compliment."

"I just meant that, you know, you were like this . . . cool . . . magical thing that came out of nowhere and might definitely stab me."

"Well, your first impression of me was surprisingly accurate," I said.

"I've still got the receipt. I can take them back."

I held the box to my chest and glared at him. "I'll kill you if you do, and not even for the life insurance. I'm never taking them off. If I die before you, bury me in them."

"We don't have life insurance."

"Yet," I said. I took off the earrings I was wearing and slipped the unicorn ones in their place. "You can breathe easy for now. I can't kill you too soon after taking out a policy. It's suspicious. How do I look?" I turned one way and then the other.

"Terrifying. Absolutely ridiculous," he said.

"Exactly what I was going for."

He reached out to touch one of the earrings, his fingers so close to my neck I could feel the heat of them on my skin. It surprised me. Not the action itself, but the way it made me feel, like I'd stuck a particularly challenging landing in competition, my feet finally touching the ground and staying exactly where they ought to be, a wave of both adrenaline and relief.

When he pulled back, I turned away to look out over the parking lot, desperate for something to smother the spark of the moment. I tried my best to remain calm, but my heart had started tumbling in my chest. Maybe I was dehydrated. It was far too hot out; it messed with the mind. Perhaps I was having a heat stroke.

But a part of me knew that wasn't the truth, because not even the hideous 7-Eleven parking lot and the Nickelback song starting up again could completely extinguish the unnerving sense that something was growing between me and Ollie. Something I couldn't allow myself to keep.

13

~~~~~~

Present day

After the emergency meeting in the wheelhouse, I don't catch a moment alone with Ollie all afternoon. Tension ripples through the crew as we sail back to Simpson Bay. We fend off the guests' questions with vague replies. *No, I'm not sure what Chef has planned for dinner tonight. Sure, I can check the itinerary for you. Of course I can get you another drink.*

The galley is quieter than it usually is during lunch service. No bickering. No banter. I'm not sure Ollie so much as mutters a single swear the entire time he's cooking.

Even though Ollie won't speak to me, over the course of the morning I've managed to piece together what happened, thanks to resident boat gossip hound Britt. Apparently, while she and I were running breakfast service, Alyssa pawned off making up the guest rooms on Nekesa, who found the drugs in the primary's bathroom. Not knowing what to do, Nekesa went to Alyssa, who didn't want to risk losing our tip by telling me or Cap. Ollie had overheard the conversation and approached Nekesa, telling her he'd take care of it without anyone knowing she was involved.

But, of course, secrets never stay secret on a superyacht for long.

Having so much going on with my team belowdeck without my knowing it was disconcerting. How was it possible that neither of my junior stews had come to me when an issue cropped up? It made me look incompetent. Like I didn't know how to manage them. And what was even worse was Ollie, whom I trusted more than anyone else on this godforsaken vessel, keeping me out of the loop. How foolish of me to assume he'd be able to put our personal issues aside when it came to work.

But even though I want to be pissed at him, there's no fire to my anger. I keep thinking about what I said about his creating more problems than he solves, and if I were really, truly honest with myself, I know I can't blame him for not dragging me into this.

By the time the guests are off the boat, an event that, unlike lunch, involves plenty of profanity, the mood among the crew has reached an all-time low. Nothing kills morale like not getting a tip, and even though I'm sick of almost everyone on this boat, the somber faces are even worse than the constant bickering I'm usually refereeing. There's only one thing other than a good tip that I know is guaranteed to raise the spirits of a yacht crew.

"We're going out tonight," I announce when everyone, save for Xav and Ollie, is assembled in the crew mess for dinner.

The intended effect is immediate. Britt shoots to her feet and does a little dance. "Can we do Lotus? Please, please, please?"

"Sure, why not?"

Britt squeals and the rest of the crew talks excitedly among themselves. "You'll love it," Britt tells Nekesa.

"Is there dancing?" Nekesa asks.

"Is there dancing? Ha!" Britt says. "There's dancing like you wouldn't believe." She grabs her radio and says into it, "Girls. Girls. Britt. Report to Nina's room for hair, makeup, and pregaming in five."

Seconds later Xav's voice comes over our radios. "Knock it off, Britt."

Britt cackles and grabs Nekesa by the arm to drag her toward the crew quarters. The rest of the crew, equally revived by the prospect of a night out, scarfs down what's left of their dinner, talking over each other as they wash dishes and disappear to their rooms to shower and get dressed.

In the span of five minutes, the crew mess has gone from vibrant and loud to awkward and silent. Alyssa and I are the only ones left. I don't like her, but having to work and party with people you'd never willingly spend time with in any other situation is the nature of the job.

I take the seat across from her as she picks at her salad. "I'm only going to bring this up once, because the situation is bad enough. You should know better than to try and hide something from me or Cap. You could've cost us the entire charter season. I ought to have Cap fire you right now, but I'm willing to give you one more chance. Does that sound good to you?"

Alyssa's indifferent expression makes me want to hurl her salad across the room. Why can't she just say, *Sure, boss!* and make this easy on me?

Instead, she stabs at her salad as if wishing it were my face. "Sounds great," she says, the tone suggesting that, actually, it doesn't sound great.

I get to my feet. "Enjoy the rest of your dinner," I say, hoping it tastes like bitterness and disappointment.

I've spent many nights dancing my stress away at Lotus over the years, but I've never needed it more than I do right now. Tonight, the club is packed. We have to force our way through it to get to the nearest bar. Lights swirl above us, drenching everything in pink and purple hues.

The bass of the music vibrates through me, shaking away the stress of the charter. It's past ten, but the exhaustion that felt bone-deep only hours ago fades as I wade deeper inside, and by the time I've got my first margarita in hand, I have more energy than I've had since I stepped on board the *Serendipity* at the start of charter season.

I've always loved a good party. Back in Palm Beach, I strive to be at home as little as possible. Boredom is the enemy, and I will do anything to avoid it. Good music, a great dress, and a strong drink are my weapons of choice.

Britt, Nekesa, and Alyssa stand beside me, shouting conversation at each other between sips of their drinks. RJ and Ollie are at the other end of the bar, silent and miserable-looking. When they notice I'm watching them, they drop their gazes to their drinks and pretend they haven't been staring at me and the girls for the last five minutes.

"Hey, Nina," Britt says. "Your man is looking pretty sad over there. Do us all a favor and hook up with Ollie. You two are so intense, it stresses me out. Look." She juts her chin at me. "I'm breaking out because of it."

"You're breaking out because you're a slob and don't wash off your makeup at night," I say. "And besides, sleeping with Ollie will never work."

"Why not?" Britt asks.

I set my empty glass on the bar. "It didn't last time."

Britt gapes at me as I dance away from her. I'll probably regret admitting to the fact that Ollie and I have slept together, but everyone already thinks it, and Britt will likely end up too wasted to remember anyway.

Ollie sees me dancing his way but pretends he doesn't. He stares down into his beer as if it's the most interesting thing he's seen in years. Only when I'm dancing right in front of him does he acknowledge my presence.

"You look like a prairie woman in space," he says, practically shouting so I can hear him over the music.

It's not a compliment or a dig, but an observation devoid of judgment. My dress, made from holographic blue lamé, is a genuine Batsheva with puffy sleeves and a ruffled collar.

I hold out the skirt and dip into a curtsy. "Thank you," I shout back. "That's exactly what I was going for."

Ollie doesn't say anything. He takes a sip of his beer and pretends to be very interested in his surroundings, though Lotus is nothing new and he is more of a pub guy.

Suddenly, the energy within the club doesn't feel like enough to carry me through my post-charter exhaustion. I wish the DJ would turn up the volume or play something I haven't heard a million times before. I wish the crowd were wilder, but it's a Wednesday night in March. Too soon for spring breakers, which is probably a good thing. Partying with a bunch of college students would only make me feel more out of place.

Earlier, as I'd gotten dressed along with the rest of the girls in my room, I wondered for the first time if Jo was right about my déjà vu being boredom. Eglé, stretched out on my bunk, taught us Lithuanian curse words between sips from a Solo cup filled with tequila. Britt's accent was so bad it made even Alyssa laugh from where she sat on Ollie's bunk tapping out texts.

I had been in the bathroom, standing before the mirror with a curling iron in one hand and a drink in the other. I'd felt entirely outside the moment as I watched Britt applying Nekesa's makeup. The two of them sat cross-legged on the floor. It reminded me of all the times Jo and I sat like that, laughing as Britt told us stories about working Med season on the *Talisman*.

But things were different now. Jo wasn't there, and though I wanted to enjoy the moment with the girls, a moment of fun where I didn't have to be Boss Nina to the same degree, it didn't feel right. It was so disorienting I had to look away. My eyes landed on Ollie's toothbrush and toothpaste resting on the sink. The girls laughed hysterically as they played Fuck, Marry, Kill, but I couldn't keep up with the conversation. For whatever reason, the splayed bristles of Ollie's toothbrush and the tight precision with which he'd rolled the bottom of the toothpaste tube were more interesting.

"Ollie, Simon, and me?" Britt said, yanking me back into the conversation. "For Fuck, Marry, Kill," she explained at my blank expression.

"I don't think you'll like the answer," I said. I set down the curling iron to zip Ollie's toothbrush and toothpaste away in his toiletry bag, the sensation that I no longer belonged there fading a bit once it was out of sight. *It's just guilt*, I told myself. Once I apologized to Ollie, I'd feel settled again.

Which is what I'm trying to do now as I stand before him, swaying along to the music. "I'm sorry about last night," I say.

Ollie points to his glass and shouts, "You want a sip of my pint?"

I lean toward him, thankful my heels boost me up enough for my mouth to reach his ear. "Can we talk? Outside?"

Ollie nods when I pull away. He finishes his beer and sets the empty glass on the bar. I take his hand and lead him through the club, trying not to think of the night I dragged him outside Mitch's and kissed him. I have kissed my way out of apologizing to Ollie plenty of times, but I have a feeling it won't work now.

My ears are ringing when we step outside. The door to the club shuts behind us. I feel exposed in the quiet. When I turn to Ollie, I'm suddenly unsure of what to say.

He shoves his hands into the pockets of his jeans with a sigh. "What'd you want to talk about?"

I settle on, "A cigarette would be great right about now."

Ollie lets out a small sigh that twists me up inside. Why is it so hard to shove away the sarcasm and jokes and just say what I mean, especially when I know it's something that needs to be said? It's so much easier to say *I'm sorry* in a crowded club than out here, where I know he'll actually hear me.

I cross my arms over my chest and look away for a moment. My eyes snag on the door to the club. Part of me wishes to escape inside so I don't have to have this conversation, but the other part of me would rather go back to the boat and watch movies on my laptop. I don't know which part of me is the real Nina. It's as if I have no idea who I am anymore. Nothing feels the same.

"I'm sorry for being such a douche canoe last night," I say when I turn back to Ollie. "I was exhausted and emotional, and you were right about that primary. I should've told Xav."

Ollie nods but doesn't look at me. He's got his walls up, and I hate it. I want the smirk and the dimples. Not this.

"And I'm sorry for what I said." I uncross my arms and take his face in my hands. "You don't *only* make problems for me. You, Ollie Dunne, make most things better." I smooth the groove between his eyebrows with one of my thumbs and feel the tension there ease. "I didn't mean what I said. *You* are not a problem. Can you please forgive me so we can go back to being pissed off at each other for the things we're usually pissed off at each other for?"

Ollie leans into my hands. "And what would those things be?" I know he's forgiven me by the playfulness that returns to his eyes. If I lift my hands from his face, perhaps I'll find a dimple beneath them, but I'm not willing to stop touching him to find out.

"Oh, you know, beef cheeks, butt cheeks . . ." I give his face a pat. "These cheeks."

"Which is your favorite?"

"That's a secret I will take to my grave," I say, wishing I could kiss him without it complicating things.

The door to the club opens. Music and voices flood outside, reminding me that we aren't alone. When I lean away, Ollie looks as if he'd like to grab me by the waist and pull me against him. I wish he would. He's flirted with me plenty over the last two months, but he's hardly touched me. I can't count how many times I've nearly dragged him into the laundry room and begged him to put me out of my misery.

But I can't make a move on Ollie, even though I really, really want to. He might think it means something. If *he* initiates, then I can just go along with it.

Which is exactly what Ollie is thinking. I know it. Because instead of pulling me to him, he leans away. "We'd better go back inside," he says. "Who knows what those gobshites have gotten into in our absence."

As if he's made a prophecy, a frantic-looking RJ waves us over as soon as he spots us in the club. He points over his head to a nearby stage used for dancing. But instead of dancing, I find two of my stewardesses screaming at each other and making one hell of a scene. I can't hear what Alyssa and Britt are saying, but their hand gestures paint a pretty clear picture. Simon stands poised to step between them, looking as if he's trying to talk them down. Eglé is off to the side with Nekesa, who sips at her drink and looks like she's trying not to cry.

"What the hell happened?" I ask when we get close enough to hear RJ.

RJ leans between me and Ollie. "Alyssa started going off on Nekesa, something about the primary and the drugs. And Britt . . ." He shakes his head. "You know how she gets."

That's all he needs to say before I'm making my way through the crowd to the stage. Britt is fun, and lighthearted, and can roll with the punches, but when someone sets her off, especially if she feels they're treating someone else unjustly, she can explode. I've had to talk her down from a fight more than once over the years.

I haul myself onto the stage and step between Britt and Alyssa. "Back off!" I shout, pushing them away from each other. "You're both drunk. Cool off and deal with it tomorrow when you're sober."

Neither girl looks ready to back down. Britt won't look away from Alyssa, who looks between me and Britt with equal disdain.

"This yacht is a joke," Alyssa says.

"Hey now, Lyss," Ollie says, forcing his way between me and her. "Let's not say anything we might regret, yeah? How about you and me go for a little walk?" Ollie takes her by the shoulders and steers her to the steps on the other side of the stage before disappearing into the crowd.

"Everyone good here?" I sweep my gaze over the rest of the crew. Nekesa and Eglé nod, but Britt starts ranting a mile a minute.

"I can't work with her, Nina. She's . . ." Britt rambles on, but it's too loud in here for me to understand her. During a lull in her monologue, I pat her on the cheek and turn her toward RJ.

"I need a drink," I tell him. "Keep her *away* from Alyssa."

RJ nods. When I hop from the stage, my bad knee nearly gives out, but I catch myself at the last second. I push my way through the crowd and find a place at the bar where I can keep the crew in view. As I watch the crowded club around me, I think of the photo I saw on Alex's Instagram page the other day. It was a selfie of him, Jo, and Greyson. All three of them had their faces covered in flour. *Too many cooks in the kitchen*, the caption read. The sight of it made me feel scooped out like an ice cream tub with nothing but freezer-burned bits left in the corners.

I missed Jo, but that wasn't the problem. The photo made me feel jealous. Jo had changed. It was a good thing. I was happy for her. But at the same time I felt . . . annoyed. I used to think the two of us were on the same wavelength. Everyone else we knew seemed to be going somewhere or pushing toward something, whether professional or personal. But Jo and I weren't like that. Other than the bucket list she did for her thirtieth birthday, we didn't make long-term plans or envision lofty life goals. We asked for nothing. We claimed our place in life and were perfectly content.

But Jo isn't just content anymore. She's *happy*. And though she still makes time for me, I can't help but feel she's left our frequency for another. One I'm not sure I'll ever be capable of tuning in to.

I order a drink and scan the room for Ollie and Alyssa, spotting them talking against the far wall of the club. Ollie nods, brow furrowed in concentration as Alyssa speaks. When she finally runs out of things to say, Ollie pats her on the shoulder. He says something short in reply, but whatever it is makes an impact, because frigid, aloof Alyssa is suddenly hugging him.

Ollie hugging another woman doesn't bother me. It's amusing to watch him awkwardly pat her on the back. It was painful whenever he dated other women over the years, but I never felt jealous. He'd seen me with other men too—no relationships, but plenty of flings. It was never a big deal. He knew none of them were serious. And I knew I could have Ollie if I wanted. I knew he'd leave anyone for me.

Alyssa eventually disappears into the crowd. Ollie casts his gaze over the nightclub and smiles when he spots me. I wave before turning back to the bar to order him a beer.

"Fancy seeing you here," Ollie says when he comes up behind me. I pass him the beer, which he accepts with a nod.

"Thanks for the help back there," I say. "How'd you talk her down?"

"Didn't," Ollie says. "Just stood there and let her ramble on. Told her I was sorry she had a rough day."

"And that worked?"

"People seem to like it when you let them finish their sentences," he says, and gives me a pointed look.

"Me? Interrupt anyone? Ha," I say.

We stand beside each other, drinking and not speaking. It's so loud in here that it wouldn't be worth the energy to try to hold a conversation. I keep tabs on the crew, relieved everyone seems to have cooled down. Alyssa has rejoined the others, though she and Britt give each other a wide berth and won't make eye contact.

"You good, love?" Ollie says into my ear.

"Marvelous."

"You look down."

Is that what's going on? The thought never crossed my mind. Between this and my conversation with Xav, I'm starting to wonder what I must look like to everyone else. I've never been the type of person to wallow for long when things don't go my way. I don't see the point in it. Everything is what it is. There's no use trying to change it. "Do you really want to know what's wrong with me?" I say.

"I know plenty of things that are wrong with you, kitten," Ollie replies. His dimples peek out from behind his beer when he lowers his glass.

"Fair enough. But what's wrong right *now* is you haven't ordered me a shot of tequila and taken me out on the dance floor."

"Well, those are two problems I *can* fix," Ollie says.

He winks, and when he turns to wave down the bartender, I find myself wondering if there aren't other problems of mine Ollie can solve after all.

When we finally leave Lotus, it's nearly three in the morning.

"I want grilled cheese!" Simon whines from where he's slumped over RJ's lap in the back of the van we've called to take us to the marina.

"You're totally langers, all of you," Ollie says from beside me.

"No one understands you," I mumble into his shoulder.

RJ, Matt, and Britt begin chanting "grilled cheese" over and over until Ollie shouts, "All right! I'll make your fecking grilled cheese if you'll just shut up!"

The van falls silent the rest of the way to the marina.

Ollie, true to his word, heads straight to the galley when we return. I hop up onto the island counter and watch him cook, tuning in and out of the conversation, drunkenly mesmerized by the seemingly endless supply of grilled cheeses Ollie makes.

"What's *that*?" I ask, swaying toward him after he pulls a delicious-smelling tray from the oven.

"Pizza rolls, what else?"

"Oliver," I whisper, leaning so far forward, I nearly tip off the counter, and Ollie has to catch me. "I love your pizza rolls. They're my favorite snack, especially when I'm drunk."

"I know that, kitten," he says, and smacks Simon on the hand with a spatula when he reaches for one.

"What the hell, man?" Simon says, rubbing at the back of his hand. "You don't have to be such a dick about it."

"I made your fecking grilled cheese. Leave my girl's food alone."

I cackle loudly and point a finger at Simon. "Ha! Hands off my snack! What are you, the South African Hamburglar? No, Pizza Roll Burglar?"

"That's an awful name," Nekesa says. "Keep it general, like . . . South African Snack Burglar."

I point to Nekesa. "You're my favorite. Britt! Text Jo and tell her Nekesa's my new favorite."

Nekesa grins, Ollie shakes his head, and Simon stares longingly at the pizza rolls.

Britt slumps against the counter with her chin propped in one hand. "Ollie's girl, huh?"

I turn to Britt, finally registering what Ollie's said. "I'm my own damn girl," I say. I fling my arms out wide, and Ollie has to lean back to avoid getting whacked in the chest. "No one owns Nina Lejeune. I go when I want, I come when I want—"

Britt pats me on the leg and hollers, "Did you hear that, everyone? Nina comes when she wants!"

"That is twisting my words," I say. I boop her nose and nearly tip off the counter again. "And you know what? Maybe I *do* come when I want. I make sure of it. Never fake it, Britt, that's the best advice you'll ever get. Don't let anyone tell you that all women should orgasm from penetrative sex. Most women only orgasm with clitoral stimulation. I know this one guy who does this thing with his mouth that's—"

"And the galley's closed!" Ollie interrupts, steadying me by putting his hand on my waist.

I frown up at him. "I'm *educating* the *youth*, Oliver. Do you *want* them to be cursed to a life of joyless sex?"

Ollie blows on a pizza roll to cool it down before shoving it in my mouth. "I want *you* to not say anything you'll regret saying tomorrow."

I mumble an incoherent response. *God, these pizza rolls are good.*

Ollie glares at the rest of the crew. "Out of here, the lot of you. Go feck up someone else's part of the boat."

Britt straightens and stretches her arms above her head in a yawn. She looks between me and Ollie with amusement. "Thank you, Nina. I have learned *so* many things tonight. I think you ought to give us another lesson tomorrow. Maybe you and Ollie can co-teach?"

"Out!" Ollie says.

Britt, who has a grilled cheese in each hand, takes a big bite out of one and then the other before following the others down into the crew mess. When Ollie helps me off the counter, I go to follow Britt, but he calls out after me. "Aren't you forgetting something, darling?"

"Right, right, right," I say. I dip into a low curtsy and put on my best Irish accent. "Thank you for the snacks, Oliver. Good night."

Ollie laughs. "You only had one, Neen. You need to sober up or you'll be miserable tomorrow."

"Mm. You're right," I say, ditching the bad Irish accent when I realize how hungry I am. "But can we eat them up on the bunny pad?"

"Where else would we eat them?" He takes the plate of pizza rolls in one hand and a bottle of water in the other. I loop my arm through his and let him lead me up to the bunny pad, where I sigh heavily onto the cushions and stare out at the ocean.

Ollie sits beside me and sets the plate of pizza rolls in front of us, then opens the bottle of water and passes it to me. We eat in silence for a while as the water, wind, and food slowly sober me up.

"You know what this reminds me of?" I say.

"What?"

"The first night we ever hung out."

Ollie laughs. "You mean the night of our drunken cartwheels?"

"Only one of us was actually doing cartwheels, Oliver. Don't kid yourself."

A smile flickers at the corner of his mouth. I want to press my thumb there and yank that smile like a loose thread on a thrifted sweater. I want to unravel him in my hands until there's nothing left, until I'm so tangled up in him I'll never break loose.

"What?" Ollie says. "What is it?"

When I kiss him, he leans back into me, and all I can think is that I've been a fool for not kissing Oliver Dunne every second since the day we met.

But after a few moments, Ollie breaks off the kiss and rests his forehead against mine.

"*Nina*," he sighs.

"*Ollie*," I reply. I lean my cheek into his hand, wondering why we aren't still kissing.

He pulls away from me with a groan. "You're going to kill me."

"Correct. I just haven't decided how."

"I have no idea what this means," he says.

"You don't know what *what* means?"

"You kissing me."

"It means I want to boink you, obviously."

"You want to . . ." Ollie laughs. "And you think I say weird shite."

"I meant what I said. I come when I want. I happen to know you are a fabulous lover with a thorough understanding of anatomy. Now, back to the kissing, please."

"What I mean," Ollie says, very much not getting back to the kissing, "is I don't know how the kissing relates to our . . . situation."

"Our . . . right." I hadn't forgotten about Ollie's ultimatum, but I'd hoped his silence on the matter was a sign he'd given up.

"We need to talk about it."

"I don't think there's anything to say."

Ollie rubs at the back of his neck. "I still don't understand why we can't be together for real."

I let my face fall into my hands. I'm too drunk for this. "I don't either," I say. It's the closest to honest I've ever been with him about how I really feel. I love him. He knows it, even if I've never said it. This should be simple. If I were watching myself in a movie, I'd be screaming at the screen by now.

Ollie doesn't say anything. Why can't he just leave things the way they are? He ought to walk away. I'm not sure why he hasn't. My commitment issues have never been a secret. I wear them as part of my whole persona. I'm not proud of it. I don't even like it. But I don't know how to change. I'm not sure I can.

"Are you even having fun, Nina?" he finally says.

I lift my head to look at him. I know he's referring to my rules. Have fun. Don't rely on anyone but yourself. I told Jo they weren't impossible. Usually they are pretty easy to live by.

Usually.

But when I look at Ollie now, when I think about getting ready with the girls earlier, about how utterly disconnected I've felt from charter season, I wonder if I've gotten everything wrong. Ollie has a point. The things that used to be fun aren't as fun as I remember. Take tonight, for example. I only enjoyed myself when I was with him. Being around Ollie is fun. Not being with him . . . isn't.

"I don't know," I say.

Somehow I've landed in a space where my rules contradict each other. I think back to the lost twentysomething I was when I made them. My parents . . . they were the catalyst for this, but a decade later, they're doing fine. It's been ten years, and Dad hasn't had a single relapse. I'm out of debt. My parents have rebuilt their life. Maybe Jo was right. Maybe my rules are ridiculous. The thought of letting them go is both thrilling and terrifying.

Ollie is right. We need to talk about it, but I can't do that right now. I'm not ready. I need more time.

"I've got an idea," I say. "We can kiss instead of talk. We can get this out of our systems. We haven't snuck off to the laundry room at all this season. You might see things differently after. Everything might go back to normal."

"As much as I would *love* to try and get you out of my system, I don't think it's possible. And besides, you're drunk."

"I'm not drunk," I say.

"You're not sober."

I boop his nose. "*You're* drunk," I say.

Ollie takes hold of my finger. "I stopped drinking right after that beer you bought me for helping you keep your stewardesses from clawing each other's eyes out." He opens my hand and presses a kiss to my palm. "Never been more sober in my fecking life."

He sets my hand in my lap, and I settle back against the cushion with a groan. "That was a shitshow, wasn't it? What's with this season? Why is it so much more chaotic than all the others?"

Ollie gives me a look I'm not sure I could decipher sober, let alone drunk. "It's always like this."

"No," I say. "It's definitely more chaotic this season."

He looks like he wants to argue with me but thinks better of it. He leans back on the cushion beside me, and I snuggle closer, throwing an arm over his chest. We lay like that in silence for a long time. I listen to him breathe and trace a finger up and down his chest, lower and lower to his stomach, until Ollie catches my hand and presses it to his cheek with a sigh.

"I think it's time for you to go to bed, kitten," he says.

"I'm a party animal. I'm just getting started." I wedge myself closer and press a kiss to his throat.

Ollie stifles a moan of pleasure and shifts away from me gently. "You're absolutely murderous. I'd like to be able to sleep tonight." He sits up and pats me on the hip. "Come now. Up you get."

I whine in protest, but it's not so cozy up here without him beside me.

Everyone else must be passed out, because the ship is quiet as we make our way belowdeck. Ollie laughs at me as I clumsily change into my pajamas, then mutters curses under his breath when I try but fail to lift myself into the top bunk and he has to keep me from falling flat on my ass. He takes me by the shoulders and maneuvers me into his bed instead.

"Did you change your mind about getting it out of our systems?" I say.

Ollie pulls his comforter over me with a laugh. "Nope." He leans closer and presses a kiss to my forehead. "This is a trade," he says. "For *one* night. You better not wake up acting like you've claimed my bunk."

"Thanks for the idea," I mumble.

He slips off my unicorn earrings, first one, then the other. "I love you, Nina," he says. The words aren't pleading, or demanding. They're certain. A statement of fact.

Even if I weren't drunk and mostly asleep, I wouldn't know how to respond. Fortunately, Ollie doesn't seem to expect a response, because the next moment he's gone. I hear him lift himself onto my bed. I know he is settling beneath my blanket. I know he is turning onto his left side, burying his face into my pillow, one arm shoved beneath it. For a moment before I fall asleep, I think of Ollie and what it would mean to make our relationship real, and for the first time my answer isn't *No* but *Why not?*

14

~~~~~~~~

Eight years earlier

Two weeks before Ollie's Immigration interview, I sat across from him on the floor of our Lake Worth apartment, a grease-stained pizza box open between us.

"We're going truth on this one?" Ollie asked.

"Yup." I looked down at the notes in my hands. Throughout most of the six months since we'd gotten married and filed the adjustment-of-status paperwork that would begin Ollie's immigration process, it had been easy to push all of it to the back of my mind. After that day, we'd never spoken about what we'd done or what information was slowly making its way through Immigration. Not until we'd received the notice to appear for Ollie's green card interview. Since then, every spare minute we'd had was devoted to practicing, making sure our stories matched and we could fake being a real couple. Our plan was to tell the truth as often as possible and keep the lies to a minimum.

"What was the question again?" Ollie said.

I glared at him. "Can you at least *try* to pay attention?"

"How am I supposed to pay attention when you're hurling the crust of your pizza back into the box? Who doesn't eat pizza crust? That's the best part."

"The sauce is the best part," I said.

"You're mad," Ollie said, finishing off the pizza crust I'd just discarded.

I pressed a hand over my eyes. "Look, Oliver, I'm really not in the mood to argue with you about pizza again. The question was *When did you and Nina meet?*"

"I met you—"

"Don't do it like that. Pretend I'm the interviewer," I said.

Ollie rolled his eyes. "I met *Nina* when she walked onto the boat looking for a job. That was in January, about a month before we set sail."

Good. "And you two hit it off right away?"

Ollie rubbed a hand over his jaw. "Nah. She was annoying. Cute, but annoying."

I wasn't sure how I felt about being called *cute*, but it was better than *scary*. I couldn't imagine the interviewer keeping a straight face with that one. "You got married only five months after meeting each other," I said. "That seems pretty quick. When did you start to develop romantic feelings for Nina?"

"By the end of the second week on charter," Ollie said. I glanced at my notes. We'd agreed on three weeks, but before I could correct him, he continued speaking. "I'd been watching her since we set sail. She'd made it clear she didn't give a shit what anyone thought of her. Most people like that, they act like they don't care about anything, but not Nina. She may not care what people think of *her*, but she cares about people. I liked watching her with the guests because she took their requests, even the ridiculous ones, so seriously." Ollie looked away from me to grab another slice of pizza from the box. "I'm a perfection-ist about food. Have to be as a yacht chef. It didn't take long for me to realize Nina was like that too, but with the smallest things. Things no one else would think are important. She'd take forever adjusting those little umbrellas in the guests' drinks so they'd look just right. I once caught her in the Sky Lounge making sure all the streamers for a party were the same length. Stuff like that."

Ollie chewed thoughtfully for a moment before continuing. "Our second week we had this charter, a bunch of empty nesters. They found out Nina used to coach gymnastics and begged her to teach them how to do flips on the floating trampoline. Dinner was marinat-ing, so I was out on the main deck watching, because, hell, it was amusing. These middle-aged gals trying to do flips and stumbling and laughing all over the place. And Nina, she was just mesmerizing, laughing along with them and looking like a real pro doing all her moves."

I kept my eyes on the notes. This was off-script but . . . good. Really good.

"When the primary finally landed a flip, Nina just barreled into this woman and hugged her so hard she nearly knocked her right into the ocean. She was so happy for this lady she hardly knew, and not because she was trying to get a good tip. I'm not exactly the most pleasant personality, especially at work, but it's just because I want every meal to be something the guests will remember. That day, watching Nina, I could tell helping people have fun really mattered to her. It was what cooking was to me. I remember standing there and thinking, *Fuck, I'm in some real shite now.*"

Ollie stared at his pizza and took another bite. It took me a few seconds to realize he'd finished speaking. Everything he'd said had happened—the trampoline and the flips and all. The things he'd said about my perfectionism, about what mattered to me . . . it was all true, though I'd never said those things to him or anyone else. But what he'd said about how he *felt* . . . That couldn't be real, right?

"Damn," I said, rubbing my bad knee. It had ached like hell after that day on the trampoline. "You're good, Ollie. I almost believed you." I scratched out what we'd originally put as the answer to that question and scribbled in a quick summary of what he'd said. "Let's keep that version."

Ollie shoved the pizza into his mouth and didn't respond. Once he'd finished his slice, including the crust, he leaned over and snatched the paper from my hands. "My turn to ask the questions."

"Bring it," I said.

"Let's see." Ollie scanned the page. "Right. Which side of the bed does your sexy specimen of a spouse sleep on?"

I rolled my eyes.

He poked my side. "No eye rolling or they'll know you're lying."

"The left side. But only because it's farthest from the closet," I said. "He's terrified of closets."

Ollie narrowed his eyes. "I wasn't before you made me watch that *Fact or Fiction* show where the kid disappears in a closet."

"It was fiction!"

"Not on the *show*! The show says it was inspired by a true story!"

"The kid was a runaway! They found him a few weeks later!"

"You read that in a fecking YouTube comment. That's not a reliable source."

"Oh, whatever. Will you focus on this, please? Next question."

Ollie looked at the paper again and grinned. "How often do you and your spouse have sexual intercourse?"

I held his gaze. I wouldn't let him think he could embarrass me. "Twice a week," I said.

He cocked his head to the side. "That's it? Shouldn't you still be in the honeymoon phase?"

"We're busy people."

"But you live together *and* work together, right? You never, you know, rock the boat a little?"

I narrowed my eyes. "I don't think that's something they'll suggest in the Immigration interview, Oliver."

"How about every other night?"

"Every other *morning.*"

"Ah, prefer a nice wake-up, do you, Neen?"

"Maybe."

"Noted." He leaned forward and snatched the pen from my hands. "Every other *morning* it is, then."

"You do realize this isn't real sex. We're pretending."

"Hush now. I'm trying to write."

"You're too goofy for this tonight," I said. My knee ached from sitting on the floor for so long, so I stood and moved to the couch. When Ollie finished writing, he brought the pizza box to the kitchen and put the kettle on.

"Do you want the lemon or the chamomile tonight?" he called.

"Both!"

"Greedy," he said, but I watched him pull out one of each and drop it into my mug anyway.

Initially, I'd worried moving in with Ollie would be awkward, that things would feel different once we were back in Palm Beach, but it had been the easiest thing in the world. When he turned around with a mug in each hand, he caught me staring at him from where I sat on the couch.

"What?" he said.

"*What* what?"

"Why're you looking at me like that?"

"I'm not looking at you."

He blew across the top of each mug and stood at the boundary between the kitchen and living room. "Yeah, you are. Your eyes are looking at my eyes right now."

"No, they aren't," I said, not looking away.

He shook his head, then flicked off the lights in the kitchen with his elbow before crossing the living room and setting our tea on the coffee table. "You're weird, Neen."

"You knew that when you entered into this arrangement." I leaned forward to grab my mug. "And thanks for the tea."

Ollie sighed and tossed a throw blanket over my lap before sitting down beside me. "Suppose you're right. Makes life entertaining. Speaking of entertaining, want to watch *Dexter*?"

"I knew you liked it!" I said.

"What can I say? You won me over."

I adjusted the blanket over my legs but let my feet poke out so I could shove my toes beneath Ollie's butt. He yelped out a curse.

"My feet are cold!" I said.

Ollie shot me a glare. "Yeah, I know! That's why I gave you the tea and the blanket!"

I wiggled my toes. "But your butt is so much warmer!"

"Your freezing feet are gonna give me hypothermia," he grumbled.

His hand brushed against mine when he tugged a corner of the blanket over his lap, and I noticed a shiny smooth patch of skin at his wrist. I took his hand in mine. "How'd you get that?"

Ollie stared down at where my thumb passed over the scar and laughed. "I started working at the family pub when I was fourteen, and this old fella, Oisin, taught me to cook. Grumpy old bastard looked like the fecking Crypt Keeper, but he sprinted around that kitchen like Usain Bolt. My first week I made the mistake of getting in his way when he was deep-frying chips. Knocked right into him just as he was pulling 'em out and a big splash of oil got me right there. And you know what he said?"

"What did he say?"

Ollie straightened up and scowled, his accent deeper and thicker as he spoke. "He said, *You're as sharp as a beach ball, aren't ya, boy?*" He laughed, and his face relaxed into a grin. "Loved that old bastard. Always effin' and blindin', but he had a soft spot for me, believe it or not."

"Gee, wonder what he says to people he doesn't like?" I turned Ollie's hand over and examined his palm. "You have a lot of scars. Do you remember how you got all of them?"

"Only the ones with a good story." He guided my hand to a barely visible scar on his thumb and told me about the time he'd nicked himself cutting a lemon behind the bar because he was distracted talking to a girl he had a crush on. We sat like that for a long time. Ollie passed my hand over each of his scars and burns until he ran out of stories to tell. Some stories made me laugh, while others broke my heart. A few scars he skipped over completely, but I knew better than to ask.

"What about you?" Ollie said. "Any good scar stories?"

I rested my hand on my knee, which was hidden beneath the throw blanket. "I've only got one, and you already know it."

Ollie pulled the blanket from our laps and let it fall to the floor. His eyes raised to mine when he gently pulled my leg into his lap. I could hardly breathe as he traced circles over the scar with his finger. He smiled. "Looks like it hurt."

"That would be an understatement." My leg was still in Ollie's hands, but I stretched out on the couch and stared up at the ceiling. I closed my eyes and felt him move away, but then the couch dipped on either side of me and when I blinked my eyes open again, I yelped at the sight of his face hovering above mine.

"Pop quiz," he said, grinning as he looked down at me.

I laughed. "What's gotten into you?" His body was inches above mine, but alarmingly, I found myself wishing he'd close the space between us and press into me, pinning me to the couch.

Ollie's eyes searched mine, and he bent his face closer. "We've got to see if you can keep your cool under pressure." He pulled back an inch, but the way he looked at me made me forget my frozen feet. Keeping my cool was most definitely not happening. I was burning all over.

"What's the question?" I asked.

"When's my birthday."

"January third."

"What's my favorite color?"

"You don't have one."

"Middle name?"

"Joseph."

"Where was I born?"

"Ireland."

"*Where* in Ireland?"

"Cobh."

"How old was I when I had my first kiss?"

Ollie saying the word *kiss* coincided with the voice in my head screaming *kiss him*, and suddenly I couldn't think.

His eyes roamed my face, pausing briefly on my mouth before flitting back to my eyes. "Answer the question, Nina."

"Fourteen."

He made a sound like a buzzer and tickled me. I inhaled sharply, laughing so hard it hurt.

"How old, Neen?"

"Twenty!" I wheezed.

He paused in his tickling to glare down at me. "Twenty? You think with a face like this, I really didn't get a kiss until I was twenty?"

Before I could respond, he started tickling me again. "Fifteen! Fifteen!" I cried.

"Bingo." He released my wrists and squeezed beside me. We hardly fit there, side by side. "Scoot over, girl, or I'll fall off."

"Serves you right," I said, but I turned onto my side and made as much room for him as I could.

Ollie turned on his side to face me. Between him and the back of the couch, I felt warmer than I ever had in my entire life. Even warmer than the day Xav had married us on the boat. All I could think about was how long his eyelashes were, how close his face was to mine, how close all of him was to all of me. His breath smelled like the mint tea cooling on the coffee table. Christmas was only a few weeks away. I'd have to see if I could find him a nice gift. He'd once said he preferred loose-leaf tea but found it too messy during charter season. Maybe I could get him one of those tea balls we'd seen in the new tea shop downtown. When we'd gone there last week, Ollie had grabbed a tea ball in each hand and asked me which of his balls I liked better. I laughed at the memory.

"What's so funny?" Ollie said.

"Tea balls," I whispered, unable to bite back the smile on my face.

"I should've known you were thinking about balls," he whispered back.

"Why?"

"That's your thinking-about-balls smile," he said.

"I don't have a thinking-about-balls smile."

"But now you will. Every time you think about balls, you'll remember this conversation and smile, and it'll be your thinking-about-balls smile."

He brushed a thumb along my cheek, pausing at the corner of my mouth.

"Why are we whispering about balls?" I said. At his touch, a feeling

I wasn't sure I could name pressed against my ribs, sharp and good and almost painful. I wanted more.

"I don't know. You're the one who started whispering about balls."

I didn't know what the hell we were talking about. The words were nothing but filler. The real conversation was in the gentle pressure of his thumb at the corner of my mouth, in the way my chest (really, I had never been more aware of being braless) pressed against his with each breath I took.

Ollie ran his thumb over my bottom lip. "Do you think we'll pull off the interview?" he said.

"Yes," I said, hyperaware of how he watched my mouth move against his thumb.

He lifted his eyes to meet mine. "How can you be so sure?"

"Gut feeling."

His hand drifted down the side of my neck, his touch so light it raised goose bumps on my skin. "Are you cold?"

"No," I said. "It's a million degrees in here."

"If we get caught, I could be banned from entering the US for ten years. What will you do then?"

"Oh, I don't know," I said, unable to imagine anything outside of Ollie's hand running up and down the side of my neck. "Take a nap? Go to jail? Add to the impossible amount of debt I have already?"

Ollie's hand stilled. "You can change your mind," he said. "You don't have to go through with this."

"I want to go through with it," I said. I wanted a lot of things at that moment. "We're really not lying *that* much."

"But the lies we're telling are felonies."

"What if . . ." I said, then let the words die. The idea was awful. It was the worst idea I'd ever had. It didn't even make sense. But right then, with Ollie's hand back in motion, gliding down my neck to my arm, and then along my side, everything he'd said about me still rever-berating in my head, it didn't *feel* like the worst idea.

"What if what?" Ollie asked.

"What if we . . . took a few lies out of the equation?"

"What do you mean?"

"What if we turned some of them into truths?"

His hand stilled at my waist. His fingers fidgeted with the hem of my shirt. "Which lies?" he said.

"It wouldn't mean anything," I said. "It would be . . . method acting. Research."

"*What* would be method acting?"

Instead of answering, I let my eyes drop to his mouth and moved toward him, slow enough for him to catch on and say no or pull away.

But Ollie didn't say anything. The space between us hardly ex-isted, but he leaned in and met me halfway. When we kissed, his mouth moved against mine, as gentle as it had been the day Xav had married us on the *Serendipity*. We pulled back at the same time, look-ing at each other as if assessing for damage after a hurricane.

"Is this . . . a good idea?" Ollie said.

"I don't know." I wondered if the kiss would break something be-tween us. I couldn't tell. At that moment, I wasn't sure I cared. I wanted my fingers in his hair. I wanted his mouth against my throat. I wanted it everywhere. I wanted to take everything he had and then some. I wanted, wanted, wanted.

It didn't have to mean anything. It was a game. The only game I could think of in which everyone who wanted to win, could.

"Maybe we should do that again," I said. "Just to be sure."

We kissed again, but this time Ollie pulled me on top of him, send-ing the couch pillows toppling to the floor. I sank my hands into his hair, kissing him again and again, but I wasn't surer of anything. I couldn't think. I could only feel. Ollie and his mouth. Ollie and his hands. Ollie and every part of him beneath me.

Ollie's mouth trailed down to my jaw. "Is this still okay?" he said.

"Yes."

"And this?" he asked, his mouth moving to my neck.

"Mm-hmm."

"You purr like a kitten."

"Shut up."

Ollie's hands slipped under my shirt, running up my sides before pausing at my ribs. "How much . . . research . . . are we doing?"

I whipped off my shirt and pulled his hands over my breasts. "We're getting PhDs."

Ollie stared at my hands over his. "Dr. Dunne, I like the sound of that."

"Shut up, Ollie."

We made out on the couch until I was positive I could write an entire thesis on Oliver Dunne's mouth and hands. If my knee ached, I didn't notice, because every part of me did. Ollie tugged at the elastic in my hair, and I laughed when it shot across the room. My hair tumbled over my shoulders like a dark wave. It probably looked wild, lumpy from how long I'd worn it up. But there wasn't a trace of humor in Ollie's expression when he looked up at me and took a strand between his fingers.

"Beautiful," he said.

I wasn't sure if the words were for me or not. I remember thinking that whatever game we were playing, we'd moved on to the next level, but I couldn't tell if this was winning or losing.

Ollie's shirt had disappeared at some point, and I delighted in the feel of his skin along mine when he rolled me beneath him and pressed me into the couch. He tilted my head to the side, laughing as he took one of my unicorn earrings between his fingers.

"What?" I said.

"I'm just glad you like them."

When his eyes left the earring and met mine again, I could hardly breathe. How much of this was proximity, and stress, and physical attraction? How much of this was acting? Could you research something this lovely? Could you know everything about it and not lose yourself in it completely?

I decided not to think about that, because if Ollie was something I could get addicted to, then I needed to stop before things went too far. But perhaps it was already too late. Not a single part of me wanted to stop.

"Do you still want to go where this is headed?" I asked.

"Where do *you* want this to go?" he said.

Everywhere, I thought, not quite sure what I meant by it. I wasn't thinking of us naked on every surface of this apartment, though I wouldn't have minded that. I thought of us talking on the bunny pad, and laughing out on the balcony of our apartment, my feet beneath his butt as we watched TV. I thought of him at the gas station down the street, pumping gas as I waited in the stillness of the quiet car and watched him through the window. I thought of things that hadn't even happened yet. Things that might never happen. Like sitting across from him at an expensive restaurant. Him rolling his eyes as I showed him some wild outfit at a thrift store. Dressing up as Dexter and Rita for Halloween. I saw him at my parents' house, out on the deck drinking a beer with my dad. There wasn't a single place or moment I couldn't picture Oliver Dunne.

It was all too much. I didn't want to think about what it meant. I only wanted to take without worrying about what belonged to me and what didn't. I wanted to steal this moment and figure out how to give it back later. I could dull the fear and longing, everything I wouldn't allow myself to dwell on, with Ollie's mouth, Ollie's hands, with every part of him.

He twirled a strand of my hair between his fingers. "And this would all be method acting, right?"

"Right. We'll make this marriage real for two weeks. Just until the interview," I said, as much to myself as to him. "That way we won't *really* be lying, and we'll have more material to draw from. Once it's all over, we'll go back to normal. Does that sound good to you?"

Ollie's eyes were bright when they met mine again. "To tell you the truth, Nina Lejeune, I think it's the best idea you've ever had."

15

~~~~~~~~

When I enter the galley to make the guests coffee on the morning of my thirty-third birthday, Ollie strides over to where I stand beside the espresso machine, his hands behind his back.

"You look awfully peppy today," I say once I finish grinding the espresso beans. "Did you overdo it watching latte art tutorials again?"

"I'm always peppy," Ollie says. "Pep is my middle name."

I roll my eyes and scoop the ground espresso into the portafilter. He's practically buzzing beside me, and I know why, but I take my time tamping down the espresso and twisting the portafilter into place. Once I've started the machine, I turn to Ollie with my hands outstretched. "The goddess will accept your offering now."

Ollie places a plate with a strawberry cupcake on it into my hands. "Happy birthday, kitten."

I swipe a taste of the cream cheese frosting. "As good as ever. You know I hate giving you compliments. Your ego doesn't need any extra inflation. I worry your head will float away."

It's strange how something as small as this can make me feel like so many versions of myself at one time. The birthday cupcake is tradition, from the flavor to the plate he serves it on. The only year I didn't have a birthday cupcake on charter was last year. Jo had asked Amir to make one, but he'd misheard her and made a strawberry *cake* instead. It was fine. I didn't mind. It wouldn't have mattered if Amir had gotten it right. He could've used Ollie's exact recipe, and it wouldn't have changed the sense that something was missing.

"We're going out tonight," Ollie says.

I set the cupcake on the counter to finish making the guests' coffees. "No shit we're going out. It's our night off."

"No," Ollie says. "I'm taking you out on a date tonight." He swipes some frosting from the cupcake and smears it on the tip of my nose.

"Not with that behavior, you're not."

"What behavior?" Ollie says. He scoops another bit of frosting from the cupcake and holds it in front of my face.

"Oliver Joseph Dunne, don't you dare." But I'm in the middle of steaming milk, unable to do anything but squeal in protest when he smears it over my cheeks.

"I'll stop if you let me take you out once we get these guests off the boat." His eyes flick to the cupcake before roaming my face again. "How do you feel about having a frosting monobrow?"

"Enthusiastic," I say.

"Mm . . . that's too bad. Let's do a frosting moustache instead."

I pretend I don't mind the frosting moustache, but once I hear Britt's voice coming up the stairs and Ollie goes in for the frosting monobrow, I've had enough. "Fine! I'll go on a date with you. But *only* because it's my birthday."

Ollie grins. He scoops the frosting from the tip of my nose and licks his finger.

"And I want the bottom bunk," I add when the milk finishes steaming.

"Oh no you don't," he says. "That deal expired two months ago."

"No deal, no date," I say.

Ollie swears. "Fine. But we're not swapping bunks until *after* the date. I don't trust you not to chicken out as soon as your sheets are on my bed."

I extend my hand so we can shake on it. "Deal."

When he puts his hand in mine, I grab the rest of the cupcake from the counter and smash it into his face.

He jumps back, curses flying from his lips. We stare at each other for a moment. He looks utterly ridiculous with frosting sliding down his face. The cupcake is in pieces on the floor. Lord, we've made a mess.

Ollie starts laughing at the same time I do. The frosting tickles my nose as it melts on my face, and I feel childish in the best way. A way I don't often feel anymore.

"Is this, like, a foreplay thing?" Britt says.

Ollie and I turn to the galley entrance and find her grinning gleefully.

"I'm not cleaning up after your weird sex games," she says.

"It's not a weird sex game," I say.

"That's for after the date," Ollie says.

"What date?" Britt says.

"It's April second," I say at the same time Ollie says, "The date I'm taking Neen on tonight."

Britt's eyes widen and she prances over. "What do you mean, *a date*? Like a *date* date?"

"A platonic date," I say.

"It's a real date, isn't it? I think my soul just left my body."

"I thought you didn't want to have to clean up."

Britt's gaze drops to the floor. "Right."

"How about you forget everything you've seen here and run the coffees up for me?"

"But I'm not on service until—"

"It's that or I shove what's left of that cupcake down your throat and hide your lifeless body in the bilge."

"Coffee it is, then!" Britt says. "Nice work, buddy," she adds, shooting Ollie a wink as she steps around me to grab the coffees.

Once she's out of sight I turn to Ollie. "You don't have to *tell* everyone about the date."

"For fuck's sake." He turns away and crosses the galley to the sink, where he gets a kitchen towel damp and wipes it over his face.

"What?"

He sighs. "If you want to hide it, then what's the point, Nina?"

"Of the date?"

He nods.

"It's my birthday. Dates usually involve free food. I want the bottom bunk."

Ollie rolls his eyes. "Don't be like that."

"Like what?"

"All . . . jokey. Is the thought of someone knowing you'd go on a date with me so embarrassing you'd threaten to murder them?"

"I wouldn't *actually* murder Britt with a cupcake, Ollie. It would be very inefficient."

He sighs and passes the dish towel to me. "Here. It's fecking hard to be mad at you with frosting all over your face."

I hold the towel in my hands, unsure if I want to remove the frosting moustache or not. Ollie looks . . . pissed off, but there's something else too. "You don't really think that, do you?"

"Think what?"

"That I'm embarrassed by you."

Ollie doesn't reply. He holds my gaze, one eyebrow lifting slightly. The look in his eyes makes me want to play dead right here on the galley floor. I'll drape this kitchen towel over my face and never take it off.

"But I . . ." I'm not sure what I want to communicate. Ollie doesn't embarrass me. The idea that anyone could embarrass *me*, the world's most embarrassing person, is laughable. "That's not what this is about."

"Then what's it about, Nina?"

"I don't want people getting their hopes up."

"People or me?"

I wince. "You?"

Ollie crosses his arms over his chest and leans against the counter, his expression serious as he watches me. "You don't have to worry about getting my hopes up, Nina. You don't owe me anything. Maybe I make it seem like you do, but I mean it. If you sincerely don't want to be with me, I'll drop it. That's what I'm trying to do. But I'm fecking confused because you're constantly contradicting yourself, and I'm starting not to know what's real and what's not. If you really don't want to go on a date with me, then we won't go. I'll even give you the bottom bunk."

I wipe my face with the towel to buy time. What to say? I'm proud of Ollie and his accomplishments. Of all he's overcome. I even find his irreverent demeanor charming. He feels like the opposite of me in so many ways—able to detach from the people who hurt him (except me, it seems), so willing to start over, so open to changing his life—and yet we're so similar, too intense, too over-the-top, too much. I love him, but I can't tell him that because the words feel like a promise I'm not sure I can keep.

I let the towel slide off my face and into my hands. The way Ollie looks at me has me all twisted up inside. I think of the fun we were having moments ago. Of my increasingly conflicted feelings about committing to him ever since the night he tucked me into his bunk after I got too drunk at Lotus. Why am I constantly pushing him away when all I really want is to pull him close?

"I want to go on the date," I say, forcing the words out before I can change my mind.

Ollie blinks at me. "You . . . do?"

"Just as long as you really mean it, that you won't get your hopes up." I twist the kitchen towel in my hands. My heart races as I look at him. "I'm not embarrassed by you. Otherwise, I wouldn't . . . it's been almost a decade, and I . . ."

"You don't have to explain."

"I don't know if I can give you what you want, but I . . ."

"Nina—"

"I'd be lying if I said there was absolutely no chance of us ending up together at the end of charter season."

Whatever Ollie is about to say dies on his lips. I'm not sure I'd have heard it anyway. The sound of my pulse in my ears is overwhelming.

"Okay," he finally says.

I busy myself by wiping down the nearest counter. "So . . . what time is this . . . date?"

"Uh . . . I thought we'd leave at four," he says.

"Marvelous."

He nods and turns away. He's quiet as he cooks breakfast. It's as if he's worried this small step forward could become two steps back with one wrong word. I'm quiet too, trying not to think about what my *no* becoming a *maybe* could set into motion as I clean up the bits of cupcake from the floor.

When breakfast is ready, Ollie passes me the first plate, a look moving between us that has nothing to do with food. In his eyes I see fear, and hesitation, and hope. I wonder what he sees in mine. I wish he would tell me. Maybe then I would know how I feel.

"Four o'clock," he says, once my arms are loaded up with plates.

"Four o'clock," I repeat, knee aching as I leave Ollie and the galley behind.

16

A year after successfully navigating Ollie's Immigration interview, not much in my life had changed, but the things that had were all good. My credit had improved as I slowly paid down my debt. We'd both quit smoking. One night during charter season, we'd made a bet to see who could go the longest without a cigarette, and neither of us gave in. We lived together in the same apartment. Another charter season had come and gone.

And despite our initial agreement that our "method acting" would last only two weeks, I still found myself waking up next to Ollie more often than I liked to admit.

So I didn't admit it. Not to anyone. We didn't talk about it either. We pretended there had never been an expiration date, just like we pretended we weren't slipping into each other's beds in the middle of the night whenever we couldn't sleep.

Which was perfectly fine by me. There was nothing to talk about.

I had everything I wanted: a decent apartment, a great job, my friend, fabulous sex. It was the simplest my life had ever been.

And then Ollie had to go and ruin it.

It had been an awful week. My second stew had quit without notice, leaving me to manage the day charters by myself. Xav hadn't liked any of the candidates so far. I was exhausted and needed something to cheer me up. One of our guests had told me about an estate sale and how the owner had been known for her eclectic fashion sense. Even if I couldn't afford a single thing, it would be enough to see it all for myself. That morning, I woke up in Ollie's bed, intending to slip out unnoticed. But as soon as I moved, Ollie slung an arm around my waist and pulled me against him, burying his face in my neck.

"Where do you think you're going?" he mumbled.

"An estate sale."

He grunted, then let go of me to roll onto his back with a yawn. "All right. I'm up."

I turned to face him. "You don't have to come with me."

"I don't mind." He rubbed his eyes, then paused to look at me. "Unless you don't want me to come."

"That's not what I meant. I figured getting up early to spend your day off at some dead lady's mansion wasn't your cup of tea."

"It's my cup of tea." He sat up with a dramatic yawn and stretched his arms above his head. "Speaking of tea, I'm gonna put the kettle on. Want me to start the coffee?"

"I can do it."

"I know you *can* do it."

I rolled my eyes. "You're insufferable."

"That's not what you were saying last night." I hurled a pillow at him, but Ollie caught it with a laugh and tossed it back at me, hit-

ting me in the face. "Right. I'll make you enough for the big tumbler.
You look exhausted, you know. Were you up late last night or something?"

"You really are insufferable!" I called after him when he left the
room.

Giant coffee in hand, I wandered the mansion with Ollie for over
two hours, laughing at his commentary as I ran my hands over the
woman's strange and beautiful things—vintage ostrich-feather boas,
and antique jewelry, and dramatic evening gowns I'd never be able to
afford, not even if I paid off all my debt.

There were a lot of horse tapestries.

The estate sale had done wonders for my mood. But then we returned home and were met by the worst smell I'd ever had the displea-
sure of smelling in my entire life.

"Shite," Ollie said as soon as we stepped inside.

"What . . . Oh," I said, plugging my nose as soon as I followed him
in. "It smells like . . ."

"Shite," Ollie said again. He pinched his nose between his fingers
and walked through the apartment, searching for the source of the offensive smell.

"It's not good, Neen," he said, meeting me at the hall that led to
our bedrooms and bathroom.

The hems of Ollie's jeans were wet. I peered beyond him, unable
to hold in a gasp when I realized the hallway was flooded.

"Please tell me that's not coming from—"

"Don't think you wanna know," he said with a grimace. In any
other circumstance, I would've laughed at how his voice sounded with
his nose pinched between his fingers. But as I stared at my shit-water
hallway, I felt uncharacteristically uninterested in humor.

"We can't stay here," he said. He guided me out of our apartment and pulled out his phone to call our landlord. Once I could form a coherent thought, I dialed Xav and asked if we could stay on the boat until our shitty situation was under control.

The two of us packed our things as quickly as we could and headed for the marina. "It almost feels like the start of charter season," I said when we arrived.

Ollie stepped from the car and slung a small duffel bag over his shoulder. "Did you really need to bring your board games?" he asked, giving my giant suitcase a skeptical look as I hauled it from the trunk.

I shot him a glare as I caught my breath. "Who said anything about needs, Oliver? This is about *wants*. What if we get bored? Besides, I can't very well leave them all at the apartment. What if they get stolen?"

"You're such a yacht stewardess," he said. "Not a bad thing," he added at my skeptical expression. "I only mean that you're always prepared for a good time. You know how to plan for fun. Most people just hope it'll happen."

"I suppose you have a point."

Ollie locked the car and we walked together across the parking lot. When we stepped onto the dock, my suitcase got stuck between two planks, and I had to pause and yank it back into motion.

"Still think bringing half your board game collection is a bit much. One or two I get. But ten? We'll only be here a night or two."

"These are valuable!" I said. "Do you know how much board games cost in this economy?"

"You bought each of those for, like, five bucks tops at World Thrift. Not even sure you've got all the pieces."

"You don't *need* all the pieces unless you want to play by the *official* rules. *I* make my *own* rules."

He laughed. "Can't argue with you on that one, kitten."

We'd made it halfway down the dock when my suitcase got stuck again. Without saying another word, Ollie grabbed it with a sigh and carried it the rest of the way down the dock.

The *Serendipity* was quiet when we stepped on board. The first thing we did was take the longest, hottest showers of our lives. Once I felt sufficiently clean, I wandered the yacht. Even though I lived on it for months at a time, it was strange to have the whole boat to ourselves without any work to do. It reminded me of those two whirlwind weeks after our first charter season together, when Ollie and I were planning our fraudulent wedding.

When I reached the master suite, I peeked inside and stared longingly at the bed. It was huge. Nicer than any bed I'd ever slept in.

"Planning to break some rules tonight, Neen?"

I hadn't heard Ollie come down the hallway. I turned to face him. His hair was damp, making it darker than it usually was. I resisted the urge to wipe away a water droplet when it fell from a strand of his hair and landed on his forehead.

"Maybe," I said. "But taking the master suite wouldn't be breaking the rules, would it? We're technically guests tonight."

He laughed. "You're not wrong."

"Am I ever wrong?"

"D'you really want me to answer that?"

"No thanks," I said. I stepped into the room and hurled myself onto the bed. "Oh my," I said, closing my eyes as I sank into the comforter. "This thing is like a cloud. I'm never leaving."

When the bed dipped beside me, I opened my eyes. Ollie's face came into view, mere inches from mine. I let out a contented sigh, and amusement flashed in Ollie's eyes.

"What?" I mumbled.

He stroked my cheek with the back of his hand. "You look cozy," he murmured. "Like a cat curled up in a patch of sunlight."

I let my eyes drift shut. "What a lovely metaphor," I said. "You talk an awful lot about cats for someone who doesn't have one, you know. Did you have one as a kid?"

"Mm-hmm," Ollie said. "Her name was Snot."

I laughed and opened my eyes again. "You named your cat Snot?"

"Not me. Jack."

"Oh," I said, unsure how best to respond. Ollie hardly ever mentioned his family. "Why'd he name it that?"

Ollie kept stroking my cheek, but I could tell his mind had drifted elsewhere. I didn't move, just lay there and waited. "Not sure. I'd guess it was because of my cat allergy. My nose was like a faucet around that damn cat, but she followed me everywhere anyway. She was the coolest. Acted more like a dog." He paused for a moment. "Probably not around anymore." There was a moment of quiet, but then he seemed to emerge from whatever memory he'd gotten lost in. His eyes focused on mine as if he'd forgotten I was there. "Did you have any pets as a kid?"

I shook my head. "Too much traveling for gymnastics to ever have a pet."

"Did you want one?"

"When I was younger."

"But not now?"

"I've never really thought about it. It wouldn't seem fair to have a pet when I'm gone for four months every year."

Ollie's hand drifted from my cheek to my earring. "Guess you're right," he said.

"We should live in this bed," I said, and snuggled deeper into the covers. "I'm staying here all night. You'll have to drag me out of it for dinner."

"Why not just eat dinner here?"

"You're a genius, Oliver Dunne," I said, snapping my fingers. "I like your style. Breakfast in bed is overrated. Dinner in bed is where it's at. Should we order pizza?"

Ollie scowled. "No way. This is a special occasion. When do we ever get to be superyacht guests? I know a yacht chef who makes the best tapas you've ever had."

"Where is she?" I said, and pretended to search the room.

Ollie stuck his tongue out at me before sitting up with a sigh. "Why don't you pick out one of your board games and we'll make a night of it."

"Dinner in bed *and* game night? I think you're trying to woo me, Oliver."

"Don't like it when you call me that," he said.

I waved a hand dismissively. "Oh, you love when I call you that. It makes you feel special."

"Maybe," Ollie said. "But I'll never admit it."

Ollie left for the galley. I'd just finished setting up Settlers of Catan on the bed when he returned with more food than seemed reasonable seeing as it was just the two of us.

"Are you expecting guests or something?" I teased. "I don't have the expansion, so we can only have up to four players."

"I may have gotten a little carried away." He passed me a giant plate before sitting opposite me on the bed and glancing at the board game between us. "Settlers. Oh Jesus, is this that game with the sheep?"

I narrowed my eyes. "This is a great game. You just haven't played it enough to appreciate it."

He stuffed a croquette in his mouth. "Once was plenty. This game is boring."

He finished off another croquette and licked his thumb. The food. The bed. The board game. It was all a bizarre combination of things I couldn't have predicted would be so . . . arousing.

"Fine, how about we make it a bit more interesting?"

He raised an eyebrow. "Making up your own rules again? I think that's called cheating, love."

I ignored the comment. "I'll admit that not everyone has sophisticated enough tastes for Settlers of Catan. But I am positive that even *you* would enjoy Settlers of Catan After Dark."

"I'm listening," Ollie said. "How do you play?"

"It's simple, really," I said, busying myself with a croquette. "Whenever one person builds a settlement, the other removes an item of clothing. What do you think?"

Ollie tilted his head this way and that, a croquette in each hand. He lifted one and took a bite. "On the one hand, I still have to play Settlers of Catan. But on the other hand," he said, looking at his other hand, "this does sound like an intriguing twist. How does a person win Strip Settlers?"

"There are multiple ways to win. And it's Settlers of Catan After Dark. Please, have some class."

"I see," he said. "You know, I don't think this is fair. You're much better at these games than I am." He sighed. "But I suppose there's nothing else to do, so why not."

It didn't take me long to realize Ollie's strategy at Settlers was far more ruthless when nudity was involved. We never did finish Settlers of Catan, though Ollie won the After Dark portion of the game easily and with enthusiasm.

"You know," he said from beside me once we'd finished the first round of Settlers of Catan After Dark, "I don't remember *wood* being such a highly sought-after resource the last time we played."

"Oh, shut it," I said, shoving him away from me.

"You have to admit I'm great at this game. I think I've become a board game enthusiast."

"But did you *really* win?" I said, still out of breath from what Ollie had called the *bonus round*. I took in his bare torso beside me. I'd lost so miserably that, even though I'd been wearing more items of clothing, I hadn't managed to get more than his shirt and socks off.

His gaze traveled over my still-flushed face with a look of smug satisfaction. "Oh yes, I'm certain I won. But I'm starting to think you may have lost on purpose." He rolled over, making me yelp when he pinned me to the bed. "Care to lose again?"

I laughed. "*You* want to play Settlers of Catan twice in a row? My, I really have converted you. I half expect to come home and find you DM-ing a game of Dungeons and Dragons."

Ollie gave me a lingering kiss. "I don't think you have to worry about that," he said when he pulled away. "For some reason my interest in games only exists whenever you're around."

Ollie's words caught me off guard. Though we'd slept together more times than I could count, he didn't often say things that sounded so . . . sincere. We'd sometimes joke around in bed or compliment each other's physical appearance, but we never talked about any *feelings* for each other outside of sarcastic annoyance or friendship. I liked it that way. It kept everything simple. You couldn't lose something you didn't have. And if you didn't acknowledge it, did you really have it? But what Ollie had said didn't *feel* insincere. It didn't feel like a joke. As I looked up at him, my thoughts ran together, and rather than respond, I pulled him down to kiss me again, steering the conversation elsewhere by ending it entirely.

It was well past midnight when we gave up on the games and turned on the TV. Ollie stood beside the bed in his underwear, searching through his duffel bag for his pajamas when I noticed a small tissue paper–wrapped package had tumbled from his bag and onto the bed.

I took the package in my hands. It was light, almost as if nothing were inside. "What's this?"

"What's what?" Ollie said. A look I couldn't decipher passed over his face when he spotted the tissue paper in my hands. "Oh . . . I, uh, got you something. At the estate sale."

"You did?" I said. "When?"

"When you were in the bathroom." He returned his attention to the duffel bag. "I was gonna give it to you for Christmas. There they are," he said, and tugged his pajama bottoms from the bag.

I rolled onto my back, still undressed from our "games," and pressed the gift to my ear. "I hope it's a horse tapestry."

"Sure," he said as he stepped into his pants. "There's a fecking horse tapestry in there."

"Do I have to wait until Christmas? You know how I hate waiting. Can I open it now? Please?"

"Fine, but you'll probably hate it," he mumbled.

"Oh shut up. You're sucking all the fun right out of this."

He sank onto the edge of the bed and watched me as I slipped my finger beneath the tape holding the tissue paper closed.

"Oh," I said once I'd opened the gift and found a small gold medal, a lot like the Saint Dymphna one he always kept in his pocket. I held it close so I could read the words beneath the saint's image. "Saint Valentine," I said. I flipped the medal over, finding an inscription on the other side. "Until death," I read aloud, feeling my heart kick on like a motor in my chest. I recognized the medal from when we'd skimmed over the jewelry at the estate sale, but I hadn't looked at it too closely.

"Guess her husband was a morbid fella, yeah? I'll get you a chain for it, of course. Unless you hate it. It's okay if you hate it."

I imagined the medal on a chain. How it would feel around my neck. How I'd tuck it beneath my shirt and know Ollie had one in his pocket. I didn't hate it. Not in the least. But this was a rather romantic gesture. *Until death* . . . Was this an inside joke alluding to our fraudulent marriage? It couldn't be because he *wanted* a real relationship like that, right? We were just friends. Friends who happened to be legally married and had frequent sex, but it was all very casual, and twenty-first-century, and . . . confusing as hell, actually.

I ran my finger along the edge of the medal. "It's lovely," I said. "Be careful, Oliver. If you keep buying me jewelry, people will think you're in love with me."

Ollie cleared his throat. I looked up at him and noticed his ears had turned a furious shade of pink. "About that," he said.

"About . . . what?"

"I . . ." He looked away from me, seeming at war with himself as he stared around the master suite. When he finally faced me again, his expression made me think, *Oh shit*.

"I do love you, Nina," he said.

"You . . . Oh." I dropped my gaze to the Saint Valentine medal in my hands, trying to come up with something to say, but I couldn't catch hold of any thoughts at all.

"I think they chopped his head off," Ollie said, breaking the silence as if he hadn't just confessed he loved me. "They keep his skull out in some church with a flower crown on it."

"How . . . interesting," I said. It was the only thing I could think to say.

When I looked up at Ollie again, the medal warm in my palm, my heart raced ahead of me, faster than could possibly be safe. *He loves me*, I thought, not sure what to make of that.

I'd thought I knew what I was getting into when I married Ollie, but I hadn't, not really. Not the day of our fake wedding. Not when we started sleeping together. I'd let him walk right into my life, into my bed. I'd broken my second rule, relying on him more than I realized. Our marriage was fake, but the feelings he'd developed were real. As for my own feelings . . . I couldn't even begin to pick through them. I didn't know where to start. I had no idea if what I felt about Ollie was just friendship or something more. I'd never let myself consider it, because it wasn't a possibility. We'd both been clear from the beginning: This was casual, a mutually beneficial arrangement. Neither of us wanted a real relationship, that was the beauty of the whole thing. That was what had made marrying Ollie such a simple choice.

But with the medal in my hands, nothing seemed simple anymore. How foolish I'd been to think anything about me and Oliver Dunne could ever be simple.

"Thank you," I said, feeling like a total cliché. I rolled away from Ollie and sat up on the opposite edge of the bed to tuck the medal away into my purse. Ollie didn't say anything, and I frantically tried to think up some way to spring us out of this awkward conversation and back into more comfortable territory. I spotted the remote on the floor beside the bed and grabbed at it like a life raft. "How much do you want to bet there are *Dexter* reruns playing on Showtime right now?" I said.

Before Ollie could respond, a crash sounded from somewhere on the deck above us.

"What was that?" he said.

"I don't know." I leapt from the bed, glad to have an excuse to get dressed. "Maybe it's Xav."

I hastily tugged on the clothes I'd left in a heap beside the bed and followed Ollie from the room and up the spiral staircase. When we reached the main deck, Ollie cursed at the sight of light leaking from beneath the galley doors.

We made our way down the rest of the hall and paused outside the galley to listen. A woman's voice sounded from inside, but I didn't recognize it. I couldn't make out a thing she was saying.

"What should we do?" I whispered. But then a loud pop sounded from within the galley, jolting me into action. Without thinking, I pushed through the galley doors, ready to grab the nearest frying pan and knock whoever it was over the head with it.

But when I stepped inside, I was met by a woman who stood at the sink with a bottle of champagne bubbling over in her hands.

"The fuck?" Ollie said when he stepped in behind me.

I scanned the galley, taking in the mess of champagne on the counters, on the floor, everywhere.

Ollie burst into laughter, but I didn't think this was funny. Not at all. The woman turned to us with wide eyes and gently set the champagne bottle in the sink. Before I could find anything to say to her, she snatched a dish towel from the counter and dropped to her knees on the galley floor, hurriedly wiping up the mess.

"Bad idea, Jo. Bad idea," she muttered to herself as she moved the dish towel in circles on the floor.

"Who the fuck are you?" Ollie said.

The directionless way I'd felt moments earlier when Ollie told me he loved me disappeared as I watched this oddly harmless-seeming trespasser clean the galley floor. There was nothing like a crisis to keep me from getting swept up in emotion. Whether or not I loved Ollie didn't really matter. Getting physically involved with him had been one thing, but getting emotionally involved would be like popping a bottle of champagne. Fun in theory, but risky in practice. Whatever Ollie and I shared, I loved it. I didn't want to screw that up by making a mess of things. I'd spent enough time cleaning up other people's messes. I didn't need to make my own.

When we finally got the woman to talk, she told us her name was

Jo Walker and that she was friends with Mr. Simmons, whom Ollie
and I knew, seeing as he was friends with the owners and often joined
them whenever they took the yacht out. Once she started talking, she
didn't stop—telling us all about her miserable night at her bartending
job and how she hadn't meant any harm.

"I didn't steal it," she said, nodding to the champagne bottle in the
sink. "I brought it from the bar."

"Obviously. We'd never keep it on board. That's an awful champagne," I said.

"It's an awful bar," Jo said, and I decided I liked her despite the
trespassing.

"You know," I said, tapping my finger against my chin as I looked
her up and down, "we're in need of a new stewardess. Perhaps *you'd* be
interested, seeing as you seem to like yachts so much."

"Me?" the woman said at the same time Ollie said, "Are you fecking nuts, Neen?"

"I'm perfectly in my right mind," I said. "Look at her. She's perfect
for the job."

I couldn't explain it, but there was something about this Jo Walker.
I recognized that look. It was the face of someone who needed a lucky
break.

Ollie and I never talked about the Saint Valentine medal or what he'd
said. A few days after that night on the *Serendipity*, I found a thin gold
chain on my nightstand. I slipped the St. Valentine medal onto it and
hoped he wouldn't read too much into it. Whenever I wore it, I always
kept it tucked beneath my shirt and out of sight.

Time passed. Ollie and I carried on the way we always had. If he
was upset that I never returned the feelings he'd admitted to me, he

didn't show it. Sometimes I wondered if it had really happened. But then I'd feel the medal around my neck and know it had. A year later, when the conditions on Ollie's green card were removed and I'd rebuilt my credit enough to start managing on my own, Ollie asked me if he should get his own place when our lease was up. I told him to do whatever he thought was best, not realizing he was seriously considering moving out until he passed me his phone one evening to show me photos of the apartment he'd leased.

"The kitchen is huge," I said, only half taking in the images as I flicked through them.

"All the cabinet doors open all the way. Every single one of them."

I glanced over to our kitchen, with its awful cabinet doors. Our apartment wasn't the best, but it wasn't *that* bad. "Our kitchen is fine," I said, and passed back his phone.

"*Your* kitchen as of next month," Ollie said.

The excitement in his voice made me want to sneak into his new apartment and glue all the cabinets shut. I willed myself not to be annoyed, because Ollie wasn't *wrong*. It *would* be my kitchen next month. His new kitchen *was* nicer. Cabinet doors *should* open all the way.

It wasn't until I found Ollie cooking dinner a few nights before he was supposed to move out that I understood why I was so bothered by his fancy new kitchen. I'd just returned home from helping Jo go grocery shopping before her nieces and nephew arrived to spend a few weeks at her place. Ever since the night Ollie told me he loved me, I'd slowly pulled away from him, and my fast friendship with Jo filled the gaps. The distance I put between myself and Ollie hadn't been intentional, and if Ollie noticed, he never said. I hadn't realized what I was doing until Ollie told me he was moving out, and in those last few weeks of living together, I found myself both constantly annoyed with him and wanting to spend as much time as I could in our apartment together.

Ollie didn't notice my arrival. I lingered at the edge of the kitchen, watching him as he stood before the stove and sautéed something I couldn't see. He wore that angry look he always had whenever he cooked. When he flipped the food, a stray bit of oil jumped from the pan, landing on his hand. He leapt back with a "Fecking hell," and stuck the knuckle of his index finger in his mouth, cursing under his breath as he continued cooking.

Perhaps I made a sound, or maybe he simply felt someone was watching him. When he turned and spotted me, his expression smoothed, except for the little groove between his eyebrows. It didn't used to linger like that. How was it possible I knew Ollie well enough to notice the appearance of his first wrinkle?

"Hey, Neen," he said. He pulled his finger from his mouth and shook out his hand. "Didn't know you were home."

I love you. The thought appeared suddenly, surprising me with its surety. Was it really that simple? One moment you don't know a thing, and then something small, something as trivial as a wrinkle, pushes you over the edge. That was exactly how it felt, as if I'd been shoved off the side of the yacht, the ocean beneath me, ready to swallow me whole.

"Just got here," I said, hoping Ollie couldn't sense the chaos that had broken loose within me. I was in love with Oliver Dunne. Probably had been for . . . God knows how long. How ridiculous!

Ollie nodded to the pan on the stove. "You're just in time. I made stir fry for dinner. Are you hungry?"

"Oh," I said, not fully tuned in to the conversation.

An amused look crossed his face. "You good, love?"

I blinked, forcing myself back into the moment. "Sorry. What did you say?"

"Are you hungry?"

"Yes," I said. The words *I love you* welled up in me again, but got caught in my chest, too heavy to force out. I did love him. There was no denying it, at least not to myself. And why admit it out loud and risk ruining things? Love was risky. It had ruined my life. It had been a completely different type of love, but love nonetheless, that had kept me from pressing charges against my father and freeing myself from his mistakes. Love had brought me to a place where every choice I made felt like a last resort: quitting gymnastics, getting into yachting, marrying Ollie.

But being with Ollie didn't *feel* like a last resort, and I had no idea if that was because emotion had clouded my judgment or because what we had was different.

I tried to be optimistic when I helped Ollie move into his new place a few days later. *Putting some space between us is a good idea*, I told myself. But it didn't feel like such a good idea when I carried his boxes out the door. Or when I helped him unpack his things in his new place with its perfectly functional kitchen cabinets. Or when it grew dark out and I realized I ought to go home to my apartment. The apartment I'd shared with Ollie for years and where he no longer lived.

"I better get going," I said, hauling my purse over my shoulder as I lingered at the edge of Ollie's new living room.

"You don't have to go," Ollie said. "You can stay over, if you want."

I wanted to, but I knew I shouldn't. I shook my head and gave him a small smile. "Don't want to take over your bachelor pad on your first night. I'll just . . . use the restroom and get out of your hair."

"Oh, okay," he said. He ran a hand through his hair and turned away from me to sit on the couch. "Better use the one in the bedroom. Haven't cleaned the hall bathroom yet."

I nodded and stepped inside Ollie's room. It was so strange seeing his bed, his dresser, his clothes, so familiar to me, but now in this
unfamiliar place. After using the restroom, I caught sight of myself in
the mirror as I washed my hands and noticed the gold of the chain I
wore the Saint Valentine medal on when it glinted in the light overhead. Some nights, as we lay naked together in bed, Ollie would take
the Saint Valentine medal between his fingers and run it back and
forth along the chain. I'd pretend not to notice, talking about everything but us as we drifted off to sleep. Ollie never brought up the
medal, but I always wondered what he thought when he saw me wearing it.

I dried my hands on the hand towel I'd placed there only a few
hours ago and unclasped the Saint Valentine medal from around my
neck, leaving it on the bathroom counter for Ollie to find. It was im-
pulsive, a way to say goodbye to the way things had been between us.
We couldn't possibly continue on in the same way now that we didn't
need each other. Looking back, I see so clearly that I should've asked
him to stay. But nothing was clear to me then. What did I have to be
afraid of? I hadn't expected Ollie moving out to be so hard on me. He
was only fifteen minutes away. The distance I was creating between us
only made my life harder than it had to be. But it had never even
crossed my mind to ask Ollie not to go. I couldn't imagine a world in
which you could love someone without damaging them. All I could
see was that Ollie and I had been living in an illusion. Letting go of the
medal felt like letting go of *him*. In my mind, it was the best house-
warming gift I could give him.

It was a good idea. At least that was what I told myself.

But it didn't feel like such a good idea when I returned home to my
half-empty apartment and Ollie's tea was no longer in the shitty cabinets that didn't open all the way. It didn't feel like such a good idea

when I didn't have his butt to keep my toes warm as I watched TV by myself on the couch.

Suddenly I wasn't sure which ideas were good anymore and which ones weren't. They all seemed pretty bad to me.

17

After we drop off the guests and the tip meeting ends, I watch from the top bunk of our room as Ollie slips on a button-down and begins folding the sleeves of his shirt to just above the elbow, revealing his forearms in the most frustratingly sexual way. The outfit is something I didn't know Ollie owned: a bright pink oxford and slim camel-colored chinos. It must be new. Something about it highlights the blue of his eyes and warms the blonder parts of his hair. It's brighter than he typically dresses, but somehow so very Ollie, the very best of him. Ollie sitting beside me on the bunny pad to watch the sun break over the ocean before the guests wake up. Ollie, eyes flashing in amusement, betraying how much he secretly enjoys bickering with me in the galley. Ollie, questioning the ridiculous things I say as if he takes them seriously—as if he takes *me* seriously.

Forget the food. I'm already salivating.

"What?" Ollie says, catching my gaze in the mirror that hangs from the back of our bathroom door.

I want to take back every bad thing I've ever said about khakis. "It's . . . your butt," I say.

Ollie cocks an eyebrow. "What about it?"

"It's . . ." *Marvelous? The eighth wonder of the world? My muse?* "A shame."

Ollie turns to face me and leans against the mirror, hiding his marvelous butt from view. "What's a shame about my butt?"

"Just . . . all of it," I say. I can't resist checking him out from head to toe. For the love of God, his socks have little unicorns on them.

"I like your socks," I say, and flop back onto my pillow. I'm dead and gone, and it's all Oliver Dunne's fault. If only he'd worn this outfit before, then all this drama between us would've been over years ago.

"Are you about to cancel on me?" he says.

"We have a deal." I probably look miserable lying here with my palms pressed over my eyes. "What makes you think I'm canceling?"

"You haven't even started getting dressed, and we're leaving in an hour."

"Oh." I lift my hands from my face and sit up. I'm still wearing my khaki shorts for work and a sassy mom tee that reads, *I love my ungrateful children.* "When you said four o'clock, I thought that was a joke to make sure I was ready on time. It's far too early for dinner."

"Do I look like I'm joking about anything related to taking you out tonight?" Ollie says. He turns one way, then the next, posing like a model at a photoshoot. It's quite the show.

I fan myself with a hand. "It's too warm in here." Ollie grins. "Because of that ego of yours," I add. "It's filling the room with hot air."

"I look *marvelous*," he says.

He really does. "I've never seen you this dressed up before," I say. "Is it a special occasion? The most important person in the world's birthday, perhaps?"

"That's not why I'm so dressed up."

"Pray tell, Mr. Delightful."

Ollie looks at me, not an ounce of humor in his expression. "It's our first date. I want to make sure there's another."

"Well," I say, unable to come up with a smart remark, or any remark at all. Ollie winks at me, then disappears out of sight to sit on the bottom bunk.

I hear him rummage beneath the bed. Moments later he reappears with a pair of shoes hanging from his fingers. "We're leaving in fifty-five minutes," he says. "I don't care if you wear that or"—he steps over to our tiny closet and reaches inside—"this."

He tosses a dress across the room, barking out a laugh when it lands on my face.

It's the gown I'd been wearing when he showed up at my apartment on New Year's Eve. The dress is an off-the-shoulder floor-length gown in lilac tulle. I have no idea how Butch managed to get a Carolina Herrera, let alone for a price I could afford. When I asked, he didn't answer.

"Won't we be overdressed?" I say.

"I assume so. You always are. You can wear an entire outfit from the costume bin for all I care. Better yet, wear nothing. I wouldn't complain if I had to carry you naked off this boat."

"Well, who would?" I say. The image of him throwing me bare-assed over his shoulder and carrying me ... anywhere ... is undeniably appealing.

Ollie steps over to the bunk and props his chin on the mattress of my bed. "You'd look beautiful in anything. But there's something about this ..." He takes the fabric of the dress between his fingers, his mind seeming to go elsewhere for a moment.

I run a hand through his hair like I had on New Year's Eve and wonder if he's thinking about that night too.

"Fifty-three minutes," he says. He lifts himself up on the edge of the bunk and kisses my cheek, then disappears out the door.

The dress feels heavier in my hands once he's gone. I stare at the waves of tulle on the skirt until they blur together. I like to tell myself there is nothing new for me and Ollie to say to each other.

But now . . . now I'm not so sure.

"A grocery store? That's your big romantic gesture?"

We stand before the entrance of Le Grand Marché, the grocery store where we'd gone provision shopping our first charter season together.

Ollie's shoulder bumps against mine when he leans closer. "I want a do-over," he says.

"For what?" We're the only ones standing still in a swirl of people whose voices ring out around us in the Saint Martin sun.

"C'mon, Neen. You remember."

Of course I do. I could never forget how he tried to brush me off or how I followed him here like a gnat, ruining his boat shoes in the process.

A decade has never felt longer than it does in this moment. I expect déjà vu, but it doesn't come. Standing here with Ollie now doesn't feel like that day at all. Yes, Le Grand Marché has changed, but I'm different too. Not whole or healed from what brought me here the first time, but changed because Ollie loves me, and because I love him back, even if I've never had the courage to say it.

When I first stood here, I thought Ollie was nothing but a chef with an ego, someone who could see nobody but himself. I couldn't have been more wrong. When we met, I was wounded and angry. He was the first to push through my defenses, with his brooding looks, and teasing demeanor, and well-timed insight. He cracked my heart open, just wide enough for him to squeeze through.

He was the first. And every other love in my life is because he tunneled his way in. Jo. Xav. Alex and Greyson. Lord help me, even Britt and RJ.

I take his hand in mine. "You're still as delightful as a grocery bag," I say.

When Ollie looks at me, it's with a knowing awareness in his eyes. I'm not sure how he does that. How he seems to understand what's happening in my head at the same time I do, sometimes before. "I'm still convinced you like grocery bags," he says.

Someone bumps into Ollie as they charge past us into the store, knocking us out of our moment and back into the present.

I drop his hand once we've stepped inside and waltz ahead as he grabs us a cart. When he catches up to me, I'm in the produce section, weighing a melon in my hand.

"This has got to be the size of a baby's head," I say.

"I've got you thinking about babies already? That was easy."

"Depends on how big you were as a baby. Though with you being a mere five feet eight inches tall—"

"Nine," Ollie says.

"I can't imagine your offspring would have a head the size of this melon."

Ollie rolls his eyes, and I set the melon back with the rest. I don't seem like the type, but the truth is I love kids. If my life had turned out differently, I think I'd have a large SUV full of them by now. Emphasis on the SUV, because I refuse to be caught dead owning a minivan.

I walk alongside Ollie as he wheels the cart to the nearest aisle. "How is taking me provision shopping a date? I thought you were more creative than that."

"This is provision shopping for pleasure, not business. I'm your man. I have to cook for you on your birthday."

"You don't belong to me."

"But I do, Nina, there's no pretending otherwise."

He might be right about that. No matter how many people we try to forget each other with, it never works. All I notice is how they aren't Ollie. Maybe there will always be a part of Ollie that belongs to me. And even more frightening, maybe *I* will always belong to *him*, whether I want to or not. *But you do want to*, the voice in my head says. *But I shouldn't, right?*

Ollie pauses in the cereal aisle and pulls me in front of him so that I'm standing between his arms, boxed in between him and the shopping cart.

"What are you doing?"

"Up you get," he says, gently prodding the back of my good knee with one of his until I stand on the bottom carriage of the shopping cart. He sets the cart into motion. Other shoppers cast amused glances as we pass. We must look ridiculous as he wheels me along the linoleum.

"So, what's for dinner, Chef?"

"I thought we'd make a game of it," he says. His breath tickles the hair at the nape of my neck. He pauses halfway down the cereal aisle, a rainbow of boxes beside us—Lucky Charms, Cheerios, Froot Loops, and Cap'n Crunch.

"I love games," I say.

"I know."

"What's the game?"

"You pick eight things. Any eight things. And I'll use them in our dinner. Let's see if you can stump me."

"So if I win, I get a shitty dinner?"

His cheek is rough against mine when he leans forward. When we first met, he was always clean-shaven. Years ago, I told him I liked a little bit of stubble on him—that barely-there, sandpapery kind—and he started using a beard trimmer instead of a razor. "Don't worry, love, you won't win."

I turn and lick his face, making him pull back with a start. He wipes his cheek with the back of a hand. "What the feck was that?"

"Psychological warfare," I say, and part of me wants to eat him up, to devour him right there in the grocery store.

I yank a box of Cap'n Crunch off the shelf and set it into the cart.

"You and your feckin' Cap'n Crunch." Ollie laughs. "Oh, Nina-Neen," he says, and shakes his head.

I squint at him, suspicious. "What?"

"I knew you'd pick that, so I may have done a bit of research."

"That's cheating!"

"Not my fault you're predictable."

We move down one aisle, then the next. Ollie kisses my neck as we glide through the store, making me feel things that are most inappropriate for a frozen vegetable aisle.

"Stop trying to distract me," I say.

"Why? Is it working?"

"No," I say.

"Are you sure? You've got goose bumps," he says, and kisses his way down my neck to my shoulder.

"I'm cold. We're in a goddamn freezer aisle." I lean forward and tug open a freezer door to reach for a bag of frozen peas. *Damn it*, too easy. I try to put it back, but Ollie catches hold of my wrist.

"Uh-uh," he says. "Rules are rules. You touch it, we buy it."

"You're a cheater," I say, and reluctantly set the peas into the cart.

Twenty minutes later, Ollie has three grocery bags looped around his arms. Inside is a box of Cap'n Crunch, a bag of frozen peas, an eggplant (which was an accident, I'd picked it up for the purpose of innuendo, and Ollie said it counted as one of the ingredients), Jolly

Ranchers, wasabi, spaghetti (that awful vegetable kind), peanut butter, and a box of Creamsicles.

I'm not in the mood to eat. I'd really rather keep the psychological warfare going.

"Do we have to go back to the boat so soon?" I say once we find ourselves in the parking lot again.

"Am I winning you over, Nina Lejeune?"

"No," I say, but it's an automatic response. The truth is I'm all mixed-up. I think of all the days and nights I've spent without him. All that wasted time.

"Well, lucky for you, we aren't going back to the boat just yet."

"Then where are you cooking all that?" I ask, nodding to the bags on his arms.

Ollie raises his eyebrows at me. "Patience, love. You'll see."

"What is this place?" I ask after our car drops us off at the back door of a building on the French side of the island.

Ollie punches a code into a panel on the door. There's a small flash of green light, a whirring sound, and then Ollie opens it and ushers me into an industrial-looking kitchen.

"Welcome to Dreamland," Ollie says. "My buddy Barnabé owns this place."

"Barnabé . . ." I say. The name sounds familiar. "Barnabé from culinary school? Your old roommate? That Barnabé?"

"The very same," Ollie says. "This place isn't open on Mondays, so he said I could have free rein of it to woo my woman. It's nice, isn't it?" Ollie's eyes roam the kitchen. "Really made something of himself."

"Dreamland," I say. "Why'd he name it that?"

"Dunno," he says. "We were always talking about shite like that back then, what it would be like to have our own place. What we'd name it. Then this bastard actually goes and does it."

"What about yours?" I say.

"My what?"

"Your restaurant. What would you name it?"

"Dunno," Ollie says. He crosses the kitchen and drops our bags onto a counter. "I never took it seriously like Barnabé did. I'd just say the first thing I saw." He sweeps his gaze around the kitchen, and his eyes land on me. "Smartass," he says with a grin. "That's what I'd name it."

I know he's joking, but as I stare around at the kitchen, I wonder if Ollie regrets the way his life has turned out, and if so, what role I've played in that.

"Don't you want your own place?"

Ollie shrugs. "Never thought about it, really."

"Why not?"

"Dunno."

He leaves the kitchen, returning moments later with a rolling office chair he gestures to as if it's my personal throne. I take a seat, watching as he sets to work. He grabs an apron hanging nearby and loops it over his head before tying it around the back, then darts to the sink to wash his hands. When he returns to the counter with our groceries, he pulls out each of the items we bought and lines them up. The groove between his brows deepens as he scans the ingredients. Anyone else might think he's angry, but he's just in another world, the place his mind goes to turn over every possible way he can use each ingredient.

The cartwheels start up in my chest again as I take in this version of Ollie. I wheel myself over and lean my head against his side. When he looks at me, his eyes come back into focus.

"Forgotten about me already?" I say.

"Nah." A smile tugs at the corner of his mouth. We've had so many moments just like this one. Quiet moments in the galley, in my apartment, in his, where something delicate blossoms between us, a small break in the push and pull of our bickering. It feels like when a wave reaches the apex of its run up the sand. There's always a pause, a moment of weightlessness right before the water gets sucked back out to sea. Maybe being with Ollie for real would be like that, just one weightless moment after another.

"If you're drooling now, just wait until dinner is done," he says.

I roll my eyes and push myself away on the rolling chair, nearly bumping into a tall metal shelf.

"Easy there, killer."

"Killer is right," I say, giving the air an uppercut before parking myself at a nearby counter to watch him work. Nothing about tonight or this season feels easy. I've always hated those movies where the couple can't be together because of a simple miscommunication. But, of course, real life is fueled by people not listening or understanding each other.

I know better than anyone that simply communicating doesn't do a damn thing. Ollie and I know almost everything about each other. We have been *almost* completely transparent about where we stand. Ollie loves me. I love him too. He knows that, even if I haven't said it. Miscommunication isn't the problem here. When I look at Ollie, I feel just as much fear as I do longing. Sometimes the possibility of having something is more terrifying than the thought of never having it at all. I've told myself for years that what we have is good enough for me, even though it's not what I really want.

And what do you really want? the voice in my head says.

Ollie, I think.

Usually I ignore the question, and not only when it comes to Ollie.

While I'd happily fill a cart at World Thrift with vintage Hawaiian shirts and mom jeans or stack the closet in my hallway with old board games until the closet itself resembles a precarious game of Jenga, when it comes to anything else, anything *real*, I'd rather not wonder. Why get all worked up thinking about what I want if it might not be as good as I hope? Or, and perhaps this is the real problem, what if I get exactly what I want and realize it's perfect and lose it anyway?

My life is good. But it isn't perfect. Why change what is working to have something that might not work out? What if getting what I want ruins everything else?

Nearly an hour later, I'm still gnawing on these questions when Ollie turns to me with a satisfied look on his face. "I've just got to plate this, and it'll be ready. Why don't you go sit?"

"I am sitting," I say, and give myself a spin in the rolling chair.

"In the dining area, smartass," Ollie says.

"Where—"

"Through that door. You'll know where."

I stare at him for a moment but decide I'd rather not ask. I get to my feet and turn away to push through the kitchen doors. I'd assumed the restaurant was empty when we got here, but Ollie has clearly had a co-conspirator. The whole place is glowing. String lights wrap around columns and hang from the ceiling. Candles flicker warmly on every table as far as the eye can see. Instrumental music plays softly overhead. It's the very picture of romance. But then I notice the glow sticks at my feet. Neon pink, and yellow, and orange—all my favorite colors, a rainbow path leading from where I stand to the brightest spot in the room, a table for two set in its very center.

"Did you look up?" Ollie says from behind me. I hadn't heard him follow me out.

"Oh," I say. A bubble of emotion bursts in my chest when I tilt my head to the ceiling. I've been so overwhelmed by the string lights and candles and glow sticks that I haven't noticed the glow-in-the-dark stars stuck above me.

"I didn't really think that through," he says. "Can hardly see them with everything else."

"It's lovely," I say, bowled over by this small, silly galaxy Ollie has made for me. I turn, wanting to reach out and touch him, but his arms are balancing plates, and beside him is a Black man I recognize from the photos Ollie has shown me of his time in culinary school.

"This is Barnabé," Ollie says. "Barnabé, Nina."

"I'm glad to finally meet you," Barnabé says. He steps around Ollie to set the plates in his arms on the table.

"I can't believe he convinced you to do this to your restaurant," I say, shaking Barnabé's hand when he extends it to me.

"I didn't do it for this asshole," Baranbé says. "I did it for me. Not sure I'd ever get him to shut up about you otherwise."

I glance at Ollie, who simply shakes his head and sets the plates he's carrying on the table.

"Well, whatever the reason, thank you. You have a beautiful place."

Barnabé smiles at me. I like him. "Don't take this the wrong way, but I'm surprised you're as beautiful as he said. He's been hyping you up for nearly ten years. I was a little worried I'd have to fake it."

"He is rather dramatic, isn't he?" I say.

"Nothing's changed, then. I bet he never told you about the time he almost got kicked out of culinary school."

"Shouldn't you be going, Barnabé?" Ollie says, clapping a hand on his shoulder.

"Oh, come on, Oliver. I want to hear the story."

Barnabé laughs. "Ah, Ollie's right. I'll hold on to that one. Then you'll have to come see me again."

"I definitely will."

Barnabé claps his hands together. "It was lovely to meet you, Nina.

Don't fuck it up, brother," he adds, and gives Ollie a back-slapping hug. "The place is yours for the night. Have all the fun you want," he says, shooting us a wink before he turns to go.

"He's absolutely charming," I say once Barnabé is out of sight. Something about meeting him means even more to me than the lights and candles and glow sticks. It's rare I get to meet someone from Ollie's past. And Ollie is proud. Neither of us likes to ask for favors. Yet he's shown me this piece of himself. And given the two minutes I spent with Barnabé, Ollie surely endured plenty of teasing to make this happen.

"He's a good fella," Ollie says. He steps over to the table and pulls out a chair. "Now will you sit down before the food gets cold?"

"Worried you're about to lose our game?" I say as I take my seat.

Ollie pushes in my chair with a laugh before taking the seat across from me. "Not at all. Go ahead, try it."

I look at the eggplant pasta dish before me, which seems perfectly normal. "I think you cheated. I don't remember picking out a salad."

"Never said I could use *only* the ingredients you chose, just that I had to use them."

"Sneaky."

"But most of what you picked is in that." He nods to the pasta. "Even your damn Cap'n Crunch."

I twirl a forkful of spaghetti and bring it to my mouth, then pause to eye him skeptically. "You didn't poison this, did you?"

"Poison? No. Love potion? Yes." Ollie crosses his arms over his chest and leans back in his chair. I want to laugh. How can he be so serious?

"I'll risk it," I say, then take a bite.

Ollie's eyebrows raise as he watches me chew. I take my time. A thousand little bites before I swallow. I set down my fork and look at him, saying nothing.

"And?"

I sigh and look up at the ceiling and catch sight of the stars. I can't help but smile. I haven't smiled this much in ages. I'm unable to bite it back when I look at Ollie again. "I hate to admit it, Oliver, but, damn, you can cook."

Ollie leans forward. His expression is all sunshine in the yellow light. "Just say the word, and I'll cook for you every night."

"The word."

"Smartass."

We eat in companionable silence. If this were any other first date, the bitchy voice in my head would say, *Pass!* I'd cause a diversion, stash every last breadstick in my purse, excuse myself to the restroom, then pay the bill up front before fleeing out the door.

But this silence is different. It's not a we-have-nothing-to-talk-about silence. It's a silence that says, *I don't need to fill this space because it's already full. I don't need to make this interesting because sitting with you is interesting enough.*

When an instrumental version of "Feel Good Inc." comes on, I finally put together the common thread between all the songs that have played.

I point my fork at him. "You didn't," I say.

"Table manners, Ms. Lejeune," Ollie says. "I didn't what now?"

"The music. All the songs are from my floor routines."

Ollie grins. "Wondered how long it'd take you to notice."

I laugh. "I don't understand."

"They're part of you," he says. "Couldn't tell what you were feeling doing your routines, but I knew you were feeling something. Plus some of them are just fecking weird, you know. You just had to go and do Led Zeppelin, didn't you? And not even 'Stairway to Heaven'! I remember watching your routine to 'Moby Dick' and thinking, *She fucking didn't.*"

"I fucking did," I say.

"Dunno how they let you win a single competition."

I shrug. "They can't penalize you for song choice. As long as you've got a version without words, you can play whatever you like. Hell, you could do the *Super Mario* theme song if you wanted."

"I'm surprised you didn't."

I press a hand over my heart. "I'm offended. I have *some* class, you know. I can't say the same for everyone here."

Ollie narrows his eyes. I'm so distracted by his expression that I don't notice the spaghetti noodle he twirls around his fork until it lands on my face.

I gasp and pick the noodle from my cheek. "What about table manners?" I say.

"What about them?"

Without taking my eyes off him, I fling a forkful of spaghetti his way. Sauce slips down both our faces. Ollie looks ridiculous. I must look just as wild, maybe even more so if my makeup is running. We're laughing so hard we can barely speak.

When we finally catch our breath, Ollie leans back in his chair with a sigh, and I try not to giggle at the spaghetti noodle caught in his hair.

"Two food fights in one day is over the top, even for us," I say, picking a piece of eggplant that's been breaded in Cap'n Crunch from my dress and flicking it onto my plate. We're a mess, but that's nothing new. Ollie shakes his head as he watches me. "What?" I say. "Bored of me already?"

"Never," Ollie says. The sincerity in his voice has my heart beating double time.

One moment I'm smiling, and the next I'm crying. I don't understand what's happening. Ollie must not either, because he sits up and reaches across the table to grab my hand. "What did I say? I didn't mean it, whatever it was."

I shake my head, trying to sort through the wave of emotion that's sucked me out like a riptide. With sauce dripping down my cheek and Ollie's *Never* ringing in my ears, I realize that even with the people I love and trust the most, I haven't been able to articulate my darkest of fears. What if I told them everything I keep to myself? All that fear, and loneliness, and hurt, and they decide it's too much. The voice in my head always has something to say, but this is the worst: *No one cares about your problems. Your problems are boring. You are boring.*

But with Ollie's hand in mine, I know that these are lies. I know he cares. He's always cared. And somehow that terrifies me more than anything else. I know we're good together. I know there will never be anyone for me but Oliver Dunne. I have no real reason *not* to be with him. But whenever I think about it, *really* think about it, I'm reminded of the first time I stepped on a balance beam after my injury. I *knew* I was physically capable of doing beam again, but my brain wouldn't cooperate.

Ollie has always feared that something in him is broken, but that couldn't be further from the truth. He isn't the broken one. *I* am. What other explanation is there for why I've spent the last ten years afraid to love him? For why the thought of having him is just as terrifying as the thought of losing him? Why else would I deny myself what I want so desperately when he's right here in front of me, begging me to take him?

What I don't know is how to convey all this to Ollie. I'm not so sure I fully understand it myself. I squeeze his hand, unable to hold back the small sob that escapes me, and he lets go. He gets to his feet, steps around the table, and kneels beside me on the floor.

"Let's get you cleaned up, yeah?" He takes a napkin and holds my trembling chin in his hand, wearing a look of utter concentration as he tilts my face this way and that, wiping away all my mess so gently it hurts.

"Ollie," I say as he pulls a stray spinach leaf from my hair.

"Hmm?"

"I'm . . . scared," I say. I feel the tears coming again. I lean into him and bury my face in his neck. I don't know what's happening to me. It's disorienting. Overwhelming.

"Oh, darling," he says. He wraps his arms around me. He doesn't say anything else for a minute, simply holds me there as he kneels on the floor. Finally, he gently pulls back to wipe away the tears on my cheeks.

"What are you scared of, kitten?"

My throat tightens, and I look away, worried I'll start sobbing if he keeps looking at me like that. "Everything," I say, hardly able to get the words out. "Of what I can have . . . and lose." *Of losing you*, I don't say.

But Ollie knows what I really mean. His eyes leave mine as he sweeps my bangs to the side, then nudges one of my unicorn earrings with a finger. "You don't have to lose me," he says.

"I don't know why I'm crying." I dab my eyes with a napkin. "You know I'm not normally so emotional. It's the . . . Cap'n Crunch, I think." A hiccup escapes me, and I shake my head. "Why do you have to go and change everything? Why now? Why not in five, ten, a million and one years?"

Ollie is quiet for a moment. He worries his bottom lip as he searches my face. "You remember New Year's?"

"Of course," I say. "You were . . ."

"A fecking mess."

"I was going to be polite and say *visibly upset*, but sure."

"I'd just gotten a phone call from Jack."

"Jack . . . your brother?" As far as I know, Ollie hasn't talked to Jack in fifteen years.

"He tracked down my number. Called to tell me Da died."

"Oh," I say. The entire night reframes itself in my mind. I'm not sure what I'm supposed to say. Somehow *sorry* doesn't feel right. "Why didn't you tell me?"

He leans back on his heels with a sigh. "I meant to, I just didn't know what to say or how to say it. I wasn't sure how I felt about it all. You wanted to know why now. Talking to Jack, Da dying . . . You spend all this time thinking time is exactly what you've got. But then something happens, and you realize you don't have as much time as you think. In my head, Jack's been a kid all these years. But he's not. He's all grown up. And Da . . ." Ollie pauses. He rubs at the back of his neck with a hand before continuing. "I always wondered what it would be like to see him again. I used to have these conversations in my head, imagining what he'd say, rehearsing what I'd say back . . . I still do sometimes, even knowing it'll never happen now. Jack, he asked me to come home and see Mum. Guess she's not taking it so well."

"You could visit home now, right? Now that your dad's . . . gone."

"I've thought about it," he says. "Part of me wants to, but the other part. Well, I'm still angry, to tell you the truth."

"Of course you are—"

"And ashamed," Ollie says, continuing as if he hasn't heard me. "I left them with him. I didn't keep in touch. That's what I said to Jack when we talked, but he told me to get over myself and . . ." The words trail off and Ollie drops his face into his hands.

"And what?"

Ollie lifts his head, leveling his gaze on me. "He asked if I'd help him run the pub."

I force myself to connect the dots. "Move home to Ireland. Permanently."

He nods.

"What did you tell him?"

"That I needed a few months to sort things out before I could decide."

"Oh," I say. *Me. I'm the thing to sort out.*

He takes my hands in his. "What should I tell him, Nina?"

"I can't tell you what to do, Ollie."

"But I'm asking you to tell me," he says. His voice is frayed and pleading. "I'm fucking begging you here."

I feel every burn and callus on his hands as they grip mine. "I don't want you to go," I say.

"I don't have to go. Tell me not to go."

I've spent so much time worrying about what will happen if I say yes to Ollie that I've never really considered what it would be like if I said no until now. What would it be like to know, really know, that I'd never have these hands on me again?

"I love you," I say. "Don't go."

Ollie's fidgeting hands still. His eyes meet mine, searching. All this time, I've never said it. Even though it was always true. Even though he's said it to me a million times.

I pry my hands from Ollie's and take the napkin from my lap to wipe the mess from his face as gently as he'd done for me. Ollie doesn't move, not so much as a twitch of an eyebrow. He stares up at me, stuck, and I wonder if I've finally broken him.

"Nina," Ollie says when I wipe away the sauce from above one of his eyebrows. "Say that again. I can't have heard you right."

I set the napkin on the table and take his face in my hands. I feel like I've torn out my heart and put it into this ridiculous man, where anything could happen to it—good or bad. I dip my face closer, and my nose brushes against his. "I love you, Oliver Dunne."

"Do you mean that?" he whispers. "You aren't just saying that because you feel bad for me, or because I make a fecking good spaghetti with Cap'n Crunch?"

I pull a spaghetti noodle from his hair with a laugh. "It's not that, though I'm sure the Cap'n Crunch helped. I really do love you, Ollie. I've loved you all this time."

We're still for a moment, just looking at each other, and then Ollie pulls me from my chair and onto his lap on the restaurant floor. I'm not sure who is kissing whom, but when I'm sure I'll pass out if I don't take a breath, I pull away, giving him a pointed look. "I will not have sex with you on a restaurant floor."

"This is working out even better than I imagined," he says.

I take one of his hands and press it against my cheek. I feel the warmth of his skin against it and want that feeling everywhere else. "Shh." I drop his hand and press a finger to his lips. "The talking part of this date is over."

Ollie laughs, then takes my hand and kisses it. "Love, if we're sleeping together tonight, you know that's not true."

18

~~~~~~

As soon as we're in the cab, Ollie is kissing me senseless again. I set my mind to *Do Not Disturb*. Goodbye, anxiety about the future, I will see you tomorrow. Goodbye, thoughts of anything other than Ollie and his mouth and every other part of him.

The rest of the crew still hasn't returned from their night out when Ollie and I board the *Serendipity*. We make our way onto the boat slowly, unable to go ten seconds without kissing each other against whatever happens to be nearby: the yacht railing where I'd first seen him, the dining table where I've served countless meals he's made.

Ollie leads me into the galley, kissing me as he guides me across it until I'm against the island counter. He lifts me onto the countertop and steps between my legs. My dress is hiked up so that the backs of my thighs are exposed to the cool granite, but Ollie's hands chase away the chill as they slide up my skin beneath my skirt.

Impatient, I release my arms from around his neck. My hands roam along the collar of his shirt until they find the buttons. I try to slip them free, but my fingers are clumsy. I'm distracted by the sheer pleasure of kissing him like this—with total abandon, without the pretense of it meaning nothing.

I'm halfway through unbuttoning his shirt when one of Ollie's hands darts over mine. "Slow down, kitten," he says. "I'm taking my time with you tonight."

He hooks his arms under my legs and lifts me from the counter, starting in the direction of the staircase that leads belowdeck.

"The master suite, doofus," I say, breaking off midkiss. "Why would I sleep with you in a bunk bed when we have the entire boat to ourselves? Fresh sheets. No guests. No crew. Except Xav. But he's probably passed out in his quarters with the TV still on, so that doesn't count."

Ollie spins in the direction of the guest quarters with enthusiasm. I laugh wildly as he carries me down the hallway, but Ollie shuts me up when he pins me against the wall for a lingering kiss that works its way down my neck.

By the time Ollie's mouth seeks mine again, I can't take it anymore. I press my hands over my mouth until he sets me on my feet. His laugh echoes after me when I drag him the rest of the way to the master suite.

I step inside and pull Ollie in after me. He shuts the door behind him, and there's a pause as we face each other in the dim light. It isn't hesitation. Not the usual *Should we really be doing this?* This is different. Another one of those weightless moments. One that ends when we reach for each other at the same time.

Ollie's hands find me again, so warm I practically melt into his lap when he backs across the room and sinks onto the bed.

"This thing is fecking comfy," Ollie mutters. "If I'd have known this was happening, I would've gotten us a nice room somewhere, you know."

"This is perfect," I say. I sink my fingers into his hair. "I am so beyond gone right now, I probably would've slept with you in that bunk bed. I'd maybe even sleep with you in a yurt." I take his face in my hands and rest my forehead against his. "Just so you're aware, I doubt I'll become less ridiculous with age."

Ollie pulls back to look into my eyes. "Does that mean you plan on being with me until you're old and ridiculous? I know you said . . . what you said, but I didn't ask if that means you want to make things between us . . . real. If you don't want to really be together—"

I clap a hand over his mouth. "Ollie, I love you. I want to be together. For real. Tonight, tomorrow, twenty years from now. But especially tonight, so will you please get your face on my face? And your clothes somewhere else?"

Ollie's laugh warms my palm. He pulls my hand from his mouth and leans back on the bed, pulling me along so that I'm hovering above him.

"What?" I say as he stares up at me.

He brushes my bangs to the side. "How fast are you aging? Because you get more ridiculous by the second."

I scowl, and he adds, "I never said it was a bad thing. I like you ridiculous."

He presses himself up to kiss me. When he pulls back, he has a mischievous look on his face.

"What?" But then he's tickling my sides, and I can't say anything more because I'm laughing so hard I can hardly breathe.

"What's wrong with you!" I wheeze.

I yelp when he rolls us over on the bed, and I'm suddenly beneath him. "Absolutely nothing," he says.

He presses a kiss to my forehead before dropping beside me on the mattress, then props himself up on an elbow and stares at me.

I turn on my side to face him, but he doesn't say anything. "What are you doing?"

"Enjoying the view, what else?" he says.

I should've known Ollie wasn't kidding about taking his time. "What view? I'm still fully dressed." I trace a finger over his collar bone, then down to the center of his chest. "And you've still got your shirt on."

"You don't think I'm pretty like this?" He flutters his eyelashes at me.

I roll my eyes. "You're utterly delightful."

"Well," Ollie says, and his expression becomes serious. "Clothed or not, you're a spectacular view."

"You're a spectacular view too," I say. I can't be sarcastic when he's looking at me like that. I have no idea how I managed to go so long without telling him how I feel, when the love I have for him is so overwhelming, I'm not sure it fits inside me. Not anymore, anyway. It feels like uncorking a bottle of champagne after shaking it as hard as I can. Big and messy, yes, but also bubbly and wonderful.

But I'd also really like to finish unbuttoning his shirt and resume the kissing. "Now that we've established how lovely we both are, will you stop looking at me and start kissing me again?" I say.

Ollie raises an eyebrow.

"Will you start kissing me again, *please?*" I say, earning myself a smile from that handsome mouth.

"If I have to," he says.

"You have to."

When Ollie kisses me, the energy between us shifts. All the humor and sarcasm flees the room, leaving only this intensity we've tried to rein in for years. The kiss is slow, every movement between us intentional in a way no other kiss has been. Somehow, my mind is numb and buzzing at the same time. I don't have enough breath to speak, but even if I did, I wouldn't have anything to say.

Ollie pulls back when the kiss ends and takes one of my unicorn earrings between his fingers. "On or off?" he murmurs.

"On, of course."

"Come here," he says. He sits up, pulling me along with him until I'm straddling his lap at the edge of the bed. The skirt of my dress pools around me, but his hands somehow find their way beneath it to run up and down my thighs as he kisses me again.

When I get the rest of his shirt unbuttoned, I toss it on the floor behind me. I don't care that I'm creating more work for myself. I don't care that I just changed these sheets and will have to change them again before the guests arrive tomorrow. I'm too busy exploring his stomach, and chest, and shoulders with my hands. My mouth travels along his neck, finding all the places he likes to be touched, the secret landmarks only a local would know. I can't think of anything other than mapping out every part of him, even though I've had him memorized for years.

I reach for the button on his pants, and Ollie catches hold of my wrists with a groan. "This isn't fair, kitten."

"I don't care," I say, already breathless.

But Ollie doesn't let go of my wrists. "Stand up and turn around."

When I do as he says, he finds the zipper of my dress and pulls it down slowly, trailing kisses along my back in its wake. I'm reminded of how he helped me unzip my dress on the day we got married. I should've known then that we were never just friends. Maybe I did.

Once Ollie's unzipped my dress, the bodice falls to just above my waist, leaving my chest bare and exposing the lace edge of my underwear. I take Ollie's hand from where it rests on my side and pull it around to where I'm most desperate for his touch.

"Bossy girl," he says, toying with the fabric of my underwear between his fingers.

"It's just a suggestion," I say.

He presses a kiss to my shoulder. "Don't I always take care of you?"

"Yes," I say.

"And do you think tonight will be any different?"

"No."

"Then be patient."

"Easier said than done."

He laughs into my skin. When he finally pushes my dress over my hips, it falls to the floor, and I kick it away. He tugs down my underwear, and I kick that away too. Once I'm fully undressed, he pulls me against him so that I'm sitting on his lap completely naked.

He wraps his arms around me and rests his chin on my shoulder.

"What are you doing?" I ask.

"I'm hugging you."

I press a kiss to his cheek. "And you say I'm ridiculous. You're the most ridiculous man I've ever met."

"That sounds like a compliment," he says.

"I suppose you're right."

Ollie's grip on me loosens. "Let me see you," he says.

He nudges me to my feet, and I turn to face him. His hands drift up and down my sides as he looks at me. He's seen me naked more times than I can count, but his gaze lingers on every part of me as if it's the first time.

"Beautiful," Ollie says, and when his eyes meet mine, there's not an ounce of teasing in them.

We dissolve into each other after that. Somehow, I'm in his arms again. Somehow, we make our way back to the center of the bed. I don't realize how desperately I've wanted all of him until I've undressed him fully. How much I've longed for his mouth on every part of me until it's there. How much I've missed him, until he's on top of me, inside of me, until I lose myself beneath him.

Being with Ollie is better than I remember, but it's bittersweet too. Before, sex was always something to get out of our systems. Or something we didn't acknowledge because it was too complicated. Until now, every night we've spent together has been about taking as much of each other as we could carry, never knowing how long it would be until we could have each other again. But even then, even in those moments when we lost control, we were always holding back. Sex with Ollie has never felt like it does tonight—open, vulnerable, a gift.

Afterward, when the both of us are spent, I rest my head against his chest, indulging in the satisfied post-sex state of him. When he's nearly asleep, I tug one of the hairs on his arm, and he blinks awake to shoot me a glare.

"What was that for?"

"For better or for worse," I say.

He rubs his arm. "Worse is right." His scowl disappears, and he rolls on top of me. His body pressed against mine stills something restless within me, making me realize how unanchored I've felt ever since he quit the boat. "Speaking of for better or worse," he says. "What are we supposed to . . . tell everyone?"

"About what?"

"About us."

"Oh," I say. I hadn't really gotten that far. "It would be weird to tell everyone we're married right? They might have a lot of questions we don't want to answer."

"Probably," Ollie says, but his expression is hesitant.

"What if we told everyone we're dating? Just for now. And in a few months we can tell everyone we've eloped."

"How long are you thinking?"

I comb my fingers through his hair. "Three months? That seems reasonable, right? Just like *90 Day Fiancé*."

He laughs, and the hesitation in his face disappears. "More like nine-year fiancé."

"Ollie," I say.

"Hmm?"

"Thank you."

The wrinkle between his eyebrows deepens. "For what?"

I push myself up to kiss that little groove between his eyebrows before resting against the pillow again. "For loving me all this time. For never giving up."

He leans down to kiss my forehead, then drops beside me onto the bed and tugs one of my legs between his. "I couldn't stop loving you if I tried," he says, one hand drifting sleepily up and down my back. "Still convinced you'll be the death of me, though, wife."

The word *wife* where Ollie would normally say *girl* skips through me like a stone on water. I'm not sure where the feeling belongs, if it's good or something I'd rather worry about later.

Future-Nina's problem, I tell myself, ignoring the voice in my head when she touches her finger to the tip of her nose and calls, *Not it!*

19

Three months later, July

"We're gonna be late, love."

I catch Ollie's eye in the bathroom mirror of my apartment. He leans against the open doorway and watches as I apply my mascara, his hands shoved into the pockets of his jeans. "Patience, Oliver. It's just lunch with my parents."

Ollie lets out a puff of breath. "It's not *just* lunch with your parents."

I cap my mascara and turn to face him. "Are you . . . nervous?"

"Of course not," he says. I raise an eyebrow and he sighs. "Feck. Maybe a little."

I can't help but smile, which makes Ollie scowl. "I'm not making fun of you." I push off from the bathroom counter and step toward him. His ears are pink. I pinch the tops of them between my fingers, and the groove between his brows deepens. "Look at you," I say. "How am I supposed to get anywhere on time when you barge in here all flustered?"

"I'm not flustered," he mumbles.

"Don't be nervous. My parents love you." Ollie's joined me for cookouts and other family events now and then over the years, but last month was the first time I brought him along as something more than a friend. I thought my mother would faint with happiness when we walked through the front door hand in hand.

"They might not like me as much when you tell them we've eloped," Ollie says. "Your dad might try and kick my arse for marrying you without asking him first."

"I should probably care what my parents think, but I don't," I say. "Telling them is just the warm-up for dinner with Jo and Alex tonight. We have to tell them as soon as we get to the restaurant, otherwise I won't be able to eat a thing, and that'll make Jo suspicious, and if she's suspicious, I'll only be more nervous."

"I'd say you're overthinking it, but you and Jo are something else," he says.

"You don't think she'll be upset that we're stealing her thunder by getting married before her? Not to mention *without* her."

"When you told her we were together, she looked like she'd won the fecking lottery," he says. "I don't think she'll be upset."

"You have a point," I say. I straighten the collar of Ollie's shirt and frown. "You don't have to be so dressed up, you know. You'll be too hot in this."

The nerves flutter across his face. "Do you think I should change?"

"Absolutely, and right this minute." Ollie laughs when I hop onto the counter and pull him to me. "This is a fashion emergency," I say, slipping the top button of his shirt loose.

"We're already late," Ollie says, but he doesn't step away when I continue unbuttoning his shirt.

"Exactly. So what's a little while longer?" Once his shirt is undone, I push it from his shoulders, letting it fall to the floor.

Ollie sighs when I run my hands over his chest and down his stomach, greedily touching every inch of skin I can. "You make no fecking sense," he says. "But it *feels* like you're making sense when you do that."

"See, Oliver? I'm always right."

"And I don't like it when you call me Oliver," he says.

"Oh hush. I'm trying to concentrate." I shoot him a glare and unbutton his jeans.

"I thought my shirt was the problem," he says.

I shake my head soberly. "No. The whole outfit . . . it's got to go."

"In that case, we ought to go to the bedroom where the clothes are," he says.

"Oh, if you insist."

Ollie lifts me off the counter and over one shoulder. I yelp, and he smacks my ass with a laugh before turning to carry me into the hallway. But he hardly takes a step when he stumbles over one of the loose cabinet doors that's swung open beneath the sink. He curses and takes a step back, managing to keep his balance until he slips on his discarded shirt. From where I'm hanging, mostly upside down over his shoulder, I'm positive we're about to tumble into the shower. I brace myself to hit the ground face-first, but Ollie shifts his weight at the last second and hits the wall with the shoulder that's not supporting my weight.

Ollie hisses but somehow manages to keep hold of me until he can set me gently on my feet.

"Are you all right?" I ask once I'm upright again. I feel his shoulder, checking it over to make sure he hasn't broken or dislocated anything.

"I'll be fine." He shuts his eyes and takes a slow breath. "This fucking apartment. I can't wait until your lease is up. We need a bigger bathroom. And kitchen. And living room. And—"

"I know, I know," I say. We've been looking at houses for weeks, but I haven't liked a single one. They've all been lovely, with beautiful yards and open kitchens and more closet space than I'd know what to do with—which is saying something. I know we can afford it. Ollie and I are both frugal, and between the two of us, we have more than enough for a decent down payment. But every house Ollie has shown me has something that's just a little off. Why settle for anything less than perfect? There's no rush.

"I really think the place we're seeing tomorrow will be the one," he says. "I can already see you filling up your walk-in closet and taking over half of mine. There are so many closets in that house, you could have two devoted to your board games."

Ollie continues listing all the things I'll love about the house. When he talks about our future like this, I want to give him everything. I'm trying to, anyway. Whenever he passes me his phone with a listing for a house he's really excited about, I agree to go to a showing. When he asked about a timeline for trying to get pregnant, I told him I'd set up a preconception appointment with my doctor, but every time I call to make an appointment, I hang up as soon as the receptionist answers.

I know I should tell him what's going on inside my head, but Ollie's been happier than I've ever seen him these last three months, and I want to keep him happy. And besides, I don't know what I'd say. I'm just adjusting. It's not a big deal. All I need is a little more time.

"Doesn't it sound perfect?" Ollie says.

"It sounds marvelous."

Ollie tugs at one of my unicorn earrings. "You'll love it, Neen. I know you will."

I'm not so sure. But I really hope he's right.

When we arrive at my parents' house an hour late, my mother opens the door and says, "There you are! Your father is out back trying to grill *brisket* of all things, and I think he might need a little help." She raises her eyebrows at Ollie.

He shakes his head. "I've warned him brisket's hardest to get right."

"You intimidate him a bit, dear," Mom says. "I think he wants to impress you."

"Well, you can tell Dad his cooking will always be my favorite," I say. At Ollie's incredulous look, I add, "What? I never said it was *true*. Just to tell him that."

"Your cooking really *is* my favorite, Oliver," Mom says.

"Thank you, Mrs. Lejeune," he replies.

Mom sighs. "Will you ever call me Erika? Mrs. Lejeune sounds so . . . old."

Ollie shrugs. "Sorry, Mrs. Lejeune, me mum raised me too polite for that."

Polite, my ass. I shoot Ollie a dirty look. He never complains when my mother calls him by his full name, probably just to bug me. Whenever I bring him around, he tucks away his surliness and busts out the Irish charm. I swear he makes his accent thicker on purpose. He catches my eye and winks before kissing my mother on the cheek.

"Speaking of me cooking . . ." Ollie holds up the Tupperware in his hands. "Brought you more of that brown soda bread you like."

"You're a dear." She takes the Tupperware from him and sighs like a smitten schoolgirl. I'm starting to wonder if *she's* in love with him too. I can't say I blame her.

We follow Mom into the kitchen, where she sets the Tupperware on the counter. She looks through the kitchen window into the yard. "Oh dear. Really, Oliver, I think you better get out there."

"Wish me luck," he says, pausing on his way out to kiss me on the cheek.

As soon as we hear the back door shut, Mom turns to me with a barely contained smile. "So . . ." she says.

"La-ti-do," I sing.

"Nina."

"Mother."

She squints at me. "You look happy."

"I am." I cross the kitchen, setting my purse on the counter so I don't have to look at her. It's not that I don't want my mother to know what's going on in my life, but nothing makes me more uncomfortable than one of her *interrogations*.

"You two seem . . . serious," she says.

"We are." I open the cupboard beside the refrigerator, but instead of the lemon-and-orange-slice-patterned glasses they've kept there since I was a kid, I find nothing.

"Where are the glasses?"

"We've got a thing of Solo cups in the pantry," she says. "What does *serious* mean, exactly?"

I only half hear her question. I've never even *seen* a Solo cup in this house. My mother doesn't cook, but the woman has always insisted on using real dishes, even when it's inconvenient.

"Did you get rid of them?" I ask. She better not have. Those glasses are adorable. Not to mention vintage.

"Get rid of what?"

"The glasses."

"Oh, no, sweetie," Mom says. "We're just packing."

Before I can ask what she means by *packing*, Ollie returns to the kitchen with my dad at his side.

"There's my girl!" Dad says. "How's that dinghy of yours?"

"Oh, you know, still floating," I say.

"This guy's all right, you know," Dad says. "Pretty sure he just saved all of us from having to order takeout." He claps Ollie on the shoulder, the one that took the brunt of our fall earlier, and Ollie grimaces.

"I worry about you on that thing," Mom says to me. "Do you know how many stories I've seen on Facebook about boats like yours stuck out in the middle of the ocean because of food poisoning? Hundreds of people, sick to death. Even the captain."

I roll my eyes. "Those are cruise ships, Mom. And really? Sick to *death*?"

"I just think it's time you found a job that'll let you settle down."

"*Mom*," I say.

"What? Is it a crime to want to see my baby? You're gone half the year!"

"It's only four months," I say. We have some version of this conversation a few times a year. Her reasons for why I should quit my job only get more and more ridiculous with time.

"I promise I won't give Nina food poisoning, Mrs. Lejeune," Ollie says.

My mother presses her hand over her heart and turns to him. "Oh, Oliver, I didn't mean *you*."

"Well he's the only one who cooks on the yacht, Mom," I say.

"I guess that's one less thing to worry about. Though there's still sharks, storms, and pirates."

Pirates! I catch Ollie's eye, but he nearly bursts out laughing and has to look away. Time to steer the conversation away from work.

"Where are you guys going?" I say.

"What do you mean?" Dad asks.

"Mom said you're packing. A BYOB vacation I get, but not BYOD." Dad scrunches his eyebrows, and I explain. "Bring your own *dishware*."

"We're not going on vacation," Mom says.

"Then why are you packing?"

There's a moment of silence. Mom shoots Dad a questioning look.

"We're moving!" he says, clapping his hands together as if this is some long-awaited announcement.

"What?"

"Surely we told you," Mom says.

"Moving . . . where? Didn't you just pay off the mortgage, like, three years ago?" I'm clearly missing something. Mom loves this house. My parents have lived here my entire life.

"We're only going across town," Dad says. "About ten minutes from the two of you, actually."

"We're renting this cute little town house," Mom says. "You'll love it."

I can feel Ollie watching me while Mom rambles on and on about their cute town house, but none of this makes any sense. She's spent every spare moment over the last thirty-odd years making this house her own. They never even considered selling it back when Dad was gambling. It wouldn't have helped. The mortgage was cheaper than rent would've been.

Something isn't right. I can read the tension beneath Dad's smile. Mom is obviously deflecting. I gaze around the kitchen, noticing things I didn't the first time. The toaster is gone. All the photos and magnets have been taken down from the refrigerator.

I lean against the counter, my thoughts spinning, spinning, spinning, as if my brain's been hurled into the washing machine on the *Serendipity*. I look between my parents, afraid to ask the question I already know the answer to. I'm not sure *who* to ask . . . Mom. Or Dad.

Fuck it. I may as well address the room.

"Did you lose the house? Is Dad gambling again?"

My parents exchange a look. Suddenly, Ollie is at my side. He says my name, but I can't respond to him right now. I can't do anything other than wait for my parents to say something. To tell me I'm being silly. That this is all a misunderstanding. That they just wanted a change of scenery.

"I don't want you to worry, sweetheart," Dad says.

I laugh, but it's something wild. Ollie is saying something again, but I can't understand it. I can only focus on Dad.

"Are you?" I say.

He doesn't have to say anything for me to know the answer. The look on his face is enough.

"But . . . I thought you were better. I thought this was over." The panic that comes over me reminds me of the way I felt whenever I attempted beam after my injury, a panic so overwhelming that it hinders my ability to think or move.

"Really, sweetheart, it's nothing to worry about," Mom says.

That snaps me out of my stupor. Suddenly, I'm angrier at *her* than him. For not telling me, for staying with him, for allowing him to ruin her life, mine. "How long has this been going on?"

"Oh, I don't know," she says, and drops her gaze to the counter. "Not long after we paid off the house."

Three years? "Why didn't anyone tell me?"

"We didn't want you to worry," Dad says.

"Well, I hate to break it to you, but I'm fucking worried."

"Language," Mom says.

"Why do you do this to yourself, Mom? How can you stay after everything he's put us through?"

"It's not that simple, Nina." Her voice is calm, but I can tell she's moments away from crying.

I turn to my dad. "And what about you? Don't you have anything to say for yourself?"

Dad sighs. "I don't know what you want me to say, Nina."

That's the moment I decide I've had enough. I need to leave. I turn to grab my purse, but Ollie already has it in his hands along with the car keys, which only makes me want to cry even more.

He places his hand on my arm, then turns to my parents. "I think it's best if Nina and I head on," he says.

Ollie steers me from the kitchen and to the door. I'm not sure if my parents follow us or if they stay in the kitchen. I'm not sure if they say anything as I leave the home I grew up in, maybe for the last time.

* * *

As soon as we return home, I make a beeline for the couch. I grab my laptop from where I left it on the coffee table and kick off my heels, leaving them in a heap on the floor. I can't sit down right now. I carry my laptop to the kitchen and set it on the counter so I can stand.

Ollie follows me into the kitchen, where I'm trying to steady my hands enough to type.

He stands behind me and wraps his arms around my shoulders. "Hey," he says, his voice soft in my ear. "Slow down, yeah? Take a minute."

"I don't want to take a minute."

"Kitten."

I lift my hands off the keyboard and press them to my eyes. "Sorry," I say.

"Do you want to talk about it?"

I shake my head, then drop my hands from my face. "My knee is killing me," I say, more to myself than to him.

"Then you ought to sit down."

"I'd rather be moving."

Ollie doesn't say anything more. He simply stands there, holding me as I navigate to the site I use to monitor my credit. I froze my credit years ago. I have every protection system in place imaginable, but you never know.

When I see nothing unexpected, I let out a quick breath of relief.

"Are you okay, love?" Ollie says.

"All my accounts look good."

He drops his arms from around me and turns me to face him. I let him, suddenly exhausted. Ollie holds my face in his hands. "But are *you* okay?"

"I'll be fine." I hate how my voice trembles, how the emotion is right behind my words. Unwanted tears threaten to slip through, but I fight them back. Ollie doesn't say anything. He lets go of my face and pulls me to him, resting his chin on top of my head.

"I don't think I can do dinner tonight," I say. My voice is a thread away from breaking, but here, tucked against Ollie's chest, I allow myself to shed a few silent tears.

"I already texted Alex and Jo and told them we had to reschedule," he murmurs.

"Thank you." My voice is barely above a whisper. I'm not sure he hears.

After a few minutes, Ollie kisses the top of my head and pulls away. "Come on," he says. "Let's see which of your murder shows is marathoning on Oxygen." He reaches around me to shut my laptop, then guides me into the living room. He takes the remote from the coffee table and turns on the TV.

"*Florida Man Murders* . . ." he mutters, eyes on the screen. He slides his gaze to me. "Is that too close to home?"

I laugh from where I've buried myself in throw blankets.

The flicker of a smile appears at the corner of his mouth. "*Florida Man Murders* it is, then. Just know I won't be able to sleep tonight." He tosses the remote beside me on the couch. "You hungry?"

"A little."

"That's a problem I can fix," he says. "You good here?"

I nod.

"Be right back."

When Ollie returns halfway through an episode of *Florida Man Murders*, he's carrying the largest plate of his homemade pizza rolls I've ever seen, and I almost start crying all over again. He sets the plate on the coffee table, then pulls the blankets off my legs—just enough so that my feet are poking out—and sits on my feet before arranging the blankets over me again.

"Look at this," Ollie says. He hands me his phone. "I forgot to show you the tile in the master bathroom. It made me think of you."

I stare at the photo. The tile *is* something I'd like, pink with a white palm frond pattern here and there. Elegant with a touch of whimsy. But I don't love it. In this moment, I've never hated anything more.

"It's nice," I say, and hand him back the phone.

"And there's this," he says, flicking to another photo. He holds out the phone to me again, but I don't take it. I glance at it but don't take in a thing.

"Cool," I say.

Ollie furrows his brow. "You don't like it? We could always see a different place tomorrow."

"Can't you see I don't want to talk about this right now?" I say, my voice harsher than I intended.

"I was only trying to cheer you up."

"Why would looking at *houses* right now cheer me up?"

Ollie opens his mouth to say something but must think better of it, because he drops his phone into his lap and doesn't say anything.

We both turn our attention back to the TV. Once my annoyance has cooled, I glance at him from the corner of my eye. He stares at the TV, his jaw set, no trace of the sunshine I'd seen there this morning. I don't know what to feel. Looking at him makes me feel everything at once. Love, guilt—and fear. It's all tangled up. Ollie is far too good for me. I've always known that. Maybe it's why I can't ever have him. Maybe that's why I've never been able to let go of him either.

"I'm sorry," I say, hoping to bring back a little bit of that sunshine. "It really does seem nice, but . . . Can we reschedule for next week? I just don't think I can look at houses right now."

"Of course, kitten," he says. He draws gentle circles on my knee with a finger and shoots me a smile. "We've got time."

He turns toward the TV again, and I watch as the smile slips from his face.

I turn to the TV too. The circles he draws on my knee are all that keeps me from panicking. The words *We've got time* echo in my head, but I'm starting to doubt we'll have enough.

20

〰〰

August

One night, nearly a month after the disastrous not-lunch with my parents, Ollie comes home after getting a drink with Alex and finds me in the kitchen washing the dishes.

"Well, hello there, Mr. Delightful. How's your boyfriend?"

"He's fine," Ollie says. He tucks his hands into the pockets of his jeans and leans against the counter.

Odd. Ollie usually gushes about Alex after they hang out. Those two are almost as bad as me and Jo. But the Ollie standing before me is downright miserable.

"What's—"

"Did you text Jo about scheduling dinner for this weekend?" he says.

"I . . . forgot," I say.

He rubs a hand over his face. "Jesus, Nina."

"What? Am I not allowed to forget things now and then?"

"Sure, but you *don't* forget things, Neen. You don't forget to text your best friend. And this is the third time you've either canceled last minute or forgotten. I told Alex I'd see him this weekend, and he had no fucking clue what I was talking about. So then I'm sitting there thinking, *Nina didn't text Jo, did she?* Didn't hear a fucking word Alex said after that." He pulls his hands from his pockets and crosses his arms over his chest. "So?"

"What?" I turn to the sink and rub at a red stain at the bottom of the wineglass in my hands. I've known this conversation would come sooner or later, but I was really hoping for later.

"So what's going on? We were supposed to tell them a month ago, and you keep stalling."

"I'm not," I say. I turn to him and hold up the wineglass. "We need new wineglasses. These are awful. I saw a set on Craigslist today that had to be worth a fortune."

Ollie sighs. "Did you have time to look at the houses I sent you this morning? The second one is walking distance from World Thrift. If we want it, we need to act quickly. We've already lost three that were perfect."

"The outlets were crooked." I look at the wineglass in my hands. "Ugh, I give up on this. It's beyond help." I set the still-stained wineglass in the sink and pick up a plate instead.

"Nina," Ollie says.

I can feel his eyes on me, but I don't look up. I don't want to have this conversation. I'm tired of it already. I see everywhere it can lead, and all the destinations are bad. "Do you think those wineglasses on Craigslist were stolen?" I say.

"Nina."

"I ought to check if there have been any news stories about missing wineglasses lately."

"Goddamn it, Nina! I'm trying to talk to you!"

I set the plate on the drying rack and turn to glare at him. "What the fuck, Ollie? If you don't want the stolen wineglasses, then you should've just said."

Ollie rubs his hands over his face with a groan.

"What?" I know I'm being unreasonable, but I can't stop myself. I don't know why I do this, why I'm always doing the exact opposite of what I *know* I should. I can't outrun my problems forever, but it never stops me from trying.

He drops his hands from his face. "I can't believe I thought things would be different this time. I thought we were past this."

"Past what?"

"*This*," he says, gesturing to me. "Our . . . in-between thing."

"What are you talking about? Everyone knows we're together."

"They think we're dating. They think I'm your *boyfriend*, Nina. We haven't even told Alex and Jo we're married."

"We haven't seen them much lately."

"Because you've been avoiding them! Why is that, Nina? I've never known you to avoid Jo, so it must have something to do with me."

"No . . . Ollie . . . it's not that."

"Then what is it? What else can it possibly be? We can't live in this apartment forever."

"We just haven't found the right house."

"If you just fucking tell me what the right house looks like, I'll move mountains to find it. I'll build it myself if I have to."

I don't think it's funny, but I laugh anyway. "I can't explain it. I'll know it when I see it."

"Would you?"

"What's that supposed to mean?"

"Would you know the right thing if it were staring you in the face? Because I'm not so sure. I think you could be standing in your dream house and not see it because you'd keep your eyes shut just to avoid it."

"That's ridiculous."

"Yeah, it is."

When I meet his gaze and see the hurt in his eyes, I feel as if I'm somewhere else. It's as if I'm watching a movie I've seen a thousand times. I know what happens next. I know the ending. But I don't see how I can do a single thing to stop it.

I turn back to the sink and focus all my attention on finding the silverware at the bottom of the soapy water.

I can't see Ollie, but I hear him sigh. "You said you wanted this . . . What's really going on here, Nina?"

What's going on is you're freaking out, the voice in my head says, but I don't say anything.

"I'm not trying to make you live a life you don't want, Nina. But I am trying to think about our future, and I can't get you to make a single decision. You say you love me. I believe you. But nothing's changed. This is the same shite we always do. Anytime I bring up the future, you get upset."

"I do not get upset!" I hurl the fistful of silverware in my hands back into the sink. When I look at Ollie, he has both eyebrows raised. "Well, now I'm upset! But only because you won't leave me alone! I haven't looked at houses because I don't want to move. I haven't told Jo and Alex we're married because I don't want them to know! And I didn't tell you any of that because I knew you'd make it a big deal, and it's not a big deal."

We're quiet as we glare at each other across the kitchen. I wonder if we'll leave it at this. We should. Ollie should sigh and go to bed. I should tell him I'm too tired to talk and finish cleaning.

"I didn't mean that," I say.

Ollie shakes his head. "I think you did," he says. "Here I've been thinking you can't tell anyone about us because it's this big thing. But really, it's because this is nothing to you. Is that it? Too unimportant to tell your best friend?"

"No," I say. "No, that's not true. I'm just . . ." But I don't finish my sentence. I'm all out of excuses.

Ollie looks away from me and stares at something across the kitchen. I'm not sure what. "I love you," he says. "But this isn't being together."

"Don't be ridiculous. We're together." I abandon the rest of the dishes and dry my hands on my jeans as I walk over to him. "We sleep together every night. I've let you use my deodorant for the last two days, for crying out loud. How much more together can you get?" When I take his face in my hands, I feel the rough stubble beneath my palms. "What am I supposed to do? Literally carve my heart out of my chest and put it in your hands?"

Ollie looks down at me and takes my hands from his face. I'm hopeful for a moment that we can fix this, that he'll keep my hands in his and know exactly what to say to prevent this conversation from blowing up. But he doesn't say anything. He brings my hands down and lets them go.

"Ollie . . ." I say, but that's all I've got. I have no idea what I'm doing. *You're fucking everything up*, the voice in my head says. *I know!* I tell her. *But I don't know why. I don't know how to stop.*

Ollie rests the back of his head against the wall. "I didn't want to do this."

"Do what?"

"If there's no future for us," he says, "then I need to go."

My entire body runs cold. "Go? Go where?"

He looks at me like I'm impossible. "Ireland. Like I've been saying for the last six months. I can't keep doing this, Nina. Mum and Jack and the pub are a sure thing. They want me there. Fuck, they *need* me. I want *you*, Nina. But I can't spend another ten years hoping you'll want me too."

"Show me the house by World Thrift," I say.

"What?"

"Show it to me. We can look at it first thing Monday . . . and we'll reschedule dinner with Jo and Alex. I just need a little more time. Not much."

"How much?"

I haven't really thought this through, but I'm desperate. "A week."

"Can you honestly tell me you'll be ready in a week?"

I fully intend to say anything I need in order to get us through this conversation, but when Ollie turns those blue eyes on mine, eyes that have seen so much hurt, I can't say anything but the truth. "I . . . well, I can't *know* with one hundred percent certainty, but I can try."

"I need one hundred percent certainty."

"Oliver, nothing is one hundred percent certain."

"The pub is. Don't keep me here if you can't do this. Please."

I can't say anything. His expression makes it hard enough to breathe.

"Can you promise me things will be different?" he says.

"I told you . . . I can *try* to be different, but—"

"Okay." Ollie looks like he wants to say more, but he only clears his throat and nods. He steps away from me and leaves the kitchen. For a moment, I'm unable to move. But then I'm in motion again, my heart beating so loud I can hardly hear my own thoughts as I follow him down the hall to our room. I stand in the doorway, feeling more helpless than I ever have in my entire life as I watch him pull his shamrock-green suitcase from beneath the bed.

"You're . . . leaving now?" I say.

Ollie doesn't look at me when he sets the suitcase on the bed and flips the top open. "I'm gonna stay on the boat until I can catch a flight."

"Ollie, come on. Let's just sleep on this."

I step into the room, but he shakes his head and turns away from me to grab his clothes from the closet. "I need to leave now." He doesn't look at me as he dumps the clothes into the suitcase. "It's too hard, Nina."

I don't know what to do. I'm torn between begging him not to leave and letting him go. I have no idea what the right thing is, which of my shitty options would end up hurting him more.

So I say nothing.

When Ollie leaves the room, I don't follow. I sit on the bed and look around at all my stuff, hoping I'll spot one of Ollie's T-shirts and have an excuse to go find him. But there's no trace of him left. I don't know how long I sit there listening to him in the bathroom, then the kitchen. But at some point, the door to our bedroom eases open, and he's there, standing in the doorway. I hope that he's cooled off and come to his senses. He'll kick over that fucking suitcase at his side. He'll cross the room and we won't even have to say anything. He'll make love to me right here and we'll forget this ever happened.

But he doesn't do any of that. He doesn't so much as come inside the room.

"Goodbye, kitten," he says. He pauses for a moment, maybe waiting for me to say it back, but I can't.

When I hear the front door open and close, I don't move. When the only man I've ever loved—*will* ever love—leaves, I do nothing. I don't even cry.

21

~~~~~~~~~

As soon as it really sinks in that Ollie isn't coming back, I call Jo. I'm only able to squeak out a summary of what's happened before I can't say anything more.

"I'll be right over," Jo says.

It's only when I open the door and see Jo that the tears come. By the time she's crossed the threshold of my apartment, I'm crying so hard I can barely speak. Jo looks alarmed. She steps inside, and her eyes flit over the living room. I know she's looking for any trace of Ollie. It only makes me cry harder.

"Oh, Nina," Jo says. She pulls me in for a hug. I'm not sure how long I stand there crying on her shoulder. When I finally catch my breath, Jo pulls away to peer into my face.

"Do you want to go to Mitch's?" she asks.

"I can't go there," I say. Too many memories.

"Do you want to stay here?"

I shake my head. I'm not sure what would be worse: being in the apartment Ollie and I once shared, the one that I can't seem to let go of, even though it's come between us, or being at Mitch's, where we've so often passed from one extreme to another.

Jo slings an arm over my shoulder. "Have you eaten? We can go to the restaurant and make Alex feed us. Or what about World Thrift? We can see who can find the ugliest outfit in under ten minutes."

I spit out a watery laugh at that, and Jo smiles. "World Thrift is closed right now," I say.

"Drat."

I lean my head on her shoulder. "Are cheese Danish on the menu yet?"

"They are now," Jo says. She pulls out her phone and sends a text, then claps me on the shoulder and grabs my apartment keys and purse. I let her push me out my door and into the hallway, thankful she knows I need her to be in charge without my having to say it.

The best thing about Josephine Walker is she doesn't ask me about Ollie. When we arrive at the restaurant, she takes me to the back entrance, and we sit beside each other in her office with our feet up on her desk, eating cheese Danish and watching episodes of *Snapped* I missed while on charter.

"How's the restaurant?" I ask. "Not sick of Alex yet?"

Jo leans back in her chair. The diamond on her finger flashes in the light as she puts her hands behind her head. It reminds me that her wedding is a mere four months away. I know it won't really change anything, but it doesn't feel that way. Alex will officially be more important. With Ollie gone, what does that leave me?

"To tell you the truth, between the restaurant and wedding planning, I'm exhausted. You'd think a small wedding would be no biggie, but I'm basically planning the most stressful theme party of my life. I don't see as much of Alex as you'd think. One of us always tries to be home with Greyson. It's a little intense."

Other than giving me a hug and a plate piled high with cheese Danish when we arrived, I haven't seen Alex all evening.

"Are you happy, though?" I ask.

A smile flutters at Jo's lips. "Can I tell you something? Don't be mad, okay?"

I raise an eyebrow. I'm not promising anything.

Jo sighs. "I didn't want to tell you before because I thought you might try to use it to convince me to work on the *Serendipity* again."

"Now why would you think I'd use any of your personal truths to get what I want?"

Jo gives me a look that says, *Don't even pretend you wouldn't.*

"Fine. You're probably right. Continue."

"I know I told you that I wanted this," she says, throwing up a hand to indicate her office. "And I did. I *do*. But I was also really nervous about it. It's been this huge change. Suddenly I'm managing a restaurant, planning a wedding, being someone's stepmom. I keep waiting for something to go wrong." She shakes her head. "God, Nina, so much has gone wrong. All small stuff, but it's been a steep learning curve. I went from being Alex's girlfriend to his fiancée, and business partner, and co-parent. It's been a lot of work for all of us to figure out what our family is going to look like, especially with Greyson's mom coming around more often."

"Shit," I say, and take a bite of cheese Danish. As in, *That's a lot, Josephine.* But also, *Shit,* as in, *I'm totally a piece of it for having made all this about me.*

"Greyson's going to California after the wedding to stay with her mom for the first time," Jo says. "I know she's fifteen now, and it's only a week, but"—she shakes her head—"I don't know . . . It's hard to think about. Grey wants to go, and Alex thinks it's a good idea, but I'm worried, even though it's ridiculous to feel like I should have any opinion about it at all. I've only known Greyson for two years."

"Two years in which you've been a part of her life almost every single day," I say. "Of course you're worried. You care about Greyson. You know how much her mom leaving hurt her."

Jo shoots me a look. "Okay, don't laugh."

"I'll try not to, but you're a very funny person, Josephine."

"I can't believe I'm admitting this," Jo says. "But a part of me is worried Greyson will have this amazing time in LA. You know how obsessed she is with aliens and One Direction—"

"She's the only person I know who can connect those two interests."

"Oh God. Her theory about Zayn being replaced by a reptilian is . . . thorough."

"It convinced me," I say. "But that's beside the point. Go on."

Jo sighs. "Anyway, Maggie has all these fun things planned. Harry Styles was in the last movie she worked on as casting director, and she got Greyson meet-and-greet tickets for the concert he's playing while she's there. Then they've got this mini road trip planned to see all the UFO sightings in Southern California."

"One of those things is definitely cooler than the other," I say.

Jo groans and lets her face fall into her hands. I pat her on the back, and she lifts her head. "I guess I'm jealous. I hope she has an amazing time, but part of me doesn't want her to have *too* much fun. What if she comes back and thinks I'm boring? What if she doesn't love me as much?"

"Josephine Walker, did you or did you not throw a Zac Efron–themed movie marathon?"

"Sure, but—"

"And go skydiving? And parasailing? You're not boring. Greyson loves you."

"For now," Jo says. She shoves a giant bite of cheese Danish in her mouth.

I take Jo's face in my hands, squeezing her cheeks as she chews. The door opens, and Alex's head pops in. We turn to look at him, my hands still on Jo's face, and he looks between us.

"Are you two having a moment?"

"Yes," Jo and I say at the same time. Jo's yes is more of a *yearsh*. Bits of cheese Danish fall onto her shirt.

"I'll leave you to it, then," Alex says before disappearing out the door.

"Anyway," I say, turning back to Jo. "One, it's impossible for anyone to stop loving you, because you are an ethereal being of light. Two, I highly doubt Greyson will ever think of you as boring, despite your severe lack of connections to the former members of One Direction. But even if she comes home after this whirlwind trip and suddenly thinks you're the most boring person in the world, it won't matter. You and Maggie aren't in competition. Greyson doesn't need you to be exciting. She's only ever needed you to be there. I'm sure Maggie is a lovely person, but she hasn't been able to give Greyson that."

Jo starts to cough, and I let go of her cheeks to slap her on the back.

"Stop hitting me! I'm fine!" she says, her voice hoarse.

I sigh, slumping into my chair. "I wish you'd have told me." Guilt gnaws at me. I wasn't supportive when she told me about the restaurant, and so she'd kept all this to herself. I know I can be a selfish asshole, but it never hurts quite as much as when the victim of my jerky behavior is Jo. "But I get why you didn't," I add.

Jo shrugs and finishes off the last Danish before pinning me with a probing look. "You had a lot going on," she says carefully.

I know this is her feeling out if I want to talk about Ollie. I wonder what he's doing. *Will he really go to Ireland? File the divorce petition? If so, when?* I sit up to grab a framed photo from Jo's desk. The photo has to be at least five years old. In it, she and I stand in front of the *Serendipity* in our formal whites, arms slung over each other's shoulders. *Ollie prob-*

ably took this, I think. It amazes me how much, and yet how little, has changed since then.

"I think it's my fault Ollie left," I say.

"Why?"

I set the photo back on the desk and get to my feet. I pace the office as Jo sits there in her chair, swiveling this way and that. "He's the one who left, but I . . . I think I was the one who really ended things."

I can't see Jo, but I imagine she's looking at me as if I've just said I'm downsizing my closet in favor of a capsule wardrobe. "What do you mean?"

I pause beside the office door and bang my forehead gently against it. Unfortunately it doesn't knock any sense into me. "I don't even know, to tell you the truth."

"Well," Jo says after a long moment of silence, "if you're interested in finding out, I have a great idea."

I don't even bother lifting my head to look at her when I speak. "If that idea begins with a *T* and rhymes with . . . Oh, forget it, I can't think of a good rhyme. If you're suggesting therapy, I don't want to hear it."

"I'm just saying, it might help."

I make a fart noise with my mouth before crossing the room to slump into my chair. "Pass. Any ideas that don't involve paying money to spill my guts to a stranger?"

It's not that I have anything *against* therapy. I'm sure it's helpful for other people. I just never saw the point. My parents tried to get me to go to family therapy with them after I busted my knee and found out about the debt Dad sank all of us in, but I'd managed to get out of it. I had my reasons. One, we didn't have money for therapy. And two, I didn't see the point. How could talking to someone I didn't know help me with my very real-life problems? Why did a stranger have to be involved in our family's business? Could a therapist fix my credit?

Could they find me an apartment I could afford? Rescue my athletic career?

No, they couldn't.

And even though the situation with Ollie is completely different, I don't see how a therapist can help with that either. *Yes, hello, therapist, my name is Nina Lejeune, and I can't commit to the man I love because I have daddy issues.* How boring! How common! How small and insignificant when there are people out there, people like *Jo*, who have had so much more to overcome.

Besides, therapy is very much in opposition to my rules. One, it isn't fun. And two, it essentially *requires* me to rely on another person. Thanks, but no thanks.

"What?" I say when I catch Jo staring at me.

"Can I ask you something?" she says.

"Depends."

"Why do I get the feeling there's something you aren't telling me?"

"Oh Josephine," I say. "There's so much I haven't told you."

"Like what?"

"Well," I say, sitting up straighter in my seat, "for one, I never told you that before I was a yacht stewardess, I was a gymnast. A good one. Almost went to the Olympics twice."

Jo doesn't look surprised, which is surprising. "Yeah, I know that."

"What? How?"

"You really think I've never googled you before? Everyone knows that about you. Heck, Greyson has a whole playlist of your routines saved. Alex was pretty surprised when he found out. That Greyson has a playlist," she adds. "The gymnastics thing didn't surprise him at all."

"You never told me you knew! None of you!"

"Why would we? You never talked about it, so we figured you didn't want us to know."

"You have a point," I say. I clear my throat. "Well, if this one doesn't surprise you, then I'm convinced you're a mind reader."

"Lay it on me," Jo says. She sets her elbows on her knees and leans forward, chin propped in her hands.

"Ollie and I weren't just together . . . we were . . . well, *are* . . . married."

"You're not!"

"We most certainly are. Nine years last month."

I'm glad Jo is sitting, because one of her elbows slips off her knee and she nearly falls from her chair. "Nine . . . I don't know what to say."

I tell Jo the whole sorry story. About my dad. About meeting Ollie. About our deal, though I leave out why Ollie wanted to avoid being sent back to Ireland. That part isn't mine to tell. When I tell her about what was really happening belowdeck the night Ollie and I caught her with champagne in the galley, she smacks my shoulder and calls me an asshole.

"I am *not* a sign that you shouldn't be with the love of your life! What the fuck, Nina?"

"How do you know you weren't a sign?" I say. "It's not like a person can just *decide* to be one. That's not how signs work."

"Fine. I'm deciding *not* to be one!" She tilts her face up to the ceiling. "I do not give my consent to be a sign!"

"Too late," I say.

She looks sincerely upset when she settles her gaze on me again. "I can't believe you used me as an excuse for your emotional constipation."

"Don't take it personally. I hardly knew you!"

Jo does a slow spin in the office chair. "You've got some serious issues, Nina. Holy shit."

I prop my legs on her knees to keep her from spinning. "Shit. Shite. Tomato. Potato. Tell me something I don't know."

"Do you think he'll really go back to Ireland?"

I think of how I watched Ollie walk out the door only a few hours ago. How it felt different from the other times he's walked away. "Unfortunately, I do."

"Are you going to be okay?"

I give Jo the best smile I can manage. "What other choice do I have?"

22

~~~~~

September

When the knock on my door comes a few weeks later, my first thought is of Ollie. It's two o'clock on my day off, and I haven't changed out of my pajamas. I've been in my pajamas a lot lately. Jo is starting to worry, though I tell her not to. They're silk pajamas at least. I'm not that far gone.

I smooth the wrinkles from my shirt before walking to the door and peeking through the peephole. But it isn't Ollie who stands in the hallway.

"Xav? What are you doing here?"

"Is it a bad time for a visit?" he says, generously pretending he doesn't notice I'm in my pajamas and my normally sleek hair looks like a bird's nest.

It's probably not the best time, but I don't really care. Xav has seen the best and worst of me; he can handle my less-than-perfectly-tidy apartment. Besides, I could use a distraction from scrolling through old photos of me and Ollie, and Xav's visit has me curious. "Come on in."

I move aside, and Xav steps into my apartment.

"Sorry it's a bit of a mess," I say, shutting the door behind him. "Can I get you some water? Coffee? I'd offer food, but I don't have any. Have you had lunch? If you're planning to stay for a while, I can order something. You like that Salvadoran place downtown, right?" I pull out my phone to look up the menu.

"You don't need to be chief stew today, kiddo," Xav says. "I'm here as your friend, not your boss."

"Well, in that case, make yourself at home. There's beer in the fridge." I set my phone on the coffee table and settle onto the couch, tucking my feet beneath me.

Xav's beard twitches, barely concealing a smile. "You want one?" he asks, starting in the direction of the kitchen.

"It depends on why you're really here," I say.

Xav doesn't respond, but when he returns, he has a beer in each hand.

"I'm going to need a drink for this?" My heart sinks a bit when he passes a bottle to me and takes a seat at the other end of the couch.

Xav sighs and takes a swig from his beer. "That depends on how you feel about it, but I figure a drink can't hurt either way."

"Every year you become more and more cryptic, you know. I fully expect you to embody Captain Nemo by the end of your career."

"Finally, someone's catching on," he says.

I take a sip from the beer in my hand. As I do, my eyes are drawn to a folder Xav has tucked beneath his arm. I set my beer on the coffee table.

"All right, let's get it over with. Either you're here to tell me you've retired and those are all the assets you're handing over to me, or you're firing me and that's my amazing severance package, or . . ." I let the words trail off. I'm fairly certain I know what's in that folder, but I can't bring myself to say it.

Xav sighs. He sets his beer on the coffee table and passes the folder to me.

"I hate to do this, Nina, but he asked that I be the one to give it to you."

I take the folder in both hands, bracing myself for a moment before flipping it open. Like it did on the first day of charter season, my name in Ollie's handwriting leaps out at me. I scan the pages. Beneath item six, there is a check mark beside the words "The marriage is irretrievably broken."

Shit. "He really did it," I say, more to myself than to Xav.

Xav clears his throat. "Do you . . . need anything?"

I lean back against the armrest of the couch and sink deeper into the cushions. I close the folder and toss it onto the coffee table, and the top page spills out. "PETITION FOR DISSOLUTION OF MARRIAGE WITH NO DEPENDENT OR MINOR CHILD[REN] OR PROPERTY," it says.

Nothing. That's exactly what Ollie and I have between us according to this divorce petition. And once I respond, officially dissolving our marriage in an uncontested divorce, as simple and uncomplicated as Ollie said it would be, we'll have even less than that.

"I'm okay," I say. I nudge the offensive page back into the folder with my toe, then set my Oscar de la Renta coffee table book on top of it. "You sure you don't want lunch? Water? Is the beer okay?" I wish he weren't here as my friend. This would be a lot easier if he were here as my boss. Then I'd know exactly what to do.

"Are you sure you're all right?" Xav says.

"I'm marvelous," I say, though my whole body seems to have gone numb. "He told me he'd do this."

"That doesn't mean you believed him."

I shrug. I knew he'd gone to Ireland. Jo told me he'd stopped by the restaurant to say goodbye to her and Alex. But part of me hoped he'd forgotten all about this.

"Can I ask you something?" Xav says.

"As my boss or my friend?"

"Friend."

"I'd rather you'd have said boss," I mumble.

"Ollie didn't sound too happy about this, considering he's the one who filed it," he says with a nod to the folder. "I'm going to go out on a limb and say this was your decision, somehow, but you don't look too happy about it either."

"That's not a question."

"Fair enough," Xav says. "Let me rephrase that. What the fuck is wrong with you, Nina?"

I glare at him. "What did you just say, old man?"

"I said, *What the fuck is wrong with you?* I'm glad you've got Jo, but she's too nice to tell it to you straight. I don't give a rat's ass if you get pissed off at me for saying this, but letting Ollie go will be the biggest fuckup of your life."

Xav has handed my ass to me plenty of times over the years, but never for something like this. Never something personal. I'm not sure if I want to slap him or burst into tears. "I think you need to go back to being my boss, Xav. What makes you so sure *this* is the mistake? The way I see it, everything up to this point has been the mistake."

"Believe it or not, kiddo, I've got some experience with love."

I try to hold on to my anger, but I can't help but snort. "I'm sorry," I say, and cover my mouth with a hand. In the ten years I've known Xav, I've never heard him talk about anyone outside of work. Now that I think about it, it's a bit strange. How could I have gone so long thinking I know everything, when I obviously know nothing at all?

"I let someone go once, someone I shouldn't have. I'm not saying I know everything that's going on with you and Ollie," Xav says. "But I know you love each other. It's obvious to anyone with eyeballs. I've known you since you were both brainless kids, and I can tell neither of you wants this."

I look away from him to pick at the hem of my shirt. "It's too late. He's already gone."

Xav is quiet for so long that I look up to make sure he hasn't died right there on my couch. When he catches me looking at him, he sighs. "He's not gone. He's just in Ireland. One day, it really will be too late. I don't have the words to tell you what that feels like. I don't want you to know. Well"—he pats my arm and gets to his feet—"I better get going. Good chat. You let me know if you need a little time off work. Or, hell, a lot. I've got a stewardess champing at the bit to pick up some shifts."

I scan my messy apartment and laugh. "Taking off work is the last thing I need right now."

"Whatever you say, kiddo."

"Go to hell, old man."

Xav smiles. He takes his empty beer bottle and disappears into the kitchen. When he returns and heads for the door, I leap from the couch, taking him by surprise when I ambush him from behind with a hug.

"Thank you," I say, grateful he can't see the tears blurring my vision. "I'm sorry I told you to go to hell."

Xav pats my hand. "I know you think ending things is the right answer, Nina, but there are just as many right answers as there are wrong ones."

"Okay," I say, not sure I really understand what he means.

Once Xav's gone, I return to the couch and tug the folder from beneath the Oscar de la Renta book. I only read through half the form's title before my mind is made up.

"Fuck you, form," I say, flipping it off before I rip the page in half right down the middle. I take the next page and rip it into smaller pieces. And the next, into even smaller pieces. By the time I'm done, I've got a pile of the world's most depressing confetti at my feet.

I kick it away from me, not caring that I'll have to pick it up later. I grab my phone from the coffee table and call Jo.

"Can you take a few days off from the restaurant?" I ask when she answers.

"Probably," Jo says. "What's up?"

"Pack a bag, babe. We're going to Ireland."

23

Forty-eight hours later, Jo and I finally arrive in Cobh. My jet lag and the ache in my knee from the long flight and subsequent train ride fades as soon as Ollie's family pub, the Local, comes into view.

"You ready?" Jo says, giving my arm a squeeze when we stop outside the pub.

"I have absolutely no idea," I say. "So we better do it."

I push through the door to the pub and step inside. It's small, but in a cozy way. The menu is scrawled on the chalkboard that hangs on the wall beside the door—Ollie's handwriting, I realize, my heart vaulting into my throat. Instead of the dollars and mementos that litter the walls and ceiling of Mitch's, the Local is decorated with framed black-and-white photographs of Cobh. Two Irish flags hang from the ceiling. Warm light falls from glass bulbs, making the clean wooden tables shine. I run a finger along the nearest table. No dust.

"I see why Ollie hates Mitch's so much," Jo says.

The place is beautiful, clean, charming. Not a Taco Tuesday menu in sight.

"Nina," Jo whispers. I look up, and she nods in the direction of the bar. Behind it, a young man holds open the door to the kitchen and hollers something I can't make out. I only catch a glimpse of bronze hair in the kitchen beyond, but it's enough. Ollie's here.

"I'm absolutely allergic to you, you feckin' Muppet," Ollie shouts. That's a new one. I have no idea what he's saying, but I'm suddenly fighting the urge to cartwheel right out the door.

He's so . . . Irish, I think. Ollie never wanted to come back, and even though I knew why, I always assumed he hated Ireland. With a jolt that sends a sliver of fear through me, I realize Ollie looks like he belongs here. It's as if there's always been a piece of him missing, and I've walked right into it.

"You're more miserable than I remember," the man behind the bar says.

Ollie's laugh floats out of the kitchen. It buoys my heart and crushes it at the same time. He sounds happy, and yet I've spent the last month miserable without him.

When the kitchen door swings shut, the young man turns to face the pub. He catches sight of us, and an easy smile appears on his face.

"Welcome to the Local," he says. "What can I do for you girls?"

Jo gives me a hesitant look. I wish I would've paused outside to do a handstand for my nerves. As I approach the man behind the bar, a feeling of recognition washes over me, because *this* is Jack, Ollie's brother. I know it without having to ask. Even though Jack's hair is darker, and his arms are covered in colorful tattoos, and he is *far* more cheerful looking than Ollie has ever been, I see the resemblance. Those blue eyes, the nose . . . They're brothers. There's no denying it. Anyone who knows Ollie as well as I do would see it.

"Hi," I say, trying to hold back a smile when I make it to the bar.

"Hello," Jack says, all charm as he looks at me, then Jo. He eyes me again and leans toward me over the bar. "You look familiar."

"I'm . . ." *Friends with your brother?* No, that doesn't feel right. Ollie and I haven't spoken once since he left. I can't imagine we're friends. "Nina," I say. *Nice one*, the voice in my head says. "And this is Jo," I add, nodding to Jo, who gives Jack a little wave.

"Nina," Jack says. His blue eyes linger on mine. They're lighter than Ollie's, less intense. He flicks his gaze to the kitchen door. "You're not . . ." He turns to me and squints, then slaps the bar top with both hands. "You are! You're Ollie's Nina!"

"I think that's up for debate at the moment."

Jack looks me over again, and his expression changes, still charming, but with a layer of hesitation. "I'm not sure if I'm supposed to love you or hate you."

"When in doubt go with both. That's what I do."

Jack nods. He straightens and crosses his arms over his chest. "What are you doing here, then, Nina?"

I nod to the kitchen door. "I think that's obvious."

Jack shrugs a shoulder. "Is it? I don't think so. From what I've heard you're supposedly the most spectacular girl who's walked God's green earth, and yet you broke my big brother's wee little heart. So why don't you spell it out for me, Nina Lejeune?"

Jack smiles at me, and I can't help but laugh. "You're Ollie's brother, all right. The two of you are absolute shits."

His smile becomes a grin. "We're two shining shites, Ollie and me. And you're exactly like he said."

"How's that?" I ask, but before Jack can answer the kitchen door swings open, and Ollie appears in the doorway, a bewildered look on his face.

"Jackie, I must be losing it. I swear I just heard . . ." The end of his sentence trails off when he notices me. "Nina," he says, my name in his mouth somehow a question and statement at the same time.

I'm too nervous to try to decipher the look on his face. "Hi."

Ollie is rooted to the spot in the doorway. I try to think of something to say, but everything I rehearsed on the flight and subsequent train ride into Cobh leaves me. It hurts to look at him. I've missed him even more than I realized.

Jack props his chin in a hand and looks at Jo. "Are they always this . . . silent?"

Jo laughs. "I wish. Usually there's a lot more profanity."

"Can we talk?" I say to Ollie.

Ollie sweeps a hand through his hair and looks at Jack.

"Oh, go on," Jack says. "I managed this place well enough before you got here."

Ollie looks at me, and I wish I could figure out what he's thinking. "I'll be right out," he says. He disappears into the kitchen, and as the door swings shut, I catch sight of him untying the apron from around his waist.

"You look like you're freaking out," Jo whispers to me.

"I'm not freaking out," I whisper back.

Jack, who is doing a shit job of pretending not to eavesdrop, sets one pint in front of me and one in front of Jo. He leans forward and whispers, "I gotta go with Jo on this one. You're definitely freaking out. You've got this twitch in your cheek."

I bring a hand to my face. "Thank God I'm an only child," I say.

Jack grins at me. "He still loves you, you know. Can't promise I know how your little gab sesh will play out, but the boy is hopelessly heartsick, you can be sure of that."

"Thanks," I mumble, and take a sip from the pint.

When Ollie returns, he joins his brother behind the bar and eyes me with hesitation. "You've met Jack, I see," he says.

"He's absolutely charming, Oliver," I say.

"Don't trust this bastard. Smiles the whole time he's slagging you," Ollie says. He slaps Jack on the back, making him splutter on the pint he's poured for himself. "Quit drinking on the job."

Jack's gaze flicks from Ollie to me. "My brother's ex and her friend walk into my pub and it's not the start of a clever joke? I'm going to need this," he says. "Say, you want one too, Ollie Wollie?"

Ollie rolls his eyes and doesn't respond. "Wanna go for a walk?" he says to me.

"Sure."

I follow Ollie from the pub. He pauses for a moment when we step outside as if unsure where to go.

"Let's do the waterfront, yeah?" he says, more to himself than to me. He turns, and I follow, trying to make sense of his body language. Is he happy to see me? Part of me thinks yes, but the other part—well, I'm not so sure. He looks stressed out, like he's fighting not to look at me.

The street slopes down as it runs toward the sea. My knee, used to the flat terrain of Florida, aches a bit after the long flight as I make my way down the hill. Ollie must think of it too, because he stops suddenly, and I nearly run into him. He gives me his arm but doesn't say anything. I grab on to his elbow, and he walks a bit slower.

Cobh is breathtakingly beautiful. Ollie's shown me pictures. He once gave me a tour of the town using Google Earth. But it's different actually experiencing it. The water is visible here, a wide expanse of blue as far as the eye can see. The cathedral towers above concrete houses in candy colors. If I weren't so occupied with Ollie, I'd revel in the view more.

The road turns to brick as we pass into Pearse Square. It's bustling with tourists and locals. *No wonder Ollie ended up in yachting*, I think as we pause at the bottom of the square and wait to cross to the other side of the street, where the road runs alongside Cork Harbour. I knew Cobh was a seaside town, of course. I can't even think of the name without hearing Ollie's voice in my head saying, *It's pronounced* cove, *not* cob. I nearly say it aloud, but decide against it when I glance at Ollie, who seems to be drowning in his own thoughts.

I let go of his arm, tempted to step behind him and karate chop the tension right out of his shoulders, but then I notice the monument beside us.

"You never showed me this," I say. I reach out to touch the stone around the plaque. Ollie watches me, an uneasy look on his face. "Well, that's depressing. This was the last port of call for the *Titanic* before it sank."

"I know that."

"Of course you do."

Great backdrop for your grand gesture, the voice in my head says.

The street clears, and we cross to the other side. We walk along the sidewalk beside the harbor. Ollie has his hands in his pockets, probably fidgeting with his saint medals.

We pass into a small brick park right in front of the water. There's so much to see—a large gazebo, flags from various countries waving above the railing that separates the promenade from the sea below, a brick fountain, a cannon. People occupy benches or lean against the railing to look out at the sea and the boats in the distance.

Normally I'd be giddy with excitement, eager to see and touch everything. But this isn't a normal Nina and Ollie adventure to blow off some steam.

Ollie stops behind one of the empty benches. He pulls his hands from his pockets and braces himself on the back of the bench, staring out at the water. I know he feels me watching him. He clears his throat, and I realize he's waiting for me to say something.

"How are you?" I say.

Ollie raises an eyebrow. *Really, I came all this way just to start with that?*

He sighs. "I'm . . ." He lets the words trail off and shakes his head. "Fuck, Nina, I don't know."

I've imagined a million different ways this could go, but none of them started like this. I brush my fingers along the back of his hand, but he doesn't acknowledge it. "I made a mistake," I say.

Ollie nods, and his gaze flicks over me before returning to the sea. He shifts on his feet, looking unsure of what to do with his limbs. I follow him as he wanders over to the railing and leans against it. He doesn't look at me when I stand beside him.

"What was the mistake?" he says.

As if he doesn't know. I stare out at the harbor too, wondering what he's looking at with such concentration. "Letting you go, of course."

Ollie rocks back and forth on his heels. He looks as if he's having an argument with himself in his head. I watch him and wait for him to touch me, or give a sigh of relief, or tell me he forgives me and we'll be okay. But he doesn't give me any of that. He gives nothing.

"Ollie?" I say when I can't take the silence any longer.

"I'm thinking," he says. He turns away from the water and walks back over to the empty bench. He sits down and clasps his hands together between his knees, not looking up at me when I sit beside him. Instead, he stares down at his hands, one leg bouncing up and down with nervous energy.

We sit in an awkward silence for what seems like another eternity. I watch groups of people walk past us, laughing and talking. I watch the boats out at sea and feel glad I'm on land.

"Ollie," I say when I've run out of things to stare at and he still hasn't spoken.

"Why?" Ollie lifts his head. He pulls his hands apart and rests against the back of the bench, looking all casual and annoyed, like he sometimes looked at me from the crew mess table when we were in the middle of an argument about last-minute menu changes.

"Why was letting you go a mistake?" I say.

"Nah. Why'd you change your mind?"

"Because I miss you." I take the hem of his shirt between my fingers. He pretends not to notice, but I feel him tense beneath my touch. "I'm miserable without you."

"It's not like we haven't been apart before. You'll get used to it."

"But it's different knowing you're here. I . . . I need you in my life."

"And this life with me in it, what would it look like?"

I glance up at him. "I don't know." I tug at the hem of his shirt. "I hadn't gotten that far. I had to see you."

Ollie sighs and releases his hands from behind his head. He gets to his feet, and the hem of his shirt pulls free from my grasp, leaving me empty-handed as I look up at him.

"That's a problem, love," he says. "Because I have thought about it. A lot. I've been thinking about it for years."

"Our life can look like whatever you want it to look like," I say. "Just come home."

Ollie turns away from me. I look out at the harbor and think of the *Titanic*, sensing that this conversation is sinking fast.

"Do you have any idea how hard it was for me to come here?" he says, still not looking at me. "I wish I could tell you everything that's happened. I've had to face fifteen fucking years away from here, from Jack and Mum. It doesn't matter that Da's dead. It was all still here waiting for me."

"How is your mom?"

He shrugs. "It's complicated. She misses him, but at the same time . . . she's relieved? And guilty. It's a fucking mess, really. I don't know if me being here is making it worse or better. Jack says better, but . . ." He shakes his head.

"I can't even imagine." I get to my feet and stand just behind him, resting my hand on his elbow.

"I wanted to call you every day, Nina. Some days, the first thing I'd do is look up what the next flight back to the US was. I've got them all memorized now," he says. "You have no idea how many times I almost bought the next ticket back to you."

"So come home," I say.

He turns to me. "I am home, Nina. I'm glad I'm here. I would've needed to deal with all of this at some point. I always said Da was why I couldn't come back here, but I could've come without seeing him. And you . . . Even when we weren't speaking, even when I was seeing someone else, I told myself that I couldn't leave you. But I was just using you as an excuse not to deal with everything I left behind. I'm sorry for that, kitten."

"What . . . what are you saying?"

Alarm passes over his face. "Oh, no, darling," he says. He steps nearer and takes my face in his hands, tilting it up to look into his. "You misunderstand me. Loving you wasn't just an excuse. I love you, for real. Always have, still do, likely always will." A flutter of relief passes through me. Finally, he's said it. Finally, he's touching me. "But . . ."

"But what?" At the look on his face, my relief fades as quickly as it arrived. "Why do I feel like you're about to break my heart?"

Ollie caresses my cheek with a thumb before letting me go. "My da was a nice guy, you know," he says. "Beat the ever-loving shite out of us, but he wasn't always like that. He could be downright likable. Most charming fella in town."

I try to follow Ollie's train of thought, but I'm not sure where he's going with this. What does his dad have to do with us?

"Home could be real stressful-like. But there'd be these long stretches of time where we had the nice version of Da, the one everyone else knew. He'd feel guilty for what he'd done and apologize. He'd surprise us—get Mum flowers, me and Jack new bikes and stuff. He'd promise never to hurt us again. And every time . . . every fucking time, I'd believe him, even though I knew I shouldn't. But he never changed, Nina. He never changed a damn thing. None of us did."

"I'm not sure I understand," I say.

"I'm not saying you remind me of my da, Nina. I couldn't. You're unlike him in a million ways."

"Then what?"

Ollie takes my hand in his and looks down at it. He traces the lines on my palm as if they can spell out everything that's happened between us. "I don't know, Neen. We've been doing the same thing over and over. Every time we got close, I told myself that this time could be different, but it never was, because *we* never changed, neither of us. Then Da died, and I thought, *To hell with this!* I thought that maybe if I put everything on the line, things really would be different. We could break out of this on-and-off and in-between thing."

He gives my hand a squeeze before letting go. "But it didn't matter that I changed, because you didn't. When you said you loved me . . . that you'd really be with me, I was so desperate to believe you. I was like my mum, hanging on to something that was never gonna happen."

"No," I say. I want to cover his mouth with a hand, to make him eat his words, to stop him from saying whatever he's about to say. "It will be different this time. I promise."

Ollie shakes his head. "I can't know that, Nina. And neither can you, because you haven't really thought about it. You don't want to lose me, but you don't know if you want what I do."

"I do!" I say.

"Then what do you want, Nina?" he says. His voice is raised, but not angry. It's desperate. "What do you see our future being?"

I fumble for an answer, but I have no idea.

Ollie nods. "Right."

"Does it matter?" I say.

Ollie's eyes are bluer than I've ever seen them. The intensity as he stares me down could burn a hole right through me. *Zap!* My heart would disintegrate, not even a fine dust left behind. "It matters, Nina. The whole fecking problem is you don't know what you want. Or maybe you do. Fuck it, I don't know. Maybe you know exactly what you want but are too stubborn to do anything about it."

"Maybe you're right," I say, desperate to turn the tide of this conversation. "Maybe I can be a little . . . inflexible . . . sometimes."

Ollie glares at me, but it dissolves into a snort and he covers his face with his hands. "If that's a gymnast joke, I swear to God . . ."

I feel a snag of relief. I know that voice, it's the *Nina, you're impossible and I love it* voice. "Ollie, I want to be with you. So maybe I don't have anything concrete to show you. But I'm different," I say. "I've changed . . . or will change."

"I want to believe you," Ollie says, all the laughter gone from his face. "But I don't. We've been married for almost ten years, and you never tried to change our relationship one way or another. You're not afraid of commitment, Nina. It was never about that. It was always about having to trust me, or, I don't know, trust yourself. You couldn't take that risk."

"But I'm here now, taking a risk."

He laughs. "Coming all this way might seem like some grand gesture to you, but it's not. It's a plane ticket and a bunch of promises. It doesn't mean anything would be different."

"What do I have to do to convince you?" I say.

Ollie shrugs. He turns over his shoulder and looks back the way we've come. I follow his gaze, eyes drawn to the cathedral that looms over the town. *He's given up on me*, I think. I never believed it was possible until now.

"I don't know, Neen. I've stopped trying to make that happen. It was never my place to make it happen, and I'm done coming up with excuses for why it should be."

"And that's it?" I say.

He sighs and turns back to me. "That's it, kitten. Should we head back?"

I sink onto the bench again. I can't just walk back down these streets with him. Walk into that pub and face Jack and Jo. I shake my head. "Will you tell Jo where to find me?"

Ollie nods. He looks as if he's about to walk away, but then, as if he's been swept up in a storm, he comes nearer and sinks onto his knees in front of me. He pulls me to him and kisses me with urgency, as if it's the last time. It very well may be. I've never cried while kissing him before, but I do now, because I know this kiss isn't Ollie changing his mind. This is a goodbye.

When he pulls away, he looks sadder than I've ever seen him. He brushes the tears from my cheeks, then presses a chaste kiss to my lips. "Don't cry, kitten," he says, his voice thick with emotion. He holds my face in his hands and kisses my forehead. "I'm sorry, Nina. I really am."

I try to say his name, but I can't. He gets to his feet and turns his back on me. I try to keep the tears from blurring my vision as I watch him walk away. I keep hoping he'll change his mind. That he'll do an about-face and run back to me again.

But he doesn't so much as look over his shoulder before he crosses the street, turns a corner, and walks out of my life.

24

~~~~~~

After Jo and I return from Ireland, September drags on, hot and stifling. I never get déjà vu anymore, though my life is the same as it ever was. Every day feels like two, and when I'm not working day charters, I desperately try to make the time pass. I haunt Jo and Alex's restaurant under the guise of wedding planning. I scroll Craigslist, but nothing seems weird or fun enough to capture my imagination. I wander the rainbow aisles of World Thrift, but not even the wildest of vintage designer pieces can break me out of my funk.

I feel like I'm waiting for something that will never come. I haven't spoken to Ollie since he walked away from me at Cork Harbour, not that I haven't tried. He hasn't responded to my emails. He hasn't answered my texts. I know he's given up his US number, because a few weeks after returning from Ireland, I nearly dropped my phone into the ocean at the sight of his name on my screen seconds after sending him a text. But my hopes of finally reaching him were dashed when I open the message and read: **Who is this?**

One day I find myself lingering in the bathroom at work, scrolling through WebMD pages because I'm convinced my lethargy is the result of a rare and serious illness contracted abroad. This never-ending malaise can't be the result of a broken heart, can it? Ollie and I have "broken up" plenty of times, but it's never left me like this—exhausted, miserable, thoroughly disenchanted with my life, with everything.

Unsurprisingly, WebMD gives me plenty to worry about but no actual answers. By the time I force myself to return to the main deck, I'm half-convinced I have a tapeworm lodged in my brain. When I step into the main salon, I'm met by a run-down-looking Britt. Her hair, extra frizzy in the Florida humidity, looks like a cloud around her head.

"There you are! Why didn't you answer when I called you over the radio? I was about to send RJ down there to check on you."

"You didn't call me over the radio," I say, and shove my phone into the pocket of my skirt.

"Okay, sure. I just *imagined* I did," Britt says.

I don't have the energy for Britt's attitude today. She's been surly ever since charter season ended. It's completely unlike the bubbly, carefree Britt who normally annoys the crap out of me. Oddly, I miss her. Perhaps she has a tapeworm lodged in her brain too. "I swear I didn't hear you over the radio. Are you sure you're on the right channel?"

"Yeah, Nina, I'm sure. Are you sure you have your radio?"

"I always have my . . ." But I let the words trail off when I pat my skirt and realize I do *not* have my radio. "That's . . . weird."

"Is it, though?" Britt says. She rolls her eyes so hard I'm worried they'll fall off the boat. "I'm going to go check on the guests," she adds before turning to leave the room.

"What's with the attitude, Britt?"

"I don't know, Nina, you figure it out," she calls over her shoulder.

"I don't know what's gotten into you, but please don't forget who's chief stew around here."

Britt turns to me. Anger and hurt flashes in her eyes. "I think *you're* the one who's forgotten!"

"What—"

"Why are you even here, Nina? You clearly don't want to be."

"Excuse me?"

"I thought you might snap out of it after charter season, but you haven't. It's only gotten worse."

Now *I'm* angry. "What's your point, Britt? I misplace my radio *once* in ten years. Jesus take the helm!"

"It's not just the radio!" Britt says. "You clearly don't want to be here."

"That's not true," I say. "I love this job." The guests' laughter floats into the salon from outside. Britt shakes her head and crosses the room to hurl herself onto the couch in front of me. She stares up at me, and it reminds me of the night I lashed out at Ollie after he sent our pervy guests to bed. A sliver of doubt works its way into my heart. I'm not over yachting, am I? I think of that moment in the wheelhouse with Xav when he told me it was okay if this job was no longer for me. I think of that night at Lotus, how I'd felt outside of it all, like I no longer belonged. I stare at Britt, who stares back, neither of us breaking eye contact. Is it really possible I don't want to be here anymore?

It can't be. Just the thought of quitting this job terrifies me. It reminds me of how I felt when my gymnastics career ended. Who am I if I'm not chief stewardess of the *Serendipity*? Especially now that Ollie is gone and Jo is getting married.

I sink onto the couch opposite Britt. "I'm just . . . having a hard time."

"Because Ollie left?" Britt says.

"I . . . yes." I hope that's what this is about, because then this feeling of not belonging might fade along with the pain of missing him. *Because that's going so well*, the voice in my head says.

"You miss him a lot, huh?" Britt says.

I stare at my knees. "Yeah."

"You love him, right?"

"Unfortunately."

"So what are you going to do about it?"

I sigh. "There's nothing to do. I went to Ireland, told him I wanted him back, and he . . ."

"He what?"

"He walked away from me. He said he didn't believe I'd changed."

"Well, did you?"

"Did I what?"

"Did you change?" Britt asks.

"I . . . no. I didn't." I'd spent so much time trying to push away missing Ollie that I hadn't even considered whether or not he was right. "I don't know if I can."

Amir's voice comes over the radio, startling us both. "Britt. Nina. Amir here. Lunch is ready."

Britt gets to her feet and gives my shoulder a squeeze. "Don't be silly, Nina. Anyone can change." She unclips her walkie-talkie from her shorts. "You've got about five minutes to find your radio before lunch service starts."

I look up at Britt, feeling as if I'm seeing her for the first time in years. She's capable of more than I give her credit for. She's no longer the greener-than-grass, gossip-loving, hot-mess junior stew I met three years ago. She still loves gossip and isn't any better at keeping her bunk clean, but she's grown up more than I realized.

"Thanks," I say. "You're a great stewardess, you know. I'm sorry I haven't said that more."

"Or ever," Britt teases.

I roll my eyes.

Amir's voice comes on over the radio again. Britt groans, whips her radio to her mouth, and presses the talk button. "Amir, this is Britt. I need you to *fucking chill*, over." She shakes her head and looks at me. "Chefs, am I right?"

Xav's voice comes on over the radio seconds later. "Knock it off, Britt."

That night, I'm sitting on my couch, my old gymnastics routines queued up on the TV, when I receive a text from Jo.

Just heard from Ollie. He'll be at the wedding. Thought you'd want to know. xo

I read the text but don't respond. I'm not sure it matters if Ollie will be there or not.

I turn my attention back to the screen, where I've paused the video right at the start of my beam routine from Olympic trials. I've never watched it before. It takes all my willpower not to look away, but I see the moment everything changes. Right before I attempt the salto, my eyes leave the beam, and my back foot is a smidge to the left of where it ought to be. That's all it takes for the salto that was supposed to usher me onto the US Women's Gymnastics Team to become the salto that ends my career and throws me into another life completely.

A moment of hesitation, a sliver of fear, a quarter inch in the wrong direction, and everything changes.

I've learned nothing since.

But maybe I can start.

When the video ends, I turn off the TV and stare at my phone. Once I send this message, I can't take it back. Jo won't let me.

I fumble with one of my unicorn earrings and think of Ollie. I can't let hesitation and fear take anything else from me. I pick up the phone and tap out a text to Jo.

Send me your therapist's number. No, I don't want to talk about it. Yes, I can feel your gloating from here.

My thumb hovers over the send button.

Just get it over with, the voice in my head says. I don't know how it can be so helpful at times and yet utterly destructive at others, but I guess I'm going to find out.

25

~~~~~

October

Carla, my therapist, flicks on a white-noise machine by the door and settles into the chair across from me.

"How are you, Nina?" she says.

It's our fourth session together. The first three were painfully awkward. Every time I pull into the parking lot for therapy, I consider downloading a voice changer app so I can pretend to be someone else and call the office to tell Carla that I've died and am no longer in need of her services. It's not Carla. She's fine. Therapy isn't at all what I expected. I haven't been asked to recount my earliest childhood memory. She doesn't ask *And how does that make you feel?* after everything I say.

Even though I like Carla, I can't seem to open up. When she asked why I was seeking therapy during our first session, I panicked and said I was having a midlife crisis.

Carla glanced at the paperwork in front of her and raised an eyebrow. "You're thirty-three, right?"

"It's an early midlife crisis," I said.

"Can you tell me more about this crisis?"

"It's nothing, really. I'm just . . . bored."

Carla asked what I meant by that, but I managed to move the conversation from boredom to board games, and despite her best attempts to coax me back around to why I was there, my verbal gymnastic skills are even better than my actual gymnastic skills used to be. I'm not sure how therapy is supposed to work, but I'm pretty sure avoiding all of Carla's more probing questions by talking about thrifting is not it.

Today I straighten in the plush armchair, fidgeting with a unicorn earring as I brace myself for Carla to jump right in and ask me about my boredom again. The only way I force myself from the car and into this chair each week is by thinking of Ollie. I imagine seeing him at Jo's wedding, and him asking me what I want, what I see our life being, just like he had that day at Cork Harbour.

If I stand a chance of getting him back, I need to know the answer.

Every week I promise myself that *this* time I'll do the work. I'll spill my guts.

And every week I talk about nothing until my hour is up.

"I like your earrings," Carla says.

My fidgeting stills. I drop my hand into my lap. "Thank you."

"I've noticed you wear them to every session. Do you wear them every day?"

"They're my signature item," I say. "I only take them off to shower and sleep."

"They're cute." Carla drops her gaze to the notebook in her lap. "Where'd you get them?"

"A friend gave them to me a long time ago."

"How long ago?"

I sigh. "Oh, I don't know. Ten years?"

"They must be a good friend if you still wear them every day after all these years."

"I don't think we're friends anymore," I say. "Sometimes I wonder if we were ever just friends at all."

Carla doesn't say anything, but I feel her watching me. She's probably worried about scaring me off. The worry isn't unfounded. This is the most vulnerable thing I've said to her in nearly a month of therapy.

The moment of silence stretches on. It's as if I've dipped my toe into freezing water and am waiting to adjust to the temperature before submerging the next body part.

Perhaps that's how change happens. Dip in a toe. Work your way up to a foot. A calf. And eventually, you're able to submerge yourself completely. Maybe a moment of bravery is as powerful as a moment of hesitation. Maybe it's enough to change the course of my life.

"What's your friend's name?" Carla asks.

When I turn to the window, one of the earrings grazes my cheek. "Oliver," I say. "But he doesn't like it when I call him that."

26

November

Two weeks before Jo and Alex's wedding, I linger at work once the guests are gone, then make my way up to the wheelhouse and knock on the door.

"Come on in," Xav calls.

I clutch the paper I'm holding tighter, trying to keep my hands from shaking, but it's no use. Instead of the voice in my head, I hear Carla's telling me to ground myself. I pause before stepping inside. I notice . . . my reflection in the door handle. I hear . . . whatever awful music RJ is playing out on deck. I smell . . . the ocean.

"Hello?" Xav calls.

I'm calm enough to open the door. I know this is what I need to do, but that doesn't make it any easier. Nothing I've done over the last three months has been easy. With Carla's help, I've picked through the junk I've been carrying around inside me for years, finally clearing enough space to loosen my grip on my current life and, for the first time, consider what other possibilities are out there. Every morning when I wake up, I think of those questions Ollie asked me and try to answer them. At first I didn't know what I wanted other than Ollie, which was a given. Every therapy session I open up a little more. About gymnastics. About my parents. About Ollie. About all of it.

A few weeks ago, I woke up and had my answer. I could see a picture of the life I wanted in my mind. It isn't complete or finished, but the life I want is vibrant, full of possibility and risk. It excites me.

I don't know if it will be enough for Ollie to give me another chance. I don't deserve one.

Carla helped me make a list of all the changes I wanted to make—big and small alike. The big ones were the hardest, of course. I didn't renew the lease on my apartment. I downsized my belongings to three suitcases. I sold my car. I bought a one-way ticket to Ireland for two days after Jo and Alex's wedding. But this . . . this paper in my hands is the last big thing. It's also the hardest.

"What's wrong?" Xav says as soon as I step inside the wheelhouse. He sits at the table in the corner of the room. It's where we've had countless preference sheet meetings, where he's lectured me a thousand times, where he's passed me a cup of coffee and asked how I was doing, just to check in.

It's where I first saw Xav on the day I boarded this boat and begged him for a job.

"I don't think anything's wrong." I take the seat across from him. My toes still hang off the floor, but it doesn't bother me like it did the first time I sat here. I slide the paper in my hands across the table. When Xav glances down at it, my life feels like a glass room, mirrored moments wink at me from all over.

Xav sighs as he looks over the paper. We've been friends for a long time, but I still can't predict what he will say or do. Especially when it's something like this. Something unprecedented.

He lifts his head. "You're sure about this?"

"I don't *feel* sure," I say, giving him a weak smile. "But it's time."

He runs a hand over his beard. "You're really going to hand chief stewardess over to Britt?"

"She's not so bad."

"Never thought I'd hear you say that."

I laugh. "She can't keep her bunk clean to save her life, but she's a great stewardess."

"I hate to say I told you so."

"No, you don't."

"Yeah, you're right."

I lean toward him over the table. "You know who else is a great stewardess?"

"Jo Walker."

I roll my eyes. "Yes, but that's not who I'm talking about."

He raises an eyebrow. "Go on."

"Nekesa. I ran into her a few days ago and happen to know she is sick of making upside-down caramel macchiatos."

Xav's smile is barely visible beneath his beard. "Sounds like I need to give Ms. Nekesa a call." He folds my resignation letter into a square and tucks it into his shirt pocket. He leans back into his seat and settles his gaze on me again. "I'm proud of you."

"Don't get all sappy on me, you senile old man." I fold my hands on the table in front of me, squeezing them together to keep them from trembling. Saying goodbye to Xav and the *Serendipity*, the very things that saved me when I needed them most, doesn't *feel* right, even though I know it is.

Xav smiles. Thankfully, he doesn't bring up the tears I've failed to hold back. "So," he says. "What's next for you, kiddo?"

"I'm not sure," I say. "But I have a lot of ideas."

27

~~~~~~

December

The night before Jo and Alex's wedding, I curl up beside Jo on her couch and tuck my feet beneath her butt as we watch TV.

The last two weeks have been a whirlwind of wedding-related activities. Though the wedding will be small and simple, I've spent most evenings at Serendipitous, hogging a table in the back with Greyson and making decorations for the reception. Jo and Alex stopped by to help whenever they weren't working, though I could tell Jo was skeptical about the need for decorations in the first place. *It's your wedding, Josephine,* I'd told her. *Not some geriatric anniversary party at an Applebee's. Decor is a must.*

Earlier, Jo's condo was bustling with activity: Jo's family, which included her sister, nieces, and ex-brother-in-law, came by for dinner. Britt stopped by too, as well as Jo's elderly neighbor Belva. I brought my overnight bag and a pitcher of Drunken Joeys, Jo's signature cocktail. As I sat there in Jo's condo, surrounded by all that laughter and excitement, it was the first time I'd truly felt okay in months. The first time I could see Jo's future and feel more happiness than loss. *Thank you, therapy.*

The condo is quiet now. Everyone else left for home or their hotel a few hours ago so Jo could get her "beauty sleep," as if she needs it. Neither of us is tired, though it's nearly midnight.

"Beth could've stayed, you know," I say as another episode of some awful reality show Jo likes begins. "I can share you. I don't *like* it, but I have to get used to it, I suppose."

"That's good to hear, but the truth is, I didn't feel like sharing *you*," Jo says. If she weren't sitting on my feet, I'd smother her in a rib cage–cracking hug.

Jo turns her phone over in her hands. She and Alex haven't seen each other today, but she's been grinning at her phone nonstop, eyes flicking out the window to gaze across the parking lot to the opposite building where Alex and Greyson live.

"Oh my God, Josephine," I say when she smiles at her phone again and taps out a quick text. "Go in another room if you're going to sext your fiancé. It's grossing me out."

Jo smacks my shoulder. "I'm not *sexting* him, Nina!"

"I don't believe you. That right there is a sexting face."

She gives me an exasperated look. "It is not! This is just my usual face!"

"Nope. That's your sexting face."

"I don't *have* a sexting face! Even if I did, why would *you* know what it looks like?"

I hold out my hand. "Come on, give it here."

She narrows her eyes. "I thought you were grossed out by sexting."

"I'm not grossed out by sexting. I'm grossed out by the thought of *Alex* sexting."

"He's *not* sexting me!" Jo says, and slaps her phone into my palm.

"I'm scared to look at this," I say, and Jo rolls her eyes.

I'm just messing with her, but when I glance down at the screen, what I see is even *worse* than sexting. "No," I say, and cover my eyes with a hand. "Josephine, tell me this is a prank."

Jo hurls a couch pillow at my face. "You're being a butthead," she says.

I uncover my eyes. "Love poems?"

Jo's cheeks turn pink. "They're songs, actually."

It's so sweet that I'm positive a bit of sugar would actually kill me right now. I double over on the couch and pretend to dry heave. "You're making it so much worse. Stop."

"I can call Alex and have him come over. I'm sure he'd serenade me in person, especially if he knows it'll annoy you."

"Too late. It's midnight. You can't see each other until the wedding. It's bad luck."

She rolls her eyes. "You know I don't believe in luck."

"How can you even say that? You own a restaurant called Serendipitous."

"That's different! Fate isn't the same as luck."

I gape at her. "Wait. Are you saying you believe in fate now? Since when?"

She shrugs. "I don't know. I guess I've come around to the idea."

A notification lights up her phone. The sight of Ollie's name makes whatever reply I had fall right out of my head. The message is nothing exciting, but it's the most Ollie thing I've ever seen.

Fecking Miami and its fecking traffic.

"What?" Jo says. She leans forward, eyebrows raised in alarm. "Please don't tell me he's actually sexting me now."

I shake my head and pass her the phone. She glances at the screen, then looks at me. "I know where he's staying. We can go over there now."

"No way." I burrow deeper into the couch. "I can wait. It's your big day."

"I really don't mind!"

"Nope! Trust me, Josephine, nothing good happens after midnight."

"Is this another luck thing?"

I laugh. "It's an experience thing. Besides, I don't want to be all mopey at your wedding if things don't go well."

"All right," Jo says. We turn back to the TV, but I don't take any of it in. *Ollie's here*, I think. I wonder what he's doing. If he's thinking about me.

Jo looks me over. "You okay?"

"I think so."

"Do you know what you're going to say?"

"Yup."

"I think it'll work," she says.

"You're biased."

She shrugs. "So's he."

"Hopefully in the right direction."

"He is," Jo says. "How are things with your parents, by the way?"

I sigh. "They're okay, I think. We still talk, but I told them I need some time before I start visiting with them again. It's too hard to be around them right now . . . I just . . . panic. I'm working on not letting their problems affect how I feel about everything in my own life. I *know* that if Ollie and I work things out, we won't be like them, but it's still hard to see."

Jo sits up and turns to face me. "You really have changed, you know. You're so much more . . . open."

"You don't miss the old me?"

She scoots closer and rests her head on my shoulder. "There is no old you, Nina. This is the person you've always been. You're just . . . more here. I get more of you now. How could I miss the way things used to be?"

"The jokes were better when I was emotionally constipated," I say.

Jo laughs. "I don't know, I think they're still pretty good."

"Oh, Josephine. I really ought to kidnap you. I'll force you to write a letter saying you've gotten cold feet, but really you'll be my hostage in some abandoned Irish castle. No one will suspect a thing."

Jo snorts. "If I'm ever kidnapped, everyone will know it was you. Except maybe Greyson. She'd think it was aliens."

"Maybe we'll get lucky and aliens will kidnap both of us."

"Grey would be so jealous. We can't do that to her."

"Yeah," I sigh, "I guess you're right. There goes my last escape route."

"You don't need one," she says. "Everything will be fine, even if it's not."

I hope she's right. Jo and I have been through it all. Who knows if the worst is behind us or not? Instead of everything that can go wrong, I think of all we've overcome and how much possibility is ahead.

Everything is about to change. In what way, I'm not fully sure. But it doesn't feel like a storm out there on the horizon.

It feels like a sunrise.

The next morning, I'm squeezed in between Britt and Jo's nieces on the couch as Jo's sister helps her into her wedding dress.

"I don't see why Greyson can't be here," says Kitty, who is fifteen. She turns around on the couch to peek through the blinds and out into the condo parking lot.

Her older sister, Mia, who is newly eighteen, smacks Kitty's hand from the blinds. "Quit it, dingus. It's bad luck if Alex sees."

"Alex's condo is across the parking lot. There's no way he could see her through a crack in the blinds, even if he *tried*," Kitty replies.

"Girls." Beth, Jo's sister, shoots them a glare. "Tone it down."

"Believe it or not, Greyson wanted to be with her dad today," Jo says.

"I wonder what they're doing over there." Kitty peeks through the blinds again, which earns her another smack on the hand from her sister.

Britt sips a mimosa and shovels dry cereal into her mouth like it's popcorn, clearly enjoying the sisterly drama.

Jo turns to face us. "What do you think?" she says. Her dress, a simple spaghetti-strap fit-and-flare gown, has no right looking as good on her as it does. I take full credit for finding it. As soon as Jo got engaged, I told Butch to put aside any wedding dresses that came in for me. Jo said I was ridiculous, but when she tried this one on, there was no question about it. It was perfect.

"I think I'm going to cry," I say.

"Please don't," Jo says, her voice wobbly. She looks away to smooth her hands down the front of her dress.

Once the excitement over the dress has died down, I disappear into the kitchen to get a mimosa before Britt finishes off the pitcher.

Jo follows me into the kitchen. "You okay?"

"I'm marvelous, babe. As marvelous as you look, which is a lot." I raise my glass to her and take another sip of my mimosa.

"You look marvelous too," Jo says. "You're the only person I know who can pull off that shade of pink."

"It's *salmon*," I say. The guest list for the wedding is so small it didn't make sense to have a bridal party, but I bought a bridesmaid dress anyway—a vintage floor-length gown with a high neck and drapey sleeves I found on Craigslist.

"You also look . . . stressed," Jo says.

I twirl the glass in my hand. "Oh yes. I'm that too. It's a big day. I'm happy for you, but I also feel like I'm about to have an organ removed."

Jo rests her head against the fridge. "Want to know a secret?"

"Stop that!" I fuss, forcing her to straighten up. "You'll ruin your hair. But yes, I want to know all your secrets. Especially the really dark ones."

Jo settles a soft smile on me, one that breaks my heart. "I feel a little bit like I'm having an organ removed too."

"Really?"

"Yup."

"Which one?"

She scrunches her nose in thought. "A kidney?"

"Good choice," I say, and boop her on the nose. "A bigger deal than an appendix, but survivable. Will you promise me something?"

"Depends," Jo says. A wise answer, given I have asked for her to promise me many ridiculous things over the years.

"I know Alex is your next of kin and all. But you promise you'll haunt me first when you kick the bucket?"

Jo doesn't even hesitate. "Of course. Alex doesn't even believe in ghosts."

We grin at each other for a moment, and then Jo sighs. "He's right across the parking lot," she says, and I know we're talking about Ollie now, not Alex. "Are you sure you don't want to talk to him before the ceremony? You don't have to wait here with me."

"I'm starting to think you're more anxious about me and Ollie than I am. In fact, I think you're more anxious about me and Ollie than you are about the fact that you are getting *married* in . . ." I glance at the time on Jo's microwave. "Shit! Five minutes. So as much as I'd love to get this over with, I really don't think there's time. Patience, dear Josephine."

I chug the rest of my mimosa and shoo her from the kitchen.

"All right, people," I say. "It's showtime."

28

~~~~~~

The ceremony takes place on the condo's private beach. Alex and his family and friends are already up there waiting. As we walk down the breezeway, the atmosphere is joyous and casual. It doesn't feel like we're going to a wedding. Jo and I never went to school together, but I feel like a teenager walking down the halls between classes, arm in arm with my best friend.

There's no procession, but I slip my arm from Jo's and hand her off to her sister and Mark, her sister's ex, who's the closest thing Jo has to a father figure, right as we near the gate that leads to the beach. Ahead is the small flower-adorned arch that marks where the ceremony will take place.

There are fewer than twenty guests, including the bride and groom. As I trudge across the sand with the others, I search for Ollie and find him standing beside Alex. He looks completely unchanged, as lovely as ever in a white button-down and cropped gray pants that fit him so well I might pass out here on the sand. The wind ruffles his hair in the morning light, putting every hue on display—from blond to gold to bronze. He laughs as he talks with Alex, and the sight of it is beautiful and painful all at once. I'm happy that Ollie is happy, but I'm also ter-rified. What if he's happier without me? What if this is the last time I'll ever see him? What if everything I've done is for nothing?

No. Not nothing, I remind myself. I'm becoming the person I want to be. It just so happens that becoming the person I want to be means hopefully becoming someone who can truly love Ollie and be loved by him in return. But with or without him, I am moving on. No matter what happens, I'll be okay.

Alex's daughter, Greyson, catches sight of me. She elbows Ollie, and when he looks up and spots me, his laughing expression fades. I'm not sure how to interpret the look that takes its place. He gives me a small nod before looking away. I don't try to figure out what it means as I circle around the wedding arch with the others to watch Jo make her way down the beach with Mark and Beth.

The ceremony is simple, but I cry the entire time. Alex's parents are folk singers and play a song they wrote especially for the occasion. Xav, the officiant, cracks a few one-liners, but I can tell he's struggling not to get choked up. It's no use, though, because Jo and Alex wrote their own vows, and no one can remain dry-eyed through them.

"Alex," Jo begins. "Hot Yacht Chef," she adds, which makes every-one laugh. "When we met, my world was so small. You walked into my life at the worst possible time." She pauses to take a deep breath, giv-ing Alex a watery smile that has me seconds away from ugly sobbing. "You asked me once if I believed in fate. I didn't. Not then, anyway. But fate didn't care if I believed in it or not. It kept throwing you in my way—at Mitch's, the condo, at work. It gave me exactly what I needed. *You* were exactly what I needed. Before I met you, I never knew how big my life could be . . ."

I wonder what Ollie makes of all this. When I turn to look, I find he's already watching me. When his eyes meet mine, I freeze, and before I can smile, or nod, or raise an eyebrow, he turns away, returning his focus to Alex and Jo again. His thoughts have never been more impenetrable.

After the ceremony, our little party disperses for the reception, which will take place at Jo and Alex's restaurant. I lose sight of Ollie but don't go looking for him. I'll wait until the reception. It'll probably be better to have a few drinks in me before I find him and ask him to talk.

I head in the direction of Jo's condo, where I need to grab a few things to drive over to the reception. As I walk down the breezeway, I rehearse everything I want to say to Ollie in my head.

"Wait up! I'm coming with you," a voice hollers after me.

"Me too!" a second says.

"Shotgun!" cries a third.

I'm suddenly flanked by teenagers. Mia, Kitty, and Greyson look so grown-up in their dresses. They're chattering a mile a minute, the conversation swirling around me so fast I can hardly keep up.

"Who says any of you is invited to ride with me?" But truthfully I don't mind. It would be more entertaining than driving alone.

"I'm riding with you even if it means sneaking into the trunk," Greyson says. "No way I'm getting stuck in the man van with Dad and Jo." She bounces up and down as she walks alongside me. "Nina! Do you think I can live with you for a few months? Just until they get over the honeymoon phase?"

"Absolutely not," I say. "Not that I don't think you'd be an excellent roommate, but I'm . . . in between places at the moment."

"Are you homeless?"

"Technically, yes," I say.

"We can live in your car," Greyson says. "It'll be great. You can take the back seat. I don't need much room."

"As lovely as that sounds, I've sold my car," I say.

We step into Jo's condo. A minute later, Jo's sister opens the door and pokes her head in. "Are these three bothering you?"

"Always. But it's all right. They want to ride with me over to the restaurant," I say.

Beth glares at the three of them. "Nice try, girls, but you're not getting out of photos. Get back up that beach right now."

Greyson and Kitty groan, but Mia laughs. "Told you it would never work. C'mon, let's go pose like the good little nieces we are."

"I'm not a niece!" Greyson says.

"You're *my* niece now," Beth says.

"Oh my God!" Kitty's eyes widen and she grabs Greyson by the arm. "We're cousins. How weird is that?"

"Zero percent weird," Greyson says. "Everything is right in the universe."

By the time Beth gets the girls to leave the apartment for family photos, the other guests have already left for the restaurant. I load the two boxes I need to bring with me into the trunk of my rental car before doing a final sweep of Jo's condo to make sure I haven't missed anything. When I step back into the parking lot, I spot Ollie staring at his phone from where he sits on the ground beside Alex's unit.

My pulse races, heart skipping away as if running toward a springboard. *Now*, the voice in my head says. I walk right past my rental and cross the parking lot.

Ollie doesn't notice me at first. He's frowning at his phone. The groove between his brows deepens as he swears at it.

"Need a ride?" I say when I stop in front of him.

Ollie lifts his head in surprise, and the wrinkle fades a bit when he sees me. "Nina."

"Hi."

"Hi," he says.

"Do you need a ride?" I say. "Or are you planning to sit here all day?"

Ollie frowns at his phone again. "This fecking thing. My roaming sucks, and I don't know Alex or Jo's Wi-Fi passwords. Can't even get a fecking Uber," he says.

"Sounds like a yes to me. Come on."

I don't wait to see if he'll come. I turn and start toward the car, hoping he will. Ollie sighs, and I am both relieved and even more terrified when I hear his footsteps behind me. I hope he can't sense how nervous I am. All the things I want to say run wild in my mind. It's like a goddamn toddler tumbling class in there.

We're silent as we get into the car. Silent as we click our seat belts into place and I pull out of the parking lot and onto South Ocean Boulevard. If he wonders why I'm not driving my convertible, he doesn't ask. The silence is unbearable. Awkward. There's so much I want to ask. How is he? How's the pub? Does he still like it in Ireland? Does he regret it? Does he miss me? Does he still love me?

One mile. Then two. My mind flits to the things I have in the center console of the car. Right there between us. We still haven't spoken a word when the restaurant comes into view. I park in an empty spot and cut the engine. Ollie mutters a thank-you and undoes his seat belt. I panic, realizing this might be the only moment I can get alone with him.

"Wait!" I say. I wrench open the center console and gather into my hands everything I have inside it.

Ollie's hand stills on the passenger door.

"You were right." One of the papers in my hands slips loose. "Shit," I say, fumbling to grab it and put it back with the others.

"Right about what?" Ollie says.

"Everything."

Ollie eyes me skeptically. I get it. It's not every day I go around telling people they're right about anything, let alone *everything*, especially him.

"When I went to see you in Ireland, you said things wouldn't be different. You said I hadn't really changed. That I didn't really want a life with you because I hadn't even thought about it. You were right."

Ollie narrows his eyes. "Jesus, if all you wanted was to tell me I was right about that, I would've rather you just—"

"No!" I say. "That's not . . . I'm not saying this right." My hands are shaking. Everything is coming out all wrong. It doesn't matter how many times I've played through this conversation in my head, the reality of it is so much more complicated and terrifying than I had imagined. "What I mean is I couldn't really want a life with you because I couldn't even imagine what it would look like. I couldn't imagine anything for my life other than what it already was. I hadn't changed at all, like you said. But I have now. I know exactly what I want, and I want to be with you, Ollie. For real. I *want* to change. I need to. I've already begun."

Ollie opens his mouth to speak, but I cut him off. "Wait, please." I shuffle through the papers in my hands, but I'm so nervous I can't take in what's in front of me. "Oh shit. I had this whole speech, but it seems so wrong now, and I can't remember most of it anyway . . . Right! Here!"

I find the paper I'm looking for and pass it into his hands. "See? I mean it."

He takes the paper in his hands. He skims it and pauses, his gaze flicking up to meet mine. "You gave up your apartment?"

"Yup. And there's this . . ." I pass him another paper.

"You sold the car," he says.

I hand him a stack of papers next, and Ollie glances over them, confused. "What is—"

"Bills," I say. "For therapy."

He raises an eyebrow. "You're telling me that you, Nina Lejeune, have gone to this much therapy?"

I nod, gaze returning to the two papers left in my hands. "And . . . there's this," I say, passing one over.

Ollie sets it on top of the others. The skepticism on his face turns into something else as he reads it.

"Is this . . ."

"My resignation letter."

"You're quitting the boat?"

"I already did. I am no longer chief stewardess of the *Serendipity*. Britt is, believe it or not. And—"

"Why?"

I stare at him. "Why what?"

"Why did you do all this?"

I look at the last paper in my hands, my one-way ticket to Ireland, and hold it out to him.

"Because you were right," I say. "I didn't want the life I had at all. I was just too afraid to change it because even if I wasn't happy, I was safe. But it didn't matter how safe I was. I lost the thing that mattered most."

He runs a hand through his hair. "What—"

"You, Oliver Dunne," I say. "You're the thing that mattered most."

He glances out the windshield, clearly distressed. "Jesus, Nina, I didn't want you to give up your life. I never asked for that."

"I know. That's not what this is. I'm simply letting go of all the things that are holding me back, and I'm hoping it'll be enough for me to deserve you."

"That's the most fecking ridiculous thing I've ever heard, Neen." He shakes his head. His expression is torn. He looks like he wants to believe all this means I've changed but isn't sure he should. "None of this has been about deserving me. It's not like I'm some catch."

"That's not true." I put a hand on his cheek, a spark of hope coursing through me when he doesn't pull away.

"When I saw you in Ireland, you asked me what I wanted," I say. Touching him is so delightful, I take his face between both hands. "I didn't have an answer for you before, but I do now."

"And what's that?" Ollie says, his voice barely above a whisper.

I run my fingers through his hair. "I want you, first of all. I hope that's obvious. I want you to withdraw the divorce petition, which I haven't responded to, by the way. I want to be your wife, and I want everyone to know it. I want to be my own boss and start a party-planning business. Oh! Right. I forgot. I want to move to Ireland. I want to live in Cobh with you. There's a gorgeous little three-bedroom I think is in our budget. I can send you the listing, if you like. I want to learn everything there is to know about the *Titanic* and any local ghosts and/or unsolved murders. I want to have a baby, sooner rather than later, and give it the most Irish name possible. But only if it's a boy. A girl would be named Josephine, obviously, but we can call her Josie to avoid any confusion. I'm partial to Ciaran for a boy but am open to negotiations." Ollie laughs, and I can see it, all of it, the life I want, right there in front of me, starting with this man whose face is in my hands. "How does that sound to you?"

"I—"

"Oh! And I forgot to say I'm sorry. For . . . pushing you away, and not hearing you about what you needed. I'm sorry it took me so long to tell you I love you, but I do love you, Ollie. I have the whole time. There hasn't been a single day I haven't loved you."

"Nina—"

"If you don't love me back anymore, if it's really over, I understand. I don't deserve another chance—"

"Nina—"

"I mean, it would be the biggest fucking loss of my entire life, but I can survive it, so I don't want you to feel like you have to—"

Before I can finish my sentence, Ollie leans forward and kisses me hard, knocking the thought right out of my head. We've shared more kisses than I can count over the years, but this one is different. I'm not sure if it's the kiss itself or me. I'm different. A person who can give everything, who can take a chance on love, on *herself*, even though she's absolutely terrified.

When Ollie pulls away, I blink at him, kissed into a daze.

"Jesus, wife, is that the only way to shut you up?"

Wife. The word skips through me like it did months before, but this time there's no fear, only light. "I want to be offended," I say.

"Did you mean all that?" he says, flicking at one of my unicorn earrings. "You know, moving to Ireland and the baby stuff?"

"Of course. I'd never joke about naming another human after my best friend."

Ollie rolls his eyes. "You know what I'm asking, kitten."

"Yes," I say, and hold his gaze. "I mean it. How does all that sound to you?"

Ollie rests his forehead against mine. "It sounds fecking perfect."

29

〜〜〜

Six months later, June

"There you are," Jo says when she finds me inside Mitch's at our usual table beside the bookcase. She scoots into the booth across from me and slides a margarita my way. "One more before you abandon me again?"

"You sound like an old man," I say. My fingers dance across the bottom of the margarita glass. "Ollie's already getting me a drink." I'm not lying, but my heart starts cartwheeling around anyway.

Jo gives me a suspicious look and takes a sip from her drink. "I've never seen you turn down a free margarita just because you've already got one coming."

"And what do you mean before I abandon you again?" I say. "It's just Ireland!"

Jo sighs. "I'm just glad you and Ollie were able to visit. The three months since I visited you have been the longest of my life. I'm fine, but I'm miserable without you. I'm not trying to make you feel guilty about leaving me forever, by the way."

"Forever? Listen to you, Josephine! You're really putting on the drama." I lean toward her over the table. "I have to say, I love it."

"Love what?" Ollie says when he arrives at the table with Alex beside him.

"You, of course. And Jo," I add. I squint at Alex. "Not sure about you."

"You love me, Nina," Alex says. He joins Jo on the other side of the table. "Don't be embarrassed by it."

"Mm, I think I should be embarrassed by it, though."

Ollie passes me a drink before scooting into the booth and slinging his arm around my shoulders.

I slide the margarita Jo brought me to Ollie. "Here, you look like you need one last Mitch's margarita."

"I don't even . . ." he begins, but I widen my eyes at him, and he changes gears, "know how to say no to that," he finishes. He takes a drink of the margarita, admirably trying not to grimace.

Jo raises an eyebrow, but before she can say anything, I cut her off. "We really ought to pat ourselves on the back, Josephine," I say.

"Why's that?"

"We've both acquired dutiful margarita-bringing husbands," I say.

Jo clinks her glass to mine. Ollie and Alex look at each other and sigh.

I take a sip of the margarita Ollie's brought me, but when I set it on the table, Jo snatches it and pulls it to herself.

"Josephine!"

She sniffs my drink, her eyes narrowed as she stares at me and takes a sip. She slowly lowers it onto the table. "Nina!"

Alex looks from me to Jo, completely lost. I feel Ollie trying not to laugh beside me.

"Anyway," I say before Jo can utter another word. "As I was saying before, it's just Ireland. And it's not forever. We'll visit you. And *you* will visit me."

"Nina," Jo says again. I'm fairly certain she's gone into shock.

"I was thinking early December might be a good time," I say.

"Nina!" Jo says. She's practically shouting now. She gets to her feet, but it's awkward since she's in the booth still, so she sits down again. She takes a sip from my margarita and makes a face when she realizes it isn't hers.

Ollie can't hold in his laughter anymore. He's practically doubled over on the table, laughing so hard tears stream down his face.

Alex, Lord bless him, looks at all three of us in turn, completely bewildered. He turns to Jo. "What's going on?" But when she doesn't answer and shouts my name again instead, he turns to me. "Did you break her? What's going on?"

I roll my eyes. "My God, Alex, it's like you've never even had a baby," I say.

"A . . ." He stares at me, then Jo, then Ollie. "You didn't."

"I most certainly did," Ollie says.

The two of them laugh when Alex holds out his hand and Ollie shakes it.

"You two disgust me," I say. "I'm nauseous enough as it is."

"Nina!" Jo shouts again.

"Josephine!" I shout back.

She stares at me for a moment, then says, in a disturbingly calm voice. "How far along are you?"

"Twelve weeks."

Jo squints as if doing math in her head. "Did you get knocked up when I came to visit you?"

I take a sip of my drink. "It's possible."

"Was I *literally* in the *next room* when you made that baby?" she says, pointing at my stomach. "Actually, don't answer that. I'd rather not know. To tell you the truth, I'm torn over whether I ought to be weirded out or honored."

"Weirded out," Alex says at the same time Ollie and I say, "Honored."

Jo takes her straw from her glass and points it at me. "And to think *you* accused *me* of having a secret fetus!"

I look down into my drink and stir my mock margarita with my straw. "And how do you feel about this secret fetus?"

"How do I feel about it?" Jo says. "How do I feel about *you*, my best friend, having a secret fetus?"

"Technically, it's not a secret anymore," Alex says. Jo and I look away from each other to glare at him, and he holds up his hands in surrender.

"Nina," Jo says, stretching her hand across the table to take hold of mine. "How could I feel anything but really fucking happy?"

"Thank God," I say. I give her hand a squeeze. "I have a feeling it would be really awkward to have a baby you hate named after you."

After we talk about the baby and life in Ireland so much that we've run out of things to say, I catch sight of the photo of me, Ollie, and Jo stapled to the wall.

"Still here." I sigh.

Jo follows my gaze to the photo and laughs. "I thought you stole it!"

"I did. But I put it back before we set sail for charter season. Didn't replace the money, though. Figure Mitch has enough grimy old dollars."

"What money?" Jo says, but then she holds up a hand. "Never mind. I don't want to know."

I reach out and rip the photo from the wall.

Jo's eyes widen. "What the—"

"Souvenir," I say, waving the photo at her before tucking it into my bra. I rummage around in my purse and pull out the mini stapler and Polaroid camera I always keep on hand.

"What are you up to, kitten?" Ollie asks.

"Well, I've got to replace it!" I say. "Alex wasn't even in that one!"

Alex slaps a hand over his heart. "You do love me!"

"Don't be ridiculous," I say. "I just love your cheese Danish."

Ollie waves down another patron to take a photo of the four of us. Once it's developed, I staple it to the wall and lean back to take in my work. "There," I say. "That ought to freshen up the place."

Jo sighs. She grabs my hand from across the table and kicks off the weepy goodbyes when she says, "I can't believe you're leaving me *again*."

We cry at the table, then move through Mitch's before lingering in the parking lot. Finally, Jo and I manage to pull away from each other and get into our own cars. I'm too weepy to drive, and though I am the designated driver by default, Ollie, anticipating exactly this, hardly drank at all and slides into the driver's seat. "Are you all right, kitten?" he says.

I find a tissue in the glove box of our rental car and dab at my eyes. When I look at Ollie, I see the hesitation on his face. The poor soul, everything I've put him through—he's worried I regret leaving.

I take his hand in mine. "I'm wonderful, Oliver. I'm excited."

He raises an eyebrow. "You are? Coming back doesn't make you wish you'd stayed?"

I press his hand against my cheek. "Not at all. I have a new job. New home. New baby. New adventures. Same old husband, though. Think I should upgrade?"

When Ollie laughs, his dimples appear, and I have to squeeze his hand to keep from leaning over to bite them.

"I've got something for you," Ollie says.

"What's the occasion?"

"Dunno," he says, pulling his hand from mine to reach into the pocket of his jeans. "Do I need an occasion to give my wife a gift?"

"Absolutely not. I *am* the occasion."

Ollie grins and pulls his hand from his pocket, bringing with it a delicate gold chain and medal. I take it in my hands, tracing my finger over the image of Saint Valentine on one side before turning it over to trace the inscription on the other.

"I'd have given it to you sooner, but I got the chain from Butch. It's vintage. Picked it up yesterday."

"It's lovely," I say. "Won't it feel weird to not have the medal in your pocket anymore?"

"Nah," he says. "It'll be exactly where it belongs."

"Help a girl out." I pass him the medal and turn around. Ollie's fingers warm my skin when he puts the chain around my neck. I think of our wedding day and how I felt when he helped unzip my dress. I want to laugh at the memory. How could I have been so clueless to think there was nothing between us? Once the necklace is fastened, Ollie's hands find my shoulders, and he leans forward to kiss the back of my neck.

"How do I look?" I say, turning to face him again.

"You look marvelous, Nina Lejeune."

"Nina Lejeune-Dunne," I say.

Ollie shakes his head. "What do you mean?"

"I changed my name."

"No, you didn't."

"Yes, I did."

The look on Ollie's face is something else. Old Nina wants to brush the moment aside and make a joke, to say it's no big deal. But changing my name, adding his to mine—I know that to Ollie, it means something.

He runs a hand through his hair. "Well, fuck me."

"Sure, why not?"

He ignores the comment and turns to me, all excitement. "I'm changing mine too." /

I laugh. "You can't change your name to Nina Lejeune-Dunne. Get your own name."

"Ollie Lejeune-Dunne," he says. "Does it sound too fancy?"

I take his hands in mine, hands I know better than my own, and press a kiss to each. "No," I say. "I think it sounds marvelous."

Acknowledgments

This book was written during the hardest year of my life and would not exist without so many wonderful people.

Wendy Sherman, you are the best literary agent in existence. Kerry Donovan, thank you for getting these characters and this story from the beginning. Special thanks for helping me finally write those two chapters that refused to be written.

Colleen Reinhart and Janelle Barone, thank you for the most beautiful cover I have ever seen in my entire life. Thanks to the rest of my team at Berkley, especially Jessica Mangicaro, Chelsea Pascoe, Christine Legon, Alaina Christensen, and Mary Baker.

Krystal Beaumont and Sasha Frinzl, thank you for reading yet another of my books at its worst and helping make it its best.

Danielle Gillette, reader of every draft, thank you for being my cheer-reader and for that line about the hunky fridge. Emelia Attridge, thank you for the late-night phone calls when I was panicking. Raven Heroux, there's no one I trust more to absolutely drag me in the best way.

To the Berkletes, this journey would be awful lonely without you. I can't believe how lucky I am to have so many amazing author friends.

To the many wonderful authors who blurbed this book: Bridget Morrissey, Abby Jimenez, Kate Clayborn, Sarah Hogle, Freya Sampson,

Elizabeth Everett, Emily Wibberley, Austin Siegemund-Broka, Martha Waters, and anyone else who blurbed it after I turned in my pass pages. Sarah Hogle, another thank-you for introducing me to Glass Animals and for being weird with me. Thanks to Chloe Liese for the voice notes and heart-to-hearts. You are an absolute gem.

To all the lovely booksellers, readers, and reviewers who supported my first book and have continued to support me with this one. Thank you, thank you, thank you. Special thanks to everyone who helped me reveal the cover for this book!

To the Weymouth Center for the Arts and Humanities, the week I spent at the James Boyd House was instrumental in unlocking this book. Thank you for the space, rest, and beauty you provided. I can't wait to come back. (Special thanks to the ghosts at Weymouth for leaving me alone while I was there.)

Here are a few random ones I must include: Dr. Amir Motameni, thanks for keeping my husband alive. Glass Animals, thank you for your music, especially the *Dreamland* album, which was the soundtrack to most of my writing sessions while working on this book. Deja Brew, thanks for existing so I could write when I couldn't work at home. Captain Lee Rosbach, thanks for tweeting with me that one time. Thanks to my therapist, Connie. Our sessions aren't anything like Nina's because I never shut up, but Carla's warmth and kindness is because of yours. To Kevin, Jason, and Virgina from the KVJ Show, thanks for letting me borrow a line from the *Whacked Out News!* jingle. Thanks to Blippi for entertaining my four-year-old so I could get my pass pages done while stuck in quarantine with him.

To my children, Carolina and Nicolas, I love you more than you will ever know. Thanks for being so patient with me.

Always last but never least, my husband, Marco Ruiz: Thank you for supporting me always, but especially with this one. You were so sick when I was working on this, and you still supported me throughout the entire process. You are the most selfless person I have ever met, the one who keeps our family from absolute chaos, and the love of my life. Thank you for understanding me, believing in me, and loving me despite all my flaws. If soul mates exist, you're the closest thing I have to one.

Above all, I give thanks to God, whose goodness and faithfulness sustain me through all things.

KEEP READING FOR AN EXCERPT FROM

Love, Lists, and Fancy Ships

BY SARAH GRUNDER RUIZ,
AVAILABLE NOW!

~~~~~~

The summer I turned thirty started to unravel as soon as it began. It was the last day of charter season, and I was ironing a billionaire's underwear in the laundry room of the *Serendipity*, the superyacht I'd worked on for the last five years, when Nina called for me over the radio.

I set down the iron and unclipped my walkie-talkie from my shorts, kicking aside a pile of dirty sheets from last night's toga party. I'd been on laundry duty all morning, but I didn't mind, seeing as it had gotten me out of earlies—the first shift of the day.

"Jo?" the radio called again. "This is Nina. Do you copy?"

I rolled my eyes, glad she couldn't see me. I knew Nina was worried, given everything that had happened, but she could at least give me a second to respond.

"Go for Jo," I sang into the walkie-talkie.

"We need you in the galley."

"Copy that."

I clipped my radio to my shorts and turned off the iron. Off the boat, Nina was my best friend, but on it she was chief stewardess, aka my boss, meaning she made my life alternately fun and miserable. But over the last three months, ever since the accident, she'd been softer on me, letting me out of earlies because mornings were hardest, not complaining as much as she normally would when I missed a water spot on the faucet in the master bathroom. I was appreciative, but the special treatment made me uncomfortable, and I didn't like how she kept checking up on me. She'd corner me in the crew mess or pass me a drink in a Bahamian bar and ask how I was holding up. *Fine*, I always said, taking a long pull of whatever tropical concoction she'd ordered for me. Was I fine? Nope. Not even close. But that didn't mean I wanted to talk about it, not even with Nina.

Other than the week I'd gone to my sister's house in North Carolina, the last four months of my life had been back-to-back charters in the Bahamas. Every week the cycle repeated: Pick up the guests, cater to their whims—including ironing their ridiculously expensive underwear (we'd googled the brand; who seriously spends $165 on a pair of briefs?!)—drop the guests back at port, flip the boat, enjoy a well-deserved night off, pick up the next guests. It was chaotic, and exhausting, and exactly what I needed. Out here in the middle of the ocean, I could pretend my real life, the one where I drove a car and wore shoes and lived alone, was on hold. But even I had to admit the cabin fever was starting to get to me.

Before Nina could radio me again, I raced up to the main deck and pushed through the galley doors where, as always, chaos was waiting for me.

"There you are!" Nina called, a wrinkle of concern on her brow. She sat at a small table, her fingers nimbly folding a mound of cloth napkins into little sailboats. "We have a beach picnic, remember?"

Beside the pantry stood Britt, third stewardess and my painfully messy bunkmate. Her curly hair shook as she dug through a plastic bin of decor, piling dried starfish, delicate sand dollars, and seashells at her feet. Once I'd asked her how she could be a stewardess and such a slob at the same time. We were essentially maids on fancy boats, after all. Britt replied that she spent so much time cleaning up after other people, she had no energy to pick up after herself.

"Fecking beach picnic," Ollie, the *Serendipity*'s chef, muttered. He whizzed around the galley like a pinball, his Irish accent rising above the hiss of pans on the stove.

"He's having a bad day," Nina said.

I glanced at Ollie, who was now hacking a watermelon to pieces. "When isn't he?"

"Touché." Nina tugged the sail of a napkin turned boat in her hands. Her dangling unicorn earrings, the ones she wore every day, swung back and forth as she looked me over. They were the only sign of the goofy Nina I knew outside of work, a stark contrast to her neat high ponytail and severe expression. Though she was tiny, and at five-two was a couple inches shorter than me, she carried herself with a confidence I doubted I'd ever have. We must have made an amusing pair: petite, dark-haired, intimidating Nina, and me, your nonconfrontational, average-everything blonde.

"What took you so long?" Nina said when I sat beside her. "Find skid marks in the primary's tighty-whities again?"

I swatted a napkin at her. "Why would you put that image in my mind?" Nina didn't usually joke about the primary—the guest who'd booked the charter—but this primary was . . . different.

Nina gave me a tight-lipped smile, then set a sailboat napkin on the table and handed me a checklist of everything we'd need to pack for the beach picnic. "Double- and triple-check it. I don't want another dessert spoon incident."

On my mental list of things that didn't belong on the beach (which included closed-toed shoes, reality TV weddings, and laptops), fancy silverware was one of them. "Because God forbid they eat dessert with any other type of spoon."

Ollie glared at me from where he stood over the sink, running watermelon purée through a strainer. "If I'm spending my entire morning spherizing watermelon, they'll eat it with a fecking dessert spoon now."

"All right, all right, I'll pack the dessert spoons." I held up my hands in surrender and backed away, joining Britt at the pantry, where her pile of seashells was growing larger by the second.

I prodded a seashell with my foot. "The picnic is on a beach, you know. That's why it's called a beach picnic."

Britt turned a conch shell over in her hands. "It's the last one of the season, so it has to be perfect." She sighed and clutched the shell to her chest. "Tell me again about your trip. I want to live vicariously through you. What's first?"

"Paris," I said, dragging a bin of silverware (including dessert spoons) onto the counter. Next month I'd be off to Europe to check off the last five countries for my thirty-by-thirty list—the list of thirty things I wanted to do before my thirtieth birthday at the end of the summer. I still had nine things to go, but hopefully I'd be able to complete them and get some great fodder for the blog I'd started to document my progress.

"And then Spain, right?"

"Barcelona and Madrid," I said. "Then Switzerland, Austria, and Scotland."

Nina joined us, dropping a handful of sailboat napkins onto the counter. "I'm horrified you're not going to Ibiza. That would've been my first port of call."

"I know," I said, inspecting a dessert spoon for water spots. She'd said as much every time I brought up my itinerary. If it weren't for the fact that one of us had to stay and work the day charters over the summer, I would've forced her to come with me.

"And why do you have to live vicariously through Jo?" Nina said to Britt. "Won't you be working Med season and making bank? I can't believe you're abandoning me. Honestly, I may never forgive you."

Britt rolled her eyes. "*Working* in the Mediterranean and vacationing there are two different things. I won't be sleeping in any castles."

Ollie banged a pot on the counter, making us jump. "Could you three shut it? I'm trying to prepare molecular gastronomy for a fecking beach picnic. That primary's a miserable little pox, and if I feck this up, I'm blaming you three for distracting me."

"Aren't chefs supposed to like cooking fancy shit?" Nina said. "Quit complaining and do your job."

Ollie gave her a look that could bleach coral. "Don't eat the head off me, Neen."

Nina dismissed him with a wave. "I swear, I hardly understand you sometimes."

Britt elbowed me and mimed sticking a finger down her throat, making me laugh. There was always some sort of tension between Nina and Ollie. We were never sure if they were about to murder each other or make out. My bet was on both.

"You'll text me if they hook up this summer, won't you? They've got way more drama than *The Bachelor*."

I raised my eyebrows at her. "Who's to say they haven't already?"

Britt gasped. "Josephine Walker, do you know something I don't?"

"Sorry." I zipped my hand across my mouth. "Solemn best friend duties. My lips are sealed."

Nina and Ollie leaned toward each other over the counter, tension sparking between them. (Sexual, or the kind that got you a special on Oxygen, who could say?) I had no idea if they'd hooked up or not. But whatever Nina felt about Ollie, it had to be serious, because she refused to talk about it, and Nina wasn't the sort of person to hold her tongue.

Though Ollie had a habit of complaining about everything, he was right about this: Molecular gastronomy and beach picnics did not go together. Everything about the food he was preparing depended on precise temperatures and chemical reactions, making sand and sun less than ideal. But on a superyacht, the primary got what the primary wanted. And I couldn't wait to get this one off the boat as soon as possible.

It wasn't that I didn't love my job, because I did. I loved the routine of it: stretching sheets taut on the beds, the thud of the lines as they hit the dock, the constant hum of the washer and dryer, planning theme parties and scavenger hunts. Most of our guests were fun and generous people. But our current guests made me wonder if I should've gone to college and found a job that required shoes, offered a 401(k), and had a regular schedule with weekends off.

Our current primary was a Silicon Valley type with a God complex. Last night, after spending the entire week working indoors in the Sky Lounge and complaining about spotty Wi-Fi, he'd chewed me out in front of everyone for not smiling enough during dinner service. *You're coming off a little bitchy, sweetie* were his exact words. What he didn't know was it had been three months to the day since Samson, my eleven-year-old nephew, was struck and killed by a car while riding his bike to a friend's house. I'd spent the entire morning crying—in the laundry room, while scrubbing toilets, as I collected leaves from a nearby island and hot glued them to construction paper to make laurel wreaths for the toga party. So yeah, my smile wasn't at full force. I'd wanted to tell him it takes a bitch to know one, but I liked being employed. Instead, I apologized and imagined all the offensive towel art I could make on his bed but wouldn't.

"Hey, hello? Jo?" Nina said, knocking on my forehead. "Can you check if the guests need a refill on drinks? They're on the sun deck."

I groaned. "Do I have to?"

Nina scowled, so I shut my mouth and marched up the spiral staircase without another word.

Though the laundry room was my true love, the sun deck was a close second. Known as the "party spot," the sun deck had a hot tub that could be converted into a dance floor, several oversized lounge chairs for sunbathing, and stunning panoramic views of the water. Another set of stairs led up to the highest point on the ship, a cushioned area called the bunny pad, where guests (or crew members looking for a moment alone) could escape for the best view on board. Mr. Silicon Valley didn't care about once-in-a-lifetime ocean vistas, however. I found him in the hot tub with his coworkers and their bored girlfriends, all of them staring at their phones.

"Anyone need a refill?" I asked, plastering my brightest smile on my face.

The primary unglued his eyes from his phone. "I'll have a gin fizz. And make sure you shake it long enough this time, Jen."

I almost said, *My name is Jo, jerk face,* but the rest of the crew would kill me if I put our tip in jeopardy, so I contented myself with a "You got it" and an eye roll once I turned away. Fussy drinks for fussy guests, go figure.

Nina and I used to play a game where we'd guess which drinks the guests would order based on our first impressions of them. After a few months, we got scary good at it. Vodka sodas were the favorite of youthful, weight-conscious girlfriends. Whiskey drinkers were contemplative types who stared silently out at the water, but when they did talk, they had the best stories. Winos, on the other hand, talked nonstop. They were the ones who inevitably ordered late-night snacks, meaning we had to shake Ollie awake to make them (we played rock, paper, scissors to see who got stuck with that unpleasant task). But they were also the guests who most frequently invited us to join the fun: dancing with us at theme parties, or requesting we go down the giant inflatable slide behind them or double-bounce them on the floating trampoline. Painkillers were for the flashy new-money types who squeezed every last perk from their trip. The margarita drinkers were my favorite, though. Fun, but not overly complicated, and I'm not only saying that because margaritas are my and Nina's drink of choice.

"Oh, and, sweetie," the primary called out. "These towels are a little damp. Mind getting fresh ones?"

And gin fizz drinkers were the worst of them all. After all that shaking and straining, they were never pleased. I shook his drink with extra vigor, imagining it were his head. I knew those towels were dry when I brought them up. What did a damp towel matter when he would get it soaked with his sopping-wet chest hair anyway?

When I finished making his drink, I stood near the hot tub and waited for his approval. All I got were smacked lips and a "Meh." But what did I expect, a thank-you?

I ran belowdeck to exchange the towels (aka went downstairs, refolded the towels, waited three minutes, and returned with the same towels), then stood behind the bar, watching the primary and his friends take business calls while their girlfriends took dozens of pouty photos. After what felt like an eternity, Nina appeared on the sun deck and joined me by the bar.

"Having fun, Jen?" she asked.

"So much fun," I said, wiping down the already-spotless bar with a damp rag.

Nina and I were peeking at the girlfriends' social media feeds (models, predictably) when my phone vibrated. At the sight of my sister's face on the screen, my chest tightened, and I stared at my phone, unable to move.

Nina squeezed my shoulder. "Take it. I can cover for you."

I nodded and stepped into the Sky Lounge, the phone still vibrating in my hands. Despite the five years between us, my sister and I had always been close. She was more than a sister to me, really. Beth had become the mother ours couldn't be after Dad died, taking me in when I was sixteen. I'd lived with her; her husband, Mark; and their kids for six years, until I moved to Florida at Beth's urging. She'd wanted me to go to college, but I'd ended up bartending instead. But now, my sister had experienced an unspeakable tragedy. We all had. And I had no idea what to do or say to be there for her.

"Joey," Beth said when I answered. "Are you ready?"

I sighed into a sleek white love seat, relieved Beth wasn't already crying. Half our phone calls started with her in tears these days. Out on the sun deck, the primary passed his empty glass to Nina with a grimace. No doubt about it, I was ready for charter season to end.

"I've never been more ready for anything in my life."

"Do you need me to send anything?"

Odd question, but then again, nothing had been normal with Beth lately. "I'd love it if you could send me some sanity. These guests are horrendous."

"I can't make any promises, but I'll see what I can do. I still can't believe he paid almost two hundred bucks for a pair of plain white briefs."

"You don't even want to know what the leopard-print ones cost."

Beth laughed, but it was thin and false, not the throaty cackle I'd always teased her for. I grabbed a nautical-themed pillow from beside me and hugged it to my chest. "How are you? Is everything okay?"

"Yes," Beth said, but her voice wavered. "No, actually. Things between me and Mark aren't great. That's why we need this break."

Break? I squeezed the pillow harder. Mark and Beth on a break? They'd been together since freshman English class in high school.

Then Beth got pregnant their senior year, the year Dad died, and they got married right after graduation. Despite it all, they were the happiest couple I knew, at least until Samson died and the fighting started. But a break? I couldn't fathom it.

"I didn't know things were that bad," I said.

Beth sighed. "We wouldn't need this time alone if they weren't. I wanted to be the one to tell you, in case the girls bring it up."

I tried to imagine Beth's daughters—Mia, sixteen, and Kitty, thirteen—calling me to vent about their parents' marriage. The girls and I were close. Samson and I had been even closer. All three of them had visited me every summer since I'd moved to Florida. In between visits we video chatted and sent each other memes, but I wasn't sure we were vent-about-their-parents'-marriage close.

"I'm sorry, B." I snapped a loose thread from the white-embroidered anchor on the pillow. "I love you, no matter what happens. Mark too."

"I know," Beth sighed. "And thanks, Jo. You'll call if anything comes up?"

"Of course," I said, thinking she was talking about the girls reaching out to me about her and Mark.

"This will be hard, but I think it'll be good for all of us," she said.

I bit my lip, not so sure I agreed. How did she and Mark splitting up make an awful situation better? They'd lost so much already. But it wasn't my job to tell her what to do. My role was to be the supportive little sister.

A shadow fell across the room, and I looked up, spotting Nina in the doorway. She gave me an *everything good?* look, and I managed a weak smile.

"Listen, B. I've got to go. I love you." I hung up, taking my time to slip my phone in my pocket so I could avoid looking at Nina.

"How's Beth?" Nina asked when she sat down beside me.

"She's fine." I passed her the couch pillow and stood, crossing the room. "Just checking in."

"And everything's good?"

"Everything's fine."

"You don't look like everything's fine."

"Is it time for the beach picnic?" I turned to the sun deck. The guests milled around the hot tub, towels at their waists, their drink glasses filled. "Did the primary complain about your gin fizz–making skills too?" I tried to laugh, but my throat was thick with emotion, and I blinked back tears, angry with myself. I hadn't cried in front of anyone since the night my mother, whom I rarely spoke with, called to tell me about the accident. Shouldn't I be able to talk about this without falling apart by now? My pain over Beth's marriage, the loss of her son, it could be nothing compared to hers. Didn't I owe it to her to keep myself together?

Nina tilted her head, watching me. Why was she wasting time sitting there? What if the primary needed his underwear ironed again?

Sarah Grunder Ruiz is a writer, educator, and karaoke enthusiast. Originally from South Florida, she now lives in Raleigh, North Carolina, with her husband and two children. She holds an MFA in creative writing from North Carolina State University, where she now teaches First-Year Writing.

CONNECT ONLINE

SarahRuizWrites.com

SarahGrunderRuiz